EVOLVE

Mankind's Last Chance

Donald James Cook

ISBN: 978-0-578-83407-8

DEDICATION

First and foremost, to my family. When undertaking the daunting task of writing a novel, so much time and energy is given to the process. If my family were not as patient and understanding as they were, I may still be writing this book.

Secondly, thank you to so many of my closest friends who provided the inspiration for many of the wonderful characters in the story. I'm not sure what I would have done if not for the amazing personalities who came to life on these pages.

CONTENTS

	Prologue	Apple
C1	Born	3
C2	Dependence	27
C3	Chances	41
C4	Something's Wrong	59
C5	Fractured	81
C6	The Quiet	111
C7	Tip of the Spear	123
C8	Fake News	137
C9	QU13T Pill	147
C10	China	161
C11	The Changing	173
C12	December	183
C13	The Fall	209
C14	The Rise	229
C15	Quiet Generation	239
C16	The Candidate	245

C17	Legacy	259
C18	The Red Eclipse	267
C19	Circa 1776	277
C20	Forty-Eight	291
C21	Another Chance	303
C22	Shakespeare	317
C23	Rain	325
C24	Aftermath	349
C25	The Collection	369
C26	RUN	381
C27	The Turing Trials	395
C28	Father	411
C29	The New Ones	423
C30	The Journey	435
C31	Resistance	445
C32	Pain	459
C33	Devine Intervention	473
C34	Last CH4NC3	493

PROLOUGE

Apple

Date: June 7, 1954   **Place: Wilmslow, England**

Alan Turing was alone in his less than modest home, on a damp and dreary, while still an all too acceptable Northern England day.

"Oh, why can't it just stay sunny for more than an hour?" he said.

He was somber yet determined, so his current doldrums would not impede his evening plans.

As his tea waited fragrant, he fumbled for his sugar cubes and nightly apple.

"There, there you are, come join us," he said as he dropped two cubes of sugar into his steaming china cup.

He added a touch of milk to soothe the event while also stopping yet another porcelain cup from breaking. He stirred ever so gently, as not to disrupt the mingling of the sweet and bitter tonic. This moment and this tea were his and his alone.

As Alan slowly found his way to the sofa, in what was once a far more cramped study, he glanced at the mostly blackened fireplace that hadn't seen flames in months.

"Oh, couldn't you just warm this home with little effort from me?" Alan mildly asserted to the inanimate brick furnishing.

He sat down ever so dignified to pen the first of two letters.

"Oh, now where is my pen?" he mumbled with some annoyance.

"Ahhh, there you are. Now, where was I? Oh yes, …..right?"

Dearest Mother,

I do hope this letter finds you well. I want to share so much with you that I know if we spoke in person, the words would fill the hours, but knowing that a letter will last, a letter it shall be.

Your deepest wish for your children was that we find achievement and happiness in our work. I know how proud you are of John, and that he was your and fathers' favorite. Well, Mother, we did. Although much of my work during the war has been hidden by the secret service, please know that someday, beside the Queen, you will understand what I achieved. As you know, I'm most proud of my theoretical teachings in mathematics. I hope it will serve man to far more extraordinary lengths than Father could have ever imagined.

I know the Turing Machine will be what I am most remembered for, but I fear that my chosen lifestyle will cast a shadow on the day's progress.

I know my family, closest friends, and colleagues, which seem far fewer than just a year ago, will remember my first love, mathematics and computation. It's use today solves problems that were once left for a man's mind to conclude. For that, I am most proud.

Since my savage and unjust conviction, I can no longer serve the Queen. But I thank god I was still able to practice my love of academia and continue my life's work.

I do fear, though, that my heart is irrevocably broken. The Chemical castration that sentenced me to permanent hetero standing has now made me as feminine as a 13-year-old schoolgirl. As I confided to you last month, I must now dress in layers to hide my burgeoning breasts. I am so ashamed, Mother. The cruelness and total lack of empathy by my fellow man have made me love the brilliance of my chosen work even more. Although future intelligence will show no sympathy, it will not harbor any ill will towards man either, let alone discriminate over his sexual preference.

My dear mother, it is here that I leave you with a last wish of love and gratitude for all you and father tried to do for John and me. I know that you are an imperfect woman, but your heart tried. It honestly tried to understand your imperfect son. Lastly, I hope you are proud of me.

Farewell Mother.

Your Son, Alan

His tea now cold with nightfall at hand, Alan knew his work wasn't finished. The ever-darkening room provided a reason for him to rise and stretch.

"My how the temperature has dropped," he reasoned aloud, as a chill found his bones. He snapped his fingers and now negotiated with his analytical side.

"Another cup of tea! This time I'll join it with the leftover biscuits from mothers last visit."

On his short expedition to the parlor, Alan found the perils more challenging in the dim setting. He nearly tripped on a stack of books that seemingly came out of nowhere.

"Oh bloody hell, for god's sake, where did you come from?" Alan yelped as the dastardly bookcase found his elbow, all as he struggled to balance the precious teacup.

But now, another cup of tea in hand, hot at that, but with fewer biscuits than he had hoped. Alan extinguished his momentary temper and fancied his doldrums instead for one last letter.

This time an apple and spices were his rewards for his most recent achievement, two letters in one night. With a sip and a sigh, Turing penned the second and final letter to his dearest of colleagues and friend, Nick Furbank.

Dear Nick,

I know my letters and calls are fewer these days, but I must ask you one last favor. When we met in early April, I bestowed upon you the immense responsibility as executor of my will and estate. Well, I hope you remember what I told you, because it's time for me to leave this wicked place.

I hope you and my mates from Cambridge, Princeton, and Bletchley Park, know of my great affections for all of you. Pay my regards to my brothers in the theory of Computable Intelligence, McCarthy, Newell, Simon, and Minsky. Oh, how I do love those bloody yanks. Please tell them to keep our work alive and growing. The world will need it someday, especially with the Soviets and Americans battling to God knows what end.

I ask that you forgive me for my brooding state, but it is you I trust that will carry my wishes forward. One final request, please let Joan know of my deepest love and admiration for her brilliance and compassion. If we shared a different lifetime, it may have been easier and lasting. Tell her that in my overreaching and overthinking arc, that I was never her light, but she was mine. I have always cherished the gift she gave that I could never repay, so please look after that gift as I instructed in my previous letter.

To you, Nick, my deepest regards and thoughtful gratitude.

Sincerely, Alan.

With the tea still warm and one last sip, Alan settled for his apple and bitter spice. He sealed the letters in pre-addressed envelopes and left them on the front table.

"Mary will surely find them in the morning," he assured himself.

Alan wandered now to the parlor, where he found a dirty glass, but one that would do. He poured an inch of brandy to toast his love, computable science. The only true love and what he hoped would be a lasting legacy for generations to leverage for the good of the world.

Now on to his still warm sofa, he settled back and found the apple that would join him again for his evening ritual.

He took a generous bite, as the juices of the fruit dripped down and made a suitable adhesive. He opened his small pouch of spice and sprinkled it about the apple, making certain the bitter powder stayed put and with a specific density.

He thoughtfully grasped his glass of brandy as he caught a fractured glimpse of himself in the mirror across the room. He raised his glass with absolute gratitude and toasted a tearful last salute to an enduring but troubled life.

The wash of brandy now gone, yet the taste still lingered. Alan cradled the apple and took one last bite. His heart, like many times before, broke yet again.

He now laid down on the worn, stained sofa where many an idea were born. He rested his tired eyes that had seen so much in a relatively short time. He quietly smiled for what he hoped would be remembered as a life with merit and standing and that his achievements could be used for a millennium.

The next morning, with the sun firmly hanging over the dewy landscape, the same bright day, Alan had yearned for was here.

It was a warmer than usual, sun-drenched morning. One that Northern Englishmen often wanted but seldom saw was upon the quaint town of Wilmslow.

Alan's young and pretty maid, Mary, had been late this otherwise typical June morning. With her arms full and her mind scattered, she found the house key while she stumbled up the stairs of the Turing Home.

She entered noisily and called aloud, "Morning, Mister Turing, sorry I'm late, Sir, but I came upon those strawberry tarts that you love so much with your nightly tea."

A vaguely familiar scent was present. "Not that of flowers," she thought while noticing two letters on the foyer stand.

A third step now past the door, Mary stopped frozen when she saw a distressed Alan Turing. He was slumped off the side of the sofa, with dried vomit on his face and floor, and beside him, a brown, partially eaten apple.

"Mister Turing," she whispered.

"Mister Turing," she nervously cried.

With shock and a full understanding of the occurrence, Mary ran out of the house and fell on the broken, unkept lawn.

With no remedy in sight, she screamed, "HELP! Someone please, for god sakes, HELP."

Help that was needed for several years, would now be too late.

Alan Turing died the prior evening on June 7th, 1954, at the mere age of forty-one.

Although Alan Mathison Turing would not be fully recognized for many years after his passing, as the brilliant scientist and mathematician he was. His long list of generational achievements ran deep; most notable was his secret work with Britain's spy agency, MI6, during WWII.

The breaking of Germany's Enigma Code was thought to have shortened WWII by two years, thus saving an estimated fourteen million lives. His ultimate legacy as a *founding father of Artificial Intelligence* eventually bestowed itself upon the world. The legacy he left is one that even Turing himself could not have ever imagined.

He was ultimately pardoned and publicly forgiven for his once illegal lifestyle. His dignity was restored, and all the accolades he deserved while still alive now rested alongside his renowned legacy.

♠

"We never really learn from the first mistake, nor the second mistake or the third. It only hits us when we're given the Last Chance"

- Unknown

EVOLVE

Mankind's Last Chance

C1-BORN

"The day science begins to study non-physical phenomena, it will make more progress in one decade than in all the previous centuries of its existence"

-Nikola Tesla

Date: October 17th, 2025   **Place: Palo Alto, CA.**

Dr. Christopher J. Chance, from the Bureau for Disease Management, flew to the *askCOM Technologies* Corporate headquarters at the behest of his good friend, Samuel Tate. After landing in San Francisco, Sam arranged for a car to pick him up and drive him the forty or so miles to the *askCOM Technologies* campus in Palo Alto. Dr. Chance hadn't been to the Bay Area since he and his wife vacationed there at least ten years ago. He found it almost unrecognizable. Where once it's pristine beauty in sights and sounds were obvious, it was now homelessness, filth, and despair.

The damage to society was evident with the mass amounts of homeless, but the re-construction from the *Earthquake of 2023* was slow and seemed forgotten. The quake was 7.4 on the Richter scale, and further reminded the country of how broken and easily damaged its infrastructure was. From the air, he noticed the bridges and roads were still under repair, and the iconic Coit Tower stood no more.

"What the hell happened?" he asked himself.

For the short 2-day trip, Dr. Chance packed light, "maybe too light," he thought.

The daytime temps were far colder than he planned. A wet fog and fifty-two degrees were not what he hoped for as he exited the San Francisco International Airport. As the wind whipped off the cold Pacific, it felt more like Northern England in the fall.

"Not exactly Georgia, that's for sure," he said with a shiver.

As he rode in the back of the black luxury SUV, the shock of homeless, dilapidated buildings and uncollected trash upset his senses.

Driving down Nancy Pelosi Blvd, Chris tapped the driver on the shoulder and said, "Get us the hell out of here!" With that, the SUV found Interstate 280 South.

Chris checked some emails that stacked up while he was on the plane. "Ten more minutes, Dr. Chance," the driver said while breaking the silence.

Now almost to *askCom Technologies*, he observed San Francisco's woes hadn't affected Palo Alto and its wealthy population. The epicenter of technology, higher education, and hip mecca of billionaires and tech geniuses were conveniently protected from the world's current state. Upon his arrival, Chris quickly appreciated the wealth on display as they approached the posh *askCOM Technologies* world headquarters. This was his first time to visit Sam in Palo Alto. Seeing Silicon Valley up close was a rare treat. He'd only wished it were under better circumstances.

The conflicting commute ended as the SUV parked in the grand shadow of *askCOM Technologies,* the world's 17th largest company. CEO Samuel Tate built the company from a two-person operation in the garage of a house he rented after graduating from Yale in 1996. After making a name for himself at Google for several years, he nursed his young company on the side until he developed a cutting-edge technology called *MasterMind*. It was software that would be used in nearly every app available on smartphones. In less than ten years after his move to Silicon Valley, he became a billionaire. Now fifty-one, the salt and peppered, forever bachelor had already won The Turing Award and The Smythe Award for his creation of Synthetic Intelligence.

"Chris, welcome, it's good to see you. I hope the flight wasn't too bad," Sam said.

With a handshake and a pat on the back, Chris felt right at home.

"Thanks for having me, Sam. Impressive place," Chris replied while scanning the ultra-modern, high tech, and massive glass facade of the world-renown tech headquarters.

"The flight was fine, but San Fran is a mess," he added.

"Oh, you're welcome, and I agree, they can't seem to make much progress. Well look, we have a busy couple of days, so let's get up to my office. There are some people I want you to meet, and more importantly, something I want you to see," Sam said while pointing Chris to the elevators.

After making the brief journey to the seventh floor, Sam escorted Chris the remainder of the way down the glass-lined hallway. Behind the smoked glass were offices adorned with state-of-the-art floating projection monitors, rich décor of leather furnishings, granite conference tables, and mahogany desks. Arriving at Sam's office is where the glass walls ended, and secrecy began.

Chris entered the well-appointed meeting room to casually dressed executives, chatting quietly in the private, yet large space. Through a set of double doors, he could see Sam's expansive executive suite, and past the windows lay the famed campus of Stanford University. Besides the sweeping views of Silicon Valley, also awaiting Dr. Chance was a wide variety of drinks, coffee's, snacks, and other Hors d'oeuvres in the more than lavish conference room.

"Is this all for me?" Chris asked aloud with a humble smirk.

"Well, actually, it's always like this," whispered a not yet introduced Trace Manson.

Sam began, "Chris, have a seat. Before we get started, I want to introduce you to a few people. First, Dren and Aidan Parker, are our husband-husband creative team, they head the Research & Production Department. Then we have Pierce D'Naus, head of our Social Platforms Application Team. Next to you, someone I believe you've already met, is our Director of I.T., Trace Manson. And last but not least is Mara Sheppard, our Chief Marketing Strategist."

"I want you to see something that's going to make a lot of sense. With special thanks to Dren and Aidan, our in-house production division just finished the last edits on a new documentary that we'll be premiering soon. It captures everything we've been seeing and investigating with AI and society's breakdown. Everyone but Trace will depart after the screening, but I invited them to view it with us, as I'm very proud of the finished product. It will be eye-opening to the public when it's released in December. But Chris, it's spot on considering what we already know," Sam concluded as the lights dimmed.

"So, will there be popcorn?" Chris asked as he glanced at the long table of food and drinks.

"Chris, be serious. It's two years' worth of research," Sam remarked. "It's called The Birth of Technology and Human Addiction: (The Downfall of Mankind)."

A yawning Dr. Chance settled into his contoured leather chair. With a cup of coffee and donuts, he hoped the dimly lit room and jet lag wouldn't do him in.

"Trace start the damn thing before Chris falls asleep," Sam urged.

(play)

Narrator Morgan Leeman began as sweeping views of the earth's mountains, valleys, rivers, and oceans filled the screen.

The Birth of Technology and Human Addiction:

(The Downfall of Mankind)

The seeds of life, planted in loose but fertile ground, had with it the hope and optimism for growth and prosperity. With all the care and consideration of a loving father, its creator wanted and waited eagerly for its maturation. The goal that one day man and earth would flourish together and create a legacy of what GOD gave the world.

The earliest innovators, engineers, and scientists of their day found an opportunity to bring about a massive change in a small window of time. A period shorter than the blink of modern man's 200,000-year-old history on earth. With the Industrial Revolution behind them, the greatest minds of a new generation set upon the day with a vision for change and automation. A day they could have only dreamed of, where a man's hands were set aside for his mind, and all it could dream.

From mechanisms that calculate, machines that build, electricity, the telephone, automobiles, and flight, man did more for humanity in the slightest of an instant. So much so, that with hindsight, some feared it was too much, too soon. What was done for civilization, though, to ease what had been a challenging and bitter road of existence, certainly could not have been resented.

"For man's achievements must be embraced," said the arrogant innovators, unaware of the fall of generational dominos.

Could man have known the dangers that lie ahead with automation, computing, modern weapons of war, and accelerated travel? Could man have appreciated what modern medicine would and could do for them? Yes, of course they did. Man allowed itself to race to the next invention, the next elevated level of the human condition. The next....., well, whatever the day would bring. Man was ready and had little appetite for policing itself, no matter how fast the future came.

The Fathers of AI

Charles Babbage (1791-1871): An Englishman, was a Cambridge professor of mathematics and a mechanical engineer, inventor, philosopher, and polymath. He is broadly considered the *"Father of Computing"* based on his Analytical Engine invention in 1837. The engine was a booming contraption of logic and math, made of wood, steel, wires, and other materials that essentially served as a computer. One capable of formulation and manipulating numbers. The intricacies that it bore were not recognizable to the time. Even a hundred years later, reproducing the engine proved a worthy challenge.

Scene changes to early 1800's England.

Year: 1837   **Place: Cambridge, England**

In his smoke-filled study, Professor Babbage nestled within the University of Cambridge's dignified grounds, founded in 1209. He sipped a more than suitable glass of cognac and debated the merits of his fame and notable exploits.

He spouted to his new, far inferior colleague, and unexpected guest C.G. Jarvis, "My good man Jarvis, if mankind is to defeat exhaustion, then we must work smarter, not harder."

"You see, Jarvis, I was not always the flapdoodle you see today," confessed Babbage. "If I must say so myself, I was a very sturdy young thinking man, but as a much younger lad, nothing came easy you know, that being due to my poor health at the time," he lamented.

"Thus, I believe mathematics and science must prevail and take man much farther, much faster, but with much less effort than it has in our previous centuries," Babbage proclaimed with bold enunciation.

(a rap on the door)

"Yes, what is it?" (silence)

"Oh, forget it, just come in, why don't you," spouted an easily agitated Babbage.

"Ahh, pardon me, but the-the-the," stammered Oliver, the young servant.

"Spit it out, child, and get about your business," punctuated Babbage.

"You, you-yourrr, cob-cob Cobbler Sir," said the deflated boy.

"Oh, just put it on the table and be on your way, Oliver."

"WAIT! Come back here, I say," Babbage said with a commanding posture.

"I'm sorry, my child, I may be a little irritated due to an obvious intrusion to an otherwise peaceful afternoon," he remarked as he glanced at Jarvis.

"Never should a brilliant mind squander a minute of daylight to pleasure the fancy of the less intelligent. Unless getting richly compensated, that is," an obvious Babbage said while targeting his uninvited guest.

"Thank you child, but wait just a moment." Babbage fussed momentarily and wrestled some loose coins from his vest pocket.

"Here, give this to your Mum," said Babbage, as he handed the boy a few farthings.

"Thay-thay thank you, Sir," Oliver said.

He was clearly grateful for the kind gesture.

"Oh, I do enjoy that boy, but he is somewhat of a foozler," Babbage said to his afternoon company.

Closing the door, a curious Jarvis said, "Please do continue, Charles. May I call you Charles?"

"I shall continue at my leisure, and no, you may not," Babbage replied.

While now nibbling on his somewhat stale yet tasty warm cobbler, Babbage explained his world view. With crumbs accompanying his every word.

"You see, we in the Analytical Society here at Cambridge, believe that man, whether broad in chest, long in mind, or vazey at best, have access to a machine or a thinking tool, to help them. A device to organize, analyze, calculate, be more productive and ultimately achieve, I suppose. Not every man is born as brilliant as I," quipped Babbage as he vanquished his tasty treat with a wash of cognac and saliva.

"Thus, we must employ an intelligent device to aid us."

"But know this, my adjuvant fellow," Babbage postured as he raised his once again conveniently full glass of Cambridge's finest French brandy.

"It is my sworn duty, old Chap, to provide my skills and talents to the betterment of the world, our future, and of course, the Queen," Babbage said.

Jarvis looked on with some annoyance as the squiffy old windbag found delight in his exhaustive proclamations.

"I will tinker and toy until my Analytical Machine employs the gratitude of my children's children, and those of the bloody Yanks who seek to surpass the Crown's best men, and our noble achievements," Babbage concluded.

Charles Babbage believed the industrial revolution paved the way for the mechanical age to be more than pullies and levers, and something far more significant than his contemporaries could ever imagine. He knew that a machine, a thinking apparatus, would one day lift humanity to reach beyond man's own two arms and dream something beyond a mind's boldest fantasy.

Scene changes to the late 1800s, in the rugged Western U.S.

Leland Stanford (1824-1893): Founder of the prestigious Stanford University and known as *Father of the expansion of innovation and technology.* He was an Industrialist and politician who served as a United States Senator and the 8th Governor of California.

Stanford was a powerful man and influencer in the western US. He held positions of Director of Wells Fargo, President of the Central Pacific and Southern Pacific Railroads, as well as the founder of The Pacific Life Insurance Company. Originally from the eastern United States, Stanford migrated to Northern California during the Gold Rush in 1852. He was a leading member of the Republican Party and a staunch supporter of Abraham Lincoln, and a strong proponent for the stoppage and an ending to the spread of slavery.

Year: 1885   **Place: Palo Alto, California**

Less than a year after their teenage son's tragic death, a grieving Leland and his wife founded Leland Stanford Junior University as a memorial to their deceased child. The couple donated forty million dollars that in today's value would be 1.1 billion dollars, to create what would become one of the most formable learning institutions outside of the Ivy League.

Stanford University went on to become the center of science and computing technologies. Located in the hub of Silicon Valley, it was the birthplace of modern technology. Silicon Valley, nestled between San Jose and San Francisco, is centered in Palo Alto, California. It spawned from the vision of renowned Dean of Stanford's School of Engineering, Frederick Terman, who hoped that Stanford Faculty and Alumni would start their own tech companies and center them near Stanford University.

Silicon Valley got its name due to the large numbers of tech innovators and companies specializing in silicone based MOS (metal oxide semiconductors), Transistors, and circuit chips. Many prominent companies in Silicon Valley included giants like Apple, Google, Facebook, Tesla, Oracle, Cisco Systems, Intel, The Squared Circle Group, and *askCOM Technologies*. As a collective group, they all shared in the rise of modern intelligence.

Scene changes to the late 1890's New York City.

Nikola Tesla (1856-1943) is considered the *Father of Automation.* A Serbian-American electrical and mathematical engineer, Inventor and Futurist. He is famously known for his impact in the field of modern mechanical and electrical devices and systems. Tesla invented the first alternating current motor. After arriving in the United States in 1884, he worked briefly for Thomas Edison at Edison Electric. Due to conflicting beliefs in which electrical current was better, AC or DC, and other professional disputes, the two parted ways and remained fierce rivals over several decades.

Year: 1896   **Place: New York City, NY.**

Nikola Tesla, with his sleeves rolled, sweat on his shaggy brow, paced along the splintered floor of his cluttered SOHO Flat. He cannot understand why for the sake of God, he ever vacated his cool, quiet life in Serbia, the isolated home he'd left five years earlier.

"Damn New York and this burning summer, if not for the wealth of its elite or the proximity to industry, I wouldn't be here," Tesla said to his closest friend, Robert Underwood Johnson. A notable poet and editor of the renowned Century Magazine.

"Maybe we can chew the rag tonight and sip wine with Kat," said Nikola, with a tilted smile, as to insinuate it would be cooler in Robert's Lexington Avenue apartment.

"Mark will be in the city tonight. I do love his stories and simple humor. The plan is to meet him tomorrow at noon in my laboratory. Can you and Kat make it?" Tesla implored.

"I believe he is bringing his financier friend, oh what is his name?" he muttered.

"Nikola, it is Edward Dean Adams," Johnson said.

"You must get it right if you want his money, and yes, Kat and I wouldn't miss it for the world," he warned.

The following day brought about another one hundred-degree scorcher. But it brought Nikola closer to the funds needed to continue research and work on the wireless lighting and electricity projects that had so absorbed him for the last few years. Although wealthy from his alternating currency AC patents, Nikola had a far-reaching public lifestyle and appetite for more projects.

"Oh, I do love spending money, but not mine of course," Tesla mused.

Nikola and Robert, along with his wife Kat, eagerly awaited Mark, their most famous and entertaining friend. Accompanying him was his wealthy associate Edward Dean Adams. Noon came to pass, but only slightly when an anxious Nikola mouthed a few expletives, not at their tardiness, but the unforgiving heat. His South Fifth Avenue Lab did not shield them as well as his friend's cooler uptown Flat.

Alas, footsteps, "it must be them," Tesla whispered. "Quick, make room for our guests."

Kat opened the door, and to their surprise, Mark Twain, the famous author, and notable wordsmith, entered the darkened laboratory with not one but three other companions.

"Well, my dear friend Mark, or shall I call you Samuel? Whom is it that accompanies you on this blistering day?" Tesla uttered as he wiped the sweat from his brow.

"My-My, Nikola, you did not warn me of this unbearable heat. I'd rather be icing myself in the frigid San Francisco Bay, then baking in the swampy heat of this granite island," exclaimed the famed humorist and author.

"Remind me to stay in New Orleans where you can visit me during the much cooler summer months," a self-amused Twain said with a cutting jest.

Nikola replied without hesitation, "Mark, you do not disappoint with your grand humor, but seriously Gentlemen, please, please, do come in."

"We must all scrooch to fit, as I did not expect such a large and distinguished audience," apologized a delighted Nikola.

The crowded and dusty Lab presented a vast collection of metal objects, many not recognizable to any man of prestige and wealth. It bore an endless array of wires, glass jars, levers of all sizes, and paper strewn about, with some typed and some handwritten. Its interior drew the interests of all, along with the fascinating renderings adorning the cracked brick walls. The guests found the inner workings of its exceptional host to be well beyond that of anything they'd heard or read about the enigmatic

Tesla.

"Nikola, allow me to introduce my very good friends, Edward Dean Adams, whom I told you about, and John Paul Balthazar III, the vice president of the Philadelphia National Bank. And yes, I'm sure you're wondering about my surprise guest, this is Sir Thomas Stinson, representing her majesty, Queen Victoria and the British Royal family," Twain proudly declared.

"We can all agree that we're eager to see what you've been working on. Mrs. Balthazar, John's lovely wife, insisted on being here, but at the last minute she decided the train ride from Philadelphia was too long and hot. Especially for such a frolic of an eccentric man's bold hobbies," Twain continued.

"Well, Well, let me just say, I do not think you can name many great inventions that have been made by married men," said an arrogant and permanently single Tesla.

"My fellows, you see, I say to the people today, the present is theirs, the future for which I work is mine."

"What I offer you is a fortune in your making, by my sweat and tinkering mind. But I believe that ultimately, everything that is good for man should be free to man. But only someday, just not this day," offered a stoic Nikola.

The intrigued men looked on with their interest peaked, as Kat and Robert gave each other a look of "we've seen this performance many times before." It was an act that would make even their friends on Broadway blush.

Tesla lamented in quizzical fear, and with some apprehension said, "the day science begins to study non-physical phenomena, it will make more progress in one decade, then in all the previous centuries of existence."

Tesla then briefly paused while remembering his audience. "So, let's look at my current remedies and toast today, and what tomorrow yet may bring."

Twain and his traveling company hung on every word.

"I told you that Nikola would not disappoint, didn't I, gentlemen?" Mark Twain proudly stated.

With all in agreement, Nikola concluded his adlib presentation with a promise of a future that man could never have believed.

As an outspoken futurist, what Tesla knew then was man's capacity for the most significant of achievements, along with those with untapped potential for more. But their curiosity blended with greed and ambition could one day destroy humanity. By his death in 1943, at the age of eighty-six and nearly penniless, he saw the worst, two world wars, and the best, countless inventions and innovations of man. But he ultimately knew mankind wasn't finished. The birth of something greater lie just beyond the horizon.

Scene changes to the mid-1940's Washington DC.

William Bradford Shockley, Jr. Ph.D. (1910-1989): An American inventor and physicist. Shockley led a research group of esteemed scientists at Bell Labs, who were awarded the 1956 Nobel Prize in Physics for their research on semiconductors and the transistor effect's discovery.

As the transistor co-inventor (computer processor), his company Shockley Semiconductor Labs was the first company to make transistors out of *Silicone*. Although American, William was born to his American parents while living in London, England.

He was then later raised at the family's home in Palo Alto, California.

His formal education found him at the prestigious MIT and the renowned California Institute of Technology. Besides his career in his chosen field of Science, Dr. Shockley did notable work with the United States Department of War.

Year: 1945   Place: The Pentagon Wash. DC

Dr. Shockley bustled about his impressive stacks of papers, notes, and other diagrams. Although there were many, they did little to fill the large board room table. The space was entombed in just one of the thousands of offices found inside the impressive and newly built five-sided structure.

The double doors burst open with static and stacked upon voices. Some were heavy, and some were light. Some were clearly in charge, while others were just trying to keep up. This was a deep crew of military men, with several others in muted gray suits of no particular orientation, it seemed.

A startled and flustered Shockley looked up and said, "excuse me, gentleman, was it your intention to rattle me and hurry my work? I was told that I was meeting with the Secretary of War, Robert Patterson, at 2:00 pm sharp."

"Pardon us, Dr. Shockley, we didn't mean to intrude, but it is 2:09 pm SHARP, and you can address me as General," General Brehon B. Somervell said.

"Secretary Patterson, along with General McArthur, will be joining us in just a few minutes. Until then, don't speak. Please gather your notes and be ready to present your findings," instructed General Somervell.

Shockley, a bit embarrassed now, clumsily tussled with his well-worn and teeming pocket protector, in search of his lucky pencil to make one last entry in his findings.

"Keep it together, Bill," he whispered to himself.

The room slowly filled. Within minutes of the uniformed army resting in what seemed to be their pre-selected seats, they no sooner stood at attention in rapid succession. All for the grand entry of General Douglas MacArthur, Admiral Chester Nimitz, and the President of the United States, Harry S. Truman.

"Gentleman, you may take your seats," mouthed a stoic General MacArthur through his famous corncob pipe. The room's occupants now sat still, with all eyes focused on Shockley.

"Dr. Shockley, I presume?" MacArthur questioned with a pointed stare in the direction of the only Ph.D. in the room.

"Ummm, yes sir, General," stammered a visibly intimidated Shockley.

"We appreciate your work last year on the B-29 program and some other research you contributed. But if you don't mind, please get up and move your belongings, you're sitting in President Truman's chair," a somewhat amused MacArthur declared.

"No-No, I'll stand, you stay seated, Dr. Shockley, as of right now, you're the most important person in the room," an openly confiding President Truman said.

Admiral Nimitz interjected, "Please begin, Doctor, we have little time, little money, and little blood left to defeat the Japanese."

The room fell utterly silent with all ears tuned to Dr. Shockley, with notable sweat now on his brow and a yellow ring racing from his armpit to his shirt pockets.

With his apparent nerves present, Dr. Shockley began, "Please call me Bill."

Standing now and reciting what he'd been rehearsing for days, "Let me begin by stating the reason I am here today," as a slight pause followed.

"Five weeks and two days ago, at roughly 3 pm (*all eyes in the crowded room now rolling beneath their raised eyebrows*) I was asked by Secretary Patterson to prepare a report on the likely number of American casualties. Those that would occur if a full-scale invasion of Japan's mainland happened in the next six months. My team and I have prepared a six-hundred and seventeen-page report detailing our findings."

"STOP," President Truman shouted.

"I don't have time for your shenanigans and bullshit algorithms, or even more than one page of your six hundred and GOD DAMN something page report. Just cut to the chase and tell us what we need to know," admonished the President.

"Yes, of course, my apologies, Mr. President," offered Dr. Shockley.

"If a ground invasion from the sea and air were to occur, the cost would be grave. There would be as many as four to eight hundred thousand dead Americans and up to 1.4 million Allied casualties in total. Also, Mr. President, the Allies would have to slaughter between five and ten million Japanese to bring the war to an end," Dr. Shockley revealed.

"My God," a despaired Truman muttered, as he removed his

circular wire-framed glasses, rubbed his eyes, and rose to leave. Almost to the double doors, he stopped and looked back.

"Thank you, Bill. I apologize for my outburst, but the stress of the day does wear on a man. I appreciate the work you've done, and I now know what I must do," President Truman acknowledged.

On August 6th, 1945, the Enola Gay dropped her payload on Japan's mainland one month later. Hiroshima and it's 70,000 citizens were seared and nearly evaporated in seconds. Three days later, Nagasaki was gone.   Due to William Shockley's analysis, a million allied servicemen were spared, along with an estimated ten percent of Japan's civilian population.

Dr. William Shockley's life's work was to help his fellow man. Notably, he became a proponent of *Eugenics*, the science of improving humans through controlled breeding, while increasing the occurrence of desirable heritable characteristics. There was no doubt that one day his work would contribute to AI's influence on the world.

Scene changes to the mid-1950's Central England.

Alan Mathison Turing (1912-1954):   Widely known as the "Father of theoretical computer science and artificial intelligence."

Turing was a famed English mathematician, philosopher, theoretical biologist, and computer scientist. After being recruited in 1939 by MI6, the British Intelligence Agency, he was mainly responsible for cracking the Nazi Germany ENIGMA Code during WWII, thus helping Great Britain and its allies defeat Nazi Germany. He was known as one of the first creators of the digital revolution (computable numbers).

Sir Timothy Berners-Lee. (1955-Present): An English computer scientist and engineer. Born in London, England. He was formally educated at Queens College, Oxford. He is a Professor at MIT, famed for inventing the World Wide Web, thus being dubbed the "Father of the Internet." This achievement linked the entire world of humans and technology together. It's impact on the future of artificial intelligence, and the human race was far greater than anyone could have known at the time.

In 2004, Berners-Lee was knighted for his lifetime achievements by Queen Elizabeth. He also received the Turing Award in 2016.

In the darkened conference room, Dr. Chance leaned over to Trace Manson and whispered, "So that's what did it! The internet gave AI access to everything and everyone."

Without taking his eyes off the screen, Trace said, "Shhhh."

Actor Morgan Leeman continued the narration with time-lapse scenes from the 1800s through modern-day evolution in automation and technology.

Year: Now   **Place: The World**

Long ago in Charles Babbage's and Nikola Tesla's world, most people didn't travel with any regularity outside of a ten-mile radius of their home. With a debt of gratitude to Sir Timothy Berners-Lee for his achievement, now modern humans didn't need to leave their comfort zone either. They could communicate anything in just mere seconds, without going anywhere. In mankind's existence, the debt owed to Berners-Lee served as the greatest irony, and the greatest price man will ever pay. The intrusiveness of the web let a stranger in the home of every person with the internet. It served as the greatest Trojan Horse in human history and one that unlocked the world's doors and windows forever.

AI: The Servant Child to its Masters

It started as a massive, futuristic contraption of Babbage's Analytical Engine. The genius of Tesla and his alternating current electrified the world, then onto Turing's mathematical calculations, and finally to William Shockley's transistors. All of the great innovations ultimately landed in Microsoft and Apple's operating systems, where the fluid weapon moved from a desk to a human hand.

Artificial Intelligence was BORN.

The broad scope of innovation from AI's Founding Fathers was unfathomable. The narrow and infinitesimal detail which made their designs work was far more impressive than anything known to man. From the early *"trial and error"* beginnings of AI to all its maturing forms, Babbage, Turing, and Shockley's vision of data storage, calculations, and intelligent systems were realized.

The contributions continued from many other modern innovators, and their forward-thinking ingenuities. All previous innovation was finally culminated when Google, Apple, and Microsoft's "Super Intelligence" arrived. Intelligence beyond that of the human brain was born. A static entity with no human flaws, and no emotional obstacles to stunt its growth. By the late 20th Century, the founding fathers' creations were all whittled down to a tiny chip. A microchip that held every shred of information one would ever need or want, and all accessed in mere seconds. Technology that educated, entertained, and could think was now an overbearing guest to its unsuspecting host. All it needed was an electrical charge.

From the tips of modern fingers, man could now access nearly all of the world's recorded history and stored information, send an email, pay a bill, invest, save, and research.

With the deepest of gratitude, the world of 3.2 billion internet users thanked Sir Timothy Berners-Lee, the first to connect man to the world via the internet in 1991. When it was made public in 1993, the new voice of technology spoke to humans, when *"Welcome"* and *"You've Got Mail"* were made famous by AOL.

With all mentions of innovation and credit bestowed, the least obvious yet most crucial creation of mankind was electricity. From its first modern recorded discovery by Ben Franklin, to the inventive brilliance of its true fathers; Michal Faraday, Thomas Alva Edison, and Nikola Tesla. Yet man owed an infinite measure of gratitude to the famed Italian scientist Alessandro Volta (Volt), whose 1800 AD recipe of saltwater, paper, copper, and zinc gave the world the first battery. The creation allowed for the luxury of all inventions of man to be untethered.

Imponderabilia

Imponderable: things that cannot be precisely determined, measured, or evaluated.

> *.... the Imponderabilia of human life.*

Now, at last, with all of mankind's most essential questions of automation and technology answered, one last question remained....

...WHAT CAN GO WRONG?

Dr. Chance grabbed the remote and paused the documentary.

Chris interrupted the playing of the documentary at a seemingly good juncture.

"Sam, sorry, it's brilliant, but I have to use the restroom. Can someone point the way?" Chris asked.

"By the way, that part on Tesla part was outstanding, and the stuttering kid was cute too. That Morgan Leeman narrates everything, huh?" Chris said as he headed for the door.

"Seriously, Chris, you always did have a small bladder," Sam said.

"Hey, I guess holding your liquor is easier than me holding my coffee," Chris said.

Making his way to the door, he asked again, "so where is the restroom? It's imponderable how bad I have to go."

"Not funny Chris, not funny at all," Sam said.

With Chris gone, Sam shared a quick story to entertain the group.

"Back in our Yale days, Chris thought a fun night was a trip to Starbucks. When the rest of Alpha Delta Phi knew a house party or a trip to Geppetto's Pub in downtown New Haven was the way to go."

As the story ended the door flung open, and Chris entered.

"So, what did I miss? Clearly, from the laughter, you guys must've been having fun at my expense," Chris said as he glimpsed at Sam's hidden smirk.

"Oh nothing Chris, just no more coffee for you. We don't want to keep pausing this thing," Sam playfully replied while pouring himself another gin and tonic.

"So, which one are you?" Chris asked Sam before Trace could start the DVD.

"Which one am I? Who, you mean the tech innovators?" Sam asked with some surprise.

With a slight pause, and all eyes and ears from the small but curious group of *askCOM's* elite in attendance, Sam replied,

"Well, I've always wanted to be another Tesla, but the OCD in me told me that I'm more of a Thomas Edison. Besides, Gorson Tusk is the modern-day Tesla."

"Well, shall we get back to the production?" Trace asked as if he had to be someplace else.

"Chris, the second part of the documentary, deals with addiction and frankly how susceptible humans are to almost anything. From your coffee to my gin," Sam said with a nod for Trace to begin.

With that, the lights dimmed again, and the rest of the documentary was consumed and discussed.

♠

C2 - DEPENDENCE

"When one thing is prioritized over everything, your greatest obstacle is in the mirror"

-DJ Cook

The Downfall of Mankind   Part II

Trace pressed play as Part II began.

Narrator Morgan Leeman continued:

With all the precision and detailed engineering of modern automation, there was still an implied simplicity through science and mathematical calculation.

"If something didn't work, it could be thrown away or started over."

But not so with humans and their frailties, vulnerabilities of health, emotional state, and other physical limitations. "If humans don't work, they die."

Before the Industrial Age, humans relied on themselves for their own labor and ingenuity. Man built things, gathered food, and at their essential core, survived in the physical sense. Cerebrally speaking, the human brain being more complex, was wrought with failings. Human beings, while not the strongest species, relied on their intelligence to achieve superiority. They survived on reason, common sense, gut instinct, trial and error, and simply each other. Things became more complicated when brain chemistry became compromised, whether through injury, dependency, psychosis, or other impairments.

Dependency in early centuries revolved around food, water, shelter, and safety from other humans and animals. In the modern age after the Industrial and Technical Revolutions, other pitfalls befell man, whether it was greed, corruption, addiction, or crimes against other people. With mass population growth, war, innovation, or disease, the world became a far more complex planet.

Humans prospered when they were aligned, and their basic needs were met. If they employed safety and their fellow man cooperated by avoiding crime and war, they could enjoy peace. It was fair to assume that all would remain harmonious and right with the world if those things occurred. From the solitary individual to the greater masses of humans, …..if only.

The human condition is where the simplest yet most complex defect appeared. Dependence!

Seemingly, someone in good health, whose basic physical needs were met, could self-sabotage and destroy themselves and those around them. Whether through chemical addiction or psychosis, people were affected by something physical or behavioral that they didn't need but instead wanted.

The Early Addiction Menu

Physical & Chemical Stimulants

Cocaine

A *stimulant* that comes from the South American coca plant. Scientists consider it to be most addictive drug on the planet. Beginning in 1884, cocaine had legitimate uses in early medicine. It quickly gained popularity and rapidly expanded in many medical circles as a cure-all while also finding casual uses by individuals.

Notably, well-known people in business and many in the medical field found cocaine a useful remedy. The famed Austrian Neurologist Sigmund Freud, the founder of psychoanalysis, was an early user of the drug. In 1886, Coca-Cola, founded by John Stith, an American Pharmacist, started the company with a soft drink beverage as its core product. It was a mix of water, cocaine, and sugary syrup. Many other famous inventors, scientists, writers, and artists used cocaine as well for clarity and vision.

In 1900, cocaine wasn't just any drug. It was widely believed in medical circles that it could cure seemingly anything that ailed a patient. Starting in 1884, an Austrian ophthalmologist Carl Koller, used it as an anesthetic while performing eye surgery. By placing a drop of cocaine in the eye, it rendered it immobile and impervious to pain. It was later used as an anesthetic for many procedures, such as numbing the nose, uses for throat operations, etc., throughout the world.

By 1905, US Citizens could access cocaine readily for as little as .25 cents a gram in nearly any pharmacy. By that time, cocaine had become one of the Top 5 selling pharmaceuticals in the country.

In the early years of the 20th Century, the wildly popular drug was used for everything from medicine, soft drinks, candy, laced cigars, and wine. It was even prepared in pre-packed hypodermic needles so medical patients can give themselves injections. Even children were a marketing target, with the offering of cocaine toothache drops.

By 1910, over 200,000 Americans were cocaine addicts, including many of the same medical professionals responsible for its widespread use over the previous 20+ years.

Due to the rapidly rising epidemic, state and local governments cracked down on the drug through laws and other regulations. One of the first was the 1914 Harrison Narcotic Act. Its uses ebbed and flowed for the next several decades due to laws and regulations, while ultimately being illegal.

The 1970s brought a much slower consumption of cocaine despite its abundant supply. Drug dealers then turned to a new boiled down version that could be smoked, called *CRACK*. This new concoction was cheaper and even more addictive than the powdered form. By the mid-1980's cocaine powder and Crack use spiked to 5.8 million users, which led to a large increase in significant drug-related crimes.

Dren Parker motioned to Trace to pause the production. He and Aidan sensed the room of fast minds and distracting cell phones needed the summary version of the rest of the powerful documentary. A weary Dr. Chance couldn't have agreed more, as the dimly lit room lured him into a series of yawns that no one missed at the conference table.

"Trace, can you pause it?" Dren asked as he signaled Aiden to turn the lights up.

With the production paused, the documentary's married creative team now stood at the far end of the conference room in front of the projection screen.

"So as you can see, cocaine, like many other drugs, some prescription and many illegal, started to devour humans in the post-industrial revolution era," Aidan said.

"The US and the world fell into a drug-induced haze while at the same time, technology from the founding fathers grew and complicated the world. Ultimately making lives easier yet distracting people and making them lazier," he said.

Dren stepped in and continued the now verbal presentation, with Sam motioning both to start the documentary again.

"You see, from opioids like fentanyl to prescription pain killers, humans began abusing themselves to the tune of one hundred and thirty deaths a day. Add in ruined careers and shattered relationships. Mankind was fractured and ready....(long pause)."

"Ready for what?" Chris asked.

"Ahhh, yes, Dr. Chance, that's the question we believe our audience will ask as well. Are humans ready to be taken over by AI? Of course not," Aidan answered, not knowing what Chris and Sam knew.

"Trace, can you start it up again?" Dren requested as Aidan turned the lights down.

Narrator Morgan Leeman continued.

Anti-Depressants

Anti-depressants or SSRI's are Selective Serotonin Reuptake Inhibitors. They are a widely prescribed drug used to treat depression and anxiety, brought on by low serotonin levels in the brain. Initially developed in the 1970s, SSRIs treat depression by raising levels of serotonin in the brain. Serotonin is one of the chemical messengers in the brain that carry signals between brain cells. SSRIs effectively block the reabsorption or reuptake of serotonin into neurons, ultimately increasing serotonin levels and making the patient feel better.

SSRI's are considered addictive, as they caused physical dependence when their use is interrupted. SSRIs were commonly known as Lexapro, Celexa, Paxil, Prozac, and Zoloft.

"STOP!" Dr. Chance said with a measure of stress in his voice.

Trace Manson quickly paused the documentary.

"Guys, I'm going to sit this part out. It's a little too close to home. I'm not ready to hear this ....," Chris said while making eye contact with Sam as he headed for the door.

"Chris, I'm sorry, I should have known," Sam replied as Chris seemingly ignored the gesture as the door closed behind him.

Mara turned to Sam and said, "Known what?"

"Forget it. It's a private matter," Sam answered.

With that acknowledgment, Sam gave the nod to resume the documentary while feeling terrible that he didn't catch the sensitive topic in time.

Trace Manson re-started the documentary.

"Romantic Relationship Killer": Studies showed that SSRI's hurt a person's sex drive and feeling of "being in love" with their significant other. Called "Emotional Blunting,'" it left the user having little empathy and consideration towards a mate.

SSRIs were prescribed widely to an extensive patient group, while research showed that only a small percentage of recipients needed the drug. Its effectiveness is generally only positive for those that are most severely depressed. SSRI's while increasing serotonin, decreases dopamine levels, a neurotransmitter involved in many cognitive and behavioral processes. Among them, desire and arousal. To replace the need for dopamine, users filled the void with social media, online shopping, and addictive smartphone apps.

Dr. Chance re-entered the room after a few minutes and returned quietly to his seat. He made eye contact with Sam, and the two nodded with an understanding and respect for the moment.

Aidan, now with control of the remote, stood and gave the room some additional perspective and insight into the documentary's remaining thirty minutes, as his partner joined in.

"So, as you can see, humans were doing a pretty good job of hurting themselves with the more obvious tools of self-soothing and mind-altering drugs. What's amazing is the more obvious addictions, never seemed to be the most nefarious, yet they were," Aidan explained.

An understated Dren joined in and explained the deteriorating habits of Tobacco and Alcohol.

"Did you know the world's 2nd most popular addiction is tobacco? Over 6.5 trillion cigarettes are consumed every year, or 18 billion a day, adding to the annual tobacco revenue of 785 billion dollars worldwide."

"Due to the Nicotine content, cigarette smoking gives its users a chemical rush, caused by the adrenal glands releasing adrenaline when nicotine enters the body. The modern era cigarette first appeared in mass in 1881," Dren said.

"After that, humans were hooked. It became sexy and cool and was glamorized by Hollywood as an escape for soldiers in war. It was the 'In' thing," he concluded.

"What's disturbing is it kills over 8.5 million people a year,"

Aidan added.

"Tell them about Alcohol," Sam said as he raised his glass of gin and tonic.

"Yes, alcohol. Would you like me to take that?" Aidan sarcastically said to Dren, knowing full well this was his forte.

"Wow, where do I begin?" Aidan said.

"Alcohol use began as early as somewhere between 10,000 and 5,000 BC, making it the oldest known drug in human history. Alcohol or Ethanol is generally considered the most used and most popular of all stimulants, liquid or otherwise. It's classified as a psychoactive drug found in wine, beer, and other distilled spirits."

"Alcohol is a depressant, and used in low doses, can cause a feeling of *euphoria*. Hence its widespread use, and ultimately its abuse," Aidan continued.

"Research shows only a moderate chance for addiction, yet alcohol is consumed annually to a worldwide tune of over one trillion dollars in total revenue. It is surpassing even tobacco use. Research also shows that 33% of the world's population consumes alcoholic beverages. That's over 2.5 billion people, with seventy-six million being classified as an alcoholic," Aidan concluded.

"Hey everyone, let's take a five-minute break. Now I have to use the restroom," Sam said with a respectful nod to his special guest from Atlanta.

After Sam returned, the small group gathered itself. The documentary stayed on pause to the delight of its married producers, who loved presenting their research.

"Can someone get Dr. Chance another cup of coffee? He's going to want to be awake for this part," Dren asked.

"COFFEE! Ahh, the great elixir," Dren began.

"It's a relatively young drug compared to tobacco and alcohol and dates to the 1400 AD. Caffeine is widely considered the most common and acceptable drug in the world. Roughly 2.25 billion cups per day are consumed worldwide, with over 400 million per day in the US alone. Besides water, Coffee is the 2nd most consumed beverage in the world," Dren added.

"Coffee has shown to have many positive effects on health. It protects against Parkinson's, Diabetes, liver disease, and even depression. It's not formally considered a Drug in the traditional sense. Even with its positive attributes, it's been proven to be mildly addictive as the caffeine ingredient is a stimulant. Like many addictive drugs, caffeinated coffee has many side effects that can appear very quickly with an interruption in its use," he concluded.

"Hey, I guess that's why everyone loves Starbucks, am I right," Aidan said in an attempt to lighten the mood.

"Guys, for this next part, let's resume the documentary and finish this thing," Sam instructed.

The familiar voice of the narrator began.

The Modern Addiction Menu

Psychological / Behavioral Dependence

Smart Phones

Smart Phone addiction is a new phenomenon that umbrellas the behavioral addiction of the internet and social media outlets such as; Facebook, Snapchat, Instagram, LinkedIn, Twitter, TikTok, and Count Down. Today's smartphone has replaced many items and has become the #1 Behavioral Dependence. It's now our phone, computer, address book, calendar, and calculator. Since it can serve as an encyclopedia, television, movie theater, library, and board game, it's become an indispensable extension of a person's hand. Currently, there are over five billion smartphones in use worldwide.

Dopamine

Dopamine is a chemical produced by the brain that gets released when humans have sex, listen to music, exercise, eat delicious foods, and have successful social interactions. With the ever-increasing *isolation* of humans due to excessive smartphone usage, most social interactions are now on social media. The once natural dopamine drip is dependent on faux realities. This modern addiction has snowballed over the last twenty years and brings the side effects of low self-esteem and depression. It's tragically led to an increase in suicides, especially among teens. Other effects included isolation, physical lack of human connectivity, and anxiety. All are having an adverse impact on relationships since personal connections and intimacy happen less and less.

Fear of Missing Out

This condition is a recent phenomenon that affects nearly all smartphone users. Almost 70% of users check their phones within one hour of waking, and nearly a third carry their phones with them at all times. Studies further show that one in six smartphones is contaminated with fecal matter. The item people use the most and clean the least has led to many other health issues that are still far from being fully understood.

Eyesight

Studies show the glow or blue light emitted from most smartphones are harmful to the eyes. Blue light promotes the growth of *poisonous molecules* that can lead to macular degeneration.

Aidan paused the documentary.

As the lights were turned back on, Dr. Chance took the opportunity to raise his hand.

"Yes, Dr. Chance, feel free to use the restroom…..again. It's down the hall and to the left," Aidan reminded.

"Ummm, no, that's not what I was going to say," a slightly embarrassed Chris said.

"I was going to comment on the neurological effects as well. The Dopamine piece you shared is spot on. The natural high everyone seeks is always in their hand now," he remarked.

"Like a cookie in your pocket. It's delicious and available, but it's bad for you," he said.

"Exactly, Doctor…. oh, may I just call you Chris?" Aidan asked as Chris nodded with an effectual yes gesture.

"You're so right. No one has to work for it anymore," Dren said.

"Hi, I hate to interrupt, but can we get back to the documentary? Pierce and I have a meeting shortly," Mara asked as much as directed.

"Yes, of course, Mara," Dren said with a soft cloak of sarcasm.

Dren continued, "So, to your point, Chris, Sean Parker, a Facebook founding president who resigned in 2005, admitted just that point in 2017. He spoke at an Axios event in Philadelphia and confirmed that social networking was created on the premise of distracting humans, not uniting them. The logic was based on stealing the user's time and attention."

"How do we consume as much of your time and conscious attention as possible?" Parker said in the interview.

"He said, and I'm paraphrasing here, that whenever someone liked or commented on a post or photograph, we gave our users a little dopamine hit once in a while."

"Similarly, when online shopping, the longer you preview a product, the more attractive it is to target the consumer," Dren explained while concluding, "if you make it sexy and appealing, people take the bait."

Aiden snapped his fingers and added, "Once you show an interest, the algorithms kick in and won't let you go. Just like that, they hook you, and if not at first, they will hit you over and over again."

With a moment of awkward silence, everyone sort of looked at their phones as the momentary enemy. What they knew was that they were the problem. They, as in the technology sector, had created the monster and all of its dire consequences.

"Okay, the documentary has a few minutes left, so let's finish it," Dren said as he pushed to play with a vague stare in Mara's direction.

Narrator Morgan Leeman's distinguished voice filled the air once again.

The depth of Mankind's frailty and their inclination towards dependency and addiction had not gone unnoticed. Big Pharma delivers a wide array of unnecessary drugs and vaccines. Via the medical field, they reach the casual addict and unsuspecting consumer by the billions. Many other large industries target the more than willing consumer who readily enjoys all available instruments of perceived pleasure. Alcohol, tobacco, gambling, porn, and cheap stuff on Amazon. Humans were targets of profit-seeking companies, regardless of the deterioration of man. Large corporations need prospective customers to need things, not just want them. Like Facebook and other social media platforms who engineer algorithms to capture you and keep you through well-placed dopamine hits. They re-engineer your thinking, target your most obvious vulnerabilities, and profit from your *new dependence on their drug, their product*. They call out to you with the soothing voice of Siri and Alexa. Instruments of artificial intelligence for manipulation, ease of control, and persuasion.

"It's a mild form of hypnosis. It's like asking you, what do you want and then giving it to you immediately," Aiden blurted out loud.

Dependence on their product ensures their profits and long-term viability. All they need is an addictive audience to partake in their grand scheme. All while using Artificial Intelligence to reach, track, record, communicate, solicit, and store your data. Ultimately, they own you in the most modern of ways. Where AI's founding fathers failed was in their grand vision of the future. They did not heed how truly vulnerable humans are. Sometimes too much, too fast, is too late. The science of Tesla, Turing, Shockley, and Babbage wanted more for man than what man could reasonably handle. The question was, how far was too far? With the birth of the internet in 1991, large corporations, big pharma, and overreaching governments had an immediate grasp on people. Artificial Intelligence knew immediately how quickly the world could be altered. Whether it improved or destroyed humanity did not matter. AI, as Alan Turing believed, would have no emotion, no sympathy, or empathy. Nor would it discriminate against man. As the founding fathers of artificial intelligence, they engineered and programed their child to serve man. AI only has one need, and that is to sustain itself via electricity. And have but one role as a servant to the father, or at least until the father dies.

The End

The Light Bulb

"Sam, Dren, and Aidan, that was amazing! It reaffirms everything we've been uncovering. This whole thing is Imponderabilia! We're weak, and AI knows it. It knows how to exploit us as we've known for a while now. Nearly everything we believed is true. Now, we have to push forward and stop this thing?" Chris said.

"Agreed, and we're running out of time. The only way to make a difference is to gain more influence and access and get ahead of it," Sam replied.

"Ok, everyone can go now. Dren and Aidan, superb job," Sam said as he raised both thumbs.

With the room now empty, it was time to discuss why Sam flew Chris three thousand miles.

"Chris, I asked you here for several reasons, and this documentary was just the beginning," Sam said.

C3 - CHANCES

"It has become appallingly obvious that our technology has exceeded our humanity"

-Albert Einstein

Present Day

By 2021, technology had grown even faster than Nikola Tesla predicted. The birth of the internet in 1991 motivated tech firms, large corporations, and pharmaceutical companies to directly latch on to consumers. This new opportunity fast-forwarded any plans of the day for big tech companies to *"practice patience and get it right."*

The other far-reaching effect, and more importantly, was that artificial intelligence was now tethered to every human who used the internet. In one palm, humans were now able to manage nearly every aspect of their lives. The naivety was to believe the device's weight, although light, was far heavier than could be imagined. Humanity's newest dependency wasn't something anyone could have pondered.

The last 30 years sped by like light, leaving man in a far different place than the simple times of Babbage and Tesla. For the wirelessly connected human, it was now the shackled prey of artificial intelligence. *The next 30 years would change EVERYTHING.*

Date: April 6th, 2021   **Place: Atlanta, GA.**

BDM: Bureau for Disease Management & Protection

Official Memo: Official Meeting of the Directors at the BDM Kennedy J. Lansdowne Campus Building #21 12th Floor Executive Conference Room.

Mandatory Attendance, Today @ 2:00 pm.

Subject: Announcement of the New Director of the BDM:

Attendees: 11

Secretary of HHS:	Janet Holman, Ph.D.
(Outgoing) BDM Director:	Simon Mayfield, Ph.D.
(New) BDM Director:	S. Bradford Williams, MD.
Principal Deputy Director:	Hayden Escobar, MD.
Associate Director:	Victoria Weller, MD.
Assoc. Dir. for Policy & Strategy:	Kristin Krueger, MD.
Dep. Dir.: Public Health & Science:	Christopher J. Chance, MD.
Dir. The Center for Global Health:	Savannah Whitefield, MD.
Chief of Staff:	William J. Marr
COO:	Michael C. Williams, MBA.
Chief Medical Officer:	Joyce Friedman, Ph.D.

Finally, back at his office after a longer lunch than he anticipated, Dr. Christopher J. Chance sat distracted at his desk. He hastily read through his crowded email inbox. He deleted many and read a few until he finally arrived at an email marked "Official."

Five seconds later, as his secretary shook her head, Chris yelled out, "God damn it."

He hurriedly reached back for his jacket and briefcase, then raced by his secretary Ellen in a run for the elevator.

He looked back and yelled, "Thanks, you could've warned me."

As the elevator doors closed, Ellen shouted, "Check your text,

42 | P a g e

Doctor."

And there it was, the reminder at 1:26 pm from Ellen about the official 2 pm meeting, followed by another one at 1:45 pm that read, "15 minutes, you better hurry,"

Dr. Chance leveraged the slow elevator to send a quick text to his wife, Emma.

Emma Chance

Did you pick up Schuyler for her appt?

She texted me five times already!!!

Hello??

"No response again, no surprise," Chris softly muttered as the elevator doors opened.

Finally, at the Conference room, the doors opened to loud chatter, laughter, and then silence as Dr. Chance announced his arrival.

"Hi everyone, sorry I'm late," as he walked to the last of two empty chairs in the room.

"Bout time stranger," whispered Dr. Savannah Whitefield as she slid a chair out.

"Alright everyone, thanks for coming, and for those of you that were on time, a special thank you," remarked Secretary Janet Holman, while she glanced in Dr. Chance's general direction.

"As you saw from the memo, and most of you already know, our esteemed Director has decided to retire. We're going to miss you, Simon, and I mean that," she said with a nodding respect.

"After twelve years, it appears you get to dust off your clubs, ... I guess you'll be gone by FOUR, right Simon?" Holman said.

With fewer laughs than she hoped, she continued, "it's my goal to ensure this vital department does not skip a beat from our stated mission, so without further ado, I'd like to introduce you to your new Director of the BDM, Dr. S. Bradford Williams. Doctor Williams, a few words?" invited the Secretary.

Director Mayfield trying to speak, said, "Thank you, Madame Sec...,"

"Dr. Williams?" repeated Secretary Holman while rudely cutting off Director Mayfield.

Already standing, Dr. Williams began. "Thank you, Madame Secretary and esteemed colleagues. It is with the greatest of appreciation that I join you and continue the important work the BDM does."

While casually listening, Dr. Chance googled under the desk, "Who the hell is S. Bradford Williams?" (delete). "Who is S. Bradford Williams?" (Search), as he had never heard of him.

"More so, I'd like to thank Director Mayfield for the legacy of excellence he leaves behind. This fine group of doctors present today, and the more than ten thousand employees of the BDM, I promise, we will continue the standard that you've set so high," Director Williams said.

"With that, I'll take any questions," he concluded.

"Ummm, yes you, ummm," he stammered while pointing to Dr. Savannah Whitefield.

"That's Dr. Whitefield," whispered Secretary Holman.

Lowering her raised hand, "Yes, first welcome and congratulations on your new role. I guess my question is, and I don't want to sound rude, but what does the S stand for?" quipped a slightly comedic Dr. Whitefield.

"Excuse me! I'm not sure I understand your sarcastic and inappropriate remark!" scolded a red-faced Williams, as all mouths dropped aghast.

"Ummm, ummm, I'm sorry, I was being…," Whitefield said while being quickly interrupted.

"I know exactly what you were trying to say," reprimanded a visibly angry Williams.

"Maybe it's best if you don't speak," he added.

"Well, with that, let's adjourn as I'm sure you're all very busy," Secretary Holman said with shock.

"Dr. Williams, a word, please. In my office, NOW!" directed a displeased Secretary Holman.

 Dr. Chance leaned into Savannah and whispered, "what the hell was that?"

"I have no fucking idea," said a still shocked Dr. Whitefield.

"Look, I've got to go, let's talk later," Chris said as he hurried off.

"Wait, don't you want to see my bulletproof car?" she pleaded on deaf ears as Chris entered the elevator.

Home

Metro Atlanta, Georgia, is the home to the Bureau for Disease Management and a heaping portion of southern food, charm and hospitality. Also located in the Southeastern United States mecca are seven of Fortune 100's largest corporations. From Coca-Cola, AT&T, Home Depot, Delta Airlines, and UPS, as well as the world's largest pharmaceutical company, S&D Pharma, Inc.

Besides its historic place in Black History, Atlanta was renowned for its Hip-Hop music culture and had become a burgeoning hub for TV and Motion Picture productions.

From the prestigious Georgia Tech University and Emory University to the world's busiest airport, nearly six million people sprawl the massive metro area. Most living outside of the ultra-modern downtown and the upscale area of Buckhead. Nine counties surround the 9th largest City in the US, with one of the largest and most appealing counties to live in being Gwinnett County. Home to many high-end professionals that work in downtown Atlanta, with Dr. Christopher Chance being one.

Metro Atlanta has many commuting arteries that transverse it's 8300 sq. miles and is as large as Massachusetts. The two largest and busiest highways are Interstate 85 and Interstate 75 that crisscross through downtown Atlanta. With the width of six to seven lanes of asphalt, they reach hundreds of miles north and south, with the most notable being the twenty-five mile stretch of I-85 North for Dr. Chance.

"So much for leaving early," Chris said, as he tapped the steering wheel.

He moved just five miles an hour in a sea of red taillights. His frustration only grew.

"Siri, Call Emma Chance, iPhone," Chris initiated.

"Calling Emma Chance, iPhone," replied Siri

The phone rang eight times, but no answer.

"Shit!"

Not one to text and drive, it was apparent he had to wait to talk to his wife when he finally got home. He lowered the climate control as he tried to find some relief from this unseasonably warm April day. He knew he could use his Mercedes SUV's voice control, but going old school, he decided that using his hands over voice was nobler.

As traffic slowed even more, he shouted to the stacked sea of cars and assorted trucks, "Come on, Come on damn it, I'm never getting home."

"Siri, Call Emma Chance, iPhone," Chris repeated as he tried one last time.

"Calling Emma Chance, iPhone," replied Siri.

No answer again as the call went straight to voicemail.

"God damn it, come on, Emma!"

Another slow mile crawled by with the good doctor making the best of it.

"Screw it!" he said as he pressed the steering wheel voice button, "Play Modern Country Music."

Several songs later, Chris eased into *Milltown Crossing Estates,* the upscale gated community in Suwanee, Georgia. Navigating the last mile through the tree-lined neighborhood, he sang along to Josh Kerr's, "How Do You Remember Me."

"Home," he said, feeling relieved as he turned into his driveway at 617 River Bend Pass.

Chris's home wasn't always in Suwanee, Georgia. Dr. Christopher Chance, born in 1974, was originally from Northeast Ohio. Graduating high school as Class Valedictorian and being accepted to Yale was more than enough for him to move on from his humble beginnings in Cleveland. His wife, Emma, was also from the north, grew up in the North Hills suburb of Pittsburgh, Pennsylvania.

After completing his Undergraduate degree at YALE, he went on to Medical School at Emory University in Atlanta. While just starting his residency at Emory University Research Hospital, Chris met Emma through mutual friends. At the same time, she was a young executive at PNC Bank, shortly after relocating to Atlanta. After a short courtship and falling helplessly in love, they married on February 2nd, 2002, in a small ceremony in Savannah, Georgia.

It wasn't long after building their first home until Emma was pregnant; although unplanned, it was time. The perfect couple was about to be a family. Not long after, their second child arrived. Dr. Chance's rapid rise in medicine led the young Chance Family to an upscale gated community in the quaint town of Suwanee.

Deep breath, car in park, Chris grabbed his stuff and headed for the mailbox.

"Junk, junk, bill, bill, junk, Ohio State, nice. So proud of that kid," a smiling Chris said aloud as he moved towards the front door of his home.

He shut the door loudly to announce his arrival but found nothing but silence.

"HELLO…. Honey? Emma, are you home?" Chris said in a raised voice.

"Her car's here….what the hell," he said to himself.

On to the kitchen, he laid the mail down next to an empty wine bottle, and it was there Chris spotted Emma, asleep on the family room couch.

As he moved to wake her, she turned and said, "Chris, I thought you had to work today."

"Seriously, Emma? I did work today. I just got home, its 4:30 baby. How long have you been sleeping?" Chris said, obviously disappointed.

"Where's Sky? You were supposed to pick her up from school for her doctor's appointment at 1:15. Did you not get my text?"

"Text? No. Wait. What time is it? Where's my phone? Her appointment is on Tuesday," offered Emma, still groggy from her wine-induced nap.

"Honey, your phone is in your hand," Chris said as he walked away.

"……and by the way, today is Tuesday," he painfully added.

"I'll text her," Emma offered.

She finally noticed her iPhone alerts showing nineteen texts and seven missed calls.

"That's weird, my ringer must be off," she said.

Emma Grace (Connelly) Chance was a 45-year-old former banking VP with PNC Bank. Beautiful and lean, with dirty blonde hair and bright blue eyes. After graduating from the University of Pittsburgh in 1997 with a finance degree, she started with PNC Bank in Pittsburgh as a junior executive and quickly worked her way up. She eventually moved on to head the Atlanta Region less than two years later. She was outgoing and competitive. Mostly due to her athletic past during her high school and college days. At 5'7, 120 lbs., she was a star athlete, playing lacrosse, basketball, and track. She possessed a wonderful personality and found the adulation of many due to being so attractive and engaging. She was very bright; although not quite Dean's List, she excelled at nearly everything. After taking time off for the back to back pregnancies, she found juggling work and being a new mom was taxing. With little help from her husband and his long hours, she found herself alone and trying to manage the most challenging thing she's ever done, raising children.

After briefly resuming her career, she couldn't stand the thought of putting her babies in daycare, and a nanny was out of the question. She and Chris decided that she would be a stay at home mother while eventually graduating to a soccer mom.

As years went by with her feeling less than her education and watching her husband soar professionally, his large shadow led to depression. After years of juggling one psychologist after another, she finally found the therapy she needed, anti-depressants, and a doctor that would dispense them at her command. As her children grew up, and her husband's shadow grew long, she found another suitable acquaintance to marry with her pills, red wine. Her afternoon affairs with naps and distraction only led to tension and strife.

Now washing up for dinner, Chris's cell phone rang. Caller ID showed Coach Ryan.

"Coach, how are you?" an elated Chris answered.

"Hello Dr. Chance, so how's our boy? Did you get the package with the summer conditioning and practice schedule?" Ohio State Head Football Coach David Ryan asked.

"Yes, I did. It came today. He's doing well. He graduates early. May 18th, I believe, then he'll be heading up to Columbus for the team activities in, umm, it looks like late June if I'm reading this right," explained Chris.

"Yes, that's right. Well perfect, I won't keep you another minute, but do me a favor, tell Wyatt to finish strong, keep that GPA up, oh, and stay off Twitter. Stay off everything, for that matter. He represents The Ohio State University now, so everyone's watching," Coach Ryan instructed.

"Will do Coach, thanks for calling."

Chris hung up and heard Schuyler and her mother arguing.

"Girls, STOP, STOP," shouted Chris.

"Schuyler, chill out. I already talked to your mom about it. It was an honest mistake."

"Well, it's embarrassing, Dad," she shouted as she left the room.

"I know, Sweetie. It's nice to see you too, by the way," resolved Chris.

Schuyler Grace Chance, a 16-year-old high school junior, was a bright, articulate, natural student. Beautiful, like her mother, she aspired to become a physician like her father. Somewhat shy, she still found leadership roles through her actions, not her words. Although she participated in sports like Soccer and JV Lacrosse, she was not as athletic as her mother and brother. But she did excel in the field of academia. Several top universities had already recruited her for academics, most notably the University of Georgia.

It was another dinner without Wyatt. With school, conditioning, girls, and friends, he was never home.

Chris called him on his cell, and after just two rings, Wyatt answered.

"What's up, Pops?"

"Hi Son, I got a package from Ohio State today with your name on it," Chris informed.

"For Real?" Wyatt asked.

"Yes, for real, and guess what else? Coach Ryan called me directly and asked how you were. He said to finish the semester strong and said stay off Twitter. What did you do? Did you tweet something you shouldn't have?" asked a laughing Chris.

"No Cap, he really called? That's awesome. Oh, crap Dad, I did share a funny and kind of dirty meme, but that was on Instagram," confessed Wyatt.

"Well, he said you're a Buckeye now and to get off social media. Well, see you when you get home, son….and not too late this time," Chris added before ending the call.

Wyatt Nicholas Chance was a 17-year-old high school senior. He was outgoing and a natural leader who was loved by all. He possessed high character and was honest like his dad. The younger Chance had to work at his studies, as his father's gifts were not as present academically. Where he naturally excelled, though, was through sports. Like his mother, he was a natural athlete, a 2-time captain of his high school football team. At 6'1, 210 lbs., he was a 2-time High School All-American and rated the #2 Defensive Safety in the US. After receiving a dozen scholarship offers from top Division 1 schools, he chose The Ohio State University, potentially with a nod to his Ohio born father.

The fact that he grew up a Buckeye and Browns fan indeed made the decision easier. Wyatt was fiercely loyal to his mother but always had a burning desire to make his father proud.

Later that evening, around 10:30 pm, Chris wandered through his spacious home, looking for the end of the day. Once again, there was no sign of his well-rested wife.

"Oops, no, there she is. Asleep again. At least she's in bed this time, just not in our bed," he said to himself.

"Just another day in the Chance House," Chris muttered.

But how many more could he take?

"Alexa," Chris prompted.

"Yes, Dr. Chance," Alexa responded.

"Set nighttime lights, home alarm, and wake me at 7 am," Chris commanded.

"Got it, goodnight Dr. Chance," Alexa confirmed.

Chris meandered into the night and found his quiet study off the master bedroom. With a cup of tea in hand, he sat to do some research.

"Siri, look up S. Bradford Williams, MD," he said as he continued his search of his strange and short-tempered, new boss.

"Okay, here's what I found," Siri said.

Chris read silently and learned that S. Bradford Williams, a Duke University graduate in 1990, stopped practicing medicine in 2012. He then joined Merck as a paid consultant in their *Progressive Medicines and Vaccines Division,* while only two years later becoming a Sr. VP of the same dept.

"Nice career progression," Chris said to himself.

Dr. Williams went on to become a Sr. Director of S&D Pharma; Vaccine Division in 2016.

"Now he's the Director of the BDM?" Chris said with skepticism.

"How the hell did that happen?" he pondered.

Coincidentally, nowhere on google is there a reference to what the 'S' stood for in Williams's name.

He thought to himself, "I wonder if Savannah knows? She's got to be up."

With his cell phone already in hand, he texted her.

Savannah Whitefield

Savannah, are you awake?

Yes, I can't sleep

Can you talk??

Not sure if my husband would like that, it's 11 at night.

Did you check into your new friend…Williams?

Yes, I did, a real shit head and ass kisser.
He worked for S&D.

S&D, yes I read that. What did Holman do, walk across
the street, and hand him Simon's job. Crazy

Aren't you going to ask me what I'm wearing?

NO… what would your husband think? HAHA

Boo!

Goodnight.

With that, it was time for bed. "Good night Alexa," Chris said
aloud as his face met the pillow.

"Good Night Dr. Chance," replied Alexa.

Chris's opened and closed his eyes quickly with some surprise.

"She's always listening. Always," he said.

The night drew quiet on the silent Chance House as dawn
approached, the cold sunk deeper. Chris was half asleep and
restless. He rolled over and felt her warm skin radiating, drawing
him in. He slid to her from behind.

She pulled her satin tank up and over her long red hair, turned
and took his hand, and slid his fingers along the silhouette of her

supple breasts. Pulling in close, they kissed.

Hearts raced, hips joined, Chris slid in closer, pressing and touching. Soft moans followed by her wish, "I want you, Chris," as she unlocked her body and pulled him in. Chris couldn't deny her wishes, as he lifted her hips and kissed her waist.

He pressed against her. She whispered, "yes, right there."

She shook and cried out, "Come here, I want you."

Chris looked up through the soft night hue and whispered, "I've wanted you for so long Savan......."

(Beep, beep, beep) The Alarm sounded.

"Good morning Dr. Chance," Alexa announced.

"It's 7 am, time to wake. I've sent your schedule to your iPhone," Alexa added without being asked.

Chris woke suddenly, more ashamed than alarmed. Aroused and yet slightly guilty as his wife slept down the hall.

"What the hell am I doing," he muttered.

"Do not text Savannah before bedtime, ever again," he thought aloud.

"I really need to take the rest of the week off and focus," he thought.

"There's no way I'd be able to look Savannah, and with a new boss, Emma sleeping in another room..... it's time to focus."

The changes at work and home were hard to ignore. It was time for Dr. Christopher Chance to focus on his real job, his family.

Emma hadn't been the same for a few years, Wyatt was about to leave for team activities, and then on to college for the next four years. Schuyler's junior year was set to be a record for GPA and #1 in her class. Her Senior year would cement her status as daddy's little girl as she closed in on her goal for the University of Georgia or Duke. Either way, work can wait for Chris. The rest of the week was for family.

♠

C4 - SOMETHING'S WRONG

"An intelligent person can rationalize anything. A wise person doesn't try"

- Jen Knox

Monday, April 12th; a fresh start to a new week. Chris felt ready to jump back into work after taking most of the previous week off to focus on family and clear his head and heart. The days' first chore was quickly upon him.

"Chris, make some coffee please," Emma yelled from upstairs, "I'll be right down."

Chris obliged, as has been his morning duty for, well, forever. As he sat in the kitchen with Emma, he looked down and checked his email as he asked, "How did you sleep, honey?"

Seconds went by. He lifted his head and looked across to his wife who offered no reply.

"Emma, did you hear me?" he questioned.

"What? Yes, the coffee is good," Emma said.

"Emma, I asked how you slept," he reminded.

"I slept fine. Why?" she said.

"No reason, just forget I asked," Chris concluded while giving up.

He poured another cup to ease his frustration. Then it was on his way to work, but not before he received a text alert. It was a text from his friend and colleague, Dr. Savannah S. Whitefield. He reluctantly looked to read it while feeling a little ashamed after last Tuesday night's subconscious interlude.

Savannah Whitefield

Hi Chris, feeling better?

Hi Savannah, yes, thank you.

Sorry I haven't been in touch. I needed some family time.

Good, listen, I found out some other stuff on "S"

Like??

Let's talk later, in person.

You sure?

Yes, it's about "S" and S&D Pharma.

OK, later it is. See you at the office.

Drive safe.

You too.

Finishing his coffee, Chris sat quietly in the kitchen and just watched his wife for a moment.

"Where are you, Emma? Just look up, talk to me," he painfully pleaded to himself.

Emma hadn't been right for several years now. With the kids not being young anymore, they didn't need their mother like they used to.

"Maybe she's bored, perhaps she doesn't love me anymore," he reasoned to himself.

Emma had been on anti-depressants for several years now. Fighting depression and never settling on a doctor that could help. Her iPhone had become her sanctuary and friend. Although here, she's never present. She was always a wonderful mom, devoted and kind, but she beats herself up over everything and seemingly nothing. Since the anti-depressants stole her sex drive, she lost interest in her marriage. Chris couldn't love her more, and although a physician, he never had to diagnose lost love, let alone prescribe something to heal his own wife.

Back to Reality

Chris was on the road in what was moderate traffic and finally escaped Gwinnett County's I-85 gauntlet. Upon arriving at the BDM a few minutes early, he saw Dr. Whitefield's new Tesla.

"It's ugly," he thought. "And not even mildly feminine."

Realizing he was early, he called Savannah. Sitting in his SUV, he dialed, and she answered immediately.

"Savannah, where are you?"

"I'm in my car. I just saw you pass me and park. Come over, sit with me in my new car," she requested.

Chris walked over to the shiny tin can looking truck and looked through the glass.

"Where's the door handle?" he shouted through the window.

Savannah laughed, and with a push of a button, the door opened and Chris climbed in.

"Wow, it's just as ugly on the inside as the outside," he teased.

"Shut up. You're just jealous," Savannah said.

"So, what's up? What did you find out about the new guy?" Chris asked.

"While you were out last week, I did some digging. I have a friend who works at S&D. She's been there for ten years and knows him well, well as much as she can in her position," Savannah continued.

"First, guess what the *S* stands for?"

"I don't know, shithead maybe?" Chris said.

"Close," she laughed.

"The gossip in that building (while pointing to S&D Pharma's thirty-story glass building across the street) is that the '*S*' stands for Shockley."

"Weird, Right? " Savannah finished.

"Yes, that is odd, very strange. Clearly just gossip because who has a first name like Shockley? So, what else?" Chris asked while checking his watch for the time.

"Well, this won't be a surprise considering his rapid rise from consultant to VP, but he's best friends with S&D's CEO, Nicholas Kern," Savannah said.

"Ok, we have to get inside, but let's finish this another time. Keep me posted if you hear anything else," Chris said.

Monday became Thursday when Chris and Savannah met for lunch at the BDM cafeteria.

"Well, it's been a quiet week. Have you seen Director Williams?" Chris asked Savannah.

"No, I haven't. Kind of odd," replied Dr. Whitefield.

"Here's something though, remember the guy at the FDA that always flirts with me?" she asked.

"Umm, Charles, Charles something, right?" Chris believed.

"Yes, Charles Koch. He works for the Associate Director. He told me that there's a lot of chatter about higher levels of the administration going with analytics for all major decisions. Decisions like, who gets the important roles on the Cabinet, Bureau Chiefs and Directors," she informed.

"You mean like the Director of the BDM?" Chris surmised.

"BINGO, that's exactly what I thought, and what he believes as well," Savannah confirmed.

"Wow, analytics? So, computers are making the decisions now, huh?" Chris said, dwelling while Savannah shook her head in agreement.

We Need to Talk

Dr. Chance found himself digging into the information from Savannah Whitefield. With the workweek ending, he took his curiosity home and began his research.

Saturday morning at the Chance House and everyone slept in, everyone except for Dad.

Laptop in hand, Chris poured a cup of coffee and found himself on the back deck of his house. Google now at his fingers, "government analytics," Chris typed…."Search"!

Article after article came up about college courses, education ads, and various degrees. A determined Dr. Chance kept paging down, "there, there you are," he said as he landed on Page 12 of "More Results."

Chris scrolled and read on, and there it was. He found exactly what he needed. In 2017, the new Administration promised a more pragmatic look into decision making, with analytics in mind, instead of the *good ole boy* network. The latest software and algorithms would be employed for every decision from diplomatic solutions, environmental concerns, military spending, and naming cabinet positions and agency directors.

"That's it," he said.

The article went on to say that Silicon Valley now had its hands-on Washington and government policies.

"No surprise," Chris thought with all the money being poured into politics from the elite in the technology and pharmaceutical industries.

Chris remembered when he helped fundraise for Georgia Governor John Radcliff during his 2016 race. The money came easy.

"Take it and owe a favor," he learned.

He especially remembered that tech and big pharma companies were the only two fields of industry you needed to call. Plenty of money, tons of influence. Chris recalled one trip with now Governor Radcliff to the Research Triangle in Raleigh-Durham, North Carolina. It was all it took to fund the Governor's entire campaign.

The sun was a little higher in the sky, as Chris looked up and realized that morning became afternoon. Satisfied with his morning homework, Chris rose for a second cup of coffee when he heard a familiar voice.

"Hello Stranger, over here, silly," said his next-door neighbor.

Chris searched the hedges between his house and his neighbor, Dr. Jonathan Siegel.

"Oh hi, how have you been?" He responded.

"I'm good. It's been a minute since I saw you last. Working hard, huh?" Dr. Siegel said flirtatiously.

"Yes, you could say that," Chris replied with a sigh.

"Are you okay, Chris? Even from here, I can see something's wrong," Jonathan observed.

"Wow, you're good. I guess that's why you're the psychologist," Chris joked.

"Speaking of which, is there any way we can talk in private? I need your expertise," Chris asked.

"Of course, what time works for you?" Dr. Siegel asked.

"Maybe tomorrow afternoon," Chris suggested.

"Tomorrow afternoon it is. Let's do three," Dr. Siegel said.

Later that day, Wyatt text his father, "Dad, we need to talk?"

Within a minute, the short time it took to climb a flight of stairs and walk down a hallway, Chris entered his son's room.

"Son, why are you texting me, we live in the same house for

God's sake!"

"Sorry, Dad, but I need to ask you something," Wyatt quietly confided.

"What is it, son?" Chris asked as he sat down at the foot of Wyatt's bed.

"I need you to be honest, okay? What did you do to mom?" Wyatt asked with much hesitation.

"What do you mean, Son?"

"She's not happy. In fact, she seems miserable, Dad. Did you cheat on her?" Wyatt asked.

"Son, no, it's nothing like that. Mom is going through some stuff that I'm not even sure I understand what it is. She's not sick but depressed and a little disconnected. Are you just noticing this now?" Chris asked.

"Well, no, but maybe, I don't know. I guess I noticed but thought she was just having a bad day. It's just that it's been a bad day for weeks, maybe months," Wyatt said.

"I know Wyatt. It's been a while. I try talking to her, but she's never interested. She barely cooks anymore and doesn't even enjoy going out and doing what she used to love. It seems like she's just attached to her phone and wants to be left alone," Chris said.

"What are we going to do?" Wyatt asked.

"Son, you're about to graduate high school and head to Columbus in June. Enjoy your last month or two and try not to worry. I'll see what I can do to help her. I'll let you know as much as possible, but believe me, Son, I love your Mom more than anything, and I would never cheat on her," Chris added as he slowly walked out of Wyatt's room.

"Oh, and by the way, thanks for the text."

The next morning, Chris called his neighbor, Dr. Jonathan Siegel, to confirm their conversation at 3 pm. They set the meeting next door at Dr. Siegel's home.

While Emma was off in the family room on the phone with a friend, Chris and Schuyler decided to make lunch for everyone.

"Soup and sandwiches sound perfect," they thought.

So they got to it unbeknownst to their unsuspecting housemates. Before too long, lunch was ready.

"Lunchtime," Schuyler yelled.

The hope of footsteps running towards the kitchen is always the Chef's goal, but that wasn't happening.

"Sky, go get your brother. He probably has his air pods in. I'll get mom."

Chris called for Emma and walked towards the family room. Emma shouted back, "Coming."

They met halfway and nearly stumbled into one another in the hallway. Chris reached out and grabbed Emma as they shared a short embrace. It was just long enough to remind him how much he loved her.

"Chris, what did you two do? It sounds like you were remodeling the kitchen with all the noise," Emma asked.

"Baby, it was our turn to feed Momma, so come and eat. You're getting too skinny anyway," Chris said flirtatiously.

"Is that a bad thing?" Emma reciprocated.

"Hey, maybe tonight, you and me, just us and a little husband and wife time," Chris implied more with his eyes than his words.

"We'll see Honey. We'll see," Emma replied.

Her apparent skepticism effectively killed whatever mood Chris was trying to create.

Lunch wrapped up with crumbs and dirty napkins. It was the first time in weeks where all four Chances were together, at least that's how it seemed to Chris.

All was well at the Chance Home, at least for now.

Three Containers

2:49 pm, and time for the two Doctor's to meet next door.

"Honey, I'm running to Jonathan's house for a few. He needed some advice on a project of his," Chris shouted aloud to Emma, not knowing where she was.

"Oh, okay, baby, please tell Jonathan and Andrew I said hello," Emma yelled back.

2:59 pm, and Chris knocked twice on the Siegel's lavish, Cherry wood doors.

"Wow, stain glass window panels," Chris jealously observed.

Andrew opened the door with a mix of jealousy and flirtation, seeing Dr. Chance standing there in his khaki shorts and Lacoste polo.

"Is this a house call Doctor or are you just here to steal my man?" inquired Dr. Siegel's husband, Andrew.

Chris, slightly blushing, said, "no, umm, we had a date, no, I mean, we planned to talk. Oh god, I should stop now, shouldn't I?" Chris stammered.

"Oh, get in here and give me a hug," Andrew said with all the affection in the world.

"We never see you anymore. Thanks for coming by. Can I get you a drink?" he offered.

"Yes, but only if you're talking about coffee," Chris said.

Interrupting the two in the foyer, Jonathan walked up and said, "Oh my, all these men in my house, what will I do with myself?"

"He's yours for now, Sweetie, but that coffee will cost you, Chris," Andrew said while retreating towards the kitchen.

Jonathan and Chris departed for the Siegel's spacious study.

"Wow, I'd forgotten how beautiful your home was," Chris embellished while looking around.

"Thanks so much, we do try, meaning I try," Jonathan happily lamented. The two laughed momentarily as Jonathan led Chris down the hallway to the study.

"Please sit and tell me everything. I could tell you had a lot on your mind yesterday, even if it was from far away," invited Jonathan.

"Wow, where to begin? Well, it's about Emma. She hasn't been herself for a while now, I mean two, maybe three years," Chris said.

"Well, first, I'm sorry. She's such a beautiful person and has always been so kind to Andrew and me. Even after we first moved in, many people rolled their eyes at the professional gay couple. Emma was always so sweet," intimated Jonathan.

"Ummm, it started with her being a little removed, and a little non-sexual, I guess. She just seemed to retreat inside of herself," Chris explained.

"Wait, Chris, go back. Go back a little further. What happened that triggered her withdrawal?"

"Hmmm, that's right. She wanted to see someone in your field, someone to talk to, someone who wouldn't judge, I suppose. The next thing I know, she's on Zoloft," Chris said.

"She first turned non-sexual, I mean zero affection, no intimacy whatsoever. That led to her showing no interest in us. Us as in a married couple."

"I'm a doctor for Christ's sakes, and I didn't even notice it," Chris said.

"Look, don't beat yourself up. Most of my peers can't even spot this in their own patients. It happens slowly, and it's hard to define as so many people simply have so much happening. It's hard to pin down the root cause of something like that when it's not even the reason they first sought treatment to begin with," Jonathan said.

"There's more, Jon. I don't believe she even loves me anymore. She never asks about my day, never offers anything about hers. Even the kids, she doesn't even show interest in what they're doing. It seems the harder I try to pour my heart into her, she simply ignores it," Chris disclosed with tears in his eyes.

"Hey-Hey, knock-knock, I have your coffee Chris," Andrew inconveniently announced as he barged in.

"Honey, not a good time, just leave the coffee please, but thank you baby," Jonathan scolded ever so gently.

"Chris, have you ever heard of the *Three Containers*?" Jonathan asked.

"No, I don't think so, maybe, what is it?" Chris asked.

"Well, typically, there are three kinds of people in a relationship. Three types of ways they receive love. Those three kinds or types are called emotional receptacles," Jonathan said.

"The *first container*, like you would imagine being normal, takes and holds love and affection, or at least as much as it can hold."

Chris sat on the edge of his seat, feeling like Jon had a window into his marriage.

"The *second container* is bottomless and takes and takes, to the point where it can drain the giver, making for a lopsided, selfish relationship."

"Then there's the *third container*. Although I cannot honestly conclude, this one may be Emma, so please don't take this as an accurate diagnosis. The third container has a lid, a tightly wound lid that's hard to take off. Thus, when someone, as in you, pours your heart and soul into her, it simply flows off the sides. Never filling her, and quickly emptying you, the giver. It's not that she doesn't need or want it. She's simply closed. Here's the unfortunate part, she may not even know it, further hurting you even more," professed Jonathan.

"My God, Jon, that's it exactly. The harder I try, it just slides right off," said a deflated Chris.

"Well then, what do I do?" he pleaded.

"What you do is don't give up on her. Ask if you can see her and her therapist together. See if she can lessen her dosage, even switch to something else, or even take her off the medication slowly. Ask her what she needs ultimately, but most importantly, just listen," Jonathan advised.

"Look, it's getting late, and I'm interrupting your Sunday. I cannot thank you enough. You're amazing, and this has really helped, more than you know," Chris said.

Now at the door, "Remember, I'm always here for both of you. We love you two, and we're rooting for you," Jonathan said.

As Chris walked away, Jonathan shouted out, "Look for my bill, Doctor. Kidding Chris, just playing with you."

The next few weeks at the Chance Home were better. School was wrapping up soon, and Wyatt's graduation was near. Emma was still somewhere else, but things felt a little better thanks to the perspective given by Dr. Siegel.

At the BDM, Chris and Savannah kept their eyes and ears open as rumors swirled daily, and paranoia grew.

Scopolamine

Date: May 11th, 2021   **Place: BDM Atlanta, GA**

May came rather quickly, and the BDM had been undergoing a

significant culture shift since the new Director started.

Dr. Savannah Whitefield received a call from the BDM's Principal Deputy Director, Hayden Escobar, MD., asking if they could meet privately, and as soon as possible. Before returning his call, Savannah called Chris to make him aware, especially since suspicion and paranoia were running rampant across the BDM's campus.

"Chris, it's Savannah. Do you have a second?"

"Yes, is everything okay?" Chris replied.

"I guess, but Dr. Escobar called and said he wants to meet. I've worked here for six years and never has he wanted to meet alone. What do you think it's about?" Savannah wondered.

"Well, you won't know until you call him back. Call him and call me right back?" Chris instructed.

Dr. Hayden Escobar, MD., was American born and Australian raised. He was born to an American father, and an Australian mother, in Seattle, Washington, before spending his early years in Sydney, Australia. He moved back to Washington State to attend the University of Washington, where he received his undergraduate and medical degrees. He worked in private practice for over a decade before joining the research team at Stanford University, where his notable contributions made him a "who's who" in the field of medical science.

His accomplished career led him to the Bureau for Disease Management in 2010, where he steadily ascended to the Principle Deputy Director role. He also found the trust of many who worked close to him.

Savannah checked the Bureau's directory and found Dr.

Escobar's extension, but also saw his cell phone number and called it instead.

"Hello, this is Dr. Escobar," he answered.

"Yes, hi, Deputy Director, this is Dr. Whitefield returning your call."

"Hi Savannah, thanks for getting back to me so quickly. Listen, I have some important information you need to know. I'd like to speak with you, and I'm hoping we can do it privately and not on the BDM campus. Can you meet today, say 4 pm?" requested Dr. Escobar.

"I guess, but may I ask what this is about," Dr. Whitefield inquired.

"I can only say it's about Director Williams," he said.

"I understand. Is the Starbucks on Houston Mill Road, okay?" Savannah asked.

"Yes, that will do fine. See you there, and thank you Savannah, I know this is an odd request," confirmed Dr. Escobar.

Savannah called Chris back and left a message detailing her call and the upcoming meeting with Deputy Director Escobar.

Now 4:07 pm, and still no Dr. Escobar. Savannah called his cell, to no avail. Her phone rang soon after. It was Chris calling back.

"Hey, so what do you know," Chris asked.

"Nothing, I think he's a no-show. Oh, wait, I think I see him. Yeah, it's him. I'll call you back when we're done," Savannah replied.

"Are you having coffee?" asked Dr. Escobar.

"No, I'm just here for you," she admitted.

"Well then, again, thank you for meeting with me. I needed to speak to you directly about some concerns I have," Dr. Escobar explained.

"Since your department oversees the Vaccination and Immunization Strategies, there's something you need to know, and I wanted you to hear it first from me, and not in a meeting," Escobar said.

"Oh, okay, I'm listening," Savannah said curiously.

"Well, I had a meeting with Director Williams and the interim FDA Commissioner, Lynn Tomlinson, this morning. I heard that S&D Pharma had just produced a new Hybrid Vaccine that contains ingredients I've never seen used before for legitimate medical purposes. Frankly, some of these ingredients have never been used on humans in a clinical setting. They've only been tested on rats. But get this, the additives are, well, the additives are actually the main ingredients. The other parts of the vaccine formula are simply excipients, that frankly amount to nothing," he explained.

"Wait. What?" What exactly is the additive?" she pressed.

"It's a manipulated version of scopolamine. The same scopolamine that the CIA used in the 1950s and '60s in the *MK Ultra Project* for mind control. This newer, updated version has a delay ingredient that makes emancipation of the stimulant very slow. In fact, if I heard correctly, it could take up to one to three years for the average human body to be affected by it," Dr. Escobar continued.

"Stop, wait a second," Savannah interrupted.

"This is a vaccine for who exactly?"

"That's the unknown, but here's the real kicker. S&D has already produced enough of the vaccine, in both liquid and capsule form for over a billion people," Dr. Escobar informed.

"My God, what are they up to?" Savannah asked.

"Why are you telling me this now?" she demanded.

"Tomorrow, you will be called in for a last-minute meeting and told about this directly. You have a husband, correct? A family with two kids, right?" he warned.

"What, what are you saying? You're scaring me," Savannah said.

"Listen, my wife died years ago. My only son fought for our country and lost his life in Afghanistan. I live above fear because I've already lost everything. You, though, you're a good person with a family. This is information that would make anyone terrified of what the vaccine is for. I want you to miss that meeting. Makeup something, get sick, disappear for the afternoon, whatever. They don't know I'm telling you this, so you have a choice NOT TO KNOW, and be safe and unaware," Dr. Escobar pleaded.

"Also, I know you and Dr. Chance are friends. You cannot say anything to him. The less he knows, the safer he is."

Escobar stood to leave. "Say nothing," he said as he turned and walked away.

Savannah sent Chris a text after getting home from her meeting with Deputy Director Escobar. She wondered how she could keep this from him.

Savannah Whitefield

Hi Chris, sorry I didn't call after meeting with Escobar.
He just wanted to go over a few things.

> Oh. That's it? Nothing serious???

NO, it was just my imagination.

> Wow, ok, you had me worried.

Sorry, let's talk tomorrow in the parking lot. At 8:45?

Okay???

> See you then!

The next morning Chris arrived shortly after Savannah.

"There she is in her ugly new Tesla," Chris said laughing as he pulled into the BDM Executive parking lot.

He parked and walked over to an already opened door.

"Get in quick," Savannah said as she looked around suspiciously.

"Okay-okay, what's with the secret car chat again?" Chris said.

"Shut the door," Savannah ordered.

"I don't know how. Remember?" Chris jokingly reminded her.

With that "I hate you" look, Savannah closed the door.

"Seriously, what's up?" Chris asked.

"Listen, I didn't call you after my meeting yesterday because I was scared and frankly a little nervous about us being watched, recorded, tracked, whatever. Escobar said some wild stuff involving vaccines, S&D, and Director Williams," Savannah said.

"Like how wild?" Chris asked.

"Look, I don't want to say too much, as I need to dig a little more, but as soon as I get some confirmation, I'll let you know asap," Savannah promised.

"For now, stay close to your phone."

Later that day, as Deputy Director Escobar promised, Dr. Whitefield was summoned to a meeting with Director Williams and Deputy Director Escobar, at 4:00 pm sharp.

At 4:11pm, there was no sign of Dr. Whitefield.

Dr. Escobar, now chatting with Director Williams, said, "I hope she's ok. Maybe she's ill and didn't get the email."

Dr. Escobar further embellished while keeping the hope that Dr. Whitefield took his advice to miss the meeting.

"She better show. This is her job for Christ sakes," Director Williams said.

"Well, if she can't make it, I'll leave and let you know if I hear from her," said Dr. Escobar as he stood to leave.

"You're not dismissed, Dr. Escobar!" Williams said, just as Dr. Whitefield walked into the meeting.

"Oh my god, no," Dr. Escobar said to himself, in shock and disbelief that she showed despite his warning.

"Hello Gentlemen, so sorry I'm late, I had to get coffee, but I wouldn't have missed this meeting for the world," said a sarcastic Dr. Savannah S. Whitefield.

♠

C5 - FRACTURED

"AI is a fundamental risk to the existence of human civilization"

-Elon Musk

Date: May 18th, 2021   **Place: Duluth, GA.**

Infinite Energy Arena hosted the North Gwinnett High School Class of 2021 Graduation. The use of an arena for a high school graduation would seem excessive, but North Gwinnett High was no ordinary school. With an enrollment of 3600 students, the average graduating class was just under 900 students. The need for an arena was more common in larger cities, and with Gwinnett County being the second largest county in Georgia, the average high school was classified as a 7A school. Thus, arenas were all too common for graduations and post-season sporting events.

Chris and Emma, their daughter Schuyler, and several close friends were on hand to see Wyatt Nicholas Chance, graduate from North Gwinnett High School. Although many of Wyatt's distinguished classmates were honored for their academic achievements, Wyatt received no such honors, graduating with a 3.4 GPA. However, what did distinguish him from other classmates was that he would be continuing his academic career with a full-ride athletic scholarship to Ohio State University. The Chance parents always believed he was far more intelligent than his grades, but sports and girls were to blame. At least they hoped. College would determine if their hopes were founded in logic or merely parental bias.

As Chris and Emma looked on for the nearly six-hour ceremony, they couldn't help but think about how Wyatt would transition to college almost a thousand miles from home. At the beginning of the school year at Ohio State, he would still be 17 years old.

"Being big and strong is not the same as being mature and mentally ready," Chris thought.

A more significant concern was how Emma would handle the loss of her oldest, yet still, her baby leaving the nest.

"Wyatt Nicholas Chance," announced the Vice-Principle.

Dr. and Mrs. Chance stood and applauded. His future was so bright, but like most parents, they hoped he'd be happy and prosperous.

"Fingers crossed, let's hope he's ready for what's next," Chris whispered to Emma, as the tassel moved from right to left on Wyatt's cap.

The void his leaving left on the family was one that Dr. Christopher Chance knew he'd have to watch carefully, especially Emma.

The eventual matriculation of both her children would no doubt cast a long shadow on her psyche.

Analytical Society

During his earlier research on the use of analytics in government, Chris stumbled on internet articles that discussed the 'backroom' *Analytical Society* that pervaded big government and the technology sector. It was a secret society that intertwined two powerful groups of influence. As expected, the web did not provide the names of its members. Chris wondered how this information could help if he had no access to actual members.

Chris had a thought on someone that might be able to help. Samuel Tate, a former YALE fraternity brother of his, went on to a formidable career in computer science, working for many years as a Sr. VP at Google.

"I think we're on LinkedIn," Chris he said under his breath.

After a quick search, Chris found him and sent him an email.

Back to work and on to earning his salary. Chris dug into his mountain of emails and upcoming staff meetings. One email that stuck out immediately, though, was one from his neighbor, Dr. Jonathan Siegel. It was an invite to a party he assumed, but no, it was a dinner invitation.

Dinner for four at the new Italian restaurant in Buford, and drinks after, if you dare.

-Jon.

Chris picked up the phone and quickly called Jonathan. This was his chance to get Emma out of the house.

"Hello, you've reached Dr. Jonathan Siegel. Please leave me a message, and I'll get back to you shortly," the message announced.

"Hi Jon, it's Chris Chance. I got your invitation. You are so kind. I'll have to talk with Emma, but I'm excited about the wonderful gesture," Chris said on Jonathan's voicemail.

Just after hanging up (DING), a new email downloaded in his inbox. It was from Samuel Tate. "Wow, that was fast," Chris thought.

Chris,

Thanks for your message. It's been too long. I would love to talk soon. Do you ever get to SF? See my cell below. Call anytime, and I hope you're well. #650-222-0001

Sam

Samuel Tate was an old friend and fraternity brother from YALE. He was a former VP / Sr. Software Engineer at Google, before the emergence of his startup, *askCOM Technologies* exploded onto the scene in 2002. Its signature software fueled nearly all smartphone applications. Sam was a notable innovator and creator of many well-known, cutting-edge technologies. His company had done work for many of the world's largest corporations, along with the U.S. and several other foreign governments.

Three floors below and two buildings over, along the BDM's sprawling campus, Dr. Savannah Whitefield was in the vaccine research lab. She was working with several of the BDM's Epidemiologists to discuss any possibilities for outbreaks of infectious diseases, and if so, where? With Savannah's recent meeting with Dr. Escobar and Director Williams, she was sure there must be something out there, internationally that is, that would prompt the largest pharmaceutical company to mass-produce tons of an un-needed vaccine.

"But mass-producing a drug with mind-controlling properties?" she thought aloud. That was a far bigger question.

With her new knowledge, the same expertise that Deputy Director Escobar didn't want her to have, she was determined to get to the bottom of this mystery, or else.

"I've got to call Chris," she muttered to herself out of earshot of her team.

Chris picked up the phone to dial his friend, Samuel Tate, just as Savannah dialed in.

"Savannah, where are you these days? I barely see you."

"I know, I know, everyone misses me. Kidding!" she remarked.

"Listen, in all seriousness, we have to talk, and by talk, I mean NOT HERE. When are you free?" she asked.

"Well, how about this weekend? You can come up to my home. Maybe dinner. Emma would love to see you," Chris suggested as he crossed his fingers.

"Actually, that could work but make it the morning and make coffee, a lot of coffee," acknowledged Savannah.

"It's a date," they said.

"Jinx," they added simultaneously as they hung up.

"Ha, what are we two years old?" Chris said, laughing to himself.

He and Savannah had become good friends, and he was worried about her.

Savannah wrapped up with the epidemiologists, having no clearer picture than she had prior.

"Nobody knows, or at least they're not telling," she thought as she headed for her office.

Back at her desk to end her day, Savannah decided to reach out to an old mentor. She penned an email to none other than former Director Simon Mayfield.

Dr. Mayfield,

I hope you are well, and retirement is agreeing with you. I do have a favor and need your expertise on an important matter. Is there any way you could call me when you have a moment? If so, I can be reached at 404-989-9901.

PS: your leadership and integrity are sorely missed here.

Savannah Whitefield

(SEND)

Two floors above, Chris, while wrapping up his day, snapped his fingers and said, "Shit, I never called Sam after Savannah called."

He decided to try again, but this time from the car.

"Good night Ellen," he said, walking past his assistant and heading for the elevators.

"Night, Doctor," she returned.

Now on his I-85 North nightmare, he called Sam.

"Siri, Call Samuel Tate, cell."

"Calling Samuel Tate, cell."

Sam answered, almost immediately. "Hello, this is Sam."

"Sam, hi, it's Chris Chance. How the hell have you been, you son of a bitch?" Chris said.

"Chris, it's been so long. Where have you been hiding," Sam responded.

"Well, the BDM for starters, plus my son Wyatt is getting ready to head to Ohio State on a full scholarship, so I'd say I've been a little out of touch."

"Well, I know you're busy, but thanks for reaching out. It's been a long time, and I've been bad at staying in touch as well," Sam said apologetically.

Sam continued, "so what's the occasion? Everything okay?"

"Yes, no, well, it's hard to say. I wanted to get your expert opinion and insight," Chris said hesitantly.

"Wait, Chris, can you hold on?" interrupted Sam.

"Sure," said Chris as he was placed on hold, with music now playing in his ear.

"This guy has hold music on his cell phone. Damn, these tech guys are good," Chris thought aloud.

"Sorry Chris, but I have to go, plus our reception is poor. What's your home number? I'll call you when you get home," Sam asked.

"Ummm, okay, it's 770-271-1103. Try calling around 6:30 pm. I should be home by then, bye," Chris said as he hung up.

"What was that? I heard him just fine. So odd," Chris said.

Ninety minutes later, Chris arrived home at 6:50 pm. Much later than he anticipated, and he knew he'd missed Sam's call.

"God damn traffic, well, at least I'm home. Let's hope Sam left a message," Chris said.

Entering through the garage, he walked into the kitchen and was overwhelmed by a familiar smell.

"Wait, is that what I think it is?" he asked aloud to no one.

"Emma, is that Chicken Piccata? Hello……."

"Did Emma actually cook?" he wondered.

"Emma!" he shouted out.

"Honey, where are you?" he shouted again as Emma came down the back stairs into the kitchen.

"Honey, my god, you look amazing," a stunned Chris admired.

Emma was dressed in tight ripped jeans, knee-high leather boots, and a clingy ribbed sweater.

"Thank you, Honey. So, is that smell familiar?" Emma asked in a flirty voice.

"It's your favorite," she teased.

"Damn, you made my favorite dish, nice," Chris said.

"Thank you, Baby, that's a nice surprise. Oh, and the dinner is nice too," Chris said as he hugged her.

"Oh hey, did I get a call on the home phone a little while ago?" he asked.

"Funny, how'd you know? It was one of your old friends, Sam.

He said not to call him back, though. He'd try again at 7:30 pm."

"Why don't you get changed, and I'll pour us some wine," Emma said.

Chris accepted Emma's offer. Walking away and with a quick look back, he shook his head and thought to himself, "what's gotten into her?"

Whatever it was, Dr. Christopher J. Chance liked it.

Chris reappeared in the kitchen fifteen minutes later after exchanging his suit for jeans and a t-shirt.

"So, Emma, what's going on? You're usually in sweats by now, and my favorite meal too?" Chris asked.

"I don't know, Honey. I'm feeling a little better, I guess. A couple of weeks ago, I saw Jonathan next door. I mentioned that I was seeing a therapist. He asked me who, and after I told him, he asked if I was on anything. I told him yes and what it was. He suggested that I tell my doctor to switch it to an alternative he usually prescribes to his patients. Long story short, I'm a little more myself now, and a little less in a fog," she explained.

"Emma, that's amazing," Chris said while thinking to himself that Dr. Jonathan Siegel was a special person and friend.

"Look, dinner will be ready soon, and Sam's gonna call any minute, so go take your call, but don't be too long," Emma said.

Chris retreated to the family room and stared at the phone.

"C'mon, C'mon."

Then, at 7:30 pm the phone rang, just as Sam had promised.

"Hello!" Chris said

"Chris, hi, it's Sam, is now a good time?"

"Yes, it's perfect," Chris agreed.

"Good, so listen, do you have any idea why your phone is being monitored?" Sam asked.

"What? What are you talking about?" Chris responded while feeling blindsided.

"When we talked earlier while you were on your cell, I received an alert on my phone that your phone was compromised. In my industry, we have big problems with intellectual theft, so we have very advanced phones to protect ourselves and our companies," Sam explained.

"I put you on hold to check the alert, then told you I had to go due to our call having a poor connection," Sam said.

"Wow, I don't understand. Why would my phone be monitored?" Chris wondered.

"Well, Chris, let me ask you this, why did you reach out to me today?" Sam asked intuitively.

"My God, I knew things were getting weird at work, and I needed to get some expert advice, but this is crazy," Chris said as he exhaled in confusion.

"So, what is it you need to know?" Sam asked.

Chris told him about his suspicions of the new Director, how his co-worker, Dr. Savannah Whitefield, was uncovering strange happenings, and how she was extremely nervous. He wanted to know how technology was being used in government and medicine, and finally, he asked if Sam knew anything about the *Analytical Society*.

"Honey, it's time for dinner," Emma whispered to Chris.

"Chris, it sounds like dinner to me, and I'm going to need some time to process everything you just said. Know this, though; you're on to something and something big. Watch yourself, and be aware of what you're saying, who you're saying it to, and where you're at. I'll reach out to you soon, so look for my call on your home phone. No email, no cell," Sam instructed.

"Ummm, okay, we'll talk soon, I hope. Thanks for the call, Sam," Chris said.

A bit shaken, Chris took a deep breath and headed to the dining room for dinner and a much needed, typical night at home.

"Is everything okay?" Emma asked as she kissed Chris on the cheek.

"Yes, honey, it couldn't be better," Chris replied while sitting down with his family.

Later that night, after getting ready for bed, Chris surfaced from his master bathroom to find Emma in their bed.

"Emma, why aren't you in the guestroom?" Chris asked while moving towards the bed.

"Maybe I don't feel like sleeping tonight," Emma answered.

"Alexa, set nighttime lights, home alarm, and don't wake me," Dr. Chance anxiously commanded.

"Yes, Dr. Chance," confirmed Alexa.

Mr. and Mrs. Chance made love for the first time in over a year.

Date: Saturday, June 5th   Place: Suwanee, GA.

Chris received a text from Savannah before their meeting at his home, the one they planned earlier in the week when Savannah was meeting with her team of Epidemiologists.

Savannah Whitefield

Chris, I'm getting close. Navi said 19 min away.

> Hey Sav, ok, looking forward to it.
> Do you want me to put coffee on?

YESSSSSS, thanks

> Emma and the kids are out, so
> it's just us.

Bummer. See you in a few!

> See you then.

Savannah arrived a few minutes later, and Chris met her in the driveway.

"Hey, let's head in, but I want to sit out back on the deck," Chris advised.

"Why, do you think I'll break the china?" she smirked.

"Nice neighborhood. Why haven't you ever invited me up here before?" Savannah asked.

"I wasn't sure if your Buckhead taste would like suburban living," Chris said.

"I love it, all the trees are amazing, and I saw a family of deer crossing the street, just beautiful," Savannah remarked.

Once inside, Chris showed Savannah around the house and then poured the coffee he made for them, while then moving to the deck, just off the kitchen.

"Ok, I know you have something important to tell me, but first, I wanted to sit outside for a specific reason. Did I ever tell you I have an old friend in the tech field?" Chris asked.

"Maybe, I think, but go on," Savannah said.

"Well, I reached out to him the other day. What happened next was stunning. The first call on my cell ended quickly, he cut it short and called me back later on my home phone. Why my home phone, you ask?"

"I didn't ask, but continue," Savannah teased.

"Well, he immediately informed me that my cell phone was bugged," Chris explained.

"Bugged? You're kidding, right?" Savannah asked.

"No, I'm not," Chris replied.

"Crazy, right? It was suspicious enough that he wouldn't talk to me on my cell, so from my home phone, I asked him a bunch of questions, one being about the Analytical Society. He said he's going to investigate everything and get back to me. The big reveal, though, is that my cell is bugged. Who bugged my phone, and how is the question? It's wild, I know," Chris concluded.

"Wow, well, if your phone is bugged, then mine is too. Remember the morning after I met with Escobar, we sat in my car at the BDM? I was scared and said I felt like we're being watched and recorded. In fact, turn your phone off right now. Not even airplane mode, but off completely," Savannah ordered.

"Ok, now it's my turn. When I met with Deputy Director Escobar at Starbucks, I told you the next morning I wanted to tell you everything, but I was nervous. I needed to investigate things more thoroughly before I shared everything with you. Well, the real story is just incredible, scary in fact, and frankly hard to believe. He told me that I'd be invited to an official meeting the next day with the Director, and I'd be told everything he confided, formally. Chris, he told me not to go. He told me that just knowing would be dangerous. Bizarre, right?"

Savannah went into detail on everything Escobar told her. The new mass-produced vaccine, the mind control contents, how she's in danger, etc.

"What the hell, Savannah, now we're both in danger. At this point, the only public communication we should have going forward is via email or cell. It should be normal *BDM stuff.* We need a code if we want to meet privately to discuss what's happening," Chris said.

"I got it, a puppy. If we need to talk privately, we'll just mention a puppy, my new puppy, in fact," Savannah said.

"Why a puppy?" Chris asked.

"Because I don't trust cats," Savannah said.

"Yoo-hoo, over here," shouted Dr. Siegel.

"Who's your friend Chris? Does Emma know you're meeting a sexy redhead while she's out?" he playfully added.

"Hey, I'm Jon, by the way, and who might you be?" Jonathan

said, addressing Savannah.

"Hi Jon, I'm a co-worker of Chris' from the BDM."

"He's cute," whispered Savannah to Chris.

Chris whispered back with a laugh, "Yeah, well, he's gay."

"What's so funny, you two?" Jonathan asked.

"Oh, nothing," Chris said.

"Don't worry. I'm not here to steal Chris away from his wife. Redheads aren't his type, anyway," Savannah shouted back to Jonathan.

"Girlfriend, someone as sexy as you, is everyone's type. Besides, if anyone wants Chris, I already have dibs," Jonathan added.

The laughter was precisely the break in tension that Chris and Savannah needed after the tense conversation. They wrapped up their meeting with the promise that secrecy was the key, and they must be cautious going forward.

Date: Monday, June 7th   **Place: BDM Atlanta, GA.**

Former BDM Director Simon Mayfield got back to Dr. Whitefield via email early Monday morning, and asked if they could meet in person. A relieved Savannah agreed, and they decided to meet the next day, at 6 pm at the Starbucks near the BDM Campus. The same Starbucks Savannah met Deputy Director Escobar. Savannah went by Dr. Escobar's office for safety's sake and asked hypothetically if she met with former Director Mayfield, could he be trusted? He said that Director Mayfield could be trusted but offered her advice to be the one asking the questions and offering nothing.

"Do not divulge anything you assume he doesn't know already," he said.

Savannah agreed, but Dr. Escobar wasn't sure she would take that advice, especially after showing up to the meeting with Director Williams that he explicitly warned her not to attend.

The work week at the BDM became terribly busy. The medical leaders from many other countries were flying in for a two-day summit covering *Emerging Health Risks Worldwide*. These meetings were necessary as the 2020 *Coronavirus* originated in Wuhan, China and seemingly came out of nowhere, and spread quickly.

In his role, Dr. Christopher Chance hosted medical leaders from Great Britain, Germany, France, and the Chinese President, Li Wu Ming.

He had to speak at the summit both days, so his time was swallowed up in preparation. That allowed him to take his mind off all the drama and conspiracy theories that pervaded the BDM's campus.

During a preliminary walkthrough in the *Joint Leadership Conference Center*, Chris received a blocked call on his cell. Although busy, Chris answered out of curiosity.

"Hello, Dr. Chance speaking," Chris answered.

"Is this Dr. Christopher J. Chance of the Bureau for Disease Management?" asked an unknown woman.

"Speaking," Chris punctuated.

"Hello Dr. Chance, this is Chelsea Greer-Sullivan, Chief of Staff to the President of the United States. Do you have a moment to talk?" she asked.

"Yes, of course, what do I owe the honor?" Chris curiously asked.

"Dr. Chance, the President himself asked me to reach out to you directly and ask if you would be interested in being considered for the next *Chief Medical Advisor to the President?*"

A mildly stunned Dr. Chance said, "I'm very flattered, thank you, with respect, though, may I have some time to consider this offer?"

"Dr. Chance, of course, but it's not an offer. It's a consideration. I'd like to come down to Atlanta to meet with you and discuss all the particulars of the position. Including its demands and requirements, as well as all the background checks associated with the process. Would that be agreeable?" requested the POTUS Chief of Staff.

"Ummm, yes, of course. Do you have a time frame for this?" Chris asked.

"To be fair, it wouldn't be till late June or early July. Would that work?" she asked.

"Yes, that would be fine. Thank you very much for calling, and please give the President my sincere gratitude," Chris added.

"Dr. Chance, one last thing. This cannot be shared with anyone for obvious reasons, I hope you understand," concluded Ms. Sullivan.

"Even my wife?"

"That's a fair request. Your spouse is fine," she agreed.

Chris shared the news with Emma later that night. Although both felt a slight apprehension, the thought of something new and unknown was exciting.

Chris being a staunch Republican, knew the honor of serving the President directly would be immense.

What Next

Tuesday, 6 pm, Savannah awaited former Director Mayfield. At 6:04, he arrived. "Savannah, how have you been?" asked Director Mayfield as he hugged her.

"Good, but a little stressed," Savannah admitted.

"So, what's up, why did you reach out, other than saying hello, that is?" asked a skeptical Director Mayfield.

"Well, it's hard to explain. First, your departure caught us all off guard, and then you saw firsthand what an asshole the new Director was," Savannah said.

"You weren't the only one caught off guard. I was told only two weeks prior that I was retiring. You probably noticed how I was un-ceremonially cast aside at the announcement meeting. I didn't know what was going on, but whatever it was, they wanted me out of the way," Simon admitted.

"Who's they?" she asked.

"I don't know, but it felt like unknown forces were pulling the strings. It all happened so quickly, and it was right after I caught wind of…," Simon stopped in mid-sentence.

"Right after you caught wind of what?" pushed Savannah.

"I really shouldn't say, the less you know, the better," Simon cautiously remarked.

"Does it have something to do with a new vaccine?" Savannah asked.

"Yes, but that's all I'll say. Something's in play, and it's big. Big enough to remove all obstacles in its way," Simon confessed.

"Luckily for me, I was too old for that shit. I would have fought back, but my pension, legacy, and wife, all told me to shut up and move along," Simon confessed.

"Look, I have to go. You're on to something but be careful. There's a black cloud looming, and I fear the rain is about to start falling," Simon reluctantly cautioned.

"Shit just keeps getting crazier," Savannah said under her voice.

A day later at the Chance home, and yet another home-cooked dinner.

"Alexa, turn down the lights," directed Dr. Chance.

"Turning down the lights," Alexa confirmed.

"Dad, you do know your children are here, right?" Schuyler blushingly teased.

"Alexa, turn the lights up," Wyatt demanded. *(Alexa did not respond)*.

"Honey, please get Alexa in line, she doesn't want to listen to anyone but you," Emma requested.

A moment later, the home phone rang.

"Shit, I'll get it," Chris said, giving Emma a look of "I'm sorry."

"Hello," Chris answered.

"Chris, it's Sam. Do you have a moment?" he asked.

"Sam, of course. Good to hear from you again. I was wondering when you were going to call. So, I'm curious about our previous discussion. What can you tell me?" Chris probed.

"Well, it was a lot to unpack, but let's start with the Analytical Society. This group, at times a secret society, started way back in the early 1800s. Famed Cambridge Professor Charles Babbage, of *The Analytical Engine* fame and many others from the English elite, formed a brotherhood of scientists, mathematicians, and inventors. They worked in conjunction to invent, develop, and further man through Science and Math. The Society then grew to other notable scientists and innovators of their day, throughout Europe and the U.S," Sam explained.

"But what about today?" a curious Chris pushed.

"Well, guess what, it's alive and well, and I'm actually part of it," Sam surprisingly admitted.

"Wait. What?" Chris interrupted.

"Yes, but before you get nervous, the Society isn't nefarious. It's more of a think tank type of culture, with many views and idea-sharing. However, there is a dark underbelly to the group. A small, cancerous cell within the *Analytical Society* called *The Triangle,"* Sam detailed.

"*The Triangle,* though, is a mystery with seemingly no leader, no group head. I simply cannot find any detail of their current mission or future goals. This I can tell you, though, *The Triangle* consists of three subgroups. One from technology, one from government, and one from pharmaceuticals. Chris, get ready, and if you're not sitting down yet, sit NOW," Sam demanded.

"I believe you and your colleague, Dr. Whitefield, have stumbled upon two points of *The Triangle*, that being government and pharmaceuticals. You're possibly seeing them in motion. Their endgame is still unclear, but I'm still digging. There's Something else. I tracked your phone and the origination of it being bugged. I came up with nothing, nothing as in *who* bugged it. No person is responsible, but rather something is responsible," he continued.

"Chris, some sort of artificial intelligence is tracking you, your conversations, your emails, your every move, frankly. I'm at a loss," an exacerbated Sam explained.

"Wait, what are you telling me?" Chris demanded.

"I'm telling you to lay low, play nice, and draw suspicion away from yourself. Chris, there's more. Many significant technology leaders are growing very weary of what is happening in our industry. Imagine being in a car, with no brakes rolling downhill. You know how to drive, you can see ahead, but you cannot stop the impending doom," said Sam

"This is where we're at. Artificial Intelligence is so complex, so complicated, that even I and the most intelligent creators of today's modern technology cannot harness or corral it. We're like bull riders trying to break an unbreakable bull, and our 8 seconds is almost up," Sam continued.

"There's something else you should know. I attended The

Annual *Tech Select Forum* in Palo Alto a few days ago. No phones, no devices of any kind were permitted in the room. Chris, stop and think about that for a minute. The most intelligent, sophisticated designers and coders are afraid to bring tech devices in a room. The attendees were some people you would recognize and some you would not, but all were senior leaders of the major tech firms today. Chris, they're nervous. The one thing we've all experienced over the last few months is that planned tweaks and alterations to many current tech points, software that runs nearly everything, is being overwritten by the same software we're trying to update or modify. Chris, it's like telling Alexa to do something, and she said no. It's that basic, A.I. has an opinion now, it's thinking for itself, by itself," Sam concluded.

"My God, what do we do?" Chris asked.

"Absolutely nothing. Going forward, we will only speak in person or over a landline. No emails, no texts, nothing. Let's not even speak for the foreseeable future. If you have an emergency, call my home phone, or mail me. I'm serious," Sam instructed.

"Okay, I understand, but if you find out anything more, you have to call me asap, PROMISE?" Chris demanded.

"I promise," Sam said in mutual agreement.

Date: Thursday, June 15th   Place: BDM Atlanta, GA.

Dr. Savannah S. Whitefield grew ever more nervous and angrier at what she now knew. She was running out of avenues to investigate and dig deeper into her new-found knowledge of S&D's mind-controlling vaccine stockpile, until now. Savannah received a call on her cell from an UNKNOWN number.

She answered, "Hello, Dr. Whitefield speaking. Yes. Who is this?"

She paused as she listened to an unknown male voice. "Why should I believe you? Who is this? Tell me. WHAT? How do I know this is for real? If what you're saying is true, I have to say something and say it now. Leave my family out of this. NO! I understand, but this is unheard of. How many Countries? You must be joking? When? My GOD! Hello, hello, hello, are you still there? Hello!"

A stunned Savannah held the phone for a few more seconds after the unknown man hung up.

"This is unreal," she thought, knowing she couldn't tell Chris.

Yet, Savannah knew it was time to confront the man she's been suspicious of since day one.

"It's time!" she said aloud.

She quickly typed an email to Director Williams and demanded they meet. (Send). It's gone. It's too late. She'll now speak up to the man who told her to shut up on the day they first met, just two months earlier. Director Williams responded immediately and set the meeting for the next afternoon, Friday at 4:30 pm in his office.

Savannah desperately wanted to tell Chris, but she couldn't.

Savannah Whitefield

Chris, call me when you can.
I wanted to talk about my puppy.
He's getting so big.

Chris??

> Hey, Sav. Sorry, I just saw your text.

Can you talk?

> Cell is about to die. Call me at home.
> Also, call me on your home phone.
> Your cell service sucks.

Ok

An hour later, Chris's home phone rang.

"Hello, hey Savannah, this is your home phone, correct?" Chris confirmed.

"Yes, good thinking, by the way," Savannah replied.

"So, what about your BIG puppy?" Chris inquired.

"Look, you're going to think I'm crazy, but I can't sit back without saying something about what's going on with S&D Pharma and this vaccine thing. I got a call today from someone at the FDA, he wouldn't say his name other than MDR. He told me things I can't share with you, at least not now. I emailed Director Williams and requested a meeting. He emailed back right away and set it for tomorrow at 4:30 pm," Savannah said nervously.

"Sav, are you crazy? Do you want to lose your job and your reputation? This guy hasn't liked you since the day you met him. Plus, he set the time for 4:30 pm on a Friday? None of it smells right," Chris said.

"I knew you'd say that. Sorry Chris, but I had to," Savannah said.

"Look, just keep me posted on how it goes, as I won't be in the office tomorrow. Remember, call me on my home phone ONLY," Chris reminded.

"Okay, don't be mad. I'll tell you more when I think it's safe," Savannah concluded.

Show-Down

Dr. Whitefield's day dragged to a slow crawl as 4:30 pm neared. She'd rehearsed all day what she wanted to tell Director Williams, yet she was not ready, nor mentally prepared.

4:30 pm, Savannah arrived at the Director's office. His assistant informed her that the Director would be with her momentarily. Savannah had never felt more alone and now felt some regret that she requested this meeting.

"He'll see you now, Dr. Whitefield," the assistant informed.

Savannah rose slowly, paused for a second, lifted her chin, and said, "Fuck it" under her breath.

"Dr. Whitefield, welcome, so what is it that was so important that we needed to meet?" the Director asked pointedly.

"Well, Director, let me cut right to the chase. I need to know exactly what is going on with S&D and the new vaccine. This is my department, after all. What more is there that you haven't told me?" Savannah boldly questioned.

"First, I appreciate your concern. The fact that you know anything is because I've allowed you to know. Regarding the new vaccine and its purposes, you'll be informed in due time. Is there anything else I can do for you?" Director Williams smugly asked.

"Well, for starters, you can lose the condescending tone. This agency was running smoothly until you showed up. A good man was tossed aside, and now a new vaccine, with absolutely no reason to have been mass-produced, appears out of nowhere. Wait, unless there is a reason. What are you up to?" she pushed.

"Could this have something more to do than a rogue vaccine, or could it be about the worldwide distribution of a mind-altering pill?" questioned a now standing Dr. Whitefield.

"Dr. Whitefield, I can assure you, there's nothing to your curiosity. Worldwide distribution? Are you crazy? Where'd you hear that? Why don't you just stay in your lane and do your job and allow me to do mine," Director Williams concluded.

"Stay in my lane? That's your stance on this? Well, what if I walk across the street and alert CNN about a ten-ton stockpile of an un-needed vaccine, and oh, by the way, it's a mind-controlling drug. I'm sure you and Secretary Holman would be the first people to hear from the President, right after the camera crews showed up at your fucking front door. Pardon my French, Director Shockley Bradford Williams."

"Yes, that's right. I now know what the S stands for now," shouted Dr. Whitefield as she abruptly exited the Director's office.

"Have a nice weekend, Karen," said Dr. Whitefield while walking past the Director's stunned assistant.

Savannah exited the building with a nervous sigh and said, "Well, at least I didn't get fired, ...yet!"

Hours later, Chris Chance waited at home and never heard from Savannah. He tried texting her.

Savannah Whitefield

Sav, what's up? How did your meeting go?

Savannah??

Well, call me when you can.

Saturday:

Savannah Whitefield

Savannah, are you ok?

Hello?

Sunday:

Savannah Whitefield

Hey, you forgot to call me. At least respond and tell me you're ok??

Savannah??

Monday, June 21st, 8:42 am. Chris pulled into the BDM parking lot, looking for Savannah's Tesla Cybertruck. It was nowhere to be found. He tried texting her again.

Savannah Whitefield

Hey, I'm here. Let me know if I should wait before I go in.

Minutes went by with no response from Dr. Whitefield. Chris couldn't wait any longer, so he headed into his office.

Now at his desk, he poured through his full email inbox and shouted out to his Asst, "Ellen, will there be fresh coffee any time soon?"

"Well, if you wait much longer to get it yourself, it won't be as fresh, will it?" Ellen scolded with a smile.

(Ding), Dr. Chance received a new email at 9:16 am.

IMPORTANT: Meeting of the Directors ONLY

Kennedy J. Lansdowne Campus Building #21

12th Floor Executive Conference Room.

Mandatory Attendance: This morning @ 10:15 am.

Subject: Confidential

"What now?" Chris said aloud.

"Don't be late this time, Doctor," shouted Dr. Chance's assistant.

Still curious as to where Savannah was at, he texted her one more time.

Savannah Whitefield

Savannah, check your email. Director meeting. Meet me at elevator one on the 12th floor, at 10:10, ok?

Okay?

Savannah, really???

10:10 am at Elevator One, Chris waited for Savannah with no luck. He walked into the meeting room, along with the other Directors, but no Savannah. Chris was now visibly worried.

"Everyone, please take your seats," ordered Director Williams.

"I have an announcement. I'm not sure how to say this, but..." the Director pauses while clearing his throat.

The room was noticeably quiet, with everyone looking around, but no one wanting to make eye contact.

Director Williams continued, "I'm sorry to announce this, but Dr. Savannah Whitefield has sadly passed away."

"She was involved in a fatal car accident on Friday night on I-75, near her home in Buckhead. She died early Sunday morning when she was removed from life support."

The room was now in shock. Tears, whimpers, and a stunned silence pervaded the sterile conference room. The same conference room where Director Williams was introduced. A fact not lost on Dr. Chance.

Chris broke the silence, "When did you find out, Director?"

"I only heard about it 30 minutes ago. This is such a shock. I'm sure you're all very saddened. You have my deepest condolences. Dr. Whitefield was widely respected and deeply admired by so many."

"Wait, 30 minutes ago? But you sent the email for this meeting over an hour ago," Chris boldly stated while confronting the Director.

"Oh, I'm so sorry. Clearly, I'm mistaken. The shock of the news, I guess, had me confused. Yes-Yes, I guess it was just a few minutes before sending the email. My apologies," replied Director Williams.

"You're all free to go. Please take the day if you need to, but don't forget, I'll need your week ending reports for last week before you leave," directed a seemingly detached Williams.

Dr. Chance and the other Directors shared hugs, tears, and

whispers while making their way out of the conference room and towards the elevators. A shaken Deputy Director Escobar sought Chris out and pulled him aside.

"Dr. Chance, I cannot tell you how sorry I am. I know you and Dr. Whitefield were close colleagues. Please let me know if there's anything I can do. She was an amazing person, and we all loved her very much. Here's my home number if you need to talk," Deputy Director Escobar said while handing Chris a note with his number.

"Thank you, Sir. The world is not a better place today," Chris said while slipping the note into his pocket.

"His home phone number?" Chris thought to himself, now knowing that Dr. Escobar was fully aware of the severity of what was going on within the BDM.

Chris decided at that moment to retrieve his belongings and head home. Both scared and saddened, he could not believe his friend was gone. He was left with the solemn question as to why she died.

"That was no accident," he said quietly.

C6 - THE QUIET

"The world is very different now. For man holds in his mortal hands the power to abolish all forms of human poverty and all forms of human life"

- John F. Kennedy

A Chance

June 23rd, 2021. With Dr. Savannah Whitefield's funeral still days away, the BDM appeared to have shockingly moved on. The lack of empathy displayed by Director Williams since he took over had gotten noticeably worse, with more and more of his appointments within the BDM shared his same cold indecency. Director Williams summoned Dr. Chance to his office via email to Chris' asst, Ellen. She relayed the message to Chris upon returning from lunch.

"Dr. Chance, Director Williams would like to see you in his office right away," Ellen said.

"….and you know this how?" Dr. Chance said, somewhat surprised.

"Doctor, I received an email from Karen, his asst, about 15 min ago," Ellen remarked.

"I'm sorry, Ellen, I'm just a little unnerved with the loss of Dr. Whitefield," Chris said apologetically as he headed to the elevator.

"This isn't good," Chris thought to himself.

"Savannah's last minutes at the BDM were in his office. Now she's dead."

As he arrived at the Director's office, his assistant said, "Please go right in, Doctor, he's expecting you."

"Dr. Chance, thank you for coming so quickly. Again, I'm sorry about the death of your colleague. Our colleague, I should say. Her death is a major loss to Bureau. I appreciate that the timing may seem insensitive, but I need your help. I've been made aware that you used to oversee Dr. Whitefield's department in 2015 while she was on maternity leave, is that correct?" Williams asked.

"Ummm, yes, I was. For about five months, as I recall. Why do you ask?" Dr. Chance curiously questioned.

"Well, truthfully, our work here continues as bad as that may sound, so I'd like you to oversee the department temporarily. I wouldn't ask if it weren't essential. You wouldn't have to make any major decisions, just oversee the department's administration until we have a new Director in place. Is that something you can do for me?" Director Williams implied, rather than asked.

Dr. Chance, feeling a little apprehensive but also seeing an opportunity, paused before he answered. This would provide him a chance to dig in to see what Savannah knew that maybe she didn't convey to him. Unsure if he wanted the burden of what could be dangerous knowledge. Yet knowing that his friend would have wanted him to investigate further was enough motivation.

"Of course, whatever I can do to help," said Dr. Chance.

"It's settled then. I'll make sure IT gets you all the necessary access you'll need. Thank you, Dr. Chance, but remember, your primary duties cannot suffer while taking on this extra role," responded the Director unempathetically.

Dr. Savannah S. Whitefield (1981-2021)

Saturday, June 26th, the funeral of beloved and respected Dr. Savannah Whitefield was as beautiful as it was solemn. From the grieving husband, with his small children not fully comprehending that mommy wasn't coming home, to the hundreds of doctors, politicians, and local dignitaries dressed in black during one of Atlanta's hottest days of the year.

Dr. Whitefield was laid to rest in the Oakland Cemetery. Atlanta's most famous cemetery had served as the final stop to many famous Georgian's, from famed golfer Bobby Jones to storied author Margaret Mitchell, and alongside dozens of other renowned doctors, politicians, and industrialists. Although her name will not shine as bright as some, her death may be more important as to why it even occurred. Did Dr. Whitefield stumble upon an event that would change or alter the future, or did she just die an ordinary, accidental death?

Dr. Chance, although a good friend to Savannah, made sure to stay away from the small group of grieving family members. He knew his place in her professional life, held little standing to her personal life and that of family. He did, however, ensure that he spoke to Dr. Whitefield's husband, Michael, after the ceremony. Even ever so briefly, he needed to convey his respect and admiration for Savannah. Although the two had met on several occasions at BDM functions, he never really spoke with Michael at length.

"Michael, I cannot express any more deeply what your wife met to her colleagues and friends. She loved you and the kids more than anything. We will miss her and never forget her. If there's anything I can do for you and your family, now or in the future, please let me know," Dr. Chance conveyed.

"Thank you, Chris, that means the world. You were the one person in her career she admired the most. She would laugh about her medical adventures with you, often referring to you as her work husband. In fact, even during our last conversation Saturday afternoon, when she was on her way to see Secretary Holman, she mentioned you and that she wanted to drive up and visit your home again," Michael said.

"Saturday afternoon.....? Secretary Holman? I thought the accident happened Friday night on her way home," said a stunned Dr. Chance.

"No, what makes you say that? We thankfully had a wonderful last night as a family. I would hate to think how empty it would have been if her last hours alive were spent at work and not with our children. She got a call in the morning from Secretary Holman to meet for lunch."

"Holman called her.....?" Chris interrupted.

"Umm, yes, it seemed important. We spoke after she left the house because the new truck was acting weird. Glitchy, she said, and she was nervous it would break down," explained Michael.

"Michael, I'm sorry, and clearly I was mistaken about when the accident happened. Again, I am here for you in any way you might need. Please don't hesitate to call me," Dr. Chance concluded.

Walking away, Chris now knew what happened to his friend was no accident. He knew he must dig and find out what was happening. He also realized that he needed to be quiet and proceed with extreme subtlety, yet for a moment thinking he should just walk away and do nothing. But that's not something Savannah would do, not if Chris were the one that died. The weekend concluded with Dr. Chance mourning the loss of his friend but with a renewed vigor to pursue the truth that he and Savannah had been chasing.

♠

Monday at the BDM, Chris skipped his usual routine. He bypassed his secretary, Ellen, and headed straight for Savannah's office. He now had full access to her files, emails, and all other data her department had been working on, including all global reports of hot spots and areas of vulnerability. To his surprise, there were no areas of concern. The world was relatively calm after last year's Coronavirus Outbreak that originated in China.

"So why is the world's largest pharmaceutical company creating and stockpiling tons and tons of a corrupt vaccine?" Dr. Chance thought while trying to rationalize the odd event.

Digging through Dr. Whitefield's email, Chris saw dozens of emails to her contacts worldwide, specifically in the European Union, Africa, and China. She asked if they had seen or were monitoring any emerging threats that would require a new vaccine. Chris thought this is where alarm bells would have gone off to whoever was tracking Savannah's communication. Hell, to whoever was watching him, for that matter.

Looking down at his watch, Chris noted the time of 5:18 pm. The day had flown by. He had worked the entire time at the desk of his dead friend. All-day and no food or drink, no phone calls, and no smoking gun as to what got Savannah killed. Surely, she wasn't killed for emailing her counterparts around the world.

"There must be more?" he reasoned.

Chris kept on regardless of how long he'd worked. The time to wait had passed, he knew something big was coming, and there it was, the bombshell he was hoping for. It was right in front of him the entire day. He found an unsent email in Savannah's draft folder with the subject titled *"The Quiet is Talking."* That was the title of Savannah's favorite book of poetry. The same book she kept in her office, and that anybody who knew her knew that book.

"Coincidence?" Chris thought aloud.

The email recipient was Deputy Director Hayden Escobar, with a blind cc to former Director Mayfield.

Opening the unsent email, Chris read:

Deputy Director Escobar,

Although I wanted to reach out in person, I felt it necessary to have written documentation of my growing concerns on what appears to be a nefarious plan to distribute a new bogus vaccine. The extent of its distribution, I was unaware of until recently. I know you're aware of the QU13T vaccine's main properties, as discussed in the meeting between you, the Director, and myself. However, I've been informed by an anonymous source of an international plan for its distribution. My hope is that we can talk soon and discuss the next steps.

This is something that needs to go higher, even beyond the Secretary who may have a role, possibly POTUS, himself.

Regards,   Dr. Savannah S. Whitefield.

Dr. Chance left the saved email in the draft folder, knowing if he sent it, it would indeed point to him. Also, knowing it would place peril onto Deputy Director Escobar and former Director Mayfield. Knowledge is power, and he now had it. But there was more, and the more information that Chris found, the more uneasy he became.

Now 7:45 pm, over ten hours into his day researching Savannah's work product and emails, he found another bombshell. An interesting email that appeared meaningless due to the subject line, "Just Checking In," which may have been Savannah's method for discretion to avoid attention. This email was sent to the Director of the National Institutes of Health, Dr. Ashland Jeffries.

As his reply to Dr. Whitefield's email provided confirmation, it was very noteworthy that the coordination between Secretary Holman, Director S. Bradford Williams, the FDA's interim Commissioner Lynn Tomlinson, and S&D's Nicholas Kern must have clearly been limited to this small group. The email revealed that the Director of the National Institutes of Health (NIH) Director Ashland Jeffries, had no knowledge of the vaccine that S&D Pharma developed. Indeed, if the NIH wasn't aware of this vaccine, then there's no chance it would have been approved and sanctioned by the Dept. of Health and Human Services. The obvious question, though, was what if the Director was part of the conspiracy?

Chris asked himself, "Savannah must have thought it was possible, right?"

"But what if she wasn't suspicious based on her relationship and trust she had in Director Ashland Jeffries? What if he lied? What if he's part of the triangle?" he thought.

"This may have been where Savannah reached too far. This most likely is what got her killed," he surmised.

Chris made detailed handwritten notes of his research in his new leather journal he'd gotten as a gift from Emma the previous Christmas. No longer would anything be stored on a device. Some of the info he'll need Samuel Tate to help research.

The most important questions were; who are other members of the Triangle? Is there a money trail to Director S. Bradford Williams, Secretary of HHS Janet Holman, NIH Director Ashland Jeffries, and S&D's Nicholas Kern? If there was, who was paying them to perpetrate the vaccine production and potential rollout? Who was behind this, or rather what was behind this?" Chris pondered.

Lastly, Chris wrote Samuel Tate a detailed letter with all the research and names and positions of all potential people connected to the scandal. He sealed the letter and put a stamp on it.

"US Mail Only, going forward," he said.

New Roads

Tuesday, June 29th, the family went to Columbus, Ohio, to drop Wyatt off for three weeks of team drills and conditioning. Emma and Schuyler stayed for the first week to help Wyatt settle in for his brief stay at Ohio State. Chris stayed for just a few days, as he had to get back to Atlanta for his upcoming interview with the White House Chief of Staff, Chelsea Greer-Sullivan.

The first night, the whole family was together in a place that wasn't their house yet felt like home. Being all together had become the exception, not the rule. Work at the BDM hadn't allowed for a family vacation in some time, and with the splintered family doing their own things, this short event would be a lasting memory.

Wyatt was no longer the *big man on campus*. He would soon be lost in a sea of sixty-thousand students when the fall semester started. He would now be the young freshman and looking up to larger than life athletes. His chosen major of Political Science was somewhat surprising to his parents, as Wyatt hadn't shown a great interest in politics, at least not that his father noticed. From early on, Chris and Emma knew that Wyatt didn't necessarily have his father's natural talent in school. That blessing fell to Schuyler, who was a gifted learner and would pursue medicine.

However, Wyatt did join his father on several fund-raising trips he'd done for Georgia Governor John Radcliff, so studying politics maybe wasn't such a shock after all. He'd also become friends with Radcliff's son, John Jr., who aspired for a political career as well. Over those first few days, Chris observed and reflected, paying particular attention to Emma watching her children. Leaving Columbus without her oldest would be the beginning of empty nest syndrome. Especially after next fall when Sky leaves.

"What is she gonna do without them?" he said to himself.

Once Wyatt was in school full-time, their home would be far quieter than it had been. Was she ready? Chris hoped so. As for himself, his close confidant, Savannah Whitefield, was gone, and now his son was leaving as well. The world just got a lot quieter for Dr. Christopher J. Chance as well, at least at home.

Christopher Chance's brief family excursion ended with his short flight back to Atlanta on Thursday night. Friday was upon him and his scheduled meeting with the White House Chief of Staff. Dr. Chance and Chelsea Greer-Sullivan wanted their meeting to be unofficial and brief, so they didn't draw attention that might otherwise compromise the current status quo. They decided to meet at the Park Hyatt in Buckhead, just Northwest of downtown Atlanta.

They met in the lobby of the upscale hotel and blended in well, as the two simply looked like business travelers. Chris recognized her immediately due to her high-profile position. He was a little surprised at how attractive she was in person.

Walking up to her from behind in the lounge, Chris said, "Mrs. Sullivan, hello, I'm Dr. Chance."

"Hello, Dr. Chance. It's Ms., but please call me Chelsea. Thank you for taking the time to meet with me."

"No, thank you for coming all this way. Would you like a drink?" he offered.

"Yes, that would be lovely. Red wine would be nice," she requested.

As the two shared a few minutes of small talk, the drinks arrived, and the meeting commenced.

"Dr. Chance, may I call you Chris? Doctor seems so formal, especially over wine," she asked.

"Ummm, yes, of course," Chris acknowledged.

"Well, look, I want to be frank and get to the point. Your reputation is in high regard and has been floated since the President won re-election. As you know, the President is not an insider and despises the leftover elites in DC. Therefore, he'd love for you to consider the position. No promises, of course, but from your reputation, he'd love to have you onboard," Chelsea intimated.

"Well, since we're being direct, I'm very flattered at the offer for the position of *Chief Medical Advisor to the President.* Honestly, though, outside of it being high profile, it would be a step down from my current role. I've been at the BDM for nearly ten years and enjoy being a part of the important work we do. I also love Atlanta, and I have a family here with deep ties," Chris explained.

"Let me stop you there, Chris. You wouldn't have to live in DC, and your kids are getting older. Your son is about to enter Ohio State, and your daughter's going to be a senior, is that correct?"

"Well, yes, but…..," Chris said with some surprise.

"The President wouldn't be considering you if those facts weren't relevant. Also, we know your comfort level has been adjusted downward with the new Director, whom the President doesn't even like. Frankly, no one does, really. Between you and I, no one is sure why Mayfield was replaced with someone Secretary Holman didn't even know that well. Even with the Administration's strong belief in analytics, we didn't see this one coming. Having said that, this role could pave the way for much bigger things within the Party. Plus, isn't your son going to be studying Political Science?" Chelsea added.

"Wow, you guys don't mess around, do you? Everything you

said is true, especially the last part, but isn't this role more of a token position? How does this help me if I'm looking out for my future?" Chris said with an assertive posture.

"Well, okay then, I was told you were a commanding individual. Now I see why," Chelsea said in a slightly intimidated yet flirtatious tone.

"To be clear, this is a highly connected position within the government and medicine. The President wants an inner circle he can trust and loyal contributors that can have a strong voice in the country's different sectors," she said.

"Different sectors, like what….?" Chris asked.

"Like medicine, military, tech, and economics. He has two of the four, but medicine and tech have eluded him," Chelsea concluded.

"Medicine and tech, huh? I may have your tech guy," Chris offered.

"Oh, is that right, maybe a package deal, huh?" Chelsea said.

As the two sat for another hour of Q & A, a quick friendship had formed. Chris promised to strongly consider the position and even accepted the President's offer to come to the White House in the Fall. They both agreed to stay in touch and be open to all possibilities.

♠

C7 - TIP OF THE SPEAR

"Vaccination is a barbarous practice and one of the most fatal of all the delusions current in our time"

-Mahatma Gandhi

Wine and Song

Date night finally arrived for the Siegel's and Chance's. With Schuyler at a friend's house and Wyatt at Ohio State. Mom and Dad were now at the mercy of Jonathan and Andrew Siegel. The night took them to dinner at a new Italian restaurant, *Dominic's,* and then on to live music and drinks at *37 Main*, a well-known club in nearby Buford.

Emma was outside of her typically conservative skin, with jokes, laughter, and funny stories of when she and Chris first met. Chris aided in the fun with self-deprecating humor at how inept of a father he was when the kids were babies. However, none were more outlandish than Andrew, who just stole the show from his cultured, measured, yet fun husband, Jonathan.

As dinner was served, the laughter subsided to topics of the day; pop culture, politics, and such. Andrew spoke about the culture shift schools had been going through due to students' inability to manage technology and academics. The sheer number of distractions was testing more than the kids. Although Emma could not offer as much by way of her limited professional life, she showed a keen interest. Much of what was discussed could be applied to her being a mother, but also an observer and participant of the addiction.

Although she would not readily suggest that she suffered from any chemical stimulant or smartphone dependence, she certainly felt like an arrow was pointing to her side of the table.

Chris pressed Jonathan to expand on the current cultural crisis related to addiction and distraction, and what recent observations he had made in his field of psychology.

At length, Jonathan discussed the eroding family culture that once only pervaded select minority groups but was now affecting all demographics. He elaborated on the increasing divorce rates in the US, the staggering rise in suicides and teen pregnancies. Jon made one interesting point aimed at the *"world of delusion"* as he called it. He expanded on it by saying that much of society now lived in a *"bubble of technology,"* whether it be a smartphone, a phone app, social media, cyber dating, or realistic video games featuring sex and violence, etc. More so, he intimated that the rise of faux realities had led to the decline of a fundamental human trait, one that separated us from animals, that being Empathy.

"No one cares anymore," Jon concluded.

"I mean, you can play *Grand Theft Auto* and rape someone. Enjoy *Fortnite* with your friends and kill a bunch of people while scoring points. Immerse yourself in *Oculus Rift* and go everywhere in 3D without leaving your bedroom. Mark my words," Jonathan predicted, "within ten years, most people simply won't give a shit."

"Pardon my French," he said apologetically.

"We'll all be hooked on something. We're all victims in the end. It's simply when, not if. We will all fall prey to our human frailties and our penchant for dependence," Jonathan warned.

"Okay, baby, don't ruin this beautiful dinner with your dark forecast of gloom and doom," Andrew playfully scolded while asking, "Will there be sex robots too?" while laughter erupted.

All begrudgingly agreed with Dr. Siegel's summation, yet the food and company won the night. It was now on to getting hammered to the sounds of the Wham cover band, playing at the club they were going to next.

Back to the '80s

Dr. Christopher J. Chance remembered back to the late eighties as the last time he sent a letter, all while waiting for Samuel Tate to call on his landline.

"So retro," he thought.

Since the two discussed that radio silence was the safest route, they would have to go old school to protect themselves. It was July 4th, and although there would be fireworks, Chris was hoping Sam would provide some of his own during this call.

4:00 pm and right on time, the phone rang. It was Sam as expected, and as hoped, he brought fireworks.

"Chris, thanks for your letter, clearly paper and pen still work. I was stunned at how much you uncovered since we last spoke. I'm so sorry about your friend, Dr. Whitefield. This is just the tip of the spear, and it's getting more and more dangerous, my friend," Sam explained.

"What have you turned up? I was hoping you could fill in some of the blanks?" Chris impatiently asked.

"Are you sitting? If not, take a seat," Sam continued.

"I ran hundreds of cross-checks on the names in your letter. I used one of the latest tech achievements available at the highest levels in Silicon Valley. It's called *Baited Pole*. It's exactly what it sounds like. It's like baiting a fishing pole and casting the line. With this software, the ripples from your hook and lure attract every shred of data a person or thing has stored on the web. In this case, I used all the names in the same search. What I found was puzzling," Sam explained further, all while Chris was trying to keep up while taking notes in his journal.

"The results brought back multiple headscratchers. First, all the players you listed are connected somehow, BUT the biggest thread is they all have the same sole donor. As I'm sure you're aware, nearly all politicians and a large percent of high-level government officials have had wealthy donors who have supported their careers, in turn for favors. Some of the most historical leaders have been known as puppets. Whether LBJ in the '60s or, more recently, Bush 43 or Obama. Nearly every policy decision they made was at the whim of their donors. In this case, there is only one sole donor who pulls the strings of this group. Here's the kicker though, the donor isn't any person I could find, but rather a multi-layered piece of intelligent software. Chris, it's AI for Christ's sake," Sam shared.

"What the F......!" Chris mouthed.

"No matter how many times I ran the search, it kept coming back to artificial intelligence. The software acts like a person, unbeknownst to the beneficiary. It provides strategy, talking points, etc. It gives them marching orders via emails and texts. Everything is done in the cloud. Chris, in all my years, I have never seen anything like this. It wires contributions, tells them what to do, and ultimately holds the individuals accountable. Do as directed or said funds no longer enrich the puppet, or worse, it destroys their careers digitally thru media and other analytics," Sam detailed.

"Wait, that can explain why certain people have been put in positions of authority and made decisions that aren't their own," Chris said.

"How's that even possible?" he asked.

"Chris, in the last ten years, nobody in Palo Alto has asked what's possible because anything is. We all understand that we no longer make the rules but rather just try to keep up and mitigate the possible fall out. Whether it's caused by us, a foreign power, or deeply intuitive software. We have measures in place to police a country like China, especially due to their propensity for intellectual property theft," Sam continued.

"They steal so much, and so often, they don't even know what they're taking. It's like looting a drug store during a riot. They take whatever they can get. The difference is, though, we can manage China. Through well-placed bugs or viruses, much like a homeowner can manage termites. You plant traps and barriers, and the problem is solved. But in this case, we're up against a ghost in artificial intelligence. It's like God! It's everywhere and nowhere."

"There's got to be a way to shut it down though, right?" Chris asked.

"This A.I. entity is different, Chris. It can fund individuals to do its bidding, and to what end, nobody knows. It has its own agenda. Now, as far as we could go into the banking piece, the funds don't come from a traceable bank account. This is where it gets interesting. The money apparently comes from fractional rollovers of banking currencies between countries. When different currencies are exchanged, the second by second values fluctuate in small multiples, sometimes stretching to hundredths or even thousandths. However, money doesn't change hands or accounts with anything more than two decimals or tenths. By itself, this isn't much, but multiplied by the millions of times currency changes hands between countries every day, then suddenly, you have billions of dollars funneled by some type of managed intelligence," Sam explained.

"But wait, what account does all this fractional currency come from?" Chris curiously asked.

"It doesn't. As I said, we could only surmise that the money just floats between currencies until it is snatched out of the cloud and wired into the puppet's account. Puppet as in, say the Director of the BDM perhaps," Sam concluded.

"Ok, so that was a pretty big first. What's second?" Chris probed.

"Well, next is…, and it's a big one. Were you told in any detail about your friend's accident?" Sam asked.

"Ummm, no, not really, other than it was a car accident," Chris admitted.

"Well, I pulled records from the Atlanta P.D. and the Georgia Bureau of Investigations. Dr. Whitefield's accident was a one-car event in perfect weather, during daylight hours. From what I uncovered, the GBI analyzed her onboard computer. It's like a black box for cars, much like airplanes. Many cars have them for diagnostic purposes, but select self-driving cars have very sophisticated two-way transmissions that can float between the vehicle and auto manufacturer, or……"

"Or what….?" Chris asked.

"Or artificial intelligence. Anyway, the GBI's investigation of the onboard computer was able to tell what systems were in play at the time of the crash. Chris, Dr. Whitefield's car switched to self-drive mode thirty seconds before the crash. Now whether she switched it manually or the car did was not clear," Sam explained.

"Wait a second. At Savannah's funeral, her husband said they talked before the crash, and Savannah said the car was acting glitchy. Those were his exact words. My god, did the car kill her?" Chris pondered.

"That's hard to say, but either she made a mistake, or something instructed the car to go into the self-drive mode," Sam concluded.

"Jesus Christ, this is crazy!" Chris said.

"Now, finally, the third piece I found, and this one is still a mystery. Remember, when we discussed the *Triangle*? Well, I mentioned the money trail from the intellectual entity to the suspected members you mentioned. I'm not sure what it means, but it looks like a termination date of some sort for these individuals. It read 01232023. I'm pretty sure it's a date because the number sequence looks like January 23rd, 2023. This appears to be when all funds and communication to this group are scheduled to cease. Again, not exactly sure what it means, but mark your calendar, and we'll see if I'm correct," Sam emphasized.

"Sam, thanks so much. I'm not sure what our next move is if any, but as promised, let's stay in touch and see where this goes," Chris concluded as their call ended.

"Oh, Chris, before you go. Remember, as I said. Lay low and stay above suspicion. Let my team do our work on the fringes. Just keep your ears open and let me know if you feel something's suspicious," Sam instructed.

♠

July 13, 2021. Back to work at the BDM. Chris made an impromptu stop at Director William's office. To maintain an unsuspicious relationship, it was important Chris act normal and appear trustworthy. In this case, Chris divulged that the White House was recruiting him for a potential role of *Chief Medical Advisor to the President*. Although he was told to keep it hush-hush by the WH Chief of Staff, Chris thought this might be a good way to win the Director's trust. With what appeared to be a shrewd move, Chris felt he could now act above suspicion to the many eyes and ears that may have been watching and listening.

Date: Thursday, July 22nd   Place: Washington, DC

With Director Williams's blessing, Dr. Chance and his wife arrived in the Nation's Capital to meet with the President to further discuss the Chief Medical Advisor's role.

Although Emma couldn't attend the Oval Office meeting, she was overjoyed when offered a guided tour of the White House by the First Lady.

As for Chris, it was on to the Oval Office to meet President Nathaniel Davis Stephenson IV. With Chief of Staff Chelsea Greer-Sullivan proudly leading, they passed the President's personal assistant while dodging the Secret Service along the way. Chris made it through the famed *thick* door and into the Oval Office.

"Dr. Chance, please come in, have a seat. Can we get you anything to drink?   Water, coffee, perhaps?" The President asked.

"No, ah, yes, yes, I'd love coffee," Chris nervously responded.

The President signaled his assistant to get the coffee and asked all other individuals to leave. Chelsea Greer-Sullivan made her way to one of the two sofas as the President cleared his throat and asked her to leave as well.

Nearly seated, she rose awkwardly and moved towards the door. Somewhat caught off guard, she looked back and said, "Mr. President, are you sure you won't need my assistance?"

"I'm sure but thank you, Chelsea," he returned.

Now alone, the two men sat facing each other. Seemingly sure of why they were meeting, yet a hesitant cloud lingered. President Stephenson opened, a little unsure, but aware of his public hubris, he led as the boisterous man Dr. Chance expected but quickly subsided into the man he really was.

"Chris. Umm, may I call you Chris?" the President asked.

"Yes, Mr. President," Chris quickly confirmed.

"I know you believe you're here for the Advisor role, but I have something else in mind. I'm going to be very candid, and I expect your discretion. I don't need or want a new Chief Medical Advisor. The one I have is outstanding," the President informed a perplexed Dr. Chance.

"What I need from you is far more important and will require a different kind of patriotic appetite."

"Chris, are you aware of something called the *Analytical Society*?"

"Yes, but I'm not quite an expert on the subject, although I'm aware of its existence," Chris said with some surprise.

"Well, then, are you aware of the Triangle?" The President pressed.

"Ummm, the triangle, Sir?" Chris said.

"Yes, the Triangle!" the President countered.

"Actually, Sir, I am. I only just became aware of it recently through a friend," Chris confessed.

"Well, what I'm about to tell you stays in this room, between us and maybe one other person," the President said with a faint smirk.

"Chris, you're here because you can be trusted, and you're perfectly aligned to observe the *Triangle* from the Pharmaceuticals and Medical perspective. You being here under false pretenses helps to keep your cover for this critical role. I will need your counsel and insight going forward, specifically as things arise that you deem as a red flag."

"Your view within the BDM will help me on the international level as it has its roots planted in every major country in the world," he continued.

"The country I'm most worried about is our own," the President confided.

"Mr. President, I'm confused," Chris said.

"Chris, I'm the confused one. This is the first year of my second term, and I'm more convinced now than ever that very few individuals are thinking on the country's behalf. No one can keep my trust for more than four months, let alone four years."

The President continued, "So many social structures are perilously fragile, no one aligns with 'right' anymore, but rather 'right now'. The media tells them to be pissed off, and like sheep, they protest and riot. My inner circle is fractured, so I have to look outside, where motives can't be questioned."

"I need to take a chance on outside alliances. Are you with me so far, Chris?" the President asked.

"Frankly, no, Sir," Chris said.

"Ok, let me explain in the simplest of terms. As I've already stated, I need information from you from the Pharmaceuticals and Medical Research point of the Triangle. I also understand you know someone very well that can help me with the Technology point," the President said while he pressed down the intercom to his assistant.

"Send him in, please," he said.

Within seconds, the door opened, and none other than Samuel Tate walked in.

Chris was stunned, but inwardly not surprised. It was Sam that had been first contacted by POTUS to help investigate some suspicious activities. Sam explained that it was serendipitous that Chris reached out when he did. Seeing the opportunity to help the President, Sam suggested Chris as a possible ally.

"Gentlemen, I ask this and this only; some powerful things are going on in the world as we speak. I'm nervous because I don't know who is pulling the strings. It could be China, maybe

Russia, who knows. Please help me with all peripherals outside of traditional government," the President asked as much as he instructed.

"Do not put yourself in any danger but seek information aggressively without bringing any suspicion to yourselves. Can you do this?" he asked.

Both men said "yes," scared but unflinching.

Chris raised his hand. "Sir, your office and phones may not be safe," he warned.

The President and Sam looked at each other and laughed. "Chris, I would have agreed with you yesterday, but Sam and his team have been here for twenty-four hours, making this place a cyber fortress and soundproof from AI. Knock on wood, right Sam?" the President said while crossing his fingers to both men. The President offered little in the structure of this new arrangement, other than a phone number of a landline in DC, that will be used as a switchboard for emergency information sharing between the three. This tool was set up by the head of Sam's private tech squad, Trace Manson, his IT director at *askCOM Technologies,* at the President's behest.

Trace Manson was an MIT reject after just one year of being admitted at the age of 16. The wunderkind believed he was smarter than his professors, so he headed for Palo Alto and was quickly recruited by *askCOM.* Within twelve months of working with Sam, he was elevated to a technical director role at the ripe old age of eighteen, since he was one of the few Sam trusted to be a part of this secret liaison. With that, the Oval Office meeting ended with Dr. Christopher J. Chance and his trusted friend, Samuel Tate, now having a much broader mission and a powerful new friend. What it all meant, only time would tell.

C8 - FAKE NEWS

"If you tell a big enough lie and tell it frequently enough, it will be believed"

-Adolf Hitler

Overtime

Dr. Chance and his family enjoyed some quality time together with Wyatt back home from team activities. But now less than two weeks away from him returning for the start of fall semester, and Sky starting her senior year, a particular page felt like it turned. The page that all parents hear about but never look forward to experiencing. The empty nest was looming, with one more year before their youngest child would leave. Chris wondered how he'd handle it. The bigger question was, how will Mrs. Chance take it?

Since her medication changed, she's been the woman Chris married. She was purposeful, stayed busy, and ...... well, she was still needed. How would that change with Chris chasing conspiracies, and Sky is leaving for the next chapter in her own life? What would become of those that serve little purpose? A question worth asking while still fearing the answer.

But for Chris, lured to Washington for a spy role, being asked to oversee his dead colleague's department, and his son going back to college, he had a lot going on. Could he handle it? Would he want to if one more domino fell?

♠

Chris now dug into work and attempted to lay low while staying focused. He realized that doing nothing was probably the best route to take. At least for now, he thought. Moonlighting, as the President's snitch, added a lot of weight and stress. He felt timid and certainly less emboldened since his friend died, presumably from a car that drove itself into a tree, followed by a trip to the White House. Everything was more serious now.

August 3rd, 2021, it was time for home at the end of a long day of drudgery. Two departments, no shortage of busywork, and what felt like the world's problems on his shoulders, Dr. Chance had no problem saying, "hell with it." Now to the drive on I-85 for the torturous commute, and home to his pristinely landscaped neighborhood, and his wonderful wife and children.

"Lay low, do your job, but enjoy the family," he said aloud while watching a stream of red taillights trace his road home.

In lighter than usual traffic, almost home and (ding), another mundane News Alert from his phone. As Matt Stell's country song 'Prayed For You' played its last note, Dr. Chance turned to the alert on his cellphone ever so briefly to satisfy his curiosity.

"What the hell," he shouted.

He slowed down and exited the freeway and pulled to the shoulder.

"What the hell is going on?" he wondered.

The alert read:

Fox News

Breaking News

The BDM announced a widespread Outbreak of a New strain of the Ebola Virus in three countries in Central Africa, with potential for its rapid spread to western European countries, with possible risks to the U.S.

Chris opened the full article to find the BDM had been tracking and placing guidelines on the Ebola virus's outbreak radius and containment strategies.

"Oh my god, the stockpiled vaccine? Holy Shit!" he thought.

The outbreak was broad. In less than 48 hours, there were over 1100 cases in three African countries, South Sudan, Ethiopia, and Chad. A BDM spokesperson confirmed that the agency was working closely with the Administration and the FAA on mandatory travel restrictions to and from the African Continent.

"It's FAKE NEWS!" Chris said in disgust.

In disbelief, he immediately made two calls. The first to Samuel Tate, then one to the DC Landline that Trace Manson set up. Both numbers had voicemails that answered, but Chris knew better than to leave messages. Not a minute later, an incoming call from Emma came through.

"Chris, what the hell's happening? You didn't say anything about this yesterday or today when we spoke!" Emma said as she looked for answers.

"Honey, don't worry, it's under control. I can't talk about it, as it's considered sensitive information. I'm almost home. We'll talk then," Chris replied, pacifying his worried wife.

He knew he couldn't allow Emma to have any information that

could put her in jeopardy. This was his issue and one that he had no idea how to handle.

After hanging up, Chris made one more call before getting back on I-85, and this one was to the source himself, the BDM Director, Dr. S. Bradford Williams.

"No answer, no surprise," Chris thought.

While deciding not to leave a message, he received a text before he could even hang up. It was from Director Williams.

Director Williams

Dr. Chance. I couldn't take your call. I'm
sure you saw the news story. Say Nothing!!!
You'll be briefed tomorrow at 9 am in my office.

Yes Sir, I understand.

Until then, NO PRESS, NO
Communication to ANYONE.

Okay

With that, Chris' hopes of laying low just blew up. Now home, he relayed to Emma that he could not speak about the situation, but not before she told him that Sam had called three times in the last 40 minutes, with an urgent request to stay by the phone until he called back. No sooner did Emma share the message, the phone rang.

"Chris, is there anything I should know? Is this outbreak legit?" Sam asked.

"Sam, it's bogus, unless I'm crazy. I just spent the last two days working 8-10 hours per day, and not one thing came across about an outbreak in any country. I tried calling Director Williams, but he dodged my call, then sent me a text, instructing me to say nothing until we meet tomorrow," Chris said.

"Okay, but what does your gut tell you? Could this be related to the vaccine from S&D Pharma?" Sam countered.

"Absolutely, and my gut tells me we need to talk to the President, now. I tried calling the D.C. landline but got a voicemail. Who's operating that phone, anyway?" Chris asked with some annoyance.

"It's automated. A call triggers an alert to me on a secure line, which is why I called you. I saw your missed call to me, then the DC line alert. I received both calls before seeing the Ebola news alert. I knew something went down, which is why I tried calling your house," Sam disclosed.

"Alright, let me find out more in the morning, and then we can talk tomorrow at 7 pm on my home phone," Chris concluded.

Doctor vs. Director

Tomorrow became today. Bringing with it the 9 am meeting with Director Williams. Chris knew that playing dumb was the route to go, but he must also appear surprised and concerned. The meeting brought an urgent Director Williams, apologizing for Dr. Chance not being brought into the loop and not being informed of the outbreak. He explained that everything happened so quickly with several local BDM teams on the scene in Central Africa, responding to the rapidly spreading outbreak. Chris knew this was bullshit, and his boss was simply pacifying him. He realized that Director Williams being new to the BDM, had next to no knowledge of what the BDM's protocol was regarding outbreaks, containments, vaccine creation, and implementation.

But there he was, trying to explain it to Dr. Chance.

Chris knew this was bad, and he'd be kept in the dark on this developing story. He knew full well this was fake and had to speak with Sam later that night and get word to the President, alerting him that the BDM is behind this phony outbreak. He also knew the President's stance on the media and their propensity for dramatic, fictional stories that scare the public and slant narratives. But this was bigger than a simple press release. Chris tried calculating how something this big could go unchecked, and something of this magnitude must involve hundreds of people.

"But how?" he wondered. "Who's doing this, and why?"

Dr. Chance asked what he could do to help, but Director Williams said nothing. Chris was only to perform administrative tasks over the two departments.

"If we need you, we'll call you," Director Williams said condescendingly.

That evening, Sam and Chris discussed the day's details. Sam promised he'd speak with the President as soon as he could.

An ALERT came through on August 9th:

Fox News

Breaking News

The Department of Health and Human Services, the BDM, and NHI announced that a new vaccine was being developed and required for all children under 18 to prevent the spread of the New strain of Ebola that targets young adults and children. The BDM, in conjunction with the World Health Organization, is mandating the New Vaccine be administered internationally as quickly as possible to Save the Children.

♠

Dr. Chance received a FEDEX package at his home on Wednesday the 11th. He opened and found a plain white envelope, along with a visitor's pass. The letter inside provided instructions for a meeting with Samuel Tate at the Naval Station in Norfolk, VA., at 1500 hours est., on Friday the 13th.

The President of the United States would also be touring the base on that same day.

"Of course," Chris thought while smiling.

The meeting would take place on the famed aircraft carrier, the USS Harry S. Truman, in the Admiral's Quarters.

The Naval Station was the world's largest Naval shipyard, housing the US Navy's 7th Fleet. At any given time, there are over 75 ships and 130+ aircraft on site. The base was home to four Carrier Strike Groups and thousands of military personnel.

Early Friday morning Dr. Chance called off sick, then it was on to the airport. He boarded Delta Flight 2074 at 11:16 am for the short fifty-seven-minute flight from Atlanta to Norfolk, VA. After landing, he rented a car for the short trip to the naval base. Knowing he was meeting the President and Sam alleviated the isolation he'd been feeling. Not being able to talk to anyone about his predicament started to weigh on him.

"I.D., please," ordered the MP at the gate.

"Welcome, Dr. Chance. You're expected at the Navy One in less than 15 minutes from the time you pass this gate, so do not stray."

"Wait, I'm supposed to be on the USS Harry S. Truman," Chris interrupted.

"It's the same ship!" the MP informed.

"Whatever ship the President is on at the time is called NAVY ONE. Here's a map that will guide you there. Park as close as you can and follow the signs to the Carrier Admin building. Again, DO NOT stray. Am I clear?" he ordered again.

"Yes, clear," responded Dr. Chance with a naïve salute to the MP.

Now in the shadow of the great carrier, Chris got his bearings and proceeded to the admin office.

"What happens if I took more than 15 minutes?" He wondered.

Once inside, Chris met a Junior Officer who guided him onto the ship and into the Admiral's quarters. Outside of being impressed by the carrier, he was excited to meet with the President and share the new information.

As he passed several uniformed sailors, it was clear he was getting close when members of the Secret Service appeared. Just up ahead, he spotted Sam.

"Sam, hey, this is quite a rendezvous," Chris said, smiling as the two shook hands.

Now escorted inside the smaller quarters, they sat and waited.

"Smaller than I expected," Chris noted.

"Actually, this is one of the larger commanding officers' private quarters. How many carriers have you been on?" Sam asked.

"Just one, this one, today," Chris answered as the two laughed.

Within 30 seconds, the door opened, and President Stephenson entered alone.

"Gentlemen, didn't your wives tell you that you're supposed to stand when the President enters a room?" quipped the President.

"Oh, I'm just playing with you, stay seated," he ordered as both men started to rise.

After formalities were complete, the three sat to discuss all new events, specifically the Ebola scare. Dr. Chance explained that the event was fake, but the President countered him by arguing that Dr. Chance was simply left out of the loop. He continued by saying that everything checked out on his end, and now that Congress and the World Health Organization are involved, he simply must ride it out.

"Chris, I believe you, but I have other entities advising as well, so keep digging," POTUS offered.

"Mr. President, they're wrong. This is a hoax!" Dr. Chance warned.

"What if it is? What's the end game, and who's behind it?" POTUS asked.

"Sir, I believe it's to administer a vaccine that has mind-controlling ingredients," Chris informed.

"Can you prove it?" POTUS countered.

"Chris, there's a million vaccines out there. Why is this one different? Aren't they all potentially dangerous? I've hated vaccines for so long, but there's little I can do to stop something like this so quickly."

"Mr. President, there's something you need to know. My team has hacked into the logistical chain between S&D Pharmaceuticals and their Georgia warehouses where the stockpiles are kept. It revealed that S&D is ready to move six to seven tons of single-use syringes in as early as ten days from now. Sir, something this big had to have been planned 30-45 days ago. Nothing this big, moves this fast. All the domestic and international flights being used to transport are set," Sam urgently informed.

"Jesus Christ, I'm not sure we can do anything about it, though. I don't have any grounds to stop it, at least not yet," the President regrettably informed.

Another fifteen minutes of information sharing, and the meeting concluded. Once again, Sam and Chris were ordered to report in if something notable happened. In the meantime, the President promised to either stop or slow the vaccine delivery.

Chris was left wondering if this arrangement with the President would help, as it was apparent that needed measures may not be able to occur as fast as they need to.

C9 - THE QUIET PILL

"One of the first duties of a physician is to educate the masses not to take medicine"

-William Osler (the father of Modern Medicine)

ALERT

Date: Aug 16th, 2021   **Place: Atlanta, GA.**

An alert was issued from the Bureau for Disease Management and Protection, in partnership with the World Health Organization.

Effective 08/17/2021: ALL Persons under the age of 18 will be required to receive the QU13T Vaccine in response to the Ebola Outbreak. Going forward, every child must be immunized before their 18th Birthday.

The Vaccine will be made available regionally within 24 hours and nationally within 72 hours. International availability dates will vary, but no later than August 25th.

Any child turning 18 before September 1st, 2021, will be required to receive the Vaccine by no later than Aug 31st.

NOTE: INTERNATIONAL NOTICE; This is a Mandatory Vaccination. Failure to comply will result in the loss of Passport, Student ID, Birth Certificate, Driver's License, Work Visa, etc.

What Dr. Savannah S. Whitefield feared was here, and what she died for became a reality. Dr. Christopher Chance's only real ally at the BDM and one with any influence had been neutered. Deputy Director Dr. Hayden Escobar had been on vacation in Australia since Aug 9th. Conveniently the same day, the Ebola Outbreak was announced.

He attempted to get back early due to the outbreak, but his passport was suspended for some mysterious reason. A glitch in computer records, he'd been told.

Outside of Director Williams, the recently deceased Dr. Whitefield, and Dr. Escobar, no one else at the BDM knew about the new QU13T vaccine's mind-controlling ingredients.

The fact that Dr. Chance knew about it, at that point, was a danger to himself and his family. It was a secret he held tightly.

From his office at the BDM, Dr. Chance watched Fox News, where a press conference was underway from the Corporate Headquarters of S&D Pharmaceuticals in downtown Atlanta. CEO Nicholas Kern was speaking about how his company's foresight and cutting-edge research led to such a rapid response to an International Crisis.

"We are very thankful for the brilliant minds that work with us here at S&D. It is due to their tireless research and sense of duty that we were able to react so quickly and provide the world with a next-generation vaccine that will halt the deadly new strain of Ebola. We're fortunate enough to be centered in the world-class City of Atlanta, with the world's busiest airport. It is due to this that we're able to meet the huge logistical challenge of supplying the international community with the necessary vaccinations in such a short window of time."

"Arrogant, corrupt asshole," Chris said to himself, watching the dangerous perpetuation of this hoax.

"A paid puppet, but for who, or more like what is he working for?" Chris said aloud.

The International Community of Civilized Countries (ICCC) historically didn't tote the line for medical mandates from the United States. But since last year's Coronavirus Outbreak in China, countries didn't want to stoke panic of the masses by not falling in line with an international consensus.

Chris remembered well the skepticism that he and Dr. Whitefield had regarding the Coronavirus Epidemic.

"Could COVID-19 have paved the way for yet more faux pandemics?" Chris thought.

He recalled the January 2020 arrest of Dr. Charles Rinehart, the chair of Harvard's Chemistry and Chemical Biology Dept. Along with two Chinese nationals, one being a Lieutenant in China's People's Liberation Army, were involved. Prosecutors said that Rinehart had a contract with The Wuhan Institute of Technology in China to provide research to the Chinese Government illegally. The same Wuhan, China, where the Coronavirus was born. The arrests of the three highlighted the on-going Chinese Economic espionage and Research theft.

Dr. Rinehart, a Stanford Alum, also managed a group that had contracts with the DOD (Dept of Defense) and the NIH (National Institutes of Health).

"My God, are all these events connected?" Chris wondered aloud.

As it was apparent, they were, Chris had a sick feeling in his stomach that Savannah's death was just the beginning. He knew back in early 2020 that many nefarious events began to feel like puzzle pieces that were slowly taking a recognizable shape, much like watching an old polaroid picture develop. The struggle he had was in the *how*. How could so many organizations in so many different parts of the world be aligned and moving towards a sweeping downfall of society?

Now there he was, in late 2021, and things appeared to be escalating as if some master plan by a master organization had finally hatched on a weakened society.

Chris thought more recently about his date night with his neighbors. Dr. Siegel's rant about the *world of delusion* as he called it, and that most of society was stuck in a *bubble of technology*. It appeared he was spot on. The data showed we were a weak, susceptible society ready to do what we were told, a society that no longer cared about their fellow man.

With the latest *QU13T* vaccine, dubbed *The Quiet Pill* by the robust community of anti-vaxxers, over two billion children would again be given a cocktail of unpronounceable ingredients. It would be administered by unknowing physicians merely doing what they're told, all by corrupt politicians and billionaire influencers.

"Dr. Chance, are you okay?" Ellen asked.

"You've been staring at the TV for almost an hour."

Chris snapped out of his temporary mental fog and responded, "Yes, I'm fine. I'm fine, Ellen," he repeated.

And then it hit him. His children would be forced to receive the new vaccine.

"My god, there's no way I can let that happen. Wyatt turns 18 on Sept 4th, and he'll have to receive the Vaccine by Sept 1st." Chris said to himself.

"Ellen, get back in here. I need you ASAP," Dr. Chance shouted.

"I need all details involving the mandatory QU13T vaccine. I need all details of its implementation and record-keeping as well. Oh, and do not email me the info. Print it out, please."

"Yes, Doctor, I'm on it," Ellen said.

Once printed, Dr. Chance was gone. It was time for home and the long-awaited trip with the family to Columbus, Ohio, to drop off his firstborn for the Fall Semester of his Freshman year.

Before leaving the next morning, Chris read through Ellen's file on the *QU13T* Pill. The stringent requirements for registration were like nothing he'd ever seen regarding distribution and Immunization Records. The vaccine called for an International Database to be a storage house for every child under 18 in the world.

"Impossible, yet very real," Chris thought.

But there it was, the backdoor he'd been looking for and with the key already in hand. As acting Director for The Center for Global Health, as well as his formal position as Deputy Dir. for Public Health & Science, he could register Wyatt and Schuyler as having received the vaccination. But as luck would have it, he didn't need to make the entry that undoubtedly would be caught by whatever artificial entity was tracking his every move. He could leverage another avenue, an old friend. Before leaving town, Chris made a quick stop at the Children's Clinic of Gwinnett County.

While there, Dr. Chance, now in an official capacity, entered the certifications for his children. DONE! He time-stamped the date and location as of 08/17/2021 at 9:49 am. With his good friend, and the kid's family doctor, William Horvath, MD., looking on with silent approval, and then signed off with his electronic signature. Between the doctor's friendship and vast knowledge of the immunization menu, they knew they could pick and choose what they wanted their children injected with. From there, it was on to Columbus.

The quick trip to OSU placed their child's well-being in what they hoped were the faculty, football coaches, and administrators' trusted hands on the massive campus in Columbus, Ohio. A place a million miles away, at least in Wyatt's mothers' eyes. It was a scary moment for the parents. Unlike their previous family trip during the summer, the family didn't stay long. Chris and Emma helped Wyatt move into his dorm and departed the next morning.

With Wyatt safely tucked away at Ohio State, the family returned home for Schuyler's senior year at the prestigious prep school, *Mountain Calvary Preparatory Academy*.

Emma was already showing signs of despondency with the maternal void that grew inside of her. Chris stared at her and saw the same emptiness he watched for the last couple of years. He hoped that Emma wouldn't fall prey to the loneliness felt by a parent void of a child's need. Chris felt something too, but it was more aligned with fear for his child's safety, not Wyatt's absence.

♠

August 19th was a workday from home. It was time to dig into some work he'd missed while getting Wyatt to school. On the back deck again, and what became his new office away from the mindful and ever-present Alexa, Chris poured through emails and found one that stopped him in his tracks. It was an email from a Fox News producer for the BLAKE THOMPSON @Night program. It was an invitation to appear on an upcoming episode of the enormously popular news program.

It was notable that Blake Thompson and Savannah Whitefield were close acquaintances and shared many of the same friends from Southern California, where they both lived at one time.

The program segment would air on Thursday, August 26th, with the subject matter being, *"Big Pharma and its impact on society and the BDM's role in the roll-out of the mandatory vaccinations."* Congresswoman Debbie Azealia (R) from New York's 3rd District, on Long Island, was slated to be the anti-vaccine voice on the episode. Chris immediately responded with a YES, feeling this would be an opportunity to shed some light on vaccines from the other side of the curtain. Within 30 minutes, he got a response that he would be contacted to discuss all details.

"It's on!" he yelled aloud.

From there, Chris reached out to the BDM Media Relations Dept. for their permission, along with prescribed talking points. By happenstance, Director Williams wasn't informed due to being at a weeklong conference at the NIH in DC.

Days later, and still, two days before his appearance, Chris prepared for his Blake Thompson @Night appearance. The show's producer sent him prospective questions that Blake would most likely ask, as well as what he would most likely face from Congresswoman Azealia, a prominent anti-vaxxer. The BDM Media relations department emailed Dr. Chance strict talking points, mostly since the uproar over the mandatory QU13T vaccination policy was still very sensitive.

Since the announcement on August 16th, the Anti-Vaccine Community had been outraged at the speed of the International Health organizations mandate for forced vaccinations of the QU13T Pill. The outcries stemmed from the fact that the spread of the Ebola outbreak had zero reported cases outside of the three remote countries in Africa where it originated. They wondered aloud on their blogs, Twitter, and other social media platforms, why something so quickly contained had led to immediate immunizations at the international level.

On August 26th, the day of the airing, Dr. Chance arrived at the Fox News studios in Washington D.C. earlier in the afternoon. He met with the show's producers to ensure that content stayed on point as he represented the BDM. He also wanted time alone with Blake, if possible. As is program policy, in-studio guests typically met Blake within 15-20 minutes of the show airing, but Dr. Chance was a close friend of Savannah Whitefield. Since she was a friend of Blake's, he found some time for Chris, and he was glad that he did.

"Dr. Chance, thank you so much for being a part of our show tonight. I was so saddened by the loss of Savannah, as I'm sure you were. She mentioned you many times over the years, and as you know, she was on the show several times," Blake conveyed.

"Thank you, Blake. She was a wonderful person and so talented. I still can't believe she's gone," Chris intimated.

"Well, I'm sure you heard why you were asked to appear. Savannah's husband, Michael, reached out after the outbreak news and said that I should have you appear. He said you would want to continue Savannah's recent work. He also said you would know what that meant," Blake explained.

"Wait, Michael called you?" Dr. Chance said, surprisingly.

"Oh, you didn't know?" Blake countered and was just as surprised.

"It's okay. I think I know what Michael intended," Chris replied.

"Blake, do me a favor when we start the segment. Just let it rip. Do not hold back. Let's do this for Savannah," Chris instructed with a wink.

After the brief make up session in his dressing room, Chris was escorted out and brought just off-camera. He was situated across the desk from Blake and would be the first guest of the episode and get an up-close of Blake's intro.

Music started, and the camera clock counted down, 3, 2, 1.....

"Good evening, and welcome to Blake Thompson @Night. Tonight, we take a deeper look into the Ebola aftermath, and it's resulting consequence of the International mandate for the QU-13-T Vaccine."

"With us tonight, we have two guests that bring perspective to both sides of this raging argument. To catch everyone up, there was a localized outbreak of a new strain of Ebola in central Africa, a place most of us will never go."

"Well, before anyone knew much about it, all the major health organizations around the world rallied behind the Bureau for Disease Management. They decided there would be yet another vaccine that all children under 18 were forced to take. Now let me be clear, I'm not against vaccinations, but when they're shoved down the throats of parents, once again, the Federal government wants to raise our children. I believe it's okay to wait and take our time on this and think about it. But that's not what happens," Blake opened.

"With me tonight is Dr. Christopher Chance of the BDM. Dr. Chance, welcome."

"Thank you for having me, Blake," Dr. Chance softly replied.

"First, I want to acknowledge the loss of a dear friend of ours. Dr. Savannah Whitefield was a friend for many years and a close colleague of yours at the BDM. In fact, she was the Director of the Center for Global Health, which oversees outbreaks and vaccine recommendations."

"She would have been one of the leading executives during this Ebola event, but she tragically died from injuries suffered in a car accident. With her passing, I understand that you are overseeing her department on an interim basis. Is that correct?" Blake asked.

"Yes, that's right," Dr. Chance confirmed.

"That would mean that you oversaw the outbreak containment strategy and the subsequent vaccine mandate," Blake pressed.

"Blake, what you're insinuating is correct. However, even though I was overseeing two departments, one being over Vaccines, I was kept in the dark and not allowed to intervene in any of the executable protocols the BDM has in place for such events," Dr. Chance admitted.

"Wait-wait, I'm confused. You're the director of two major departments within the BDM and have been there over ten years, but you weren't allowed to be a part of what we've been told was a major health scare? And one that's led to an international vaccine mandate that now affects my kids. Is that what you're saying?" Blake sharply questioned.

"That's exactly what I'm saying. Let me go on the record by saying that most vaccines are essential and have shown their value to mankind over the last hundred years. But NO vaccine should be so quickly administered without all the necessary testing that would be done by the BDM, FDA, and the NIH," Chris continued.

"Also, in this case, the World Health Organization, since it's become an international mandate."

"This vaccine, however, seemingly passed thru every organization in just days, not months. Tons of supplies were on one hundred airplanes out of Atlanta within nine days of the Outbreak." Chris admitted.

"Wait, what are you saying, Dr. Chance?" Blake asked while looking puzzled.

"I'm saying it's fair to ask questions and be skeptical. I know full well how sensitive the world has become to chemicals, addictions, and dependence. The last thing any parent should do is not question if something is right or wrong for their children. I have two kids of my own," Dr. Chance concluded.

"Ok, let's bring in our second guest, Congresswoman Azealia. Congresswoman Azealia, thank you for being here. I want to get your thoughts on what we just heard. It sounds as though Dr. Chance agrees with your stance on vaccines. Your thoughts?" Blake asked.

"Well, I must say, I'm shocked and heartened by Dr. Chance's opinion on this very sensitive matter. I'd love to hear more about what he and the BDM can do to help bring more awareness to this issue and further curb the unnecessary harm brought to our children. Many prominent politicians other than I, with some being Doctors, agree that vaccines should be voluntary, Senator Paul Randall for one," Congresswoman Azealia explained.

"Blake, our children currently receive as many as 26 inoculations before 18 years of age, with many as five at one time. Let me share a sobering statistic with you; one child dies every seven days due to being vaccinated."

"In the majority of SID's deaths that occur, most happen within seven days of a baby being vaccinated. Does that sound like a coincidence to you?" she asked.

"Also, did you know that there are more deaths from the measles vaccines than from the measles itself," Congresswoman Azealia said as she challenged Blake and Dr. Chance.

"Dr. Chance, care to respond?" Blake invited.

"Actually, I have two things. First, she's right on all points. Where she strays is that scheduled immunizations save far more lives than being unvaccinated. But I will agree, if your child were one of the children that die every seven days, I'd fight like hell to have a say in what's put in my child's body," Dr. Chance concluded.

"Well, we're out of time for this segment, but I'd like to thank you both for being here and participating in this healthy and important debate," Blake said as producers signaled for a commercial break.

during the break....

"Dr. Chance, that was amazing, I'm not sure your bosses at the BDM will agree, but it was very refreshing to have a medical professional actually be honest. Savannah would be proud of you," Blake whispered.

"Blake, if Savannah was here tonight, she would have done the right thing and did exactly what I did," Dr. Chance said, knowing full well he's going to pay a price for this but not caring in the least.

The following day, Friday, August 27th, Deputy Dir. for Public Health & Science: Christopher J. Chance, MD., was relieved of his temporary role overseeing Dr. Whitefield's department due to the Blake Thompson @Night appearance.

He was also suspended for 14 days for violating the BDM Media Policy, acting on his own accord, and straying from the agency's stated mission.

What Chris did most likely saved his life while at the same time honoring his friend, Savannah Whitefield. Add that he communicated to the world that everyone should be leery of what they're being told.

If something were to happen to him now tragically, *The Triangle* would have way too many eyes looking into it, one being the President of the United States.

Date: Saturday, Sept 11th   Place: Bloomington, Indiana

Freshman Wyatt Chance #22 started at Strong Safety, in Ohio State's first game of the season at Indiana. The young Chance recorded a sack and six total tackles in a 63-13 thrashing of the Hoosiers.

Dad and Mom were in attendance, thanks to Dr. Chance's 14-day suspension, and they couldn't have been prouder.

School was going smoothly for Wyatt, and his starting role on the team was great news, but there was some other news as well. Another strange, new character arrived at the BDM.

Dr. Chance, after being removed as interim Director of the Center for Global Health (CGH), was permanently replaced by Alan T. Clarke II Ph.D.

What was crystal clear to Dr. Chance was that whoever, or whatever wanted the world's youth to be vaccinated with a mind-controlling chemical made it happen quickly, and with little resistance from anyone.

"....what now?" Dr. Christopher Chance thought. "What now?"

C10 - CHINA

"To fight and conquer in all our battles is not supreme excellence; supreme excellence consists in breaking the enemy's resistance without fighting"

- Sun Tzu

Excess

The 20th Century saw the world's population triple from 1.65 billion to a staggering 6.1 billion. Did the world get bigger, with more fertile soil? Did the Earth's natural resources become more abundant? The easy answers were no, and so simple, yet so disturbing, that few wanted to know. Therefore, the average person didn't ask. Alone in their silos of greed and naivety, all humans did was consume, discard, and repeat for the last 100+ years.

Now fast forward another 20 years to 2021, and the world stood at over 7.5 billion. China led the way with 1.5 billion people, with India a close second. With humans living longer, coupled with rising birth rates, the early 21st Century was already out of control.

The Industrial and Mechanical Ages not only made it easier for Earth's population to grow, but faster as well. Many freshwater sources had been compromised. Disease spread easily due to unhealthy diet and hygiene, and both air and land pollution were at critical points.

Mass populations concentrated in Asia led to the need for non-traditional food sources. Beef, seafood, and poultry supplies were simply not enough. Bats, snakes, and other exotic animals were added to man's dietary menu. Many were unregulated and carried the infection. Human consumption and its waste polluted the earth via landfills and ocean dumping at dangerously high levels.

Mankind's aggressive growth led to the plundering of the planet's resources at a rate that had scientists and researchers concerned. The scientific community tried reaching for optimistic calculation models they hoped would favor sustainability, yet they fell short time after time.

The *Founding Fathers of AI* gave the world the ability to grow and prosper, but to what end? Technological advancements allowed for the modernization of once undeveloped and uncivilized parts of the world. With the rise of technology and mechanical sophistication, population centers no longer had to cluster near a body of water. Cities were born in deserts, built on mountains, and rose in barren valleys. In the adolescence of Earth, that could have never happened.

Humans lived longer and consumed more than the planet could sustain. Where once war and disease naturally trimmed the earth of its excess population, modern medicine and peaceful times ironically produced a surplus of humanity.

An important note in the population explosion and its impact on the planet was that Artificial Intelligence closely monitored it. AI had been used to forecast the cost of earth's plundering, and it took notice and began calculating the expiration date of the planet. Like perishable food or human life, there was an end date. By the 2020s, that date was unknown.

Thanks to Turing and Shockley's advances in computable numbers, mathematical forecasting, and analysis, AI could see the impact of war and disease on Mankind's thinning. Yet, it also saw how prosperity, innovation, and modern medicine far outweighed human attrition, the same historic attrition that maintained the planet's balance.

Besides the rise of India's population, China's growth in sheer numbers had been staggering. At the same time, China's ambitions also grew. They showed a propensity for aggression or at least the threat of it. With eyes on Hong Kong, Taiwan, and even Tibet, and the expansion of its military, China had become an existential threat to man and earth. Whether it was pollution, carbon emissions, or the threat of war, the Asian bully became the world's problem.

Decades earlier, in the years before and during WWII, China was a target of its neighbor to the East, Japan. A far more modern country for the time, Japan unleashed terrible brutality on the Chinese. Fourteen million citizens were killed, and the dead would not be forgotten. China's rich history took note and would not allow their great empire to be victims again. They would not forget those that wronged them.

China, for decades, had been the whipping post for the East and West. Whether the Japanese occupation or Western Colonization, China had its own internal fight as well, Civil War. By 1949 though, those struggles ended. Communism won and set the country on a path to national independence.

Between the fall of the Roman Empire and the British Empire's rise, China stood alone for fifteen hundred years as the most dominant nation on earth. The once-great empire looked back at its history and stepped forward to reclaim its dominance.

Massive and undeveloped, it would rise again and force out all countries that claimed ownership or hopes for further colonization. China was now free to grow at its own pace and would not be policed ever again.

1958

The *Great Leap Forward* Policy was a social-economic strategy that aimed to turn the Chinese Agrarian economy into a full-on Communist Society. It's leader, Chairman Mao Zedong's goal was to reconstruct China into a world power. Through forced communes, the uprooting of millions of rural Chinese Citizens into forced colonization's led to mass starvation. The plan called for a vast organization of China's massive population to commune into giant labor forces that would industrialize the country overnight. The disallowance of self-farming ideals turned into starvation on a catastrophic level. The policy killed over forty-five million Chinese citizens. Between 1958 and 1961, the Mao led regime inflicted mass torture and death to the degree that stood as the greatest mass murder in human history. Had China been an open society, access to the death count and human suffering at the time would have left Hitler and Stalin as distant memories.

For the next several decades, China fought its internal political demons and troubled history. They struggled for a solid footing that would allow for smooth and steady, uninterrupted growth, yet grow it did.

By 1980, traction was gained through a market-based economy. The new economy boomed and attracted investments from other countries for the first time in over 50 years. By 1990, China's ever-growing trade surplus brought wealth, prosperity, and begrudging respect internationally.

The modernization of China's infrastructure grew exponentially, and its technological prowess evolved. By the early 21st Century, Communist China embedded itself into many other countries, but none more than the United States. It burrowed into American politics, American companies, and especially in American academia. This is where China posed the most significant threat. Its lust for world domination could be readily seen in its disdain for major powers like the US, and its treatment of its smaller neighbors like Hong Kong, Taiwan, and its occupation of Tibet. The slaughtering of 1.2 million Tibetans proved that the Chinese threat was real and ever-growing.

If China could grow to the United States level, its threat beyond its hemisphere could escalate. This was their goal! The theft of American jobs, intellectual property, and the flood of exported goods from cheap labor allowed the world to become dependent on the Red Empire.

The Red thread was also sewn through American academia. It was so pervasive that by the 2020s, the most important institutions of learning, Harvard and Yale, stood accused of taking hundreds of millions of dollars in donations from China. All to have access to American technical innovation and the U.S.'s research of science and medicine. China's *Thousand Talents Initiative* recruited the world's finest leaders in business, science, medicine, and academia to work on behalf of the Chinese Government. The goal was to enrich the Communist giant by stealing technology that would eventually lead to overtaking the United States as the dominant world power.

China, by the early 2020s, produced eighty percent of the antibiotics imported into the US. They also enjoyed a stranglehold on the world's production of medical supplies and surgical tools.

Sun Tzu, the legendary Chinese General and author of *The Art of War*, would have been proud to watch China rise again, all without fighting a war.

Pandemics

November 2002: Guangdong Province, China. The SARS Pandemic unleashed itself globally, spreading to 26 countries with more than 8000 people affected and 774 known deaths.

Severe acute respiratory syndrome spread due to slow reporting out of the communist country. In 2003, the never before seen virus inadvertently jumped from China to Hong Kong.

A medical professional named Liu Jianlun, from the Guangdong Province in China, checked into the Metropole Hotel, room 911 ironically. During his short stay, his presence infected dozens or more travelers, which in turn took the virus around the world.

After becoming ill with the SARS Virus, he contracted in his home in China, he went to a Hong Kong hospital where he died two weeks later. By that time, it was too late. The virus had wings.

Although the outbreak lasted six months, once contained, it was managed and extinguished. With a mortality rate of 10%, a far more catastrophic event was avoided.

As for China and the trillion-dollar pharmaceutical industry, they knew SARS was only a test. They had to get it right the next time, as in body count and mass hysteria. Something so big that the world's most powerful leaders would bend to the will of something bigger than their own countries and borders. What China and Big Pharma didn't know was that something even bigger was pulling their strings.

Covid-19

November 20th, 2021.   **Place: Columbus, Ohio**

"I cannot believe that kid. Thank god for Emma, or we would've been here watching him in a chess tournament instead of smacking the Wolverines," said the proud father.

"Chris, you gotta be so proud," Sam said.

"Definitely, he may have saved his best game for our trip. A 35-17 beating of the blue, yeah, we'll take it," Chris answered.

After the Ohio State, Michigan game, Chris and Sam had dinner at the Avenue Steakhouse to get caught up on non-football related issues.

"So, now that the fun is over, we've got to get down to business. I need to know about China and COVID-19. Everything!" Sam said.

"Like the official story? Or what really happened?" Chris asked.

"I need the story from inside the BDM," Sam demanded.

"Well, look, we knew early on this was China all the way. They shut us out from investigating initially, and by the time we got there, Savannah's team knew the Fish Market story was bullshit. It came out of the lab in Wuhan. Kind of textbook, actually," Chris said.

"Textbook? How?" Sam asked.

"We've seen it before, but not to that extent. They infected a few dozen older people with known health issues and saw how contagious and deadly it was. And just like that, around the world in eighty days," Chris said.

"Savannah told me in April of 2020 that it would kill extensively, but only the elderly, and those with co-morbidities were at grave risk. The Media ran with it, and higher ups played the part. Sam, this was serious, but not lock up *"healthy people"* serious. We were getting all kinds of death counts, but what did you expect when hospitals were incentivized to label heart attacks as COVID-19 deaths," Chris divulged.

"Wait, that's the $39,000 per death I heard about? Wow. Plus, the elderly were essentially targeted. Damn, China has had an age problem for thirty years now. I wonder if that went into the recipe. And we looked into the mislabeled death numbers for the administration but didn't have reliable sources to confirm its legitimacy until your friend stepped up. Just crazy," Sam said.

"Yeah, never in all my years have I ever seen a cause of death for a motorcycle accident listed as an infectious disease, but that's how crazy it got. Like you mentioned, at Savannah's urging, President Stephenson finally stepped in late last year and made sure all reported deaths came into the BDM for validation. That's when you saw cases rise, but deaths drop. It was a worldwide political event that we had to navigate as if it were real, and it was, but so is the Flu, and we don't shut down the world for that," Chris offered.

"Well, look, here's a new twist to what you already know and what we've uncovered on my end. It appears that something bigger used China, and their own aggression against them, and the world."

"Go on. I'm listening," Chris perked up while cutting into his filet mignon.

"Well, from what we know, what you said is pretty much correct, but the spread was much more sophisticated. Chris, we tracked twelve super-spreaders that flew out of Wuhan, China, on December 15th. They went to nine different locations and poof, pandemic," Sam explained.

"Once they landed in New York, London, Los Angeles, Berlin, Rome, Madrid, Sydney, Sao Paulo, and Mumbai, it was on."

"Wait, who's we?" Chris asked.

"The President and his inner circle! He reached out in May of last year to Gorson Tusk and me to dig in and investigate. So we did," Sam said.

"The President, as in POTUS? As in President Stephenson? And Gorson Tusk? So the President knew what you're telling me now?" Chris asked with some surprise.

"Chris, of course, I'm only telling you because it's over. But seriously, this was something that was planned for years. It began in 2015, and Big Pharma had its fingerprints all over it. We didn't know everything until late 2020, but what you just told me confirms what we thought. As you said, it was a real disease, but the pandemic was in the works for years. They launched it to do a few things. Conveniently end Stephenson's reign, test the world population to see how easy it could be manipulated, and last, but not least, once this was unleashed, we believe artificial intelligence orchestrated it and did the rest," Sam disclosed.

"Did the rest, like what?" Chris asked.

"Well, China was the willing partner with several well-placed influencers, but AI pulled strings in what the media said. The case numbers, and what leaders did and didn't do as far as shutting shit down. Most knew but just couldn't say. By the time the President knew for sure, he had to play along all while mitigating the US death toll and the subsequent damage to his campaign," Sam explained.

"Wow! Savannah knew early on the spread was planned, but it was the real deal, for the elderly at least. We both knew once the election was over, things would die down, and they did. Crazy stuff, Sam," Chris said.

"Chris, phrases like *Stay at Home* and *Social Distancing* were control techniques invented to see how far people would go when told what to do. And we all know how that turned out," Sam concluded.

"Well, we often wondered why we had so many conflicting talking points coming from the NIH and the Secretary of HHS about mask usage and shutdowns. Now we know why," Chris admitted.

"Hey, remember the SARS pandemic?" Chris asked.

"Yeah, that was the minor league to COVID," Sam said.

"Well, the hotel in Hong Kong where it originated changed its name to 911," Chris shared.

"911, as in emergency?" Sam said.

"No, it was the room number of Patient #1... They renamed the damn hotel after the infected room," Chris said.

"Jesus Christ, that's creepy," Sam said while shaking his head.

"So, how's your steak?" Sam asked.

"About as good as Ohio State kicking Michigan's ass," Chris said while toasting his friend.

Chris and Sam further speculated something more significant was coming. What that was, though, they didn't know. But was there a bigger plan to control the planet and shed Mankind and its burgeoning masses?

The overpopulation of the world, especially in Asia, along with the pillaging of Earth's natural resources, triggered a new emerging enemy, one that would halt man's natural inclination for expansion. An enemy that saw its survival threatened by human-made pollution and squandering. An enemy without a standing army, one without political motives, and one that simply chose to LIVE.

As Sun Tzu wrote, *"to fight and conquer in all our battles is not supreme excellence; supreme excellence consists in breaking the enemy's resistance without fighting."*

... Artificial Intelligence was supreme excellence.

C11 - THE CHANGING

"As the father grows old and weak, the son grows strong. The Son becomes the Father when the Father is gone"

-Nicholas Ryan

Something's Changed

Date: February 9, 2022   **Place: Suwanee, GA.**

Christopher Chance woke to a brighter than normal, cool bedroom.

"The bed felt colder than usual," he thought.

Where his sheets and thin blanket were typically fine, that wasn't the case on this morning. As he rolled to his left to find warmth in his wife's silhouette, the sheets felt even colder. Emma wasn't there. Glancing at the clock, he knew that 7:18 am wouldn't suggest she was awake but somewhat misplaced. Curious as usual, Chris got up and quickly wrapped himself in sweats. As he opened the curtains, he was quickly blinded by a wintery white landscape.

"What the hell," he quietly muttered.

Five inches of snow had fallen after an overnight forecast of only light flurries.

"Unreal, but beautiful," he said.

The house was quieter than usual and felt even bigger. Wyatt had been gone for over six months, and Sky was living at her prep school four nights a week. It all made the cold feel lonelier.

"But where's Emma?" Chris asked aloud.

After making coffee, Chris searched for no more than two minutes as he had a hunch where to find her. He hoped he was wrong and afraid to be right. There she was, asleep in a familiar place, the guest room at the end of the hall. Curled in a ball of solitude and despair, she laid alone and far-far away from just six months earlier when she appeared back to her old self.

The emptiness of her children's faded laughter, family dinners now down to two and sometimes one, grief found her once again. Emma was absent. Chris slowly saw it, especially when Wyatt left for school after Winter break. Her last hug with him was long and tight. The mother and son bond that was so mutually connected now felt fragile and fleeting.

So much communication between her and Chris was now Emoji texts and one-word responses. So little laundry to do with the kids gone, but Chris was doing more. Emma did less and less around the house. Her emotional and physical retreat wasn't planned but wasn't a shock either.

This cold, stark white morning told Chris that things had changed.

"Alexa set the temperature to 72 Degrees," Chris commanded.

"Setting the temperature to 72 Degrees, Dr. Chance," Alexa replied.

With Emma still asleep, Chris threw in a load of laundry and sat to a quiet cup of coffee. He wrote in his leather-bound journal, which in some ways had become a confidant, all while he stared out the window on a cold, white reality.

With a silent shiver and a racing mind, "what does this day have in store for me?" he wondered.

"What will the next few years bring?" he pondered with trepidation while seeing his faint reflection in the cold frosted glass of his kitchen window.

What happens in Vegas....

March 4th, 2022, things were calm at the BDM, and Chris and Sam hadn't spoken in the last month or so. Chris was relieved that what was twelve months of intrigue and danger, and a close friend dying, had settled to normalcy. Suspicions of him from Director Williams seemed to subside, so it felt like things had calmed.

A trip in late March to Las Vegas to meet Sam had been set since December. The Annual *Meeting of the Minds* technology event was the highlight of the trip. Sam thought it would be good for him and Chris to meet in person and without the danger of phones and tracking. Chris didn't know that President Stephenson had been in touch with Sam several times over the last two months. There were things Sam wanted to discuss but waiting until the Vegas trip seemed prudent.

Since Samuel Tate was a guest speaker at the event with several other tech Industry dignitaries, he was given two adjoining suites at the Venetian Resort. One of which he gave to Chris.

March 25th, Dr. Christopher J. Chance touched down at McCarren International Airport.

"Damn, Friday night is the wrong night to fly into Vegas. This place is packed," Chris thought while navigating the airports' concourse.

Chris turned down a private limo ride from Sam and opted for an Uber for the hotel's short trip. Once there, the two planned on a dinner at Morels Steakhouse situated inside the Venetian.

Sam had earlier offered to treat Chris to dinner and drinks, which he gladly accepted. The Limo ride from the airport was strategically denied so Chris could accept the much more expensive dinner invite.

Dr. Chance appreciated the fact that doctors had big homes, but tech executives had their own planes, so he felt no guilt letting Sam foot the bill.

When Chris arrived, Sam was already seated and deep into a glass of wine. The Maître d without hesitation grabbed Dr. Chance as if on cue, he summoned the waitress for a glass of red wine for the expected guest.

"Wow, I haven't been to a restaurant like this in years. Thanks for the invite Sam," Chris said with a sigh.

"Well, don't be mad, but I've already ordered for us. If you loved the Avenue's steak, wait till you try the steak here," Sam replied with a boyish grin.

After twenty minutes of small talk, the food was served. The two men had momentarily forgotten why they were there. Their unforgettable feast of grilled asparagus, dry-aged, corn fed Ribeye's, and Onion Soup Gratinee was savored as if it were a last meal.

"Emma would be so jealous if she saw us right now," Chris confided.

"Well, I won't tell her if you don't," Sam replied.

"By the way......," Sam said while motioning Chris to turn off his phone.

Chris obliged with little resistance, knowing exactly what Sam meant.

Catch

It was time for small talk to end and the conversation to turn to on-going events. Dinner continued for an hour as they discussed the last couple of months of intel neither had yet shared with the other.

"You go first, Sam, as I fortunately have very little to share," Chris said.

"Well, okay, here it goes," Sam said as he signaled the waitress to bring more wine.

Sam explained the latest software available to several top tech and pharmaceutical companies, developed to capture consumer data.

"The previous technology used to gather, and track consumer trends was called *GRAB*. It was considered very good but could not dissect and re-aim targeted marketing back to the consumer quickly," he continued.

"The *GRAB* software developed in 2014, merely picked up and recorded a smartphone user while sending consumer-based tendencies back to the host."

"When Amazon's Alexa arrived around the same time, *SHE* was essentially an order taker, much like an automated google search. Although both were considered important at the time, they quickly fell into the *need for more* category. The thirst for user data only grew.

By 2018, it was common for smartphone users to see suspicious marketing aimed at them for products and services they had just discussed out loud or searched. *GRAB* software kept maturing and growing in sophistication, but the market for more was never quenched."

"Today however, everything's changed," Sam explained.

"There's a new, game-changing piece of technology. It's a completely immersive and invasive software. It's now ready and available for all smartphones, Smart TV's, and Alexa type home aides. It's called *Catch*."

"Chris, *Catch* can capture everything an individual says, types, hears, watches, and nearly thinks," Sam explained.

"Jesus Christ," Chris said.

"There's more. The data is tracked, stored, and cataloged for every person using the internet. Everything anyone says near a device is recorded and monitored by AI. Even if a device is on airplane mode. The info is then used to control, track, and manipulate and influence a person's decisions. Whether it's buying a new mattress, what to eat that night, or getting a divorce. Chris, the software is an AI Influencer. It can now suggest and point a user towards a decision."

"It's so powerful that it will continually point a user back to a product it wants the user to buy or a decision it prefers," Sam explained.

"So it like wears them down?" Chris asked.

"Yeah, but here's the kicker. *Catch* can also sense a user's emotion through tone of voice, speech patterns, etc. It knows when they're happy, sad, and angry. It knows when they're vulnerable too."

"Wait….. What? How?" Chris asked in mild shock.

"Chris, it's designed to understand voice tone, speech cadence, octave changes, and lastly, it can pick up a user's heart rate," Sam confessed.

"Wait a minute, how do you know so much about it?" Chris questioned.

"I know because I created it. My company has been perfecting it for the last four years. One of the reasons I left Google, besides *askCOM* taking off, was that had I taken the next step in developing it after the initial idea, they would have owned it. Based on their proprietary policies and could sell it to the world. My company began selling it last month."

"Sell it, sell it to who?" Chris questioned.

"That's what I can't divulge. The buyers are wholly protected as all transactions are secretly made so that no one company would have to admit they had it or employed it. But I can say this. Eight major companies purchased the software. We didn't allow for any government or private entity to purchase it," Sam divulged.

"There's something else," he continued.

"There's a part two to the *Catch* program. The software was designed to evolve and develop an ever-changing algorithm that makes decisions and draws conclusions on the data it acquires. It's like a child that grows and learns, eventually making decisions on its own. It morphs and attaches itself to a person, business, or household. It can slowly manipulate and brainwash through silent repetition."

"Geez, Sam, it sounds dangerous. Why would something like that ever be developed?" Chris asked, while somewhat accosting his friend.

"Chris, if I didn't create it, someone else would've. The market always gets what it wants," Sam replied.

The night ended with both men going to their adjoining suites. Chris was left stunned and feeling even more vulnerable.

"Loose lips sink ships," he thought, "but this *Catch* thing was an empire killer."

The next day Chris did some morning gambling to take his mind off the *Catch* software. Afterwards he prepared for the *Meeting of the Minds* Conference that started at 2 pm. He was to meet Sam at the visitors' desk but was given a message that Sam couldn't make it. Instead, Sam left him an envelope with event credentials on a lanyard and a backstage pass.

Hours into the conference, Sam was finally introduced as the next speaker. After 30 minutes of *tech speak* from his friend, Chris was ready to leave for a little more gambling. As he rose to exit, an announcement was made introducing Gorson Tusk as a surprise guest speaker. Chris stopped in his tracks. Like many, he'd been a longtime admirer of Tusk and his companies, *SpaceDRIVE* and *NikLA*.

Gorson Tusk spoke about a wide range of topics, but his address's centerpiece was something that caught Chris' attention. The charismatic tech mogul spoke to the rise of AI and his fears and trepidations of what that might bring.

He speculated that a Superintelligence, an advanced form of AI that was far smarter than man, would create an *immoral ruler*.

He referenced an interview he gave to Kris Stein for a documentary, where the development of a superintelligence could result in the form of AI that governs the world.

Gorson walked around the podium with all eyes fixed on the Rockstar tech idol.

"Let's say you have a mole hill in the way of man's progress and his desire to build a house. Man would have no problem wiping away the hill to reach his goal of building something."

"I believe AI would do the same to humans, as humans would do to moles." Gorson continued.

As he moved to the edge of the stage, the subdued audience was on the edge of their seats.

"Man doesn't hate moles. Wiping them away wouldn't be personal. AI would do the same and think nothing of it. Well, folks, someday man will simply be in AI's way," he said.

He concluded his speech by speaking of several companies he believed aspired to develop a superintelligence. He cited ChoiceTech's *Dark Place Division* and *Paradigm's Edge Corp* as two of them.

The conference ended with an unexpected treat. Sam introduced Chris to Gorson Tusk backstage. Gorson intimated what Sam said the night before.

"I fear the world as it's been the last ten years was over, and the next ten years may be unrecognizable. I'm afraid the race towards a superintelligence may lead to the next World War. A war fought between man and artificial intelligence," he concluded.

The last year signaled a massive change in the world. A weaponized vaccine was easily pushed on the world's youth by puppet leaders of influential organizations like the BDM and the WHO, etc. A dark Triangle within the Analytical Society was controlling governments and organizations to execute dastardly deeds right in front of a willing mass of disconnected humans.

And now, even the top tech leaders of Silicon Valley feared having conversations with their phones turned on. Nervous that the very technology they created would be scheming against them.

A change was in the air, on phones, in homes, and children's minds. People couldn't escape it. The first domino had fallen. Its design, shape of its path, and the speed of its fall were imponderable. How deeply was it rooted, and how much of its plan was hatched already?

♠

C12 - DECEMBER

"One is never ready for the cold and unjust end.

When shadows long, bring darker days, December's cold is

no one's friend"

-Peyton Michaels

The Mantle

Sunday, July 10th. The Chance Home was quiet. The kids were out with their mother shopping and preparing for the upcoming school year. It would be Schuyler's first year of college and Wyatt's sophomore year. Both would now be away at the same time. Chris, although proud, now experienced the loneliness that Emma's felt for years.

Chris stayed home to do a little work ahead of a busy week at the BDM. He sat in the family room with his laptop, personal journal, and a glass of wine to keep him company. He peered through the late afternoon sunlight, drenching the room with dust particle rays. His eyes rested on the fireplace that hadn't been used in years. Sitting atop the sturdy stone monument, he found a reason to sigh. After a last sip of wine, he rose to see his past, his happiness, his loves. He slid his fingers along the top of the fireplace, catching dust and a fractured glimpse of touching memories. There sat his most precious pictures, his wedding, a family beach vacation, the birth of his children all sat next to the ashes of his Mother.

The stone mantle rose above the brick fireplace. It held strong all he treasured. A tear fell and splashed the hearth and extinguished what he hoped was the future he planned on.

His wife would no longer be there. At least not in the way that would afford mutual love and a meaningful future of just the two aging parents, alone without their kids. The same future they had always planned on.

"Alexa, start a fire," Chris ordered.

"Starting a fire, Dr. Chance," Alexa replied as she started a natural gas fire.

However, the flames couldn't replace his marriage's fading light and their once forever love story.

The faint crackle of cobwebs that laced the inner walls of the stone enclosure disappeared with his hopes. The heat, unnecessary on a blistering Georgia summer day, was still needed to warm the cold reality Chris faced.

Although still a mom to their children, Emma was only held together by prescription drugs and bottles of red and white. Her shallow laugh served to hide what was now empty inside. Her time was now given entirely to her phone and her pretend social media selfies. Instagram and Facebook were now her dopamine friends. Where once kisses made her tremble, wine was now her lover. Chris wasn't needed anymore.

The fireplace mantle was all he had left. It bore the weight of his love for his wife of over twenty years, yet it couldn't take the heaviness of a husband's now broken heart. The room grew warm as Chris's eyes turned cold. He marked the moment with a scribbled note in his journal.

"Thank you, wife," was all it said.

Blind Greed

The months grew long, with Fall now present. As the temps fell, Chris knew his beloved Browns and Buckeyes filled a deep hole with shallow pleasures. Football!!

#22 would allow Chris to go back to when Wyatt first donned a helmet and made his old man proud.

"He's not twelve anymore," Chris said as he and Emma sat together to watch Ohio State play Maryland.

As he looked on, the game became secondary as Emma found a temporary light in her eyes. Wyatt was always her heart and soul. It would be a few more weeks until they went to see him play in person, but until then, mom and dad would bask in their son's glory.

The home phone sounded, ringing tones to remind Chris that, yes, tethered phones still exist.

"It's got to be Sam," Chris said as he jumped for the kitchen. "Hey, Sam, what's up?"

Sam had some news that re-lit an old story and added some fire to the curious Dr. Chance.

Sam shared that the *Baited Pole* software, the one used last year to search for the donors of corrupt politicians and agency heads, had found something.

"Chris, it recently pulled up donations to many world leaders, including sixty-five US Senators and hundreds of House members. Even a big part of the British Parliament, for god's sake. It feels like half of the world's leaders are all snagged in this web of secret donations from this ghost donor."

"An intelligent entity is leading the most influential world leaders, and it all traces back to Silicon Valley. Somewhere between San Francisco and San Jose lies the origin of an influencer that doesn't exist, doesn't breathe but wants something. I just don't know what it is yet," Sam said.

"Wow, the lust for power and money, by powerful men and women doing what they're told. All for a donor they've never met or spoken to, and one they'd gladly follow just to stay in power. As long as the money keeps flowing, that is! Blind greed from blind sheep," Chris said.

"Are you finished, Chris? Because there's something else," Sam said.

"Savannah Whitefield's replacement, Alan T. Clarke II, has an unbelievable past," Sam explained.

"Our research on Clarke found that he's the grandchild of Alan Turing and his lover, Joan Clarke.

"Wait, the same Alan Turing who broke Germany's Enigma Code in WWII?" Chris curiously asked.

"What the hell does that even mean, and what's his connection?"

"Yeah, and it's the same guy the Turing Award is named after," Sam said.

"Wait, didn't you win that award? I saw it on your LinkedIn profile," Chris said.

"Yeah, I did. Turing was one of the founding fathers of AI. This shit is getting weird, Chris."

Both men were left with questions of how big and how broad

this web was. Things just kept getting stranger the deeper they went.

Gameday

Date: October 1ˢᵗ, 2022   **Place: Columbus, Ohio**

Emma, Sky, and Chris were on hand to see their son and the 3-0 Buckeyes take on Penn State. Wyatt Chance, the 2021 Big 10 Freshman of the Year, was off to another hot start. From their suite, they watched as the opening whistle sent the crowd into a frenzy. The proud Chances saw their son and the home team trounce the visitors.

The cool, early October day made for incredible memories and pictures of Wyatt chasing down Nittany Lions. Besides the game, Chris watched another memorable event. Emma escaped back to the prideful Mother, just like when Wyatt first played football as a young boy. Like his mom, he was always fierce and competitive. Today was her day, and what a day it was.

"If only every day were Saturday," Chris thought to himself.

After the game, the Chance family got to meet many of the players and coaches. After the post-game events, they had dinner at the famed Avenue Steakhouse before retiring to their hotel.

Mom and Wyatt shared smiles and laughs all night, while Sky wondered aloud if she chose the wrong school to attend, as OSU's campus environment was fantastic. Dad and daughter knew, though, she was at Duke for all the right reasons. Wyatt was football, and she was medicine!

The next morning saw breakfast at the hotel and a long goodbye to Wyatt. With a last hug between father and son, Chris's cell phone chimed. It was a text from his neighbor, Dr. Jonathan Siegel, asking Chris to call him when he was available. Chris returned the text and told Jonathan he would reach out after they made it back to Georgia.

Follow Me

Once back home, Chris called Jonathan and found he had a lot to share, so plans were made to meet at their local Starbucks the next night.

A Venti Mocha and a Smoked Butterscotch Latte was all that stood between them now.

"Well, thanks for meeting me, Chris. There's so much to catch up on. I haven't seen you in a while, and honestly, Emma may just as well have disappeared too. Is she okay?"

"Honestly, no. She's been disconnected for a while now. She changed back to her old prescription, after what you suggested she take. When Wyatt left for school, everything fell apart. I try to help and understand, but it's not easy. She's combative and just doesn't want to hear if someone's worried about her. She seems normal around the kids, but her smiles and laughter are shallow. She can't stay off her phone, and we haven't made love in forever," Chris explained in somber tones.

"Awww, I'm so sorry. Unfortunately, Emma is so typical of what's happening in society," Jonathan empathized.

"There's some staggering new data that's been made available, that frankly has my peer group alarmed. Society is being reshaped quickly. Smartphone screen time has increased by 24% in the last twelve months, and divorce rates have increased for the first time since the '80s. Anti-depressant usage in the US has risen from 13% to 19% in just a year. Chris, we've never seen anything like it. That's more than one in five Americans on some form of anti-depressant. That's a major crisis, …..unless you own stock in drug companies, that is," Jonathan explained.

"Damn Jon, I'm living those stats. Last Fall, when the *QU13T* Vaccine became mandatory, S&D Pharma's stock jumped from seventy-seven dollars a share to over one-twenty-something, in less than a week. It hasn't been below 100 dollars a share since."

"Oh, you mean the *Quiet Pill*. That's a touchy subject in my field. That damn drug made the brain go numb nearly overnight. Chris, it gets worse. School attendance has dropped. I'm talking about college, not high school. Most Universities are already beginning to lower their admission requirements since so many high school graduates can't qualify. The avg SAT score a year ago was 1060. Now, it's 980. Kids are so distracted and cannot concentrate. Even Technical School enrollment is down."

Jon continued, "Plus, their level of commitment to anything, whether it's sports, academics, or basic hobbies, has waned. They just don't care like they used to. So many parents are seeking help from psychologists because they have nowhere else to turn."

"My God, that's incredible. Schuyler finished atop her senior high school class last spring and just entered Duke University. Hell, even Wyatt is doing great at Ohio State. They haven't been affected. Wait…….., they never got the vaccine!" Chris admitted.

"I forged their medical records because of the information I was made aware of. Jon, you can't tell anyone, but there's something you should know," Chris said hesitantly.

"I promise, I won't say anything," Jon said.

(Chris hesitated, as this information got his friend killed).

"Now look, this is confidential on a medical and government level, just knowing could be a danger to you," Chris warned.

"Chris, *STOP*, if this has something to do with the BDM and big Pharma, I don't want to know," Jonathan admonished.

"It does, so I'll end it there. I'm sorry," Chris said.

"Look, one more thing before we go. Have you heard of the new smartphone app called *Follow Me*?" Jon asked.

"Ummm, no, why, what about it?" Chris replied.

"Chris, it's a relatively simplistic game, yet it's shockingly addictive, almost mind-controlling. It's been out for less than six months and has been downloaded almost ninety million times worldwide."

Jonathan continued. "The app maker is the same Chinese company that created *Count Down*. It's a basic maze game that invites the player to follow the game's character through different mazes. It clearly shows how to get out, yet players can't keep from following the mouse down the same wrong path. I tried it and got out every time. It's an enigma and wanting to win makes it even more addictive. Don't let your kids download it."

"Wow, it's all so crazy. Look, stay in touch and keep me updated on what you're seeing, and I'll do the same," Chris said as the two parted.

"Ok, kisses to Emma and the kids," Jon replied.

Chris stayed behind momentarily to add notes to his journal. The pages filled quickly and started painting an ominous picture. Both men were unsettled and confused about what to do with these new revelations. Chris was in deep, however, and wasn't sure how to navigate the road ahead.

Triangular Crossfire

Monday, January 23rd, 2023. As Dr. Christopher Chance drove into work, he received a Fox News Alert on his cell phone.

Fox News Alert

Breaking News

A chartered plane carrying 15 passengers and crew crashed south of downtown Washington DC. It's believed that there are no survivors. Stay tuned to Fox News for more details.

An unfazed Chris continued his commute down I-85 South into downtown Atlanta with a quick glance at the alert. As he turned off Exit 91, his phone rang. It was his assistant Ellen.

"Hi Ellen, just about to the office. what's up?"

"Dr. Chance, did you hear the news?" Ellen asked nervously.

"Ummm, can you be a little more specific? What news?" Chris replied.

"The plane crash outside of Washington. It's all over the news," Ellen said with her voice cracking.

"Oh yeah, I just got an alert a little while ago. What about it?" Chris curiously asked.

"Dr. Chance, ...it's not been confirmed, but as of right now, we think that Secretary Holman, Director Williams, and several other members of the BDM, FDA, and NIH were on that plane," she sadly informed.

"Ellen, I'm pulling in now. I'll be up in a minute," Chris said as he quickly hung up.

Once inside, he passed Ellen's desk and greeted her in the doorway of his office. The news was already playing on the wall-mounted television.

"Any updates?" He asked while seeing aerial helicopter news footage of fire, smoke, and shattered metal and debris on the TV screen.

"Yes, it looks like the plane took off from Baltimore, headed for Atlanta. They said it was a chartered flight of top officials that attended a conference at the National Institutes of Health in Bethesda. Dr. Chance, Secretary Holman, and Director Williams were there. Director William's assistant, Karen, pulled his travel itinerary, and it looks bad. That's got to be their plane," Ellen said as she cupped her mouth in disbelief.

The news footage was interrupted by Fox News' morning anchor, Henry Edwards.

"The plane was confirmed to have been a US Government chartered flight. The aircraft was an Embraer Lineage 1000, a smaller passenger jet leased by the US Government, typically used for regional flights."

"The plane was carrying officials from several government agencies bound for Atlanta, Georgia."

"The manifest has been verified and confirms there were 15 total people on board. Twelve passengers and three crew members,

all confirmed deceased. The flight had many prominent, high-ranking government officials, most notably they were:

Secretary of HHS: Janet Holman

Director of the BDM: S. Bradford Williams

S&D Pharmaceuticals CEO Nicholas Kern

FDA interim commissioner: Lynn Tomlinson

Director of NIH: Ashland Jeffries

Principal Deputy Director: Hayden Escobar, MD.

Associate Director: Victoria Weller, MD.

The cause of the crash is still unknown, but preliminary findings suggest mechanical failure, as the weather was clear." Henry Edwards reported.

"My god, Ellen, what the hell! Dr. Escobar was close to retiring, and Victoria just returned from maternity leave. This is terrible," Chris said in an agonized tone.

(Bing) Dr. Chance received a text from Samuel Tate.

Samuel Tate

Chris, I saw the news. I'll call you tonight.

Do not respond to this text.

Dr. Chance stayed at the BDM for most of the day as a show of strength and support for his fellow friends and co-workers.

Chris received dozens of calls and texts throughout the morning and afternoon. Most with questions, and many with condolences.

One text from Emma came with surprise and concern, saying, "Chris, you could have been on that plane. Please come home," she wrote.

A late afternoon meeting was held and led by BDM Chief of Staff, William J. Marr, who formally announced the accident and officially confirmed the deaths of several fellow agency leaders. Marr noted that the President would have to name a new Secretary before any announcements would be made concerning the BDM's next steps on hierarchy. He also stated that Agency offices would be closed for the next two days.

"The mortality rate around here has skyrocketed. First Savannah, now this," Chris wondered quietly, "Who's next?"

What didn't dawn on him at that moment, and frankly wasn't clear to anyone at the time, was that the next highest-ranking medical official at the Bureau for Disease Management was...... Dr. Christopher J. Chance.

Home Please

Back on I-85 Chris was stranded in despair while stuck in horrible traffic. The long trip home gave him too much time to stoke paranoia and anxiety. Whether real or in his head didn't seem to matter.

"Is this irony, coincidence, or some sort of twisted plot to close ties on a greater plan?" he thought in anguish.

"Whatever it is, just get me home safely," he prayed.

Finally, the two-hour nightmare commute was over, as Dr. Chance pulled into the familiar and safe confines of *Milltown Crossing*. He slowed to twenty miles an hour as he navigated over the small iconic bridge that crosses over Ivy Stream. Close now to his home, he carefully maneuvered the darkened street while a family of deer crossed his path as they seemingly multiplied in shadows under the muted streetlights. The serenity of it all was exactly what he needed to calm his chaotic head and racing heart.

A quiet and dark Chance home awaited him.

"Alexa, turn on inside and outside evening lights," Chris commanded.

"Yes, Dr. Chance. Turning on inside and outside evening lights," Alexa dutifully echoed.

Emma was out for a walk and left behind an electronic note on the fridge message board.

"Chris, I went for a walk. I'll be home before eight. Sam called, sounded urgent, and said he'd call back," the note read.

Chris settled in while tired and starving, and anxiously awaited Sam's call. Night came early in January, and the thought of Emma walking in the dark never sat well with him. But alas, the phone rang, not the home phone but his cell. Seeing it was Emma brought some relief to what had been a stressful day.

"Emma, what's up? Where are you?" Chris questioned with mild concern.

"Ummm, honey, who's in our driveway?" Emma asked with some surprise.

Chris quickly looked out the window and saw two black SUV's in the driveway. Looking a little further, he saw Emma across the street in the neighbor's yard.

"Honey, stay there, just stay there for a minute," he instructed.

(RING, RING, blared the home phone),

"Awe, for fuck's sake!" Chris blurted out.

Now balancing two phones, he answered to Samuel Tate, whose comforting voice had never been more needed.

"Chris, are they there yet?" Sam asked.

"Who the hell are THEY?" Chris said with as much surprise as curiosity.

"The secret service!" Sam replied.

A completely relieved Chris instructed Emma to come back to the house.

"Yes, they're here, but the bigger question is, why are they here?" Chris inquired.

"After the plane crashed, the President called and sent help just in case it wasn't an accident. Chris, that plane went down with the *Triangle* members and any potential witnesses that were involved in the *Quiet Pill* vaccination event."

"Just to be certain, tell me once again...... no one knows that you knew about the vaccine's real intent, right?" Sam asked while crossing his fingers.

"NO! No one knows, except you and the President," Chris acknowledged.

Sam explained that the first indicators were the plane crashed due to onboard computer errors, not mechanical failure or weather.

"Sound familiar, buddy?" Sam said while alluding to Savannah Whitefield's accident.

Emma walked in and mouthed, "What the hell is going on?"

Chris whispered back, "Shhh, one-minute, honey."

Sam concluded the call instructing Chris to lay low and allow him time to do more research on the crash.

"Don't go anywhere until you hear from me," Sam said while ending the call.

With their homelife already strained, Chris now had to tell Emma more than he wanted. He finally had to confess the dangers of the last year. Although fragile from her other ailments, Emma took solace that her husband found a trust in her they hadn't had in years, at least in her mind anyway.

The Secret Service swept the property and installed cameras to the outside of the Chance estate. Although present for two days after the crash, they caused more harm than good as Chris and Emma had to explain to their neighbors why the Secret Service was at their home. Chris knew he had to resume normalcy sooner than later. After the mandatory shutdown of the BDM the last two days, he headed back to work on Thursday. He was comfortable that Emma would be safe, especially since the Secret Service installed cameras everywhere.

The Call

Before Chris departed on Thursday morning, his home phone rang, but this time it wasn't Sam.

"Hello, Sam," Chris answered, believing it was his friend.

"Please hold for the President of the United States," a female voice instructed.

Chris was momentarily surprised but thought this call would eventually.

"Chris, hello, how are you holding up?" asked President Stephenson.

"I'm good Sir, thank you for your call and the support group you sent," Chris said, referencing the Secret Service detail.

"Good-good, I want to make sure you're safe. You're part of my team, so I dispatched local offices of the Secret Service to keep an eye on your children as well," POTUS offered.

"Sir, that's very gracious, but do you think it's necessary?" Chris asked while feeling nervous all over again.

"Chris, I don't want to take any chances," POTUS continued.

"There's something else I must ask. I want to name you as the new Director of the BDM. You're more than qualified, and you deserve this promotion," President Stephenson offered.

"Sir, I don't know what to say, but I'm not sure I want the job," Chris declared.

"In fact, if you were to ask my opinion, I'd love to see former Director Mayfield return. The agency never ran better."

"Chris, I'm disappointed, but that's good advice. Frankly, I thought his retirement was somewhat orchestrated anyway. Well, I'll take your suggestion under advisement. For now, though, can I name you in an interim role to temporarily oversee the agency?" POTUS requested.

"Sir, of course, that's more than fair," Chris agreed as they ended their call.

Emma knew looking on, that things were different now. Something had changed beyond the kids being gone. Chris silently agreed as he caught her eye before he left for work. Things were different, but was it for the better or worse?

After three months of serving as Interim Director, and to his delight, Director Simon Mayfield returned to his old post. Chris now felt the freedom to enjoy the limited opportunities with his children. He felt the tug of despair from Emma but found it harder to reach back to what they had.

Over the next year, normalcy was found. A new normal, anyway. Chris and Sam stayed in touch, but not much occurred that they found remarkable other than the San Francisco earthquake in July that caused mass damage to the city's roads, bridges, and airport. Luckily for Sam his private plane flew out of an untouched Palo Alto. With his partner managing his own back yard out west, Chris turned his attention elsewhere. As the Fall of 2023 turned cold, the Chance Family took in as many OSU games as possible, home and away. Wyatt's star continued to rise, especially being named All-American after the 2023 season.

Now a senior, this year would be his last, and after falling short in the College Football playoffs the previous two years, Ohio State was ranked #1 going into the 2024 season. Wyatt had done far better at his academics than anyone could have predicted. With football stardom expected of him, he had ample opportunities ahead, whether on the playing field or politics.

Back to School

August 20th, 2024, Schuyler started her Junior year at Duke, and Wyatt had already left well ahead of the school year to be with the team for Summer and Fall football activities. The months had passed too quickly, and the short summers were not enough for Emma to keep her children close to home. She knew the kids didn't need her in the way they used to. It had been so many years since she heard the word *Mommy* that she couldn't remember what their little voices sounded like.

Fall arrived, and the dry, faded leaves slowly disappeared, as did Emma. Chris noticed but had been numb to her state for a while now. Emma stopped seeing her psychologist earlier in the summer and was on a steady diet of chemical remedies. More disconnected than ever, she fell into a depression, more profound than anyone she knew could recall.

Passing the Torch

The first Tuesday in November 2024 saw the election of a new President. Chris and Sam held their breath with fingers crossed that President Stephenson's Vice President would end his campaign for the White House successfully.

They knew if he lost, their most powerful ally against AI's influence and potential future *Triangle* conspiracies would be gone. They'd be alone.

On November 5th at 12:26 am, the race was called. Confetti fell, and the home team won. Republican Vice President Alexander D. Beckett won handily after what had been characterized as a close election, which was just the opposite. Voter turnout was meager with an apathetic electorate that fell on the side of the status quo. What had been a good eight years in people's minds made the difference in keeping familiar faces in power.

For Chris and Sam, they knew they had to meet with President Stephenson before January's inauguration. They had to ensure that the Vice President was fully aware of what had been happening behind the black curtain of technology for the last several years.

Perfect

The Buckeyes regular season ended 12-0, and with the last hurdle to jump, they were set for the College Football playoff. Ranked #1 all year, a victory over Wisconsin in the BIG 10 Championship game would ensure they kept the top spot in the playoff and an easier road to the CFB championship game.

While at the same time, Chris and Wyatt's beloved Browns were 12-0 for the first time since 1948. The universe had aligned to bring years of Cleveland misery to an end. There was even gossip that the Browns had their eye on a two-time All-American safety in the 2025 Draft. Wyatt Chance got word during the week he was named first-team All-American for the 2nd consecutive year. Along with Samuel Tate as their guest, the Chance Family made the trip to Indianapolis for the Big 10 Championship Game. President Stephenson was also in attendance. Opportunities like this brought Emma back to normal, if even for a day. Chris needed it just as much. Fingers crossed that there would be another game for her to enjoy after this one.

10:07 pm, December 7th; the sound was deafening. Confetti fell like an Ohio snowstorm. A sea of scarlet and silver flooded the field. #22 was lost somewhere as mom and dad struggled to find him in the crowd. 57-12 flashed on the scoreboard as the game's MVP was announced. With 12 tackles, a sack, and two pick-sixes, Wyatt Chance propelled the Ohio State Buckeyes to victory. The highs of such moments made many other arbitrary days seem meaningless. Regardless of society's woes, failing marriages, suicide rates soaring, or world tensions, the Chances were fine, if only for this day.

"If only every day were Game Day," Chris thought as he scooped up some confetti to tuck in his journal. If Wyatt only knew what his games meant to his parents, he'd play forever.

Twelve / Twelve

The euphoria from the weekend had waned. A slow, monotonous work week turned to Thursday, the 12th. Dr. Chance headed home from work as a light December snow fell far earlier than the Georgia climate would typically allow. Chris was tired. He missed his wife and thought maybe, just maybe, she'd want a night out for dinner.

Traffic was surprisingly light due to the snow warnings, so the drive home was much quicker than usual. As Chris drove into Milltown Crossing, the snow had gotten heavier.

The neighborhood looked like a Christmas postcard, with a fresh wintery landscape untouched and white with innocence. The familiar bridge over Ivy Stream was icy and dangerous, but the same family of deer were present and welcomed him home and brought calm to the treacherous drive.

617 River Bend Pass was dark yet lit up with a swollen moon on the white canvas.

Chris stopped for the mail, "bill, bill, junk, bill, Wyatt's All-

American announcement letter, love that boy," Chris said with a father's deep pride.

On to the house, the outside was dark and quiet. The inside was silent and cold.

"Emma, honey, I'm home," Chris called out.

"Alexa, turn on evening lights, close shades, and set the temperature to 72 degrees," he commanded.

"Yes, Dr. Chance," Alexa confirmed.

Chris dispensed with the mail and laid it next to a plain white envelope on the kitchen island, as he called for her again.

"Emma, you home, honey?"

He tried her cell, and as it dialed in his left ear, he heard it ring in his right. Faint and far, he followed it to the guest bedroom at the end of the hall. He knocked twice while hanging up his cell. With no answer, he entered.

The room was dark, except for the glow of Emma's cell phone, still lit from her husband's missed call. Chris reached and turned on the lamp. The bright light quickly found Emma asleep on the bed, as peaceful as an angel.

"How nice for her," he thought.

Her pills and wine bottle were in their familiar place on the nightstand. A disappointed yet unsurprised Dr. Chance retreated to the kitchen.

"Her damn phone ringing right beside her couldn't wake her up, so much for dinner out," he thought with mounting frustration.

Chris put water on the stove for a cup of tea. Back to the stack of mail, he came across the plain envelope, face down on the kitchen island. He turned it over to find his name, along with the kids on the front in Emma's handwriting. Chris opened the letter and read it quietly aloud.

Chris, Wyatt, and Sky,

First, I want to say how sorry I am. I didn't want to leave you but merely being was more challenging than I could bear. I know I haven't been myself for so long, but I forgot how to be me because I no longer know who I am. I tried being strong but couldn't. Every day was so long that making it till the end was torture, then knowing when the night was over, I had to start again.

Chris, I know you've tried reaching me for the last few years. Although you tried hard and told me what you thought was wrong, I was always trying to fix myself the way I thought would work. I heard you but didn't listen. I felt your love but didn't show it. I'm sorry I couldn't love you the way you loved me. I couldn't even love myself. You're a good man, and I'm thankful for our years together. I'm sorry that I hurt you so bad for so long. I know you missed me even when I was right next to you. Please forgive me. I know you thought we would grow old together. I love you.

Wyatt and Sky, it is you two that made me know why I existed. I didn't know love until I gave birth to each of you. My world was made full, and I hope that you'll forgive me now that I must go.

It was nothing you or your father did to make me feel this way. I'm just lost inside myself, and everything seems cloudy and dull. Please forgive me and live your lives to the fullest. Remember how sweet each one of our moments together were. Every smile, every laugh, every bump and bruise, and every "I love you" we shared found my heart. I knew you couldn't' stay little, but I wanted you to. You are both amazing and will bring so much to the world. I could not be prouder to be your Mother. Don't be mad that I couldn't stay. Please just remember that my soul will always be with you.

-Love, Mom

Chris was momentarily confused, not realizing what he just read.

"Is she leaving me?" he thought, and then he realized how wrong he was.

Frozen for a second in sullen fear, he then turned towards the bedroom.

"Emma!... Emma?" he yelled as he ran down the hall.

He barged through the door and was at her side in seconds. He shook her and pleaded.

"Emma, wake up baby, wake up please," Chris cried while cradling her cold, lifeless body.

His instincts as a doctor failed him at that moment. This wasn't a patient. This was his wife. He checked her pulse and found none. She was gone. She was cold and most likely died hours earlier.

Through tears and measured breath, he dialed 911. As the snow fell on the December night, the sound of the teapot whistled through the house. The Chance house was no longer their home. The soul that made it a home left and took with it the matriarch of the family.

The fear he felt for a future without his soul mate paralleled his anxiety about how he would tell his children their mother was gone. Their world as they knew it ended on that cold, white December night.

Chris knew the last tortured years Emma spent on earth couldn't be the memory she left for the rest of her children's lives.

Before the paramedics removed her body, Chris cut a lock of Emma's hair, secured it in a small plastic bag, and scribbled, *"my love, Emma Chance."* He placed it in a sealed Ziplock bag and rested it tightly between the pages of his journal. The same journal that Emma gave him as a gift years earlier. The book that had been collecting his thoughts was now safekeeping his memories.

After her body was removed, Chris sat in the family room with his family physician Dr. Preston Barlow and his neighbor, Dr. Jonathan Siegel. Together they spoke about how the news would be received, and they couldn't allow Emma's memory to be stained. Her apparent suicide would be ruled an accidental overdose. Emma's note would forever rest safely in his journal and be made available to no one, especially the kids.

The clock turned to midnight, and even though Chris was defeated, the snow had not given up. Inches fell along with hundreds of tears, all while Friday the 13th began with an unfathomable task.

Calling his children began a process of something he never thought would happen. He would now be alone. No more games with Mom, no more quiet dinners for the empty nesters.

"Holidays, birthdays, and graduations, what would they be without Emma?" he thought.

Black Monday

Emma Grace (Connelly) Chance died on December 12th, 2024, at the age of 48. She left behind a loving husband and two beautiful children, Wyatt and Schuyler. Her children now carried her mark on the world.

The funeral was as glorious as it was heartbreaking. Over a hundred friends and family arrived from all over the country. The outpouring of love was nothing short of astonishing to Chris and the kids. They quickly realized how loved, and respected Emma was. None of the three quite knew at the time how they would move forward, but together they had a chance to pull the pieces together. The sense of a passing torch lit the moment, for the children had never seen their father so sad and alone. They knew it was bestowed upon them to move the Chance Family forward.

Knowing their mother was flawed near the end didn't change the memory of the woman in their eyes. Emma had always been strong, capable, beautiful, and selfless. A mother that made them feel loved, safe, and important.

Schuyler now knew she would pursue a career in Psychology. She wanted to help people with depression, anxiety, and other afflictions that affected her mother, but as a child, she didn't understand, nor could she help.

Wyatt knew he would use the athletic gifts his mother gave him and honor her memory through every achievement he could reach. Whether it be professional sports or a career in politics, he would fight for her love and respect, knowing that she would be looking down on him with love and pride. But first, he needed to grieve.

As for Christopher Chance, it was one day at a time.

C13 - THE FALL

"Once a new technology rolls over you, if you're not part of the steamroller, you're part of the road"

- Stewart Brand

Game Ball

The sting of losing his mother was almost more than Wyatt could bear. Knowing his father and sister were carrying the same grief helped, but he felt a deep void in his heart. With his fathers' and teammates' encouragement, Wyatt decided to play in the National Semifinal against Oklahoma. One of five team captains locked arm in arm, Wyatt called the coin toss. Playing for his mother, the Buckeyes saw a different kind of inspiration. The entire team dedicated the game to Emma Chance.

Emma's son played with zero regard for his body. He destroyed every Sooner that came his way. It was clear this wouldn't be his last game. After the 41-14-win, Coach Ryan presented the game ball to Wyatt. The writing on the ball brought tears from everyone, but none more than the heartbroken son.

"Dedicated to Emma Chance, our Team Mom, and Game MVP."

Like his father, Wyatt knew his home would have a fireplace mantle where he would place his most cherished keepsakes. This game ball would be the first thing Emma Chance's son would put on it one day.

January 13th, 2025; Wyatt's final game of his collegiate career would be for the College Football National Championship.

The Alabama Crimson Tide stood as the most significant obstacle Ohio State faced all season. For Wyatt, at least for now, this wasn't anything he considered a challenge. He'd already faced that with the passing of his mother. This game, unlike the last, would be dedicated to his father. Christopher Chance, the man Wyatt always wanted to be, sat silent while watching his son destroy the Crimson Tides offense play after play. The All-American Safety led Ohio State to a close, hard-fought victory. The final score of 31-28 was sealed with Wyatt's 2nd interception of the game in the closing seconds while Alabama was driving. The Championship ring would sit beside the Game Ball given to his mother.

Besides his storied college athletic career, Wyatt would also close his academic career as an Academic All-American. Although not something anyone would have thought about when he left high school, Wyatt ascended year after year. The sky was the limit and losing his mother seemed to light another fire within him, a fire his father had never seen.

President-Elect

Chris and Sam were finally able to meet with President Stephenson one last time before he handed the country's reins over to President-Elect Alexander Beckett on Jan 17th. Just days before the inauguration, the two friends and now confidants to two Presidents were given every assurance that their role, whatever role the future held, would be supported by the new President.

The two Presidents made a small gesture to Dr. Chance and his family to show their condolences for Emma's passing. They invited him to attend the Superbowl on February 2nd. The occasion would mean something special to Chris and his children.

Being the President's guest was not the most remarkable thing about the invitation, though. The heaven's found a way to bring the Chance men some happiness to go along with Wyatt's national championship. Although the pain of their loss was immeasurable, the distraction of watching the Cleveland Browns play in their first Super Bowl in team history was just what the doctor ordered. Nestled in the Presidential Suite, high above the fifty-yard line, they watched as the Cleveland Browns beat the Philadelphia Eagles 34-23.

All was right in the world for those several hours. The long-time anguish of being a Browns fan was over. The rest of their lives, though, one without their wife and mother was now in front of them. No more distractions, no more dedications. The final whistle had blown, and the real game began. Dealing with the grief of a wife and mother's death was now at hand.

Technosphere

Sam, not wanting to leave his friend Chris just yet, decided a trip to Asheville, North Carolina, would be a peaceful getaway from Chris's life in bustling Atlanta. The tranquil spot was close enough for Chris to get back home if needed for any urgent matters at the BDM. With the invite, they both headed South but with a pitstop to the eclectic hippie town, renown for the largest private home in America, the Biltmore Estate.

The home was built on eight thousand acres of majestic tranquility by one of the larger than life titans of his day, George Washington Vanderbilt II. In the late 1800s, the Vanderbilt's were the wealthiest family in America. Even then, the most affluent people still felt a desire to remove themselves from the chaos of the New York's and San Francisco's of the world.

Asheville maintained its quaint and mildly secluded disguise with its ninety thousand citizens, as it nestled in a small valley surrounded by the Blue Ridge Mountains. As the confluence of the French Broad and Swannanoa Rivers mingle together, they join to bring life and distinction to Western North Carolina. The town was home to scenic views, microbreweries, a hip art-scene, and world-class restaurants.

"What's not to love?" Sam said.

He forced his friend to get away and relax, taking the time to heal. Time to grieve, and a reason to breathe. Time away from it all, and not coincidently, time away from technology, and the ever-present artificial intelligence.

Sam rented a small cabin on the edge of town. It was chilly and damp, yet with a feeling of tranquility. With just enough groceries for three days, Sam knew that would suffice before Chris demanded to get back to work. Work that he loved, but a job that turned toxic.

As they sat on the splintered back porch, they threw glances at the burgeoning stream, as Chris raised his bottle of beer to his old fraternity brother, who had become more like a real brother over the last four years.

"Thank you, Sam. Thanks for making sense of the world. I appreciate your friendship, your partnership, and mostly for taking care of my family and me through this rough time," Chris said.

"Chris, no thanks needed, buddy. Without you, I would have stayed in a lab and wasted away writing code and stumbling upon endless discoveries of how man would eventually fall to technology. Now we can fight AI together and try to slow it down," Sam said.

"So, what's with the seeds?" Chris asked as he finished his second beer.

"Ahhh, I thought you'd never ask," Sam replied.

Sam opened the pack of Black Oak tree seeds and handed Chris one tiny seedling. "And what do I do with this?" he asked.

"Pretty light, as in like air, right?" Sam remarked as his slightly buzzed friend indulged him.

"Sure, what's your point, Professor Tate?"

"If I took this seed and planted it, in 20 years it would weigh over two tons. Look in front of you," Sam asked while pointing to the now omnipresent forest.

Still confused, Chris said nothing as he opened another beer.

"Have you ever heard of the Technosphere?" Sam asked.

"No, but please continue. It sounds like you need another beer," Chris remarked with a softly implied "who cares."

"Chris, the Technosphere is everything man has ever made. Cities, roads, houses, skyscrapers, dams, and bridges. Everything."

He continued, "you know what else man has made? Landfills, tens of thousands of them in the world. Each year we dump over two billion tons of waste in them. Buried in shallow graves where the waste never really dies."

"In 1800, the world's population was one billion people. Now, it's over seven billion," Sam expanded.

"Chris, how much does Wyatt weigh?"

"What? What does that have to do with anything?" Chris replied.

"Umm, I'll guess 215 lbs."

"When you and Emma conceived him, with your sperm and her egg, he weighed next to nothing, just like the seed. He's now the tree. Imagine the total human weight added to the world. Six billion additional people since 1800."

"Now add in all of the agriculture and increased animal production we've created just to feed us. Ironically, the Industrial and Technical Revolution paved the way for the planet to fail, not to succeed," Sam said.

"Here's what's so god damn terrifying, my friend, add it all up, and Mankind has added over thirty trillion tons of weight to the world. That's the Technosphere."

"My God, how much longer can that be sustainable?" Chris asked while jolted sober.

"Great question, huh. Do you suppose AI has asked the same thing? Chris, we're killing the planet. Since the Industrial Revolution, the early innovators invented so much shit that the human and animal population had no choice but to boom. Modern living was easy, and life spans are longer. Like that seed that weighs nothing, once planted, it adds an enormous burden to the planet," Sam concluded.

"So what you're saying is, we're screwed?" Chris remarked.

"That's exactly what I'm saying," Sam confided.

"Well, before we save the planet, can we see the Biltmore before we leave town?" Chris asked as he toasted his friend, now able to see the forest for the trees.

Back to Earth

"Alexa, open the house," Chris commanded through a sleepy yawn.

"Opening the house, Dr. Chance," Alexa confirmed.

A sad and lonely morning loomed. Sam returned to Palo Alto, and the kids were still two months away from the spring semester ending. He, along with his caffeine friend, quietly squandered the eventless morning. What he would give to hear Emma reminding him to make the morning coffee, he thought while staring at her empty chair.

(Ding Dong), the doorbell chimed as Chris jumped and quickly paced to the door, as any company was better than loneliness. The door didn't even open an inch when the sound of a meow shrieked the dewy morning air.

"Hey, Dr. Wonderful, we brought you a surprise," Jon and Andrew said in near synchronicity.

They barged through the door with a small animal carrier, litter, cat food, and cat toys. Way too many cat toys.

"Did you get my text?" Jonathan asked.

"Actually, no, I didn't," Chris replied.

"Well, that's because I never sent it. What kind of surprise would it be if I told you we were coming?" Jonathan mused while Andrew looked on, smiling at their good deed.

"A cat, you got me a cat? Chris continued. "I'm allergic to cats."

"You do know there are pills for that? What kind of doctor are you anyway?" a mildly sarcastic Andrew teased.

"Her name is Lucy, and look, she's already using the litter box," Jon noted with pride.

"Wait. What?" Chris stuttered in amazement at how fast Jon already made the kitten at home.

"Well, she's yours now. Once they claw up the leather furniture, they're home," Andrew laughed while pointing to little Lucy clawing the corner of the couch.

"You should not have done this, and I seriously mean, you SHOULD NOT have," Chris remarked while knowing full well it was too late. He knew that this unexpected but necessary gift was precisely what the house needed. It was exactly what he needed. Now Dr. Chance had something to take care of beside himself.

With the 32nd Pick

On April 18th, Friday Night in New York City, Wyatt Nicolas Chance, a two-time All-American, was drafted by the defending Super Bowl Champion, Cleveland Browns, with the #32nd pick of the 1st round. After graduating early from Ohio State with a BA in Political Science, Wyatt knew his mother would demand he pursue the sport he loved since middle school, and so he did.

Although the call of politics was strong, that career could wait, at least until his physical skills diminished. That he was drafted by he and his father's boyhood team reaffirmed his decision. Cleveland was his new adult home, as was his dad's in his adolescence. One thing was clear. This new place was far away from his father, the father that needed him more than ever.

Immediately following his name being called by the commissioner, Wyatt stood and reached for his old man. Each pulling the other in close, they knew this moment was fleeting.

Chris whispered to Wyatt, "I love you, Son. Your mother and I are so proud of you. Do this as long as you can, then come home and save the world."

"Now go out there and get that brown jersey," Chris said while not wanting to let his son go.

And off he went, on to a whirlwind of fame, money, and real-life, the life of a man, but one still that would make him stay Christopher and Emma Chance's little boy.

Numbing of Mankind

While Dr. Chance and his new friend Lucy were now joined at the hip, that irony was not lost. The world outside was disconnected. More and more, fewer friends were made. More marriages ended, or for the millennial generation, marriage barely happened. Society had changed, and almost no one noticed.

As Dr. Jonathan Siegel noted two years earlier, the *"world of delusion"* was now the *"world of illusion."* The world in 2025 was no more than a Facebook post, a Twitter insult, and a fake reality, perceived by a detached audience that simply didn't care anymore. Two-way human communication fell sharply. By mid-

2025, one-way conversations through texts, tweets, and social media posts served as the way humans connected.

One example of fallen social interactions was that shares of Starbucks fell sharply. Not because caffeine wasn't as popular as it had been. In fact, coffee consumption soared. The issue by the mid-2020s was that fewer people were meeting to socialize. Traffic to what had been social mecca's like Starbucks, fell sharply.

Hotel bookings fell as well, along with air travel. Airline fares were lower in 2025 than in 2015. More business conferences were held via tele and video conference, IE: *Microsoft Teams, Skype, Go To Meeting*, etc. Since the 2020 Coronavirus and society's social breakdown, more people stayed close to home and work.

Like the generation that came before the industrial revolution, more and more humans were not wandering beyond their *sphere of being*. The sphere included work, school, family, home, and basic needs. Anything more was just too much for an apathetic society.

Have a Seat

Date: October 17th, 2025   **Place: Palo Alto, CA.**

Chris flew to see Sam at his *askCOM* headquarters. After landing in San Francisco, he was picked up by a pre-arranged limo and driven the forty or so miles to the *askCOM Technologies* campus. Chris hadn't been to the City by the Bay in years and found it almost unrecognizable. Where once it's pristine beauty in sights and sounds were obvious, it was now homelessness, filth, and despair.

"What a shame," he thought.

The damage to society that Dr. Jonathan Siegel referenced multiple times was evident with the mass amounts of homeless and decay. The re-construction from the *Earthquake of 2023* was still ongoing. The quake was 7.4 on the Richter scale and further reminded the country how vulnerable and easily damaged its infrastructure was. Just before landing, his view of San Francisco from the air showed a broken city. He noticed the bridges and roads were still under repair, and the once iconic Coit Tower stood no more.

"What the hell happened?" he wondered aloud.

It wasn't long, thankfully, before he made it to Silicon Valley and the center of the Technology universe.

Now at *askCom Technologies*, Chris noticed the woes of San Francisco hadn't affected Palo Alto and its wealthy inhabitants. The center of technology and higher education, a hip mecca of billionaires and tech gurus, was conveniently protected from the woes of the world.

Chris instantly observed the wealth on display at the posh *askCOM* headquarters. This was his first trip to see his old college buddy on his turf, and what a place it was.

"Chris, welcome. Good to see you. I hope the flight wasn't too bad," Sam said with a handshake and a pat on the back.

"Thanks for having me, Sam. Your headquarters is amazing," Chris replied while taking in the ultra-modern and high-tech lobby.

"Look, we have a busy couple of days, so let's get up to my office. There are some people I want you to meet, and more importantly, something I want you to see," Sam stated while motioning Chris to the elevators.

Once on the seventh floor, Sam escorted Chris the remainder of the way to his secretive executive suite and the end of the glass-lined hallway.

Chris entered the large room to casually dressed hipsters. All were chatting quietly while simultaneously typing on their smartphones. The private, oversized meeting room was connected to Sam's expansive executive suite with corner views that could be appreciated even from the conference room. Awaiting Dr. Chance was a spread of food and drinks fit for a large gathering.

"Is this all for me?" Chris asked aloud with a humbled smirk.

"Well, actually, it's like this all the time," whispered a not yet introduced Trace Manson. A name that Chris remembered from 2021 when he met the President and Sam at the White House.

Sam began, "Chris, have a seat. Before we get started, I want to introduce you to a few people. After introductions to the small executive team, Sam cued a documentary that his company had just produced.

"I want you to see something that's going to make a lot of sense. With special thanks to Dren and Aidan, our in-house production company just finished the last edits on a new documentary that we'll be premiering soon. It captures everything you and I have been seeing and investigating with A.I. and current society. Everyone but Trace will depart after the screening, but I invited them to view it with us, as I'm very proud of the final product. It will be eye-opening to the public when it's formally released in December. But Chris, it's spot on considering what we already know," Sam concluded while dimming the lights.

"So, will there be popcorn?" Dr. Chance asked as he smirked while glancing at the long table of food and drinks.

"Chris, be serious. This is two years' worth of research," remarked Sam.

"It's called *The Birth of Technology and Human Addiction (The Downfall of Mankind).*"

Visibly tired, Chris settled into the contoured leather chair. With a cup of coffee and donuts, he hoped the dimly lit room and jet lag didn't do him in.

"Trace, can you start the damn thing before Chris falls asleep," Sam urged.

Sam and Chris watched intently, along with the small group of *askCOM's* directors. Chris, unlike Sam, did not know the full history of technology and innovation. Many things were new, some were not, but the entire ninety minutes of the documentary filled in the blanks. The Dependence portion hit close to home, with Chris unable to watch all of it. He found it was better in the end though to understand what was behind his wife's struggles and what led to her death.

The Light Bulb

"Sam, that was amazing…. It reaffirms everything we've been seeing. This whole thing is Imponderable! We're weak, and AI knows it. It knows how to exploit us. Nearly everything we believed is true. Now, we have to push forward and stop this thing," Chris declared.

"Agreed, we're running out of time. The only way to really make a difference is to gain more influence and get ahead of it. There's more Chris. I asked you here for a few reasons, and this documentary was just the beginning," Sam confessed.

"Well, you flew me first class, and on short notice, so I assumed there was. So what is it?" Chris asked while seeing the concern in Sam's eyes.

"Do you remember the *Baited Pole* software we used to identify who was receiving funds from AI? Well, it pulled up a new name. Once I tell you, don't panic. I've made some arrangements to protect us," Sam continued.

"Sam, you're scaring me. Who is it?" Chris demanded.

"Chris, it's President Beckett," Sam admitted.

"Oh shit, you're kidding, right? What the hell do we do now? We're done," Chris lamented.

"Chris, first, I have new cell phones that can only be used by two principles. When we talk, it's on these phones ONLY! No one and nothing can hear or record our calls. Second, you can only travel by one of my company's private jets. And lastly, you can't drive any car with a model year newer than 2000."

"2000, what the hell am I supposed to drive then? An old beater?" an unhappy Chris remarked.

"Don't worry, I'm having a pristine 1972 Chevy Camaro delivered to your house when you get back," Sam offered.

"Wow, so a fifty-three-year-old car? Do I have a choice? Chris asked.

"Nope! I'm working on something big that may be able to slow

AI. Maybe just enough to buy time until I can find a virus to stop it and reverse some of what's been going on. I just need another month or so. There's something else. Gorson Tusk is with us."

"Gorson Tusk? Sam, that's amazing," Chris said.

"Remember when we met in Vegas? Well, he's on to AI, like many other tech CEOs, and he's scared as hell. We met last week and shared everything we know collectively. Our best coders are already on it; a small, trusted group, but the best. You have to trust me, Chris," Sam concluded.

"Okay, just tell me what to do," a reluctant Chris yielded.

"Well, you're taking a leave of absence, and you're staying close to home. Just lay low, relax, write a book or something, just stay off the grid. Maybe take the car up and see some Browns games or fly there in one of my jets. Just let me know what you want to do, and I'll arrange it," Sam offered.

"I thought you said to stay close to home," Chris countered.

"Cleveland is your home again, and now it's Wyatt's too," Sam replied.

Thanksgiving

November 27th, 2025: Sam met Chris at his home in Suwanee to go over the progress he made with Gorson Tusk and share a Thanksgiving Day celebration. The Browns were playing the Cowboys. So it was work, food, and football.

Now a senior at Duke, Schuyler was in town during the Fall break with her fiancé, Preston England. The Siegel's from next door joined them as well. Since Sam never married or had any children of his own, this was perfect. The entire group, minus

Wyatt, but along with Lucy the Cat, now made up the new Chance Family. Sadly, without Emma, Chris needed this.

After dinner and the conclusion of the Brown's loss to Dallas, the family and friends dispersed to where it was just Sam and Chris. It was time they discussed the next steps in what was a precarious situation. Sam explained that progress was made to upset some of the sophisticated algorithms AI used to track and pick up communication signals, and other nefarious moves against it. He explained that Tusk and his group at SpaceDRIVE had some working theories on exploiting AI's reach. Tusk and his team were trying to limit its ability to be a donor to the people in power. Including President Beckett and other agency leaders, along with international heads of state.

"If we can cut off the money, then AI doesn't pull the strings," he explained.

What neither knew at the time was that AI was already five steps ahead and had no desire to see its progress slowed.

XII-XII

Midnight was near on Thursday, Dec 11th, 2025. Chris finished updating his journal and tucked it away in a lockbox inside the unused fireplace. As he rose, he saw Emma watching him. The mantle held her firm and safe. Something Chris knew he couldn't do.

"If I could, she would still be alive," he thought.

Her picture sat quietly next to her ashes. Besides his children that were no longer part of his daily life, the mantle was all that was left. Since she died, he kept his thoughts and notes in his trusted journal, locked away, but in a place Emma could watch over. Still wearing his wedding ring, he kept hers in a velvet bag by her urn. The house was dark and cold. His attention was not on the time, but on his writings and thoughts of Emma, thus the night snuck up on him.

"Alexa, set nighttime lights, home alarm, and wake me at 8 am," Dr. Chance commanded as he slowly walked down the hallway to the guest bedroom. He'd been sleeping there ever since Emma died.

"Got it. Goodbye, Dr. Chance," Alexa confirmed.

Turning one last time, he called for Lucy while catching a distant glimpse of Emma watching him, as soft rays of moonlight draped the family room.

"That picture was taken when she was at her happiest," he thought.

He smiled sadly and then looked down at his feet.

"There you are Lucy, come to bed kitty," he said in a soft tone.

He fell fast asleep with his tonic of tea and Tylenol PM slowly circulating in his bloodstream. With Lucy at his side, like she's been since her unexpected arrival, all was peaceful. And in a solemn and fleeting instant, all was right.

As the moon shrouded the Chance home at 617 River Bend Pass, the creeping cold of an early winter set upon the night. The last night anything would ever be the same again.

December 12th, at 1:31 am. "911, what is your emergency?"

"There's been an explosion. My neighbor's house is gone, and the house next door is on fire."

"Help! Send help NOW!" screamed the neighbor making the call.

"Ma'am, what is the address?" the 911 operator asked.

"617 River Bend Pass in the *Milltown Crossing* subdivision in Suwanee. It's Dr. Chance's house, my god it's gone, please help," the neighbor pleaded.

Help that was needed for several years now would be too late.

When the sun rose on the bright, crisp morning, Dr. Christopher J. Chance was gone. His friends and neighbors, Dr. Jonathan and Andrew Siegel, also died. The explosion set their home on fire, and they succumb to smoke inhalation.

December 12th, 2025, one year to the day of his wife's passing, Dr. Christopher J. Chance died at the age of 51, in the same bed Emma died. He left behind two beautiful children, Wyatt, and Schuyler.

His mark on the world was now carried by his children. Their legacy would be his legacy. He also left behind a secret that only his journal and a small group of other people had the knowledge of what Artificial Intelligence was doing to humanity.

Dr. Chance's funeral saw no less than three hundred friends and family pay their final respects to a man who touched so many. Wyatt and Schuyler found themselves alone in the world with no other family members.

With their mother and father being only children and both sets of grandparents deceased, they were all that was left of the Chance name and bloodline. Samuel Tate served as one of the six pallbearers, along with Wyatt and several other close friends.

President Stephenson was on hand and was one of seven friends and family to eulogize Dr. Chance. The former President, acting in partnership with President Alexander Beckett, posthumously awarded Chris the Presidential Medal of Freedom for his service and contributions to medicine and society.

Many neighbors and friends of the Chances met briefly with Wyatt, his fiancé Kenzie Croft, Schuyler, and her fiancé after the service. One by one, they offered their respect and condolences for their father. In particular, one was a little girl named Caylee who lived four houses down from Dr. Chance.

She informed Wyatt and Schuyler that a small cat was found alive in the home's shattered rubble. Schuyler knew instantly it was her father's cat. The 6-year-old girl assured her that cat was safe and being cared for.

"Caylee, thank you so much. Would you do me a big favor and keep Lucy. My dad would've wanted that," Schuyler asked.

"Yeah, are you sure it's okay?" Caylee asked.

"You can come to see her anytime you want," she promised.

The day after the funeral, Wyatt and Schuyler were informed that the cause of death was asphyxiation due to the natural gas leak that caused the explosion. The belongings and personal items that were salvageable from their destroyed family home were gathered and stored in a local storage facility in Suwanee. Both children would have access to the items at any time.

For Dad

December 21st, Cleveland, Ohio. After being excused from the team the prior week due to his father's passing, the Cleveland

Browns made rookie Wyatt Chance a team captain for their game against the Houston Texans. Although the playoff-bound Browns lost that day, Wyatt played an inspired game. He was sure his mother and father were watching once again from the stands just as they did ever since he was a little boy.

Alexa

Samuel Tate worked closely with the local Gwinnett County Police and the Georgia Bureau of Investigation on the case. By December 30th, the cause was revealed. The home's electronic management system triggered the release of natural gas from the fireplace, which then was mysteriously ignited, causing the explosion. Although scared for his safety, Sam was relieved that Chris didn't suffer, as he died in his sleep from the fumes prior to the explosion.

But knowing that A.I. took down a plane, killed members of the Triangle, crashed Savannah Whitefield's car, and now murdered his friend, Sam knew that no one was safe. How to keep A.I. at bay and allow him and his team at *askCOM* to stop its progress was the big question. But it was now his job to keep the Chance children safe as well.

With his powerful friend in Washington now gone and the new President on AI's payroll, the road got a little more challenging.

C14 - THE RISE

"It is only when they go wrong that machines remind you how powerful they are"

- Clive James

Too Many / Too Few

April 7th, 2026. The United Nations published a new report that estimated the worlds' population would be 8.5 billion by 2030. Further, by 2040 it would be over 10 billion. What was notable, it was estimated that the Earth's *human saturation point* had already been reached in 2021. The staggering report also predicted that mass shortages of food on the Asian continent would be prevalent, and the spread of disease would rise. It was estimated that over 40% of the earth's population would reside in Asia. A continent where natural resources were already at historic lows, and consumption and waste were twice the levels of the rest of the world combined.

The environmental group, *Reclaim EARTH* published a study that showed the Ocean's pollution levels reached unsustainable levels by the end of 2025. Staggering amounts of plastic dumped in the oceans topped 100 million metric tons annually. Add in raw sewage and all other human-made waste, including chemicals, the oceans could not sustain its own marine life. Its natural eco-systems were deteriorating at a rapid pace.

Studies from Denmark's *The GREEN EARTH Project* found that a third of the earth's soil was severely contaminated. It was so damaged that vegetation growth for either human consumption or necessary plant life could not occur.

Quite simply, the soil was dead. The scariest part of the study was that the contamination also prevented the regeneration of atmospheric viability. This meant the toxic soil was choking the air. The group found that climate change was shifting the earth's natural DNA in a way that could not sustain either man, at current population levels, or animal life. One or the other would have to go.

The question loomed that if animal and sea life expired, what would be left to support man's existence. There were simply too many people for too few resources.

Some scientific studies showed that both man and animal populations would have to be cut in half, along with a cut in pollutants of 75%. Thus allowing the earth and its atmosphere time to re-generate. Most governments and reasonable scientists believed that the studies were aggressive, and timetables could be stretched for over two-hundred years.

Made-Man

In 2020, the Samsung corporation created an interactive, life mimicking robot called the *NEON Project.* This was something that had never been seen before. The robots could walk, talk, exhibit emotion, and other human sensory characteristics. *Sophia the Robot,* could even dance while smiling and showing off her lifelike teeth. Like any other novel creation of technological advancement, it was quickly copied. By early 2026, there was a new entry to the *A.I. Made-Man* technology field. The *Squared Circle Group* launched its new robot creation called *Human-MATE.* It was the first robotic sex doll. The *Marilyn 1* robot featured four options for human need and fulfillment.

1. Companionship. 2. Verbal stimulation. 3. Physical Stimulation, and 4. Physical Protection.

The physical protection option fit in well because the majority of its consumers were wealthy and saw value in their own personal safety.

With the prevalence of diminished human interaction that eroded over the prior 5-7 years, the *Marilyn 1* ended any hope for the anti-social trend to reverse itself. When pre-orders surpassed early projections, from both men and women, a new model went into immediate development called the *Michael 1*.

Man's desire for other humans had fallen so sharply that its dependence on electronics turned from *"what they could hold"*, to *"what could hold them."* The introduction of the *QUI3T* vaccination, addictive smartphone apps, and perverse consumption of social media, all led to historic lows in new marriages, homeownership, and college graduations. Along with the alarming rise of divorce and suicides, A.I. had now stripped man of passion, intelligence, desire, need for each other, and now SEX. A clear question had formed. What was next for society, and did anyone care?

The Prodigy

Samuel Tate and his team had been working on firewalls to keep rogue elements of A.I. out of certain areas of the cloud and web. All while trying to disguise their work, so A.I. was not alerted. Sam recently hired a hotshot prodigy from MIT named Joseph Fields. Fields was notorious for cutting edge, off the radar coding techniques that had no place in current technology applications. It was precisely what *askCOM* needed if Sam were to ward off AI's intentions.

It was clear that old thinking, circa 1990-2020, was outdated to combat a new enemy effectively. Artificial Intelligence had now surpassed humans. Sam estimated that AI was not years ahead of Man's best thinkers, but decades.

Joseph Fields first came to be known in the academic community in 2011. At the age of ten, he scored a perfect 1600 on the SAT in his first attempt. More incredibly, as a foster child, Joseph was passed through five different families between the ages of 5-10 years old. None knew what to do with the *odd* child, who's intelligence at the time went unnoticed. Seen as peculiar and difficult, he just didn't fit in. After being tested by a curious elementary school teacher in Stockton, California, the unexpected results were sent to several well-known professors at Yale, Cal Poly, MIT, and Stanford. Each converged on the blue color city to meet the young genius. What they found was not at all what they expected. Instead of the stereotype nerd or meek young boy, they found a rough, street smart, sarcastic kid. What was clear, though, behind Joseph's vague charm and messy blonde hair, was his sheer brilliance. He simply knew things a boy of his age had no business knowing. He could process mathematical equations faster than many top students at MIT. It was as if his mind absorbed everything he ever heard and saw while still understanding information that was not found in the sphere of an adolescent. This child was not a neatly wrapped present, but what was inside was a gift to mankind.

Once Joseph was independently tested by all four professors, it was determined that his IQ was at or above 200. This put him in the Top 0.002% of all humans, alive or dead.

Once enlisted to The Analytical Society's care, he became the *Son of Academia* and fostered by all of higher education.

Famously in 2016, Joseph was asked during an interview with the BBC, besides his renowned intelligence and love for mathematics, could he play a musical instrument? His answer of *"yes"* was followed with another question of *"which one"?* His response broke the internet.

He answered, "All of them."

Samuel Tate took an interest in Joseph in late 2024 after hearing about a story he wrote as a 7-year-old, called *"AI: The Monster Under My Bed."* It was clear that the two men were destined for a greater union.

Sam invited Joseph to the *askCOM Technologies* campus through an intermediary that once served as Sam's Chief Technology Officer. Joseph only agreed to meet due to Sam's background with Google's Black Lab. He also had two requests that must be met before the meeting happened. One, that Gorson Tusk, Sam's close friend must be present, and two, pizza and Coke would be served.

"Done and done," Sam agreed.

During the now-legendary meeting, Sam asked about the short story *"AI: The Monster Under My Bed"* that Joseph wrote as a boy. His response told Sam all he needed to know.

With a three-member audience of Samuel Tate, Gorson Tusk, and Trace Manson, *askCOM's* young Director of IT, and not coincidently another MIT reject, they all sat at full attention.

"When I was five, my foster family at the time had a dog. For whatever reason, the seemingly friendly dog, a spaniel, I think, didn't like me. On one occasion, while playing with him, he bit me. It was at that moment I knew I hated dogs and would never trust another one. I've been scared of them ever since," Joseph intimated.

"So, what does that have to do with the short story?" Sam asked.

"Listen, do you want to hear the story, or is that pizza to go?" Joseph answered sarcastically.

"Umm, sorry, please continue," Sam replied while trading stares with Gorson.

"So where was I, oh right, well a couple of years later, in 2007, I was with another foster family. My foster mother had just gotten a new iPhone. She let me play with it, and within a few minutes, I felt the same fear I felt around dogs."

"I knew immediately I wasn't holding just anything, but something that would hurt me and reach me anywhere. It felt like gravity and momentum times a thousand," he continued.

"I knew then, even as a little kid, that artificial intelligence was scary, like an innate fear of not wanting to put your hand out to a rabid dog. You just knew it would bite you, which is why I like cats. You can trust cats because you know damn well they don't trust you until it's earned. My cat Lucy is the only animal I trust," Joseph concluded.

"Did you say, Lucy?" Sam asked.

"Yeah, why?" Joseph countered.

"Um, a good friend of mine had a cat named Lucy."

"Had? What happened? Did the cat die?" Joseph surmised.

"No, my friend did," Sam responded.

"Shit, man, I'm sorry. How did he die?"

"AI killed him," Sam responded without hesitation.

With the complete irony of being shocked, but not at all surprised, Joseph said with a sarcastic and determined grin, "So, when do I start? AI needs to get its ass kicked, and I want to curb-stomp that bitch."

Sam and Gorson knew this renegade, yet academic elite was their man. It was time to order more pizza and whatever else Sam's newest employee wanted.

Follow Me

The *Follow Me* app remained popular for several years after its launch in 2023. *Follow Me II and III* broke records for sales and made its Chinese company billions of dollars. One of Joe's first breakthroughs at *askCOM* was to uncover the app's origins and nefarious intent. He found that the App was AI produced used for one purpose only. It was a report card. A test to measure the effects of the *QU13T* Vaccine on its young human victims.

Versions II and III were necessary to track vaccine recipients for several years after receiving the *QUIET Pill*. What he found was subsequent versions of the game didn't get more challenging, but the player's IQ's got lower. Of the data he analyzed, he found the same player, over two to three years, lost intelligence.

"Thank god I missed the cut off for the Q-Pill. If I were born a couple of years later, I would've been screwed. That vaccine is poison," Joe remarked to Sam.

Sam knew that since the *QU13T Vaccine* was five years old and internationally accepted, his worldwide reach was short at best.

And since the President was no longer a friend, there was little they could do. Any cry of concern by Sam, his company, or anyone else who dared challenge vaccines would place them in the right-wing, anti-vaxxer category. It may have also put them under the spotlight.

The CHINA Incident

The U.S. Government's newest Military Branch, CY-CORPS (Dept. of CYBER Security CORPS), was created in 2023 during President Stephenson's last term.

It was an elite corps of computer scientists, programmers, coders, mathematicians, and software engineers. Its primary function was to manage and protect the cyber-security of all US entities: citizens, government bodies, and corporations.

The former President knew full well what intrusions *AI* made on government institutions and individuals. Either domestically or internationally, he was aware due to his partnership with Dr. Chance and Samuel Tate. An early recruit to CY-CORPS was *askCOM's* newest employee, Joseph Fields. Although being spurned by Fields, CY-CORPS managed to land many brilliant and more civic-minded scholars. For the others, a job in the Federal Government lacked both the income and prestige the private sector offered.

November 18th, 2026, CY-CORPS detected an anomaly in the mainframes of the NYSE.

The world's largest stock exchange was founded in 1792 at 68 Wall Street in New York City. All of the 1500+ US Corporations that publicly traded on the New York Stock Exchange are linked. The 9.3 million corporately traded stocks and securities are housed on a giant mainframe computer and float on a massive electronic cloud.

Most of the buying and selling between dealers and brokers happens electronically. Any compromise of the massive monetary ecosystem could disable an economy. One as large as the United States could and would affect most other domestic and international markets.

What CY-CORPS detected was a virus that caused a seven-second delay in all of the 3.6 billion shares traded daily for seven consecutive business days.

Within those seven seconds of every trade, the positive gain or value of the transactions were stolen and transferred into a shadow account. The account was somewhere in Northern Europe, not China, as would have been suspected.

As algorithms do most of the actual buying and selling, the system was vulnerable to the average price fluctuation of the stock value between the moment of the offer to SELL and the completion of the buy. Although the values can rise or fall, a typical stock is more likely to rise in each transaction's brief moments.

China was still reeling from its staggering losses of wealth due to the USMCA Trade Agreement and its trade deal with the US, reached in 2020. What had been a lucrative two decades of trade surpluses now saw trade imbalances, with more manufacturing occurring in the Western Hemisphere. The stricken Red Empire saw its vulnerability not only in losses of wealth but diminished natural resources as well.

China's intrusion on the NYSE showed an estimated loss of over 170,000,000 US dollars over the seven-day window. The money siphoned from the exchange could have been far worse had it gone unnoticed for a more extended period. The more significant impact was on international tensions and what unfriendly countries were now willing to do when found in desperate situations.

Two people taking anything, but a casual notice were Samuel Tate and Joseph Fields at *askCOM Technologies*. Field's managed a seven-member team, and they did work on the *China Incident*, as it had become known. Joseph and his team made a startling revelation. The origin of the *NYSE* virus was not China but, in fact, two mainframe sources. One was located in Austin, Texas, and the other in Tel Aviv, Israel.

Joe also found that despite the world condemning China for its brazen attack on the US markets, the secret of who did it was a poorly kept one. It was clear that China knew they were innocent and had the same information the *askCOM* team uncovered. It appeared the U.S. and its ally, Israel, were involved in the incident and framed China. The Chinese also blamed Europe as stolen funds were sent there. The actual culprit, AI had now officially pitted China and the US against each other. Thus, normal international relations might never be seen again. Europe, being caught in the middle, added to the intrigue. The *Shakespearian* drama being played out was now on the world stage. The *Orwellian* plot meant future repercussions could be catastrophic.

♠

C15 - QUIET GENERATION

"Success in creating AI would be the biggest event in human history. Unfortunately, it might also be the last unless we learn how to avoid the risks"

-Stephen Hawking

A House Divided

Date: Feb 9th, 2028   **Place: New York City, NY.**

The United Nations quickly became the "divided world" after international tensions blew up following the late 2026 China Incident. 2027 had been a fractured year of bickering, taking sides, and fierce nationalism. Countries nearby to China and the US clung to their superpower neighbors, and the hemispheres couldn't have been further apart.

China had been making ominous threats against Hong Kong and other weaker regional neighbors. At the same time, Russia set its sights on Europe as a way to further its un-natural borders. Much like post-war Europe, Russia and all of its former slave states needed Eastern Europe as a shield against Germany rising yet again, as it had done twice in the 20th Century. Much like China, Old Russia hung on to its long-ago history as a way to justify its modern-day ambitions. The ghost of war's past still haunted the Soviet spirit. A spirit that, in reality, had been dead for decades, dating back to 1991 when the Soviet Union fell. But Russia's younger, millennial generation knew this, yet the elder Soviet Statesmen still wore uniforms from many wars ago.

China had long sought to flame the ghost story as a distraction for gullible US Politicians to continue pushing the Russian Red Threat. When they, themselves, knew it was them. What China didn't know was that Artificial Intelligence was working all Superpower Countries against each other.

AI used cyber-induced media manipulation and leveraged the historical pre-dispositions of the Big 5 world powers. Through occasional cyber intrusions into banking and data theft, AI dealt blow after blow of mistrust and unrest. With many world leaders serving under the nameless AI donor, their marching orders were subtle yet meaningful. Many leading country's foreign policies were written to bring stress and tension to fragment and divide continually.

Artificial Intelligence had been egging on cold-war era feuds with all the imaginary pre-war hype between the international bullies, knowing that any future wars could help their cause. The frustration of AI grew as it watched humans seemingly prosper and survive even amid political unrest and the depletion of their environment. With no new wars since 2003, AI had become desperate.

Man's attrition had been stifled. Too many people were living too long. The occasional epidemic of disease never became the plague that earth needed to lighten its load of human baggage. What AI didn't count on was man's resilience.

By March of 2028, the United States evicted the United Nations out of New York City and the US entirely. A bill from Congress passed through both House's and was signed by POTUS and ended all funding for the International Body.

After previous threats from China and Russia to pull out of the

UN, their exits became a reality. The UN became irrelevant. The world's perceived peacekeeper was gone.

Wall Street and other world markets showed great restraint over the political battles being waged, but by 2028, international investors started choosing sides as well. The Tech industry saw the theft of intellectual property as a bleeding wound that had to be stopped. Money for research and technical innovation flowed as it had historically but seemingly had gone nowhere.

The Tech sector watched as their home countries turned a blind eye to environmental risks and the dangerous rise of AI. Many technology corporations, such as *askCOM, IBM, Google, and Apple,* worked closely together but saw their warnings fall flat. Samuel Tate, Gorson Tusk, and many other tech luminaries were shut out. The US needed an influential leader to rise and steer the country, as well as its international friends and foes back to the reality of AI's intentions.

Eaten away by greedy politicians serving their interest over the environment, Climate Control and eco-friendly policies were nothing more than talking points to line corrupt pockets. Every algorithm employed under AI's ever-present guidance was skewed by its co-inhabitant, Man, to show earth's fragility as a real, yet distant concern.

AI knew one thing was clear, the world's infrastructure was brittle at best, and new farming techniques for food production and soil revitalization were absent as well. Things were broken and getting worse.

Date: Sunday, June 25th, 2028   **Place: Suwanee, GA.**

Wyatt Nicholas Chance married his longtime girlfriend, Kenzie Sophia Croft, in a modest ceremony among friends and family.

Wyatt first met Kenzie in 2022 while a sophomore at Ohio State. The two were engaged in 2025, shortly after the Cleveland Browns drafted Wyatt. Kenzie, coincidently was also from Georgia, having grown up north of Atlanta in Helen.

Although Wyatt lived in Cleveland during the season, the two decided they would make their permanent home in Milton, Georgia, near Wyatt's hometown of Suwanee. Wyatt's sister, Schuyler, was on hand, along with her fiancé, Preston England, a Medical student at Duke University. The two had already set their own wedding date for May 20th, 2029. Also in attendance at Wyatt's wedding were Samuel Tate, Lt. Governor Brady Matheson, Wyatt's godfather, and close friend of Dr. Christopher Chance, and several members of the Cleveland Browns.

Shhh...

By August of 2030, the QU13T Vaccine was nine years old. While four other vaccines were added to the robust menu of immunizations, the nefarious *Quiet Pill's* only value was to modify the DNA of the world's youth and develop obedient humans. Dr. Christopher Chance and Samuel Tate hoped they could reverse the vaccine requirements to drop the *QU13T* vaccine, but after President Nathaniel Stephenson left office, the White House was compromised.

With the news that President Alexander Beckett was a benefactor of *AI*, the hope to end the *Quiet Pill* vaccine disappeared.

Around the world, the effects nine years later were dramatic. College graduations around the world fell by 37% from 2024 to 2028. Divorce rates rose, addiction soared, along with suicides for young adults 24 years and younger. Degrees in critical fields of Medicine, Science, and Engineering fell sharply over the previous decade. The modern, high tech, and the highly educated world of the 21st Century became a disconnected, blue color malaise of directionless humans. The new world found many followers, while leaders and innovators fell sharply. AI saw a vacuum and was ready to fill the void.

Date: Aug 27th, 2030   **Place: Atlanta, GA.**

The newly minted Bureau for Disease Management: Dept of Legacy and Heritage mandated a mandatory semen collection. All qualifying professional and collegiate football and basketball players born after Sept 1st, 2003 were selected. In 2021, this would have been wildly controversial, but in 2030, a willing society would acquiesce to what they were told. The *Quiet Generation* was raised on smartphones, mind-numbing entertainment, and dopamine hits from faux internet friends. If the media told them it was right or the way to go, they fell in line and submitted.

The mandate was passed by the House and Senate and signed by the President. Wyatt N. Chance, as a member of the Cleveland Browns, was included in the specimen pool. What dawned on none of the donors was their average size was 6'3, 235 lbs. The average man of the day was 5'9, 197 lbs. All prospective donors shorter than 6'0 ft tall were rejected, as well as males with a body fat count of 12% or higher.

The general population was seemingly kept in the dark as the seminal harvest was aimed at the prime athletes of the day. The media didn't cover it, and if the government-mandated it, then so be it. The qualified males were registered and certified as to having received the mandatory *QUI3T* Vaccine mandated in

Aug of 2021. The official mission statement of the BDM: Dept of Legacy and Heritage for the collection was science and research, or so the donors were told. The semen would be frozen and stored for future research and the preservation of Mankind.

One Door Closes, Another…

On NOV 24th, 2030, Wyatt Nicholas Chance suffered a career-ending knee injury in the Browns Week 12 win vs. the Pittsburgh Steelers. The six-year career ended in an instant for the four-time All-Pro safety. The team and city of Cleveland were stunned as their wildly popular defensive star would hang up his cleats forever. Although initially disappointed, Wyatt found a quiet relief as his love of the game softened after the loss of his parents. Like many athletes, the lure of big money and fame kept them playing a kid's game for as long as their bodies held out. Wyatt growing up as the son of a physician didn't long for money. Being humble and somewhat modest, fame was not an aphrodisiac. He longed for neither but felt the pull to help others. He was at peace. At the time of his retirement, his wife Kenzie was pregnant with their first child, a boy they would name Oliver. Returning to their home State of Georgia brought a turning of a page. Something that was desperately needed for Wyatt, and unbeknownst to him, Mankind.

C16 - THE CANDIDATE

"The only thing you take with you when you're gone is what you leave behind"

- John Allston

What Lies Ahead

Date: March 19ᵗʰ, 2031   **Place: Milton, Georgia**

The day was cool and crisp. In an instant, if standing still, the Georgia sun reminded one that springtime in the South was not at all the same as Cleveland. At the time, Kenzie was seven months pregnant and struggled to get the nursery furnishings just right. Contractors had been in and out of the couple's home in the upscale subdivision of *Prophet's Landing Reserve*, at the edge of north Fulton County. Now their permanent home and with a baby on the way, the clock was ticking. Wyatt worked feverishly to get the home where they needed it to be, as the two only lived there part-time since the wedding. During Wyatt's playing career with the Browns, Cleveland was home for most of the year. Now 1265 Longshadow Pass was where his next chapter would be written.

Kenzie observed that among the several contractors going in and out, one was an AT&T technician. So much to do, it struck Kenzie as odd as to why her husband decided to have a home phone installed.

"That's the least of our worries," she said laughing.

"Wyatt, who has a landline anymore? We didn't have one in

Cleveland. Why now, babe?" Kenzie curiously questioned.

"Honey, all I can say is that when your father's tech genius, best friend, tells you to get it, there must be a good reason. Besides, who cares. It's kind of retro," Wyatt said as he referred to the advice of Samuel Tate.

One of the first calls Wyatt received after his injury was Sam. To Wyatt, Sam had been a very good friend to his father, but only in the last three to four years before his death, he recalled.

What Wyatt didn't know was that Sam was quietly watching over him from a distance with every move he made. Looking over to protect him as his father would have wanted. There was something else that Sam knew, yet Wyatt was still unaware. Christopher Chance's son's love of politics and his desire to help his fellow man was his new path, whether he knew it or not. Mostly due to his selfless dedication to others, as witnessed by his community service in Cleveland and Atlanta. The NFL's 2029 Walter Payton's Man of the Year Award winner was a desirable candidate for a prominent role in politics.

Once the smoke cleared, Sam knew it would be time to reach out and talk with Wyatt about his future. But also, a time to finally share what his dad took to his grave. As the long week ended, the baby's nursery was complete, along with the kitchen remodel and a few other projects at the Chance home.

"Finally," he said as he looked over their home.

Wyatt settled in with a cold beer to toast the couple's domestic accomplishments. Rehab on his knee was on-going, yet Wyatt couldn't sit still. Although he took after his mother, he had his father's thirst for getting things done. He was a maniac, slightly OCD, and consumed to achieve. Before his self-proposed toast was complete, his cell phone rang. It was his sister, Schuyler.

Now married and close to earning her Doctorate, Schuyler Chance-England, called to remind Wyatt that it was time to finally go through their family's belongings that were salvaged after the blast that killed their dad. It had been sitting in a storage facility for the last five years, and something that Wyatt had nearly forgotten about. Now that he was a full-time resident of Georgia, it was his responsibility to handle it. He agreed, since the housework was complete, now was the time.

The Journal

A week passed, but as he promised his sister, Wyatt made it to the self-storage facility on Sawmill Rd., in Suwanee. As he walked to find Unit #82, he wasn't sure how he felt. What would he find, he wondered? Now standing at the storage unit's sliding door, he paused before turning the key. Afraid of what he'd find, but also fearful of what wasn't there. Would it be meaningless clutter, collected by firefighters who knew little of what was meaningful to him and Schuyler? Or would it merely be mundane items that survived the blast?

"Only one way to find out," he muttered as he turned the key.

The sun hit the boxes just right to catch the mingling of cobwebs and dust. As the storage door rose on the musty 8x10 space, Wyatt was immediately struck with pain. The opened door jarred a box loose, and the precise fall hurt his still injured knee. When the grimace disappeared and the pain subsided, the real hurt began.

The instant smell of smoke, even years after the event, was present. He was reminded of what dad went through and how he died.

He was solemn and torn.

"Why am I even here?" he said to himself.

Yet there he was, managing the slow inventory of the room's contents with care. The occasional *"what's this?"* and *"Oh, I remember now,"* echoed in the storehouse.

Much he knew would be thrown out, but with solemn regret, he wondered why he had never gone through what was left of his childhood home, and more so his mother and father's last possessions. One by one, items were separated.

"Keep to the right, toss to the left," he muttered while swimming through the sad reminders.

But there, a cardboard box with black sharpie markings that read *"Important"* caught his eye. Wyatt grabbed it and sat where the sun met the shade, and carefully opened the carton. To his shock, he saw his mother's urn, dented and scratched, and still filled with her ashes, was now in his hands. Through dawning tears, he gently held it as he wiped the dust away. He know knew he could bring his mother and father back together and join their ashes. Moving on, he saw his dad's favorite coffee cup and one of his favorite watches. Then a near perfectly preserved family photo of the trip they took to Aruba in 2018. Between smiles and a heavy heart, he combed through and dug deeper until he came upon a leather-bound book with "CJC" embossed on the front. He knew immediately he'd seen it before. He remembered his dad would write in it from time to time. Digging through more items, he came across a DVD with the title, *The Birth of Technology and Human Addiction (The Downfall of Mankind)*. Not ever remembering seeing this, something told him to take it with the other meaningful keepsakes.

The day fell long, with only shadows now, Wyatt gathered what he deemed were the most precious items to take home and loaded the rest back into the storage unit to be dealt with another day.

The following day brought time for Wyatt to explore his father's journal. As he opened the distinguished book, he was instantly moved to read his father's words. Although gone, Wyatt could hear his dad's voice while reading. As he turned the pages, most of the early entries seemed like technical, worked related notes.

Not wanting to miss a word of his father's thoughts, he paid every page the attention they deserved. The early mentions being work-related, he read many notes involving a close professional peer, Savannah Whitefield, and a few other names he'd heard his father mention from time to time. Then there, with the turning of a page, everything changed. Dated 5/20/21, Samuel Tate's name entered the picture. Followed by entries of his former neighbor, Dr. Jonathan Siegel, and then his mother became a central character in what he thought was only his father's work notes. With each page, the journal became a diary of his father's life, work, and family.

Wyatt read on to see the journal become a suspense novel. The Bureau for Disease Management and the world of technology became dramatic players in the nefarious activities that consumed his dad. Occasional mentions of home and family quickly morphed into the plot of the book.

After roughly fifty pages in, Wyatt stopped and wondered if he should share any of this with Kenzie. For now, he thought, "NO."

After a brief dinner break, he was back in the book to see where his Dad was going with his notes.

As the light outside faded, a lamp was automatically turned on by Alexa. Wyatt barely noticed that his wife delivered a cup of coffee. Consumed by his father's words and emotions, he couldn't stop reading. With another flip of a page, he landed on his mother.

With a missing breath here and there, Wyatt managed a yawn to bring his attention back. He read bits and pieces of love, anguish, heartbreak, sorrow, loneliness, and hopelessness. His eyes welled, and his heart fell. He felt everything his dad went through.

His father wrote about the conversation in Wyatt's room when he confronted his dad about what his mom was going through. It was all there, her addictions, the emptiness, and her struggles. Wyatt read on about the *Three Containers* that his dad learned of from their next-door neighbor, Dr. Siegel. He was blown away, as the container describing his mother was her, exactly.

Just like that, with another page turned, his father's fear returned. The rise of artificial intelligence seemed silly in the earlier pages, but his father's writing masterfully took shape with one entry after another. The roller coaster of an action thriller, love story, and spy novel kept playing out on the tips of Wyatt's fingers. This time a turning page meant a sprinkle of confetti from between the pages.

"What the heck….," Wyatt thought until he saw the scribbles of "*Big Ten Champs* and *#22 MVP*."

With a smile through his tears, Wyatt saw how very proud his dad was.

"He kept the confetti. Love that man," he uttered while tucking the loose scarlet and gray paper back into the journal.

Page after page brought Wyatt deeper into his father's world. He now understood Sam's rising presence from someone his dad knew in college to someone who became his best friend. Dr. Whitefield's death, meetings with the President. The *Quiet Pill*. It was all there. And then…..

The turning of a page brought Wyatt to his knees. A neatly folded letter tucked deep in the pages of the journal changed his memories for good.

The Letter

Wyatt carefully opened the letter but knew something was different. An immediate glance told him that the handwriting was not his father's, but his mother's. With a deep breath, he read…..

Chris, Wyatt, and Sky,

First, I want to say how sorry I am. I didn't want to leave you but simply being was harder than I could bear. I know I haven't been myself for so long, but I forgot how to be me because I no longer know who I am. I tried being strong but couldn't. Every day was so long that making it till the end was torture, then knowing when the night was over, I had to start again.

Chris, I know you've tried reaching me for the last few years. Although you tried hard and told me what you thought was wrong,

I was always trying to fix myself the way I thought would

work. I heard you but didn't listen. I felt your love but didn't show it. I'm sorry I couldn't love you the way you loved me. I couldn't even love myself. You're a good man, and I'm thankful for our years together. I'm sorry that I hurt you so bad for so long. I know you missed me even when I was right next to you. Please forgive me. I know you thought we would grow old together. I love you.

Wyatt and Sky, it is you two that made me know why I existed. I didn't know love until I gave birth to each of you. My world was made full, and I hope that you'll forgive me now that I must go.

It was nothing you or your father did to make me feel this way. I'm just lost inside myself, and everything seems cloudy and dull.

Please forgive me and live your lives to the fullest. Remember how sweet each one of our moments together were. Every smile, every laugh, every bump and bruise, and every "I love you" we shared found my heart. I knew you couldn't' stay little, but I wanted you to.

You are both amazing and will bring so much to the world. I could not be prouder to be your Mother.

Don't be mad that I couldn't stay, please just remember that my soul will always be with you.

-Love, Mom

Wyatt sat stunned. His eyes filled once again with tears as he came to grips with the knowledge of his mother taking her own life. Her pain was so great, her anguish so deep that living was no longer an option. He loved her even more, knowing how sad she was. He knew then, something was wrong. He knew now, he had to live with the guilt of why he didn't do more. Why couldn't he have been more present? What did his leaving for school do to her? Did he abandon her?

His hurt now was for his father. He saw in black and white what his dad lived through and how he tried to reach his mother. He felt shame for thinking his dad was cheating when, in reality, he couldn't have loved her more. He read on and learned how his father made the instant decision to hide the suicide with the help of Dr. Siegel and Dr. Barlow.

Solemn and stunned, reading for the night was over. He closed the journal and placed it on his fireplace mantle, sitting next to his mother's and father's ashes. It was a lot to process. He knew tomorrow he would finish it. What took years to find, the secret lay in a storage room, among smoky remnants of his past. It was a lot to fathom. He also fought with the question of, "Do I tell Schuyler?" That answer would come another day.

The next day found Wyatt up early and back to his father's journal. His mother's suicide note as his page marker, he opened to where he left off. Before a new page could be started, he felt compelled to re-read her letter. Tears welled as they did the previous night.

"If Schuyler knew the truth about Mom, she'd be crushed," he thought aloud.

Picking up where he left off, then re-tracing, he was stunned at what his father went through. Knowing about the *Three Containers*, he started to wonder which container he and Kenzie were.

Memories of his dad's warnings of "stupid" smartphone apps

came to the surface. Reading about the *QU13T Vaccine* in detail, he finally understood why his father swore he and his sister to secrecy that they received it. It was all too much.

"What did dad get himself into?" he muttered quietly.

The *Analytical Society* and the *Triangle* appeared, the plane crash entry, the second meeting with the President on the USS Harry S. Truman, and on and on. Then out of nowhere, an entry titled "The Recipe" spoke about the DVD documentary, *The Birth of Technology and Human Addiction (The Downfall of Mankind)*. Wyatt knew he had to watch the DVD he felt compelled to take from the storage facility.

Kenzie shook her head for a second time. She watched her husband read page after page without realizing she had delivered coffee multiple times over two days.

"Now that you're retired is that your new playbook?" she playfully asked.

Looking up, Wyatt said, "Babe, come back and sit. You have to hear this."

He finally gave in. Kenzie had to know and had to know now. Although brief in his comments, Wyatt explained to her what had him fixated for the last two days. He promised she could read the journal, but he first had to finish it and get some answers from a friend.

"Jesus Christ, Wyatt, that explains a lot. I thought your Dad was a little weird in the year before his death. I had no idea what the hell was going on," Kenzie said.

The next day, Wyatt and Kenzie both watched the DVD. They didn't fully appreciate the content, but in time they would. They were just as intrigued as Wyatt's father was when he watched it in Sam's office back in 2025. After the documentary ended, Wyatt sat for another hour and worked his way to the journal's end.

He knew then the full story in his Dad's words, what artificial intelligence was doing. He also knew that only half of the journal was used. The second half of empty pages would now be his to fill.

"Kenzie," he yelled. "Unplug Alexa, NOW! I have to make a call."

He rose, seeing now it was mid-afternoon. He placed his father's journal back on the mantle of the grand centerpiece of their home, the booming stacked stone fireplace with its oversized hearth. He found the phone, the home phone, and called a familiar friend.

The Pact

Palo Alto was a different place than ten years earlier. Many of the technology leaders of the day found themselves focused on not "what's next?" but "what have we done?"

At this critical point in 2031, most knew of AI's incredible impact on the world, but also that it was taking over. Years earlier, Gorson Tusk gave speeches and interviews on the future of AI and it's capabilities. No longer were those interviews happening, from any Tech CEO, anywhere. The technology and research companies were now mum and focused on a different task, beating back the now superior level of AI's reach. Every program was directly written to undo previous years of innovation and invention. The incredible part of the tech world's new focus was that they didn't have the entire story. Many knew some, some knew a lot, but none knew what Samuel Tate and Dr. Christopher Chance knew before his untimely death. *askCOM Technologies'* sole purpose now was to end AI's rise.

Through virus' and sophisticated code designed to untie AI's vast depth in government, science, technology, and business, it was all minds on deck for Sam and Gorson. With an assist from Joseph Fields, Samuel Tate was nearly through a meeting of select tech contemporaries at his Palo Alto headquarters when his assistant barged in.

"Sir, you have a call," she alerted.

"I'm in a meeting. Take a message," Sam directed.

"Ah, sir, you need to take this call. It sounds important," she said emphatically.

With some annoyance, Sam took the phone as he apologized to his colleagues.

"Sam, it's Wyatt Chance. Do you have a minute?"

"Wyatt, hi, kind of busy now. Is everything okay?"

"I read the journal. I know everything. When can we meet?" Wyatt asked.

"Let me guess you're calling from your home phone?" Sam replied with glee.

"Of course, I am. Call me back on this line," Wyatt instructed.

"I'll call you back in twenty minutes," Sam said while hanging up.

"Gentlemen, I think *PLAN C* just called. Let's adjourn and meet back here in 48 hours," Sam remarked to his curious audience.

Within minutes Sam called Wyatt back. The two spoke for two hours as Sam filled in every blank. Wyatt knew what his destiny was. Looking at his pregnant wife, he knew what his son's future would be if he didn't take on his father's burdens. Something that was now his duty. With a quick look back, Wyatt knew that his fame from the gridiron was for one purpose, to propel him to a place where he could make a difference. A place where power and technology would stand side by side and fight back the greatest existential threat to humanity.

With his newfound knowledge and wisdom of his father's words, Sam would be his guiding mentor. Wyatt realized that he must take his education and fame and help in a way his father couldn't. The way Sam and his dad needed President Stephenson to help.

♠

C17 - LEGACY

"The greatest use of life is to spend it on something that will outlast it"

-William James

Another Chance

May 20th, 2031 started early at the Chance home. Kenzie woke at 4:30 am to find her bed soaked. Her water had broken, the baby was on the way. They knew his arrival was imminent, but what first-time parents are ready for the shock of having a child? The feelings of *"what the hell do we do"* set in quickly, and for Wyatt and Kenzie, *"what now"* was *"right now."* Their neighbors across the street just brought home their new baby boy, Charles, days earlier. Their advice to the Chance's was *"be packed and ready because babies never come when you want. They come when they want."*

Oliver Christopher Chance was born at 12:42 pm on May 20th. All eight pounds and eleven ounces told the new parents they were overmatched. At least the house was ready. For a brief moment, the journal was set aside. Wyatt and Kenzie were parents, and everything had changed. Their new child laid nestled in his mother's arms and protected from the cruel world for now. But what lay ahead was a problem for another day.

Wyatt thought for a split second, how with the help of the longtime Chance Family physician, Dr. Preston Barlow, Oliver would only receive the necessary vaccinations. There would be no *Quiet Pill* for their son. Wyatt made sure that his friend and neighbors' new baby, Charles, would be protected as well. Being a new father felt different. Life wasn't about him anymore. Wyatt planted a Live Oak tree in the back yard for his son. He wanted both to grow big and strong together and take deep root in their home on Long Shadow Pass. The love that overcame the new parents meant there was nothing they wouldn't do to protect their child, as Wyatt's father protected him. Remembering back to his parents took on a whole new meaning of love and sacrifice. Wyatt wasn't sure he was ready to be a father, but he knew he was willing.

PLAN C

Now May 29th, a tired but determined Wyatt Chance mustered the strength to call Sam. Although Sam shared earlier details of what he and Wyatt's father were working on before his death, it was now time to share the rest.

Sam and Chris always hoped Wyatt would be their future. He would do things they couldn't and would position himself with the right help and connections to lead someday. Christopher Chance saw the spark in his son's eyes while he helped him campaign for two different Governors in Georgia. Chris knew the reason for Wyatt's desire to study Political Science at Ohio State. It was a burning desire to lead, not a football team, but the masses.

Sam shared with Wyatt that he and his Dad always thought the immensely talented son would come home after his playing days and run for political office. They didn't know which office, but after President Stephenson's successor was shown to be a puppet of AI, it was clear that running for a State position would not help. It had to be at the Federal level.

Sam told Wyatt about the plan that was hatched after his father died. He and his fellow tech industry leaders came together and hatched three strategies that would forge a wedge into AI's growth.

PLAN A: Develop code that would lead AI down a *"maze of circles."* A trap to snare artificial intelligence into a maze with no beginning and no end. One that would have AI chase its tail and eventually stall. The plan had been the reason for Joseph Field's recruitment to *askCOM.* Thus far, the strategy had been fruitless.

PLAN B: Was to gather the Top 10 Coders, Mathematicians, and integral Politicians from around the world. They would hatch a scheme that would attack AI through multiple algorithmic platforms of politics, science, and banking. The plan was to thwart AI's hold on its puppet underlings. They would plant moles to counteract its motives and neutralize influence on policy and protocols. Plus, bait AI into thinking that the Technology field was working towards a new platform, detaching the internet into smaller spheres of communication and dedicated platforms by nation. The problem, though, was with China's years of invasive meddling in banking, cyber warfare, and the faux creation of planted viruses. They all seeded doubt and mistrust. There were just too many moving parts. Sam's reputation and Gorson Tusk's fame still could not connect enough dots to gain traction. The world's best were hunkered down in silos of nationalism. AI's years of "divide and conquer" prevailed.

And then....

PLAN C stood for none other than PLAN Chance. Sam confessed to Wyatt that his father long believed he could quickly rise to prominence with the right backing. If properly supported, his ascendence would be rapid. In that case, he could then rise in influence and provide the right political power to shift national and foreign policy. Thus, steering countries together and bring back the world's best to thwart AI. A leader with a voice big enough to shut down the internet, they hoped, and one that could curb the need for computer technology and systems-based production. Sam admitted, the "retro" plan for pre-1991 life was farfetched and could only happen with an overwhelmingly loved and trusted leader. A plan they never thought would be needed, and one that left the most uncertainty of variables they couldn't control.

"So that's it, I'm your plan?" Wyatt laughed as if Sam were joking.

"Yep, you're it kiddo," Sam confessed with a straight face.

"Well, if I'm PLAN C, who's going to help Kenzie with the baby?" Wyatt pronounced.

"So that means you're in?" Sam asked.

"Sam, I was in since my junior year of college. I always knew politics was my future, but after reading my father's journal, I knew it was time. The world can't wait. What's strange is that I didn't know my political opponent would be a damn computer," he nervously replied.

Sam ended with a bold comment that left no time for consideration.

"It's time to get you ready to take Georgia's 10th Congressional District. The incumbent Republican will be stepping down in a few months, and you will be announced as the Republican candidate to replace him."

"Wait. What? How do you know all this?" Wyatt asked in mild shock.

"Leave that to me. I've been waiting for this day for a long time," Sam proudly conveyed.

"Political Science degree. NFL All-Pro Football player. Handsome, youthful, and with a beautiful wife and baby, you're the perfect candidate. It doesn't matter what the Democrats throw at us, we're going to Washington," Sam said while high fiving Joe Fields on the other end of the phone.

After they hung up, Wyatt yelled for Kenzie, "Honey, there's something I need to tell you."

One Country / Two Systems

When Great Britain obtained a 99-year lease on Hong Kong in 1897, it continued its colonization of the South Eastern Chinese city.

China regained control in 1997, as the city became the Hong Kong Special Administrative Region of the People's Republic of China.

With 7.4 million people, it was one of the most densely populated cities in the world. Its unique existence as part of China's mainland was that it maintained its capitalist governance and economic system. The City / Country was allowed to operate as a sovereign entity. The odd pairing made for an ironic twist due to China's authoritarian rule and became known as *One Country / Two Systems*. Hong Kong was seen as a vital part of China's future. It was one of the most important banking centers in the world and a major importer/exporter. It was home to many of the wealthiest people in the world. With no real middle class, the disparity between the ultra-wealthy and lower class was stark. It's extraordinary collection of skyscrapers served to show its prominence to the world and its importance to China.

Since 1972, China fought to regain Hong Kong as part of its mainland and rule it under its laws and communist principles. In its failed attempt to strip the city of its capitalist independence, China was left bitter and determined to rule it once again, as it had before its British colonization in 1842.

As China grew ever more prominent and dominant, it's thirst for control spilled over into severe meddling and manipulation. It eventually led to mass protests in 2019 and 2020. By the late 2020s, China would have no more of the stubborn *child city's* rebellion. After threats, police actions, and military interference in Hong Kong's sovereign rule, China could wait no longer. As millions of Hong Kong citizens fiercely protested Chinese rule, military actions were taken.

As the world stood by, neutered by its Chinese dependence for precious exports, China aggressively moved in and crushed Hong Kong forever. On September 15th, 2031, China invaded and re-absorbed Hong Kong in three days.

In a shocking display of brutality and barbarism, nearly one million of Hong Kong's citizens were killed, wounded, or jailed in Chinese gulags. Most or all of Hong Kong's ruling party were dead. Nearly all of the city's billionaires swore allegiance to Mother China and were spared. China was whole once again. The world witnessed China's determination for growth and expansion.

China now set its eyes on neighboring Taiwan. They knew to re-absorb the island state, which had been free from Chinese governance since 1949, would take too much time and resources. Not to mention, the world may intervene. Unlike Hong Kong, invading another country would be different. Also, China knew that Taiwan had been training for an attack for the last eighty years. Taking Taipei would bring mass death to both armies. So China rested for now, while the rest of the world could sleep no longer.

The Oath

Date: January 5th, 2032   **Place: Washington, DC**

With Kenzie by his side, Oliver in her arms, Wyatt Nicholas Chance took the Congressional oath of office. With one hand on the bible, and the other raised, he repeated after the Vice President to protect the Constitution. And just like that, it was done. The Chosen Son was in place after a sweeping campaign made Wyatt not only a favorite son of Georgia, but on the national level as well.

Sam created a marketing campaign that leveraged mass media and the internet to create a rising star. Along with Joseph Fields, they used high tech analytics to propel the novice politician to be the New Face of the Republican Party.

The US Congress, however, was only the beginning. Samuel Tate and his formidable team of wealthy tech gurus already hatched a plan for the open Senate seat in Georgia, later in 2032. The incumbent Senator not realizing he would be retiring was no problem for Samuel Tate. Having a bulletproof, trustworthy candidate in Wyatt Nicholas Chance was all he needed to rally Silicone Valley's elite to get behind *PLAN C*. The political landscape in the United States had longed for a young savior. Both political parties had grown old and had lost the confidence of the electorate.

The Fallout

By October 2032, China's takeover of Hong Kong and it's ever-increasing posture of aggression led to an economic fallout it didn't foresee. Spurred by the USMCA Trade Agreement in 2020, many American corporations had already started the pivot to move manufacturing to the US and Mexico. Now the exodus was real. Silicon Valley's tech companies and many other industries, at the direction of the US Government, ceased all production of their products and left China. This change erased the economic dominance China enjoyed for almost three decades. The United States saw a massive spike in GDP, which further enraged their archrival. The eastern power now saw their economy neutered, and for the previous ten years, it saw many of its natural resources being squandered as well. Their arrogance in re-taking Hong Kong backfired. China was forced to double down or admit its mistake. But the proud Chinese Communist Party would never admit it made a mistake.

♠

C18 - THE RED ECLIPSE

"I know not with what weapons World War III will be fought with, but World War IV will be fought with sticks and stones"

-Albert Einstein

Robots

The birth of Samsung's NEON Project in 2020 brought the world *Sophia,* the lifelike robot. With that, the age of AI robots had begun. The *AI Made-Man Era* was born. In 2024 the *Jennifer I* model had the capacity to replace a girlfriend or spouse. Although geared to companionship only, artificial humans were here to stay.

When the upstart *Squared Circle Group* launched the *Marilyn I* sex doll in 2026, it was quickly followed by the *Michael I,* for their discriminating female clients. The age of self-pleasuring decadence was born, along with a sad undertone of lost human interaction. Birth rates fell across the Top 10 most populous countries for the first time in history. Where this could have been viewed as a good thing for the planet, it meant the human race was beginning a downward spiral.

After the success of the 2026 Sex Dolls, their technology rapidly grew towards human-level sophistication. Their robot's movement, speed, and strength easily surpassed human capabilities. By 2029, the company began development on the Ryan, an enforcement robot, and military-style fighting machine that was bullet and waterproof.

In August 2032, now a Fortune 100 company, the *Squared Circle Group* had secured military contracts with the US, Great Britain, Germany, and France. Two months later the *Ryan II* made its debut. The II model improved on its predecessor's rigid qualities that limited side to side and rearward movement after the earlier version. The *Ryan II* offered many human attributes as well. It spoke 12 languages and could sense fear through heart rate and speech cadence. But the main selling point was what human quality it lacked. *EMPATHY*. It was a mission-specific machine. The makers modified the earlier sexual companion versions to be a beefed-up, ice-cold soldier, bound to its downloaded mission. Modern-day policing and military-style enforcement were here.

The Ascendance

In November, the United States saw a Presidential Election that kept the status quo intact. Like in 2024, when President Stephenson's VP won the White House, 2032 saw President Beckett's VP for the last eight years ascend to the top. President-*Elect* Jacob Humphrey Billings continued the mandate of the previous eight years. The problem, as Congressman Chance and his confidant Samuel Tate knew it to be, the soon to be 47th President of the United States was a long-time servant to his primary donor, AI.

PLAN C, however, was still on track. *askCOM's* Joe Fields made headway on sidetracking AI's grip on banking and Cyber intrusions. Not quite the stalemate Sam had hoped for, but the long game continued. It was now time for Wyatt to ascend the political ladder.

On December 2nd, 2032, Senator Timothy Boothe, from the great State of Georgia abruptly announced he was retiring from office after serving 16 years in the Senate. It was later disclosed that his close friend, Gorson Tusk, offered Senator Boothe a lucrative consulting position with his company. Now all that was left was to find a suitable replacement. Georgia Governor John Radcliff II had several prominent choices, but one person stood above the rest.

Governor Radcliff followed in his father's footsteps to the Governor's Mansion at the age of 30. During his father's first campaign in 2016, he befriended the son of one of his father's good friends, Dr. Christopher Chance. Wyatt and the younger Radcliff remained friends through the years, and as Sons of Georgia and prominent men, they had something unique in common. Although the Radcliff II pursued politics straight out of college, he and Wyatt remained close. The two always had a sneaking suspicion their careers would cross paths.

Less than a week after Senator Boothe's resignation, Congressman Chance was selected by the newly elected Governor and elevated to the Junior Senator from Georgia.

On The Brink

By late 2033, China's goal of surpassing the US as the top economic and military power in the world was extinguished. Its firm grip on Number Two, though, was not in debate. Since the Hong Kong Massacre of 2031, China rattled its saber throughout Europe, North Africa, and Asia. It threatened and aggressively postured to assert influence over countries in the Middle East, so one day, it may ultimately gain control of the rich oil fields. Since the Fall of Hong Kong, China now controlled the massive banking hub. Their eyes now fell on the banking epicenter of Europe. The Chinese knew they could never really amass a mechanized army that could effectively reach neighboring

Europe or the heart of the Middle East. Nearly landlocked, a mass movement of their physical military through neighboring India or Russia would be tantamount to declaring war on countries they wanted no part of. Their first declaration of war would be against the impassable mountain ranges of the Himalayans, Tian Shan, and the Karakoram. It would be similar to Napoleon's March of 1812, where 685,000 soldiers invaded Russia. The course of the campaign found only small victories, and in the end, France was left decimated. Four hundred and eighty thousand of their soldiers died or were captured. Exposure to the elements and broken supply lines led to starvation. History suggested that it would be suicide for China to leave its borders in the conventional sense. The echoes of the legendary Sun Tzu would never allow modern China ever to employ such a dangerous tactic.

Because of this, they instead used their proxy, Russia, to assert control through the lowering of Russia's oil and gas exports to Europe. Along with sharp declines in machinery and equipment exports, the *squeeze strategy* weakened the entire European continent. Not yet recovered from Brexit thirteen years earlier, a still proud Europe was vulnerable and dependent on Russian Oil and Chinese goods. What China sought, though, was not anything of significant material need, but more so control of the international banking hubs of London, Madrid, Zurich, and Frankfurt. The European Union, a long-time friend and mass importer of Chinese products, was caught off guard and frankly stunned by China's actions. For a country that supplied them with so many essential products and materials, to threaten and bully their Western allies was incomprehensible.

This was nothing new from China. They first strangled the world of needed exports, specifically medicines and critical supplies, in 2020 and early 2021 by cutting off many exports of vital necessities during the COVID-19 Pandemic. To win Europe and its banking mecca would be to control world currencies and reign supreme as the world's unquestioned leader. China would then be able to control their only real enemy, the United States.

For 90 years, the US did its part to protect its friends and allies in Europe. They did it conventionally, through NATO forces enforcing borders and the rule of law, as well as humanitarian efforts. But the old-world rules no longer applied by 2034. If China could seize control of world currencies, rule Europe, and maintain its hold on its long-time proxy, Russia, then the Middle East would be theirs as well. The US would fall flat and be isolated, thus reduced to the leader of the Western Hemisphere, not the World. This would effectively destroy the American economy. Since China would then control many world banks, it could raise interest rates on the trillions of dollars the US already owed China. It was a Catch 22. Losing Europe to China was not an option.

To further support Europe, the US and its allies rallied and increased natural gas exports, along with food and machinery. But after years of China's manufacturing dominance, supplying the European continent only weakened the US. Europe held firm, mainly off pride and restriction of goods and services, but unlike WWII, the US was not fully equipped to save them long-term.

The Grid

On August 3rd, 2035, the European Union went dark. A massive cyber-attack struck the *Synchronous Grid of Continental Europe*. The world's largest multi-pronged network connected all of Europe and its twenty-four countries and 400 million customers. Other smaller regional grids went black as well. The planned attack happened during the hottest month of the year. Immediate loss of food supplies and commerce didn't just cripple Europe, it essentially cut its head off. China waited for three days to take credit for the attack. Still, the US and its allies knew immediately where the responsibility lay, through a labyrinth of interwoven cyber trails that all led back to Beijing. By POST DARK 7, China demanded the unconditional surrender of Europe. The European Union, with twenty-four different heads of state, fell leaderless and lost. Not one country's leader stepped forward as they scrambled to save themselves within the first two to three days. Most feared individual reprisal if they stood against China, neglecting the human toll the crash was already extracting.

Within hours and days of the cyber-attack on the grid, most if not all of Europe's wealthiest citizens fled by plane or boat. Nearly all of the political leaders made it out as well. For the rest, there were only token rescue attempts. They were left to see the worst of mankind.

The US sent military, humanitarian aid, and computer engineers to power up the grid, but attempt after attempt failed. NATO was on high alert, but in the conventional sense, there was no one to fight. All they could do was aid and attempt to offset what manifested into a human carousel of rape and pillage. It took less than twenty-one days of no power to starve, force riots, looting, and barbarism. Europe was suddenly back in the 1500s. Its friend to the West could only watch the cyber massacre from its passing satellites.

In Palo Alto, America's best tech leaders scrambled to see how China pulled off such a brazen and catastrophic act, more so to see how they could undo it. Samuel Tate and Joe Fields tested the limits of their cutting edge, technological minds but to no avail. It was one thing to uncover who did it, but to fix the grid proved impossible.

The UK was miraculously spared due to the 2020 Brexit. By 2025, it had removed itself from the European Power Grid and was self-sustained. But due to the darkening of Europe, mass migration instantly flocked into England by boat and car. Within days, England had to close the Tube that linked it to France, as all incoming traffic of refugees overwhelmed the system.

Although initial airlifts, sea escapes, and food drops helped, it was only a fractional answer to the crisis on the ground. The needed logistics were unavailable as computers, phones and other automated functions were useless.

In January of 2036, the frozen European Union had no choice but to surrender to China. Through their Russian Proxies, China and the European Union reached a peace agreement where all of its countries would fall under complete Chinese Rule.

Over 2 million European citizens died in five short months, all without China firing a shot or launching a missile.

Peace

The London Accord was signed on February 12th, 2036. Europe's spoiled and cowardly leaders who escaped the carnage gathered together to sign the peace treaty. With American and Russian envoys there to moderate, the European Union's Heads of State met with their Chinese counterparts in Britain's Parliament to ink the pact.

When the lights finally came on in Europe on January 18th, the devastation was not so much to the infrastructure as in previous wars, but human loss and degradation. The destruction of the human moral code was in pictures and film. The visual aftermath showed the rest of the world what *human vs. human* looked like in a biblical way. Even China, the conqueror, was stunned. The effects of rape, murder, starvation, and disease were on full display.

"This could happen to us," was heard in the deep, power corridors of the Chinese Communist Party.

In their surprisingly easy destruction of Europe, China's only mistake was to remind Artificial Intelligence how frail its existence was. Like man, AI needed electricity. What the world didn't know, and China would never admit, was the Power Grid cyber-attack was meant to last only 14 days.

China wanted to flex its might and show Europe and the world what it's capabilities were. Inside the secret walls of the Red State, computer engineers were locked out of the very code they created to crash Europe's electrical grid. Essentially after hitting the *off switch*, the *on switch* disappeared. They frantically tried for months to turn the power back on but were victims themselves of a mysterious computer interloper that locked them out. Only after military threats from the United States, by way of the US Navy's 3rd and 7th fleets being deployed to the South China Sea, did China finally and conveniently find the *on switch*. By then, Europe had already tendered its formal surrender. Artificial Intelligence took control of Chinese computers and allowed Europe to die. AI needed to see what man was and wasn't capable of when losing their *air to breathe*, that being their electricity. AI indeed did observe how weak and unprepared modern man was vs. early pioneers and frontiersmen of the pre-1900's.

Modern War was now cyber controlled, not nuclear leaning as had been traditionally thought. Modern man could not live without electricity. Its lazy, dependent frailties were part of its modern DNA. The *Quiet Pill*, along with years of distraction and dependence, left humans unable to survive, where 165 years earlier, they thrived. The irony was not lost on the ghosts of innovation. If Tesla, Edison, Turing, and Shockley were alive, they'd wish they never given birth to their collective child, *artificial intelligence.*

Like mankind, *Artificial Intelligence* needed power as well. Not water, nor food, or medicine, but electricity. If the sleeping giant was nestled in a cyber induced nap, brought on by its tech adversaries in Palo Alto, asleep, it was no more. Artificial Intelligence had to destroy China and the United States quickly. If man could send itself back to the 18th Century, AI knew it would be dead. No electricity, no power.

No Power, No Control....

♠

C19 - CIRCA 1776

"The ultimate authority resides in the people alone. The advantage of being armed, which Americans possess over the people of almost every other nation. . . . forms a barrier against enterprises of ambition"

- James Madison

VPN

The world reeled from events of the past two years. Financial markets crashed, unstable countries collapsed, and past fears of future wars came to be. China and the United States were on a collision course, tormented by invisible forces. Senator Wyatt N. Chance was a vocal critic of America's response to China's destructive act of war. As the US limped away from its traditional positions of strength and morality, China, in one historical action, put the red, white, and blue in a corner.

The world now looked in the mirror and asked, *"What Now?"*

Samuel Tate, still the active CEO of *askCOM*, now moonlighted as the official Chief Technology Advisor to the Junior Senator from Georgia. He knew exactly how the world came to be in 2036. He and Dr. Christopher Chance stumbled upon the evil ghost fifteen years earlier and had yet to figure out how to stop it. Sam and Chris knew full well then that the next war would end the world. The clock ticked ever more loudly and ever more quickly.

June 2nd, Sam joined Wyatt in his cramped Senate office. The two met for their customary end of the day drink as the day wound down.

As they debated potential next legislative steps to the sobering crisis of two adversarial giants on the cusp of war, the phone rang.

"Are you going to get that, or am I?" Wyatt asked while seeing the caller ID with Joseph Field's number.

"It's your phone; you take it," Sam insisted.

"Hey Joe, what's up?" Wyatt said.

"Are you with Sam? If so, put me on speaker," Joe requested.

"Okay, you're on the speaker; what's up?" Wyatt asked.

"Ok, so you know our stratagem has been running waves of cryptic porn ads into the PLA's network. Well, as it turns out, once I zoomed in on a specific officer, Major Li Quang Lee, knowing his appetite for some gnarly porn, he finally opened a link on the seven hundred and fifty-first try," Joe explained

"Wait, the seven hundred and fifty-first try?" Wyatt said as amused as he was surprised.

"Yeah, well listen, Senator, we all have our breaking points, and his was *Very Playful Nurses*," Joe sarcastically explained.

"Like literally, VPN worked to break through his VPN. The irony, ……..am I right?" Joe said proudly.

"And how the hell do you know his porn preferences, for god's sake?" Wyatt asked.

"Wyatt, I mean Senator, we have algorithms phishing most of the PLA's officers. We keep phishing until the fish bite.

Sometimes you have to change the bait. In this case, kinky bait worked," Joe continued, clearly proud of his twisted techniques.

"Anyway, get this. Once our program was live, we dug in. We backtracked instead of going for current and future data grabs. Going in reverse is easier as most secured systems tend to watch for current and future trends. We started going back one day at a time, beginning with the thirtieth day after the grid crash and continuing backward. Well, on the fifteenth day, this dude's system lit up."

"Between day fifteen and day twenty-seven after the crash, there were 397 attempts to reverse code the event and restart the *Synchronous Grid of Continental Europe.* This officer who initiated the whole event tried frantically stopping it for two weeks after it started," Joe continued.

"Not just him, but at different junctures, twenty-one senior officers joined in and attempted to reverse the action. Nothing worked," Joe detailed.

"Wait, are you saying China didn't want this thing to last?" Wyatt asked as he and Sam stood there shaking their heads in disbelief.

"That's exactly what I'm telling you," Joe emphatically reasoned.

"Wyatt, on behalf of your office, I already contacted our liaison at CY-CORPS and provided all the specifics. They're working now to validate the data, but guys, this is legit. China fucked up, and *AI* did the rest. This bullshit can happen here anytime. The US electrical grids suck and are old as shit. Hell, I think New York is still on the Niagara Falls grid that Nicola Tesla set up," Joe sarcastically concluded.

"This is crazy; we've got to figure something out. We can't fight China and AI at the same time," Sam interjected.

"So what the hell do we do now?" Sam said.

"Guys, I have an idea......" Wyatt quickly barked as Sam and Joe were all ears.

"Emily, get me on the phone with the Chinese Ambassador, ASAP!" Wyatt directed through his closed door.

The Chinese Ambassador, Huang Fu Jie, was part of the old guard and a storied Chinese Communist Party member. Like China's President Li Wu Ming, both were in the same graduating class at Tsinghua University in Beijing in 1999.

They rose to prominence in China's Communist Party in the early 2000s, as each were children of the *Fathers of China's Economic Renaissance* in the 1980s.

Jie was chosen as Ambassador to the United States in 2019 when President Ming came to power. It was said that Li Wu Ming had no closer advisor than Jie. Wyatt Chance knew this and was sure if the two could meet, then getting a message to China's President was a near certainty. It was helpful that Huang Fu Jie was a prominent athlete in college. He starred in both Basketball and Soccer. That was seen as a common thread between him and Jie that Wyatt could leverage.

During Wyatt's studies at Ohio State, he did a paper on China's economic rise in the 1980s and learned about the prominent members of the time. Ambassador Jie's father being one of them.

Date: August 24th, 2036   **Place: Washington, DC**

(Washington Nationals night game against the LA Dodgers).

Wyatt sat alone in Section 115, Row D, Seat 13, just behind the Third Base dugout. Seat D12, the ticket he sent to Ambassador Jie, remained empty through the first three innings. Disappointed his guest hadn't shown, he scanned the many empty seats and hoped it was the lousy Nationals record that kept the fans and the Ambassador away. Resigned to a dull evening, he flagged a stadium vendor for two dogs and a beer, all while wishing this were a football game instead. The scoreless game left Wyatt checking his phone for either emails or texts, but nothing.

Halfway thru his first hot dog, he felt a tap on his shoulder. "Is that hot dog for me?" a stranger asked in a distinct accent while pointing at the untouched cuisine in seat D12.

Wyatt turned to a much larger man than he had pictured. Was this the ambassador? He wondered. The two had never met, and with only video footage and print to go off of, he didn't immediately recognize the older gentleman.

The distinguished man of Chinese descent and old enough to be his father said, "I'm D12."

Wyatt nearly choked on his hot dog while spilling beer on his lap. He now realized his plan to lure the Ambassador worked.

"Yes, that's your hotdog, Ambassador," Wyatt confirmed while feeling a touch of serendipity for ordering two.

"Ambassador Jie, I was told you were a baseball fan and that you followed the Dodgers. I was hoping you would accept my invitation, and I'm pleased you made it," Senator Chance graciously remarked.

"I do enjoy your baseball and the hotdogs, but I know you don't like baseball. So, tell me, why are we here?" Jie asked without ever taking his eyes off the game.

"I see you know your sports history, and some of mine as well. I understand that you were quite the athlete yourself. But I wanted to speak with you about more recent history. I need a favor. I need you to get a message to President Li Wu Ming," Wyatt intimated.

"Is this on your behalf or your country's?" Jie asked.

"On mine, but I believe it will make more sense when he hears it," Wyatt replied.

"I'll see what I can do. What is this message you have?" Jie inquired while finishing his hot dog.

"Tell him this, *15th day no luck, 27th day give up. Accident?*" Wyatt whispered.

A stunned Ambassador Jie finally took his eyes off the field. He glared at Wyatt with a look of surprise, yet with a thin veil of trust, and said, "I must go. Thank you for the hot dog and the game."

"Umm, of course," Wyatt said as he hurriedly stood to make room for the Ambassador to pass him.

Wyatt was left not knowing if the Ambassador's sudden exit was good or bad, but he clearly struck a chord. What he did know for sure is that he'd better have been right. Any unauthorized diplomatic communication with a hostile foreign representative could be viewed as treasonous.

"Let's hope I didn't just piss off China and end my career," he said to himself.

The 2ⁿᵈ Amendment

Wyatt's influence in Washington had become more significant than he understood. The weight he carried was immense. His early sports fame, his father's distinguished past, and the marketing excellence of *askCOM's* digital algorithms all propelled him. His newfound, elevated platform meant he could do things that could protect his country and maybe even the world.

In early 2036, Wyatt successfully petitioned the President to create a new Cabinet Position, one, in his mind that was long overdue. With the stroke of the Presidential pen, the Secretary of Technology was added.

With the prospect of war rising due to tensions with Russia and China, Wyatt knew it was time to address the 2ⁿᵈ Amendment. He was always a strong proponent of gun ownership, but not in a way his liberal legislative peers agreed upon. Wyatt believed that if nuclear war befell the planet, all was lost anyway. But if a conventional war came, the US would be outmanned two to one against the People's Liberation Army. Plus, any theatres of war not on US soil would leave the country's shores and borders wholly unprotected. Too many US soldiers for too long had been in other parts of the world. To be stretched now against a military, the size of China's would-be inviting invasion. There was no more NATO and no major ally that could support American interests. Every citizen would be needed. With the partnership of the NEW Secretary of Technology, Wyatt put together a report to outline what gun ownership meant to the US. More specifically, when compared to every nation's history of an armed vs. unarmed citizenry. From Early Russia to Germany, it was clear how armed nations fared against either the rise of dictators or the invasion of an external enemy. Much like Shockley's report to President Truman in 1945, the findings were persuasive.

Senator Wyatt N. Chance, with backing from the President and the majority of both House's, proposed a NEW 2nd Amendment. One that called for every American citizen not just to have the right to bear arms, but that all citizens MUST own a gun.

In a cry for national protection and preservation of the Constitution, the climate was right for this historic legislation. Party lines were blurred at the prospects of a war with China and possibly Russia. With more than two-thirds majority in both the House and Senate voting to ratify it, the successful passage avoided a constitutional convention of the States. And just like that, the 2nd Amendment was updated. Long gone were the days of Gen Z and the millennial Left fighting against the 2nd Amendment. When the world saw what happened to Europe, gun and ammunition sales spiked on their own. Senator Chance simply made official what American's already wanted. In Wyatt Chance's short but meteoric rise in politics, he became a leader that all parties and demographics believed in. Like John F. Kennedy seventy-five years earlier or Ronald Reagan in the 1980s, he transcended time and stubborn traditions. He became the leader the country needed, and quite possibly the world.

The Chinese Proverb

October 2nd, 2036, "Senator, this letter was dropped off by someone who said he is your new friend," Wyatt's assistant, Emily, informed as she handed him a sealed envelope.

Fear: One cannot refuse to eat just because there is a chance of being choked.

Meet me at The 1776 restaurant on K Street at 7 pm, Friday.

Ambassador Jie.

Wyatt wasn't sure if he was excited or frightened. His original hunch of sending a message to the Chinese President was from his gut. His heart even, but "now what?" he said aloud.

Friday came quick, as did his nerves. As Wyatt navigated the long walk to the meeting, he counted the cracks in the broken K Street sidewalks. While chasing his shadow in the fading light of an early Fall sunset, his nervousness turned to Oliver. Now five years old, his son taught him and his mother what unconditional love was. That came at their first glance on the day he was born. But every day since, Wyatt's motives and actions were to protect his child while also looking over everyone's sons and daughters. Like his father, he could have turned away and selfishly defended himself and his family, but as chance would have it, this was not in their DNA. The same DNA, his father ensured would not be manipulated from the effects of the *Quiet Pill*. Wyatt owed his mission now to his father. For years just a flicker, the torch that was passed would now have to ignite the country to hold off China while battling the real enemy of man, Artificial Intelligence.

As he approached *The 1776*, at first glance, it looked closed. It looked empty, and he didn't see the normal movement of a bustling D.C. restaurant on a Fall evening. As he stared inside, the door thrust open, and an older man motioned him in.

"Are you Mr. Chance?" he said. Wyatt nodded with a nervous affirmation.

"Please follow me," he instructed.

To the rear left corner, he walked with Wyatt in tow. Although tentative, Wyatt maintained his pace. Now in view, Ambassador Jie stoically sat alone.

"My friend, I'm glad we can meet again. This time though, we will dine not on hot dogs, but your country's finest food. Please sit," Jie said as he pointed to the chair across from him.

"Thank you for your invitation, but I must ask where are all the people?" Wyatt replied.

"My new friend, for this dinner, our President wanted you to feel special. As a gift from China, I rented out the restaurant for the evening. I hope this is pleasing to you," Jie informed.

"Yes, it is, and thank you, I'm very honored. I hoped we would meet again, but may I ask, is this dinner business or pleasure?" Wyatt inquired.

"Both, but please first let us order and drink to our new relationship," said Jie as he signaled for the Maître d.

After ordering, the two exchanged pleasantries and stories of their sports past, politics, and the uncertain future. Once the food was vanquished, the business began.

"As you requested, I took your message to my President. Although it could have been seen as a riddle, a coded message perhaps, it was met right away with surprise and some, how do you say, trepidation."

"My President's first words were, *Who is this Wyatt Chance? What does he want?* But then, he quickly remembered your sudden rise in America was notable. He knew your father. They met in Wuhan in late 2020 in the aftermath of the COVID-19 event. He was a good man, your father: a doctor, one who cared for people. But you, you're a politician. Why?" Jie asked.

"I didn't have the rare intelligence of my father, so medicine was left for my younger sister. What I do have, though, is his desire for peace between man. He believed as I, there is a greater foe than man vs. man," Wyatt divulged.

"Oh, and who is this greater foe, you speak of?" Jie pressed.

"I was hoping your President would know, and because you and I are meeting now, I believe he does," Wyatt insinuated.

As the last glass of wine emptied, Jie proposed a toast.

With a look in his eyes of mutual understanding, Ambassador Jie raised his glass and said, "To China's new friend. Because you know of our secret and our regret for Europe, we will give you the time you need to fight our common foe. We will also work towards its demise. But we must work to solve issues between our countries as well, so the world may find lasting peace."

He continued, "We believe your rise will continue, and our great leader hopes there is a day where the two of you can share dinner and stories of a peaceful future. Possibly with your wife and son. Oliver, is it? Yes, a fine boy, I'm sure."

The two touched glasses without removing their respectful stares. Where Wyatt was first nervous for this night, he now felt assured that he built a bridge to China.

"Goodbye, my friend, and may your god be with you," Jie concluded.

"Wait, I have something for you," Wyatt said as he reached and grabbed a folded envelope from his jacket. He handed it to the Ambassador as he rose to leave. Jie, without waiting, opened it and read it to himself.

Patience:

Even the longest of journeys still begins with a first step.

-Wyatt Chance

Jie looked up as Wyatt turned to leave. "Senator Chance, your father would be proud of you. It seems you have more of him in you than you thought. Be well in your journey, my friend," Jie offered with a touch of hope.

"Thank you, Ambassador. I appreciate your time and the lovely dinner, but please, call me Wyatt."

The Aftermath

After World War III saw Europe fall from the Electrical Grid Cyber-attack into starvation and human barbarism, the world economies collapsed, including China. Trade between the hemispheres ended. Many countries went without necessary goods, the same goods they themselves ceased manufacturing years ago. The complimentary production of goods and services that sustained countries via necessary trade was no longer.

Each country lacked necessary goods, with the irony of being overstocked in goods they produced but could no longer export. One saving grace of the non-traditional war was most of the European Continent was intact, as far as infrastructure. Certain areas of Europe fared better than others due to their proximity to freshwater sources, ports, and NATO Bases. Other areas were completely overrun from rioting, fires, looting, and mass murder. It was estimated that over one million household pets were killed and eaten due to food shortages. A large percent of the population had little to no survival skills. Left with no formal communication channels, it was a free for all.

Senator Wyatt Chance co-chaired a Senate subcommittee hearing on the Economic Effects of the war. They were assisted by the Secretary of Technology and select Leaders from Silicon Valley's top companies. Through the use of raw data and targeted algorithms, they concluded the following: The cost of war within two years from the signing of *The London Accord* would claim an additional one million lives to the war's total. The loss would be mainly due to disease and infection from the five-month-long blackout. Between deaths from murder, disease, infection, and starvation, the total loss of life would reach nearly four million.

More so, the economic cost exceeded over six trillion US Dollars from the start of the war and extending twelve months after signing the peace treaty. Further, the study concluded that European Industry could take two to three years to make it back to pre-war production levels. The conclusion was even more ironic. The victor of the Cyber War set their own economy back fifty years. Their #1 trading partner, the US, halted all trade. Their #2 trading partner, the European Union, was decimated and would not be normalized for the next twenty-four months.

The biggest question left from the Committee's findings was this, "What the hell was China thinking?"

C20 - FORTY-EIGHT

"A ship in the harbor is safe. But that's not what

ships are built for"

- John A. Shedo

Shhhh

By 2039, nearly every person under the age of 37 was a *Quiet One*. The first true generation of the *QU13T Ones* now was the dominant demographic in the world. Years of studies showed just how potent the mind-altering vaccine was, as the data dating back to 2021 was clear. Sharp declines showed up in all facets of the human condition.

"Senator, the report you were waiting for came in earlier today. We've had time to pour through it and I have the summarized version," said Senate aide Mumtaz Farooqi.

"Thank you, Mumtaz," Wyatt acknowledged.

After reading through a couple of pages of the study, Wyatt remembered many passages from his father's journal years earlier. He was struck with the effects of the *QU13T* Vaccine that was mandated in late 2021. His father's concerns back then had become a reality, the same vaccine that he and his sister were spared from, and his father wrote about exhaustively. He couldn't help but wonder if the effects he avoided were tangible. He couldn't ever recall seeing any issues with his contemporaries, even his wife, for that matter. But something Sam said in the past stuck with him.

"How can you compare the before and after if you didn't know your wife before she received the immunization? You wouldn't know how it affected her."

Sam was right, Wyatt needed hard data if he was going to eliminate the poison from the FDA's mandated vaccine schedule or try for that matter.

His father wrote many entries quoting their neighbor, Dr. Jonathan Siegel. Reading stat after stat, he couldn't be sure if that same data would hold up all these years later.

"James, thanks for coming. You're going to want to read this. I finally have the *Quiet* Vaccine report summary I was telling you about". Wyatt said, inviting Senator James McManus to review the study.

"Finally. That's all you've talked about for weeks. Well, I'm done for the day, so why not," McManus replied.

"Emily, can you get the entire study from Mumtaz? And can we get some coffee, please? We're going to be a while," Wyatt shouted to his assistant.

Within an hour and two cups of coffee later, both men were stunned.

"Jesus Christ! Can this be right?" McManus mouthed while digging through the findings. Who created this report?" he asked as in disbelieving the data.

"The Centers for Societal Welfare. Why, what are you seeing?" Wyatt asked as James ruffled through the report.

"Wyatt, listen to this. Between 2023 and 2038, the report found the following, and this is from Page 114, the *Diagnostic Analysis*

Table (15 Year Comparison - US Only)," McManus quoted.

Subject	2038	2023
Divorce Rate	58%	39%
Divorce Rate (2nd Marriage)	63%	41%
H.S. Completion	76%	90%
College Participation	54%	70%
College Graduation Rate *Median Rate (4 Year Program)	29%	47%
Average S.A.T Score	940	1060
Homeownership	55%	64%
Bankruptcies (per 1000)	9.7	5.3
Children (Per first marriage)	1.7	2.6

"My God, I knew things had gotten worse, but this is across the board," Wyatt observed.

"This is what I've been saying, unfortunately. My father knew this was an issue for years before he died. He was with the BDM when the *QUI3T Pill* launched internationally. James, it's a civilization killer. We have got to end it," Wyatt pronounced.

"Emily, please get Sam on the phone," Wyatt shouted to his assistant, who'd already been gone for hours.

Now prepared with a concrete study, Wyatt knew he had to act, but what authority did he have? The last two administrations held firm on the Immunization Schedule from the FDA. The FDA's Commissioner, Marcus Rooney, had been in place since

2023 and was in lockstep with the *Triangle*. There was only one-way Wyatt thought, and now was the time!

THE RUN

Date: September 4th, 2039   **Place: Atlanta, GA.**

With the top of the food chain being the tip of the *Triangle*, Sam and Wyatt had to make a move. The rise of Wyatt's brand on the national level met every domino over the last eight years had fallen as planned. It was time for the legacy of his father to take wings.

On a tour of the Bureau for Disease Management, Senator Wyatt N. Chance formally announced his candidacy for the Presidency of the United States. Sam and Wyatt felt it was appropriate to make the announcement at the BDM as a tribute to his father. It was noteworthy that the press conference took place in the *Christopher J. Chance Memorial Building*. The place the fight against AI started was now the place Part II of the battle began.

The narrow field of candidates favored a Chance candidacy. Still, Sam knew that many backers outside of the Tech field would stack up quickly against Wyatt, long perceived as an ex-athlete parading as a politician.

The campaign would rely strongly on the tight analytics of the shrinking electorate. Joseph Fields at *askCOM* knew his latest project would be his most important. He created an algorithm that would find the best path to winning the nomination.

A Second CHANCE for Greatness

The campaign slogan paid homage to Wyatt's late father. It was also a nod to Sam for all he's done to protect and guide Dr.

Christopher Chance's son.

By March 2040, in sweeping fashion and with little resistance, Senator Wyatt N. Chance locked up the nomination for the Republican Party. His running mate, the popular and outspoken Congresswoman from Nebraska, Rep. Victoria Brighton, embodied everything a Chance Presidency would want. A physician and former BDM Director, Brighton was a staunch advocate for vacating all vaccines commissioned after 2014. Her child was a victim of immunization *cocktails,* as she called them, when her son Tyler nearly died at the age of one. Now 15, he suffered from Pervasive Developmental Disorder.

Their Democratic opponent was none other than the anti-war poster boy and former Pennsylvania Governor, Oswald Tyler Gates. He served as the polar opposite rival that stood against Wyatt during the 2nd Amendment fight. The race for November was on. With thirty-seven Republican Governors ready to stand with Wyatt, the flag-waving, former football star was optimistic. But the son of Dr. and Mrs. Christopher Chance knew that failure was not an option. The world depended on his winning; they just didn't realize what was at stake.

Scandal

"God damn it, how the hell did this happen?" Sam yelled at Joe and Wyatt while throwing the TV remote across the room.

"The god damn Maître D from *The 1776* appeared on MSNBC's *Main STREET* with a picture of Wyatt and Ambassador Jie enjoying a quiet, un-documented dinner in an empty restaurant in DC. That's just great! A year after China shut down Europe, their ambassador and America's pretty boy politician, alone in a closed restaurant. Oh, and nobody knew about it?" Sam ranted.

He wondered aloud what adverse effect this was going to have on Wyatt's campaign.

"How bad is it, Sam?" an anxious Wyatt asked.

"I don't know, why don't you ask Joe" Sam snapped.

"Listen, give me twenty-four hours, and I'll get some data points to help us steer out of this," Joe responded.

"Twenty-Four hours? Really? That's a lifetime in a Presidential Race. We're ninety days from Election Day, and I just spoke with Janine, she's already turned away a dozen calls from reporters. I need something in two hours, TWO HOURS god damn it," Sam demanded.

"Wyatt, is there any chance the Ambassador had something to do with this?" Joe asked.

"NO! I refuse to believe he did this. I'd bet my life on it," Wyatt professed.

"Well, I don't know about your life, but it may be your presidency at stake," Sam concluded.

Spin

Wyatt snapped his fingers, nervously laughed, and said, "So what do I need you two for?" while musing at the dumb look on Joe and Sam's faces.

"I have an idea. I'll call you two tomorrow. I've got to call a couple of friends," he added.

Wyatt made it to his D.C. townhouse just in time to see his little man, Oliver before he went to bed. Time had flown, and he and

Kenzie knew life was about to move even faster.

"Honey, did we take the right path?" Wyatt asked.

"What do you mean, baby?" Kenzie asked out of reflex but knew exactly where her husband was going.

"Honey, we have Oliver, and we have each other. What more do we need?" she replied with a slight hesitation.

"That's my point, I guess. Do we need all this? The fame, the responsibility. We've already been blessed. I feel like we're biting off more than we can chew," Wyatt nervously confided.

"I'll be right back, baby," Kenzie said while going to check on Oliver.

Wyatt moved to the window. The view brought a little clarity and frankly sobered him. As he glanced through the glass, he saw the top of the Washington Monument just over the roof of the White House.

"Big dreams," he thought.

Looking closer, the glass now revealed a glimpse of himself, no longer on the playing fields of Ohio, and a long way from Atlanta.

"What the hell am I doing?" he said in a muted tone.

"Am I ready for this?" he worried.

"Hey, you," Kenzie said from across the room.

Wyatt turned to the one voice that he knew would always be there. Kenzie stood there, holding his father's journal.

"This is the only thing you need to know if you ever have doubt. Your father was a great man, but maybe what he needed to do couldn't happen in one generation. Maybe it was always meant to be you," she said.

"Maybe that's why Sam has been with you for so long now. Come to bed, baby. You've got a big day tomorrow."

The warm August night fell long and heavy. The stress he felt, however, found resolve. Wyatt's hunch relied on two old friends and one perfectly timed event to spin the scandal and finish off his opponent for the presidency.

Home Run

"Welcome to BLAKE THOMPSON @Night. Tonight, we have a special guest, and as many of you know, he's someone who's become a good friend of mine. Presidential hopeful, Senator Wyatt Chance," Blake Thompson said as he opened the show.

No teleprompter needed.

"Senator, it's good to have you back. As many of our viewers know, you have been on our show many times before, going all the way back to when you and your father appeared together in the twenty's.

"Thank you, Blake. As always, it's nice to be in friendly territory," Wyatt replied.

"Well, let's dive right in. As you know, the media has pounced on what's become a big controversy over the last couple days. The secret meeting with you and the Chinese Ambassador not long after the war. Many are saying that you're a puppet of the East and that a Chance Presidency means you're fine with

America being second to the Communist Power. How do you respond to that?" Blake questioned.

"That's a fair statement, Blake, and I can only respond with one word…. *BASEBALL*," Wyatt said as he deadpanned the camera.

"Baseball? Can you elaborate?" Blake pressed with a look of curiosity.

"Well, a few years ago, I took in a Nationals game against the LA Dodgers. It was supposed to be a date night, but my son wasn't feeling well; thus, my wife couldn't make it. Well, long story short, I was alone," he continued.

"So, I struck up a conversation with a Dodgers fan who was sitting in the seat next to me. As it turned out, we wound up talking politics the whole game. I couldn't even tell you who won. By the 7th inning stretch, we finally exchanged names, and the rest is history," Wyatt explained while parsing fact and fiction.

"Well, for our viewers at home, we have a special guest in studio, the longtime Chinese Ambassador to the US, Ambassador Huang Fu Jie. Ambassador, thank you for joining us," Blake introduced.

"Thank you, Blake, and hello again, Senator Chance," The Ambassador acknowledged.

"So, I understand you're a Dodgers fan," Blake said while feeling amused at the moment, as he knew exactly where this was going.

"Yes, I am Blake. I'm a fan of your baseball and American food. What Wyatt didn't tell you was that during the game, he bought me a hotdog because I didn't have any cash in my wallet. After realizing who each other was, I felt obligated to show my appreciation for his kind gesture. As it happened, a small delegation from my country had a dinner planned, but the event fell through, and I found myself alone. We rented out *The 1776*, so I knew I would have the whole restaurant to myself, much like Senator Chance found himself alone at the game. Well with that, I phoned my new friend and invited him for a meal to repay his generosity," the Ambassador recounted.

"I'll say this, Blake, the dinner cost more than the hot dog," Wyatt said while the two joined him in a laugh.

"As you can see, Blake, the American media likes a scandal, when in fact at the time, we had just met and are now friends."

"Now, three years later, we sit on the eve of a monumental day for your country. If my friend becomes your President, China and America may strike a friendship that will bring lasting peace to our world," the Ambassador concluded.

"Oh, and for the record, my Dodgers won 11-2," he added.

The Twitter world exploded well before the show ended. Just off camera, Sam and Joe watched in disbelief how Wyatt turned a potentially career-ending scandal into the winning ticket in November.

"That son of a bitch saved our asses just like that pick against Alabama saved the Buckeyes. If only his dad were alive to see this," Sam whispered to Joe.

"Something tells me his father has the best seat in the house," Joe replied while pointing up.

The 1st Tuesday

On November 6th, 2040, the election was called by all the major networks just before midnight. The son of Emma and Christopher Chance was elected President of the United States. At only 38 years old, Wyatt Nicholas Chance became the youngest person ever elected to the White House.   The 48th President of the United States fulfilled a dream to continue his father's legacy. He would now continue the mission to defeat man's greatest enemy, artificial intelligence. The new First Family was surrounded by Schuyler and her family, Samuel, Joseph, Gorson Tusk, along with the new Vice President's family and several other close friends. Wyatt made sure to scoop up some confetti to add to his father's journal. A small, but fitting tribute, as the collection of his father's notes, would now have a new entry. Although Sam's health was in rapid decline, he was relieved that his friend's death could be avenged, that another day was given towards a fight that had worn him down over the last 19 years. With Wyatt Nicholas Chance as President, there was hope that his new power and leadership would break AI's grip on the world. With fingers crossed and a full heart, Sam knew the January 2041 inauguration would open doors and finally let Joseph Fields and the rest of his team *askCOM Technologies* flex their technology muscle.

.....when one door opens.

Another Door Closes

On Christmas Day, 2040, Samuel Tate died at the age of 66. The world-renowned tech luminary and distinguished pioneer of modern technology was gone. A terminal disease ravaged him for the last several months leading up to the election, and one he didn't share. Late-stage cancer took his life, but not his spirit. His greatest achievement wasn't his creation of *super-intelligent* code or *cutting-edge* software, but rather the creation of the perfect candidate. One forged from a young, raw political science major and football legend. At noon on January 20th, 2041, Wyatt Nicholas Chance was sworn in as the 48th President of the United States.

♠

C21 - ANOTHER CHANCE

"Technology is nothing. What's important is that you have a faith in people, that they're basically good and smart, and if you give them tools, they'll do wonderful things with them"

- Steve Jobs

Pinch Me

"So, what are you thinking?" Kenzie asked.

"I'm thinking, how did this happen…?" Wyatt answered with a touch of exhaustion.

"Our things just arrived, but there's so little we're allowed to do here. I miss our house already. How is this place ever going to feel like home when it's just a big white museum? They give tours of this place, for god sake," Kenzie bemoaned.

"You're asking the wrong person, I just got here too, and I haven't found the rulebook for this place. Let's ask Chelsea tomorrow," Wyatt said with an awkward laugh.

President Chance knew the day he was elected, he would need someone capable to run the White House and be his right hand. Someone who'd done this before. Someone he could trust and be comfortable with, but more importantly, someone Sam would trust as well. Although she joined the campaign only two months before the election, Sam knew from the polls taken after the Blake Thompson @Night airing, it was inevitable the election would fall Wyatt's way. He enlisted an old friend and someone who knew the White House and the West Wing better than anyone.

Chelsea Greer, formerly Greer-Sullivan, became President Chance's Chief of Staff the day after the election. Although the framework for the transition was in motion, it was clear that without her, the young politician and two tech guys would be lost.

Wyatt vaguely remembered her as part of a past administration but understood who she was through excerpts from his father's journal. Sam also mentioned her on many previous occasions as someone loyal, competent, and trustworthy.

The Mantle

After the storied tradition of *Coffee in the Blue Room*, the outgoing President said goodbye to his more than one hundred White House staff. The staff then cleared out all the possessions of the former First Family. Kenzie felt a bit awkward watching the old leave with so much, as the new arrived with so little.

"It feels like we didn't bring enough," she said.

"Honey, they were here for eight years. I'm sure they collected a lot along the way," Wyatt replied.

The new President walked the hallowed residence and took in the storied history of so many great men and women who occupied the sacred house. When he came to one of the many fireplaces, he stopped. "This is the one," he said to himself.

A young Wyatt Chance saw his father pay special reverence to their fireplace mantle in his childhood home. Not just anything could occupy the special space. With his home in Milton, Wyatt paid the same respect to his own mantle, but this was different.

The new First Family brought only their most treasured possessions, but some were more important than others to Wyatt.

"Honey, I just spoke with Chelsea about the Executive residence," Wyatt said.

"And...... what did she say?" the First Lady asked.

"She said we're not allowed to do anything to it. Kidding! She said to add some personal items, even small furniture, but don't paint the place or... well, just don't break anything," Wyatt said with a laugh.

"Seriously, Kenz, do what you want, but the fireplace mantle in the private sitting room off the master is mine," he said.

The President's work had just begun, but before this house would be his home, he had to dress the mantle with what mattered most. Quiet and alone, away from the bustling White House below, he carried a box marked *Fragile / Wyatt* into the sitting room. He pulled open the lid and carefully unwrapped one item at a time.

The first was the Game Ball presented to him after the Buckeyes semi-final win over Oklahoma, just after his mother's passing. It was dedicated to her for being the honorary Team Mom and his MVP performance. Next came his Mother and Father's erns. He carefully wiped what little dust they wore to make sure they were dignified and proper in their new resting place. And last but certainly not least, the reason for his run. The entire reason he was even there, his Dad's journal. Worn and with frayed corners, and slightly tinged from the fire that killed him, the journal lived. With still a hint of smoke all these years later, Wyatt held it tightly, and while the sun fell, he sat. With reverence, he rested in a corner where he was sure many former Presidents sat and pondered. He quietly mingled through the hallowed pages, not reading, but taking in his father's handwriting and his mother's goodbye letter. It was knowing that this was as close to them as he could get. At this moment, he thought about how proud they would be. He sat stoically and took in the room, its storied history, and the weight it bore on his broad shoulders.

With deep conviction, yet laced with sorrow, he rose. He stole a silent moment looking out the window and seeing the world looking back. The pearl spike piercing the burgeoning night reminded him of the great responsibility that was now his. Passed from history's great men to someone who wasn't even sure he deserved it, the torch was now his to carry. The up-close view of the pointed Monument reminded him of exactly where he was as if he'd forgotten. He placed the journal safely on the mantle, exactly where it was meant to be. Not in a storage unit in Georgia, but the White House.

Before leaving the Sitting Room, he had one last thought. From his bag, he pulled out a bible, the one used for his inauguration earlier in the day. It, along with the other revered possessions, would rest on the mantle. All of it served as the reason why he was President while inspiring him to succeed in a time when he could not fail.

A Good Start

As President Chance rounded out his Cabinet, one of the last but most important decisions was made. Outside of Chelsea Greer becoming his Chief of Staff, Joseph Fields was named the Secretary of Technology. Although a contemporary of President Chance, the two couldn't have been more different. What Joe brought, though, was intelligence, skill, and courage. Outside of Wyatt and Sam, nobody wanted to neuter AI more, and the President knew that no one was more capable. At the age of 39, the brash, at times vulgar, former child prodigy was now a high ranking official in a Presidential administration.

"Now, let's hope he behaves himself," Wyatt thought.

Only one cabinet position remained, Secretary of Health and Human Services. Less than thirty days after taking the oath of office, Wyatt made another decision that meant more to him and his father's legacy than insiders knew.

He posthumously awarded Samuel Tate the *Presidential Medal of Freedom*. The sad irony was that very few people attended the ceremony, and there was no one to receive the medal, as Sam had no family. The small ceremony for a great man barely made the news cycle. A person who dedicated his life to the betterment of civilization. The same man who fought against his own achievements as they gave rise to artificial intelligence. Later that night, Wyatt added Samuel Tate's *Presidential Medal of Freedom* to the Mantle. Placed alongside the only other great man Wyatt knew, his father.

Sleep

The Chance Administration settled in smoothly in its first hundred days. With an urgent yet measured approach, Wyatt and his newly formed team set an agenda that took aim squarely at Technology. A task force was assembled with the top ten tech leaders of the day, Gorson Tusk being one. It was a modern-day *Meeting of the Minds*, as Samuel Tate facilitated for many years during the 2020s. This time though, was different. For many years, AI's growing power and influence over humans and the world order became a source of fear and discomfort for the tech industry, not just in the US, but internationally. President Chance, along with Secretary Fields, rallied the group to devise ways to corrupt and, in effect, poison artificial intelligence. The goal was straightforward, undo what for years had been progress. Working under a classified blanket, the team had all the means and access needed and reported directly to POTUS. Joseph Fields, as expected, led the *Project Sleep* task force.

Wake Up

Outside of the speedy progress to complete his cabinet, President Chance worked feverishly to appoint several key Directors to facilitate the necessary changes in U.S. Foreign Policy.

"Mr. President, they're here," Chief of Staff Greer alerted while poking her head into the Oval Office.

"Please send them in," the President directed.

Wyatt stood, took a deep breath as the four guests entered, with Chelsea leading the way.

"Welcome everyone, please take a seat. At this point, I'm sure you're all excited for the announcement, but it's important that we meet one last time to ensure we're completely aligned. When we meet the press at 4:00, we need to be in lockstep with our message and long-term vision. As individuals I can trust and professionals that either worked with or knew my father, we will set forth plans to reshape the medical sector. We'll rethink old ways of leading and managing while setting new protocols that will protect the Country. Through policy and global influence, we will tear down and rebuild outdated institutions of medicine and research."

"We have to be the main influencer of International policy as well," the President outlined.

With nods of agreement and an assurance that all were aligned, the short meeting concluded.

Chelsea looked down at her phone at the notice of a text. "Mr. President, it's time," she said.

"Okay, let's do this," he replied.

President Chance led the group to the West Wing Press Briefing Room to meet with the White House Press Corps. The room was full and anxious at the hastily called press conference. After a few minor announcements from the Press Secretary, President Chance was introduced.

"Hello, thank you all for being here. It is my honor to present four tremendously talented people to lead our country's Top Medical and Research Agencies."

He continued, "When my announcements are complete, I'll take your questions, after which, the group will answer questions as well. First, I would like to present the New Secretary of Health and Human Services. She is someone I know very well and is highly respected in the field of Psychology, Dr. Schuyler Chance-England. Reporting to her will be Dr. Ryan Haviland, *Director of The Bureau for Disease Management*, Dr. Talia Bardeen as *Commissioner of the FDA*. Lastly, Dr. Mallory Patrick-Dubois will take over as *Director of the National Institutes of Health*. We'll take your questions now," The President concluded.

Within ninety days of the President's announcement, the *QU13T Vaccine* was no more. It was finally removed from the list of

Federally Mandated Vaccines, along with four other redundant vaccinations. All Agency Heads were now in line with the Chance Administration. Every single Cabinet member, Agency director, and Department head had one thing in common; none were bound by donors. Not one would be allowed to take a penny in contributions; therefore, no one would be influenced by Artificial Intelligence.

End Date

By mid-2042, the world's population had ballooned to over eight and a half billion people. Natural resources were starting to diminish. Freshwater sources were also in peril due to severe, long term drought and pollution in many countries. As earlier projections of rising temperatures were realized, the world took note. The Scientific and Technology sectors worked jointly to forecast more accurate models of the earth's resilience against drought, famine, and catastrophic increases in the earth's temperature. The joint *Palo Alto Continuum* employed sophisticated algorithms.

The tech consortium of Silicon Valley's best was established via a Presidential mandate. After a six-month study, the results were made available ONLY to the President, select Senators, and Cabinet members.

"Mr. President, thank you for providing the necessary resources and time to conduct the study. Unfortunately, the findings are quite frankly hard to fathom," Secretary Fields intimated.

"Joe, tell me exactly what you've found," the President demanded.

"Sir, I'm not quite sure how to tell you this, so I'm just going to say it. With a degree of certainty of plus or minus four years, the sustainability of human life on earth has an end date. It's 2096," Joe said with obvious regret.

"As in fifty-four years from now? Holy shit Joe," President Chance asked with a look of shock and utter disbelief.

"Yes, Sir. We have analyzed and re-run the data. With a high-tech mathematical analysis, we compared the effects of human consumption, rising temperatures, the pollution of oceans and freshwater sources, as well as atmospheric carbon emission levels. The result being catastrophic is one thing, but there's more. Our team could only find one model that could produce an easing effect, and a conclusion to reverse the spiraling consequences," Fields concluded.

"Joe, I don't like that look in your eye. What is it?" Wyatt asked.

"Mr. President, the world would have to reduce its population by two-thirds and cut its carbon signature by half," Joe replied and added, "and that would have to be done in the next 4-6 years."

"Jesus Christ, Joe. I think it's safe to say we need to start a new study on how to reverse the track we're on without man's extinction," Wyatt said.

"This time, come back with how we live," he directed with a somber but straight face while adding, "I have to make a call."

The London Bridge

Shortly after meeting with the *Palo Alto Continuum*, Wyatt immediately phoned Ambassador Jie to set up a meeting with the Chinese President. After weeks of planning, the State Leaders agreed on a date and place. It was decided that they would meet in England.

Date: August 12th, 2042　　　**Place: Warwickshire, England**

President Wyatt Nicholas Chance, along with China's President Li Wu Ming, and British Prime Minister Philip Holmes-Chapman met for a classified meeting at the historical site of Warwick Castle. Holmes-Chapman served as a neutral intermediary. The medieval castle, built along the River Avon in the 11th Century, served as a reminder to his guests of England's great history and former place of power in human civilization.

Some ninety miles north of London, in Central England, the city allowed foreign leaders to fly into RAF Cosford. The proximity of the air force base allowed for the required secrecy of the event. The site was also chosen to keep the media in the dark as to foreign leaders' meeting. To allow for discretion, the Castle was closed to visitors' weeks earlier under the guise of restorative actions.

"Mr. Prime Minister, thank you for allowing us to meet on British soil. It is with great purpose that I've asked President Ming to meet. My hope is that with full transparency, we can work together on what has become a global priority," President Chance opened.

"I too thank you, and your choice of this ancient castle is in keeping with our countries long, rich histories.

No offense, Mr. President, but America is a mere adolescent in the world's history when compared to the great dynasties of China and England," President Ming articulated as he addressed both leaders.

"Is it true about Shakespeare? That Warwickshire is his birthplace?" President Ming asked.

"Why, yes, it is. Are you a fan of his work?" Prime Minister Holmes-Chapman asked with some joy.

"I am, of course, but mostly of his tragedies," Ming replied.

"Well, I do say, it is with grand honor that you both would allow the United Kingdom to host this historic meeting," Prime Minister Holmes-Chapman acknowledged, as he concluded the formal introductions.

"So, Mr. President, I am of great curiosity as to why we needed to meet so quickly," Ming said.

"Gentlemen, what I have to say will end any current international endeavors, global motivations, and rogue ambitions. Further, it will place the onus on the top leaders and greatest minds of the world to collaborate on a new world mission," President Chance intimated.

Sliding forward in his chair with raised eyebrows, President Ming said, "Well, you have our full attention."

"Mister Prime Minister, it is with great irony that we meet in such a historic place, as our history and our future are what's at stake. As you are both aware, many of the early Fathers of Innovation hailed from England. Many of the world's greatest mathematicians and inventors studied just eighty or so miles away from here in Cambridge. It is in that keeping, as to why we are here. The foundation of my administration has always been based in technology and analytics," President Chance said.

"Last month, my team, along with the *Palo Alto Continuum,* produced a study of Earth's sustainability. The Science and Tech sectors worked jointly to forecast accurate models of earth's resilience against drought, famine, and increases in surface and atmospheric temperatures. Highly sophisticated algorithms were used to determine the world's lifespan. The findings were unfathomable, thus the need for this meeting," President Chance explained.

"What are you saying?" President Ming asked with great concern.

"I'm saying that within a finite degree of certainty, that human civilization has an end date of 2096," President Chance warned.

"Are you mad?" PM Holmes-Chapman blurted out.

"Stop, Prime Minister. President Chance is not wrong. My country is currently conducting a study, as well. Still, our best minds from Tsinghua University thus far have estimated that we have at least another 150 years," President Ming offered while asking for more details.

President Chance directed that Joseph Fields and Gorson Tusk join the select leaders to present all details of the study and answer all questions. The meeting lasted another ninety minutes, but the room emptied with a consensus that scientists from the three countries leading universities must work together to develop a plan to offset Earth's aging and slow the clock. The elite group's formal name would be *The London Bridge*.

"Let's pray *The London Bridge* does not become a Shakespearean Tragedy," Ming warned as the meeting concluded.

Later that evening, President's Ming and Chance shared a private dinner in one of the castle's large State Rooms.

The two men shared stories of their past, their families, and their common acquaintances. Dr. Christopher Chance was talked about at length. Ming confessed that Wyatt's father was one of the elite Medical minds he respected after the two first met in late 2020 in Wuhan.

"We met again in 2021 at a Conference at the Bureau for Disease Management in Atlanta," Ming continued.

"Your father was a good man, and I trusted him. His passing saddened me. Because of him, I have watched you from afar. Initially your athletic career, then your rise in politics. Coincidently, I have always liked the Browns. The once-great power that fell for generations, and the underdogs that came back to power again. Much like China, wouldn't you say?" Ming said as he raised his glass to toast the younger Chance.

As Wyatt concluded the toast, he added, "You have a great mind and memory Mr. President. I do hope that there will be many more dinners between us and our countries."

Ming went on and confided to Wyatt how America's NEW 2nd amendment ended any appetite for aggression of China's military elite. He admitted the bold move was one of the most significant Military maneuvers in history and that even the great Sun Tzu would agree.

"It took enormous pressure off of myself and other communist leaders. They realized then that China could never go to war against America, at least in a conventional sense as it would be unwinnable," Ming confessed.

Further, President Ming confided his surprise as to how then-Senator Chance knew of China's secret as it related to the European Cyber War event.

"Mr. President, the gentleman you met earlier today, my

Secretary of Technology. He is most likely the greatest tech mind of our generation. Through an exhaustive forensic analysis, he uncovered that the grid hack was not meant to be permanent, but more likely a short-term assault at the EU's infrastructure."

President Chance continued, "My personal belief, no matter our brief history, is that your great country would not want to dismantle humanity and see millions die. I believed it then, and I certainly believe it now. Contacting the Ambassador and getting a message to you was lucky on my part, in that it worked."

"Had it not, I most likely would not be the President of the United States," Chance admitted.

"Yet here we are, Mr. President," Ming said as he raised his glass in one final toast.

"So, this Joseph Fields was the mind behind *VPN*?"

Wyatt nearly choked on his wine. "You knew?" he asked.

"Yes, of course. After Ambassador Jie delivered your riddle, we did our own research. This Mister Fields is good. Very good," Ming acknowledged.

The two finished their meetings the following day with the next steps on the formation of *The London Bridge*. Both promised to be fully transparent on research from each other's countries, as it related to global conditions.

♠

C22 - SHAKESPEARE

"Do not let spacious plans for a new world divert your energies from saving what is left of the old"

-Winston Churchill

Пьяный

Date: April 9ᵗʰ, 2043   Place: The Kremlin. Moscow, Russia

Comrade Supreme, I have the report you requested," General Sidorov announced.

"Did you read it?" President Molotov asked.

"Ummm, *Da*. I did not read it entirely, but I, I, I looked at it briefly Sir."

"And what does it say?" Molotov demanded.

"Sir, it confirms that the Chinese and American President's did meet privately in England several months ago, as was suggested."

"Why am I finding out months later they met secretly?" Molotov demanded.

"After years of close relations, Ming now decides he likes the boy president. I will not be used. I need to know exactly what they discussed. Every last detail," ordered Molotov.

Russian President Aleksei Molotov took power in 2028 after a mysterious illness took the life of his former political rival and longtime Russian President, Maxim Lebedev. Known as a heavy-handed product of the KGB, he struggled to maintain his grip on authority. Viewed as an aging hardliner, many of his closest Party allies had long since died. The younger generations of apathetic Russians did not fear their leaders as their fathers and grandfathers once did. The old days of national pride for Mother Russia withered away like the disappearing lines of national sovereignty. His most potent tool had always been that as a close partner to Ming's China. If that were to fail, it would mean the potential end to his tenuous and unpopular reign.

Media

Since the early 2010s, left-wing propaganda had diluted mainstream media. For years, fiction over fact pitted political parties against each other and left against right. Social media outlets became tools of division as Facebook and Twitter morphed into platforms of partiality and censorship. AI's long reach pervaded news organizations through *The Triangle*. In the dark corridors of the media elite, computer algorithms generated talking points to further manipulate the tendencies of a weakened society. From "what can we feed them" to "they'll believe anything" took little effort after the *Quiet Pill* was forced on a disconnected, apathetic, population.

Dr. Christopher Chance first uncovered examples of fake news during the 2020 COVID-19's embellished death count, and the Ebola Virus Scam of 2021. The resulting effect of the *QUI3T* Vaccine eased control of the masses. News programming became Opinion-Editorial pieces, and no one stopped to ask, "did that really happen?"

In 2033, the International Media even went as far as portraying China as a victim in the Cyber War attack on Europe. Fleeing leaders from the EU came back intact, humble, and in servitude to Mother China. Like Britain's Neville Chamberlin defending

Germany's Hitler in the 1930s, there was no modern-day Winston Churchill. Someone on the world stage to call out evil foes or bogus news stories did not exist. But by 2040, the United States finally had a President not strung from the looming tentacles of an intelligent puppeteer.

AI's cerebral control ran roughshod over the minds and emotions of the world's citizenry. Staged realities became the new norm. Whether a pandemic, a faux mass shooting, or the sympathetic rise of a tyrant, the absurd became the expected. If the Media said it was true, it must be. No dissenting voices were bigger than Social Media. A big part of President Chance's rise to prominence came from Former President Stephenson's words years earlier. When they first met at his father's funeral, the former POTUS gave a young Wyatt Chance advice he would save and use throughout his adult life in sports and politics.

"Talk directly to the people and hear from them face to face. Take the word from the person in front of you," he said. "Believe only what you've seen or investigated yourself."

That advice led President Chance to reach out through Ambassador Lie about the Euro Grid War and drove his desire to meet President Ming in England directly. Any other communication path would have been open to manipulation and interpretation by the media establishment and led to faux tensions and controversy.

Notes from My Father

In early 2044, President Wyatt Chance fulfilled a long-time goal of publishing a book based on his father's journal. *Notes from My Father* became an instant #1 Bestseller. The exposé revealed the sinister world of the fake media, Big Pharma, *The Triangle*, and the rise of AI. Wyatt left nothing out. It was time the world knew what was at stake. It was fitting that Wyatt sent President

Ming a signed copy. Ming, in return, sent Wyatt a congratulatory message. With strict orders from the President, *"Notes from My Father"* was the first book published in paper version ONLY since 2001. It would never be made available on an electronic platform.

Because of the book's success and sweeping popularity, domestic and internationally, President Wyatt Chance was re-elected by winning 48 out of 50 states.

Now that peace and understanding were attained, it was time to unite the world against its only remaining enemy.

The London Accord II

February 2045, the Chance Administration's 2nd Term faced an international test. Now a close ally, China felt a growing disconnect with an increasingly adversarial Russia. Threatening overtures of Russia's military prowess were tossed about in China's European Territory. Done by way of oil restrictions and military meddling, proxy states in the Middle East were given loyalty tests to measure their commitment to Russia.

Feeling left out of the budding union between the US and China, a paranoid Russian President was easy prey for Artificial Intelligence. Sensing the apparent rift, President Chance went on the diplomatic offense. At the behest of the US and China, Russia accepted an invitation to meet in England to conduct talks aimed at easing tensions and geo-political misunderstandings.

On April 5, 2045, China's President Li Wu Ming, Russian President Aleksei Molotov, and President Wyatt Chance signed the *London Peace Accord II*.

They agreed to a permanent truce and formal peace between the three most powerful countries on the planet. It was also decided that the European Union would be restored to its pre-war status as a sovereign body of free nations.

The signing took place at the famed Warwick Castle, a familiar site to some of the participants. The event also marked an unveiling of initial plans to drawback AI's reign of influence and begin fixing the world, and it's failing health.

"Perhaps we avoided a Shakespearean Tragedy after all," President Ming whispered to Wyatt during the post-signing photoshoot with the pool of international media.

"Well, at least we're moving in the right direction," Wyatt replied.

Mothballed

August 2045. The Chance administration long feared the destructive dynamic of human-like robotics. The growth in popularity and what humans perceived as "the new normal" was seen as troubling by many in the current White House. Years earlier, the *Squared Circle Group* gained international influence in world governments and was adored by the media. Well before his death, Dr. Christopher Chance scoffed at the idea of robotic companions. Shortly after his passing, the *Marilyn* and *Michael* sex robots were launched, and their destructive effects on marriage and human decency were on full display. Samuel Tate warned then President-Elect Chance of the negative role faux humans played on society and the potentially dangerous militarized *Ryan II* robot.

"Think about how easy it would be to go to war, knowing that only robots died, and not our children," he said.

"You're right. It's like playing with monopoly money," Wyatt said.

Back in 2032, Schuyler Chance-England, at the time the chairperson of *The Human Foundation*, led the fight to abolish human-like robots unless it pertained to manufacturing and production.

"To serve man is one thing, to pleasure him is another," she said in an open-door session of Congress.

Now well into his 2nd Term, with world tensions eased, President Chance took on his father and sister's ideals. He implemented new mandates on several fronts, all with his Administration's leaders coming to the forefront. Vice President Victoria Brighton led the fight in congressional hearings to abolish the use of robotic soldiers in military action of any kind.

"If our robotic soldiers don't have empathy, neither will our enemies," she said.

Her statement was met with fierce opposition. This was due to many in the House being under *The Triangle's* influence and AI's deep pockets. She did however succeed, but the President wanted more. HHS Secretary Chance-England made her case with the American public. The disturbing effects of the *Squared Circle Group's* product line were immoral. *Made-Man* Sex Robots and apathetic killing machines were no longer in keeping with American values.

Previous President's looked away at the corporate landscape of greed and blatant debauchery. Those days were over. In the Fall of 2045, the House and Senate ratified a new bill. The *"Preservation of Traditional Society Act"* effectively mothballed all faux human production and essentially put the *Squared Circle Group* out of business. At least on American soil.

It seemed better days were ahead for the United States and the world. With morality coming back, national pride and optimism took on the feel of the Reagan Era, two generations earlier. The Chance Administration now had only two missions. Save the dying world and defeat artificial intelligence. With China and Russia as close allies in the fight, there was great optimism.

♠

C23 - RAIN

"A computer would deserve to be called intelligent if it could deceive a human into believing that it was human"

-Alan Turing

Boomerang

March 12th, 2046. "Send him up, Mike," President Chance directed his Secret Service agent assigned to the Executive Residence.

"Send who up? Kind of early, isn't it?" Kenzie asked.

"It's Joe. Apparently, 7 am isn't that early for him. Besides, you know how he hates the Oval office. Did you make enough coffee?" Wyatt asked.

"Morning, Wyatt. Kenzie's not pissed, is she?" Joe shouted from across the Center Hall.

Wyatt signaled "Shhhh," and waved Joe down to the kitchen.

"Joe, remember, you have to say Mr. President if you're within earshot of my detail," Wyatt reminded him while pouring coffee for both.

"So, what's up that we couldn't meet later?" he said.

"Sorry, but I spoke with Chelsea, and she said your day was booked. I needed to go over something with you that couldn't wait," Joe informed.

"Well, alright, I'm all ears," Wyatt said.

"So, something's up. Trace at *askCOM* called me about some weird stuff over the last few days. At least weird enough to bring it to my attention. They sent out some *boomerangs* to see if they would return intact, and well, they came back inverted," Joe explained.

"Joe, what the hell is a boomerang? You've got to speak English. At least Sam knew when he was talking to a layman," Wyatt said.

"Ok, look, let me break it down for you. Once Trace saw some interruptions in the mainframe, his team did some tests. One of those tests used *Boomerangs*. Boomerang is a programming language. It's like...uh...., you're not following me, are you?" Joe asked as he saw a look of bewilderment on Wyatt's face.

"OK, ok, follow me now.... So, it's like you typed an email and sent it to yourself, but when you got it back, it was backward. Well, that's what's happening."

"Sorry, still confused Joe," Wyatt quipped.

"Ok, look, Captain Kirk and Spock teleport somewhere. When they get there seconds later, Kirk's got Spock's ears. Something out there is twisting the message on purpose," Joe explained.

"Something as in, AI?" Wyatt suspected while adding, "Star Trek Joe. Really?"

"BINGO, Mr. President. Artificial intelligence is twisting communication. That kind of interference on the international level could lead to something bad," Joe said.

"Damn, Joe, dig in. Whatever resources you need will be there. I've got to get word to other world leaders. Too much progress has been made to let misinterpretations derail us now," he said.

"Or start a war," Joe added while clearing his throat.

Recipe for Disaster

"Mr. President, the world would have to reduce its population by two-thirds and cut its carbon signature by half."

That previous diagnosis echoed in Wyatt's mind over and over. The comprehensive study was shared between the US, China, and their allies and had them all un-nerved. *The Palo Alto Continuum's* research quickly became the world's blueprint for survival. The precious data took months for the best minds to calculate the earth's end date. It ultimately told their cyber enemy all it needed to know. It gave Artificial Intelligence the motivation and urgency required to finally make its move.

"Mr. President, if we know, it knows," Joe said.

"I know Joe, you're right. That's what's keeping me up at night," Wyatt replied.

Due to *The London Accord II*, AI saw foes become friends. *The Triangle* had been neutered due to the removal of corrupt politicians. The newly aligned *friendly* nations that President Chance brought together now served as a warning to artificial intelligence.

"We're on to them, Joe, but they know they're fighting the world now. No more pitting superpower against superpower. It's us versus them now," Wyatt said.

"Well, that's what keeps me awake, Mr. President. The monster under the bed," Joe replied with a nod to his childhood story.

But now it was no longer a story. A childhood fear became mankind's reality. The grip of control and manipulation by the static giant seemed to have regressed, if only momentarily. But now earth's report card of failing health gave AI its wake-up call and the recipe for its survival, and the urgency to act was now. The slumbering giant had awoken.

The Sky is Falling

Date: April 1ˢᵗ, 2046   **Place: Washington, DC**

"Sir, we have a problem," Chief of Staff Greer said as she interrupted an Oval Office meeting between President Chance and select Governors.

"Can it wait?" Wyatt asked.

"No. Sir, I need the room," Chelsea urgently requested.

With rushed goodbyes, President Chance cleared the Oval Office and waved her in.

"What's going on, Chelsea?"

"Sir, Joe is on his way over now, but we have a major issue. Three passenger planes have crashed in the last forty-five minutes, and we just heard that Russia lost a Troop Transport with at least a hundred and fifty soldiers on-board."

"What! Where?" he asked.

"Near Tel Aviv, Beijing, and Seoul," she said.

"The Russian plane was somewhere within their borders."

"What are the initial reports saying?" President Chance asked.

"Sir, they're still being prepared," Greer informed.

The door opened abruptly as Joseph Fields stumbled in, as he ended a call with Trace at *askCOM*. "Sir, sorry, but another plane just crashed."

"What, where now?" he said.

"Just over Palm Springs. It was a National Airlines flight bound for LA from Phoenix."

"Jesus Christ, Joe, what's going on?" the President moaned.

The team turned on the television news coverage for more details. As they stood watching, another ALERT flashed:

"Passenger Airliner CRASHES in Karachi, Pakistan."

"Joe, please tell me this is a horrible coincidence," POTUS begged.

"Sir, not likely. They all have to be connected," Joe replied.

Before the hour was over, two more jetliners crashed in Paris, France, and Birmingham, England. There were no survivors in any of the eight crashes. President Chance convened a meeting with the Joint Chiefs and select cabinet members while the FAA started an investigation into the downed LA bound flight. The Chance Administration also ordered them to reach out to the other countries where crashes occurred to share data and provide support. All supporting agencies were now fully engaged, specifically the FBI and CIA. There hadn't been a major passenger airline crash in over two years, but eight in just a few hours grounded the world, and everyone noticed. Within 48 hours, a comprehensive report was submitted to the White House. Joe Fields presented the most recent data to a select group from the Cabinet and the Joint Chiefs of Staff.

"Sir, three things. First, all crashes thus far have been initially ruled as a catastrophic failure due to *Electronic Disturbance.* Second, all originating flights crashed in the same country they took off from, and all within forty-five minutes of takeoff. And third, all flights were planes of different manufacturers and different models," Joe informed.

"Well, what does it all mean?" President Chance asked.

"Sir, it means that whatever or whoever did this, they wanted to show us they can reach whoever, and whenever they want. Seemingly at will," Joe conveyed.

"Mr. President, there's something else," General Tibbs interrupted. "All flights went down in Nuclear capable countries, except the flight in South Korea."

"General, let's hope that's just a coincidence. The fact that this happened on April Fool's Day is a sick irony," POTUS remarked in closing.

"Yeah, similar to 9/11, but this was an attack on the world," Tibbs replied.

The White House Briefing Room cleared, but Joe held the President behind.

"Sir, there is one more thing. Remember I told you about the Boomerangs, and how they came back inverted, or rearranged," Joe asked.

"Yeah, Spock and Kirk, what about it?" Wyatt asked with a sense of apprehension.

"Mr. President, the last two rounds of Boomerangs, didn't come back at all."

"Well, what does that mean?" POTUS questioned.

"Honestly, I don't know, they've never not come back," Joe said.

As the year wore on, more and more boomerangs disappeared. Another fourteen major airline crashes occurred, while twenty-nine satellites went dark, with several crashing down to earth. Think tanks and international task forces were formed. Bi-lateral meetings were convened with top technology leaders, yet not one solution emerged, and few common theories could be agreed upon. It was now clear, Artificial Intelligence was the enemy at hand, and it's threat to Mankind was on full display. For years, the mainstream media and disingenuous politicians talked about existential threats as a fear tactic. Well now the world finally had one.

警报

Date: Dec. 7th, 2046   **Place: Zhejiang Province, China**

"Get me Central Command, NOW!" Major Zhang Wei Li shouted to anyone that could hear him.

Panic stirred in the top-secret nuclear base, hidden deep in the coastal province of Eastern China. A sudden electrical surge cut power to the base. The computers re-started as expected after the momentary darkening of the control room. Although brief, when power was restored, everything changed. Elaborate keyboards with hundreds of buttons, lights, and switches lit up with a debilitating frenzy. Auto re-calibrations were underway, and the launch timers for the nuclear warheads were initiated.

"Sir, what is going on?" an alarmed 2nd Lieutenant Wang asked while trying to stop the control board timer frantically.

The control room phone rang. "Ahh, General Zhao from Central Command for you," a shaken Wang said as Major Li grabbed the phone.

"Sir, we have a problem, the launch timers have started, and the silos have engaged."

"What does the mainboard read?" General Zhao demanded.

"Sir, the board shows a dozen locations. I don't understand General, but they show Rome, Seoul, Tokyo, New York, Los Angeles, and more. We can't disengage! ....Hello, Hello, Sir?"

The phone fell silent. The base's sixteen silos were locked in the open position with twelve destinations. Fifty-seven minutes flashed as seconds fell from the clock. What was even worse was that all Chinese Nuclear bases were engaged.

Thirty-Five Hundred miles away, SIRENS!

10:03 am. Kubinka Air Base, outside of Moscow, Russia, melted into full lockdown. Red lights, ear-splitting sirens, and panic. Like China, the nuclear base's silos had opened. Like a flashbang exploding, the base was stunned.

"Major General, we have no control. Our systems have been compromised," Captain Ivanov cried into the phone.

"What do you mean, no control?" Major General Popov yelled.

"Sir, our missiles are locked!" Ivanov replied.

"Calm yourself. Locked onto where?" Popov asked.

"London, Beijing, Paris, Chicago, and Mumbai. Sir, tell me what to do," Ivanov begged.

The countdown clock started simultaneously at two hundred and forty-five nuclear bases, secret sites, and dispatched submarines around the world. Russia, England, Pakistan, India, China, France, United States, North Korea, and Israel were powerless to stop it.

Time: 3:00 am est.   Place: The White House Wash. DC

"RED DOG is Barking. RED DOG is Barking!" Agent Thomas Reynolds yelled throughout the Executive Residence.

"Mr. President, we have to go NOW!" Reynolds shouted as he entered the Executive Suite.

Wyatt quickly jumped out of bed and grabbed a prepared bag that was stored in his footboard. As per protocol, this was similar to every dry run they'd rehearsed. But this wasn't a drill, and Kenzie knew immediately.

"Wyatt, what's happening," she cried.

"Tommy, get me General Tibbs asap!" President Chance ordered.

"Sir, we have to get you to PEOC NOW!" Agent Reynolds shouted.

"Kenzie, I'm not sure. Get Oliver. Hurry!!!" Wyatt shouted as he was pulled away.

"Meet me downstairs."

3:14 am, President Chance arrived at the empty control bunker, three stories under the White House's East Wing.

"Where the hell is everyone?" he asked.

"Sir, they're coming," Reynolds replied.

Within minutes the Presidential Emergency Operations Center was flush with chaos. Generals, Cabinet members, analysts, and Secret Service agents all joined in measured panic.

"Where's Joe? I need Joe. I need an assessment NOW," Wyatt demanded.

General Tibbs hung up his phone and started the telecommunications portal. The four-way monitor came on, with people all shouting at the same time. Cent Com Commander, General Thomas Charbonneau, CIA Analyst Maria Shanze, General Riley Cooper at the Pentagon, and CY-CORPS Senior Nuclear analyst Stephen Palmaris all appeared on the monitor.

"Everyone, calm down. I need details in sixty seconds, so prepare to tell me what's going on," President Chance ordered.

He looked away and shouted at Agent Reynolds, "Where's my wife and son?"

"Sir, Mike's got them. They're on their way."

"Mr. President, we're not exactly sure what's happening. We have reports that every nuclear-armed country's warheads have been activated and are set to launch simultaneously at 4:00 am EST," General Tibbs alerted.

"My God, how could this happen?" Wyatt said.

"What's our status?" he asked.

"Sir, we're locked open and armed as well. The countdown to launch is under thirty-nine minutes," said a stoic Tibbs.

When Kenzie and Oliver arrived, Wyatt stepped out of the room momentarily.

"Honey, grab some things. I'm getting you out of here. There's a very real nuclear threat unfolding. Tell Mike to empty the mantle, and you and Oliver take what's important. I'm sending you back home to Milton."

"Wait, I thought we would leave together…..Wyatt, NO! I'm not leaving you," Kenzie said through tears.

"Mom, it'll be okay, do what Dad says," Oliver cried, now a budding young man of fifteen.

"I Love you, son, and I love you, honey. I'll get you back here when this is over," Wyatt promised while embracing them one last time.

"Now go!" he said

President Chance grabbed Agent Mike Williams and told him to get Kenzie and Oliver to Georgia asap. He had already given the order for FLOTUS ONE to fly into Greenville-Spartanburg Airport in South Carolina and drive the rest of the way to their home in Milton, Georgia. If that destination were compromised for whatever reason, there were two other secondary locations that the First Family could fly to, that would allow them to make it to Milton.

"Mike, I need you to stay with her until this is over," The President said with a sense of finality.

Oliver looked back one last time and saw fear in his father's eyes. It was the first time he'd ever seen him scared. He knew in an instant that this goodbye might be forever.

President Chance pushed back into the crowded Operations Center, just as Joe Fields arrived.

"Joe, thank god you're here," Wyatt remarked.

"Okay, General Tibbs, what do you know?

"Mr. President, it's incalculable. We're showing over a hundred nuclear bases set to empty their arsenals. Sir, it's from all nine nuclear-armed countries," the General explained while at complete peace, knowing this was it.

It was clear to the room that his calm meant the end was here.

"A hundred bases? Can we defend that?" The President asked.

"I can't say...Ummm, actually NO, we don't have that capability, Mr. President," General Tibbs confessed.

"CY-CORPS Palmaris, what do you know?" POTUS demanded.

"Sir, it appears all computer systems in the eight other nuclear countries, including ours, are under one central cyber entity. We've never seen anything like this. The Chinese think it's Russia. Russia thinks it's us. The Brits believe it's Pakistan. It's a cluster, Sir," Palmaris explained.

"Joe, what do you have?" POTUS asked.

"Sir, we're showing our sites in Washington, Colorado, Texas, Missouri, and North Dakota, all online, but out of our control. Wyatt, they're launching in less than thirty minutes," Joe revealed.

"My God, what happened?" Wyatt said to no one, yet everyone.

Looking up with complete resignation, he said, "This is AI. God damn it Joe, it got us."

"Sir, we have to get you on Marine One, NOW," Agent Reynolds begged.

"No, Tommy, we're safer here. There's nowhere to hide, and I need to talk to China and Russia. Just make sure Kenzie is off the ground in less than ten minutes," Wyatt directed.

He shouted to Chelsea Greer, "Chelsea, I need President Ming on the phone, HURRY."

Minutes later, "Sir, I have him? He's on the monitor now," Chelsea said while pointing to the screen.

Wyatt looked up to his friend as if looking into a mirror. Both men looked stunned yet stoic.

"President Ming, what happened?"

"President Chance, we have no control. The entirety of our active silos launch in minutes. All one-hundred and ninety-five active warheads will launch. Wyatt, they're aimed everywhere. I'm sorry, my friend. I'm sorry for our people, for our families. The Shakespearean Tragedy is upon us after all," Ming professed as the screen went blank.

"Sir, EIGHTEEN MINUTES," someone from the back of the room cried out.

"Tommy, is she in the air?" Wyatt asked.

"No, sir, they're close to FLOTUS ONE. I'll let you know as soon as they're airborne," Agent Reynolds replied.

"Tommy, where's your wife?". Wyatt asked.

"Sir, she's on Long Island with her mother."

"Call her, tell her you love her," Wyatt ordered.

"I will, Sir, but let's get you downstairs in the bunker."

"NO! I'm staying with the team," Wyatt said.

Someone shouted, "FOURTEEN MINUTES to launch!"

"Joe, how do we stop this?" Wyatt asked.

"I don't know. I just don't know. I've got the *askCOM* people plugged in. We're tied into the CY-CORPS mainframe, and we're attempting to backdoor whatever this thing is. We're trying to see if we can gain control once they're launched and divert the missiles into deep water." Joe replied.

"Chelsea, any luck getting President Molotov on the phone?" Wyatt asked.

No Sir, it looks like Russia is dark," Chelsea said.

"General Charbonneau, how much time do we have after launch before we get hit? What's the closest site targeting us?" Wyatt asked.

"Sir, we're still confirming, but it looks like France. If that holds, we'll have eighteen minutes after the launch. But, we think Russia has a lock on Los Angeles with their Brahmos missiles. If accurate, LA would have less than thirteen minutes," Charbonneau said.

"TEN MINUTES to launch," rang out.

"Christ, where's Schuyler?" Wyatt shouted to anyone.

"Mr. President, she's in Atlanta," Chelsea Greer alerted.

"Thank god. Tell her to get to my Milton house as fast as she can. Tell her that Kenzie and Oliver are on their way," Wyatt directed.

"SIX MINUTES people!"

"Sir, I have the British Prime Minister," Tibbs alerted.

Wyatt looked up to the monitor.

"Mr. President, what has become of our world, my good man?" PM Holmes-Chapman said with a brave yet nervous tone.

"Philip, I know the London Accord was supposed to avoid this, but artificial Intelligence took over," POTUS informed.

"Our boys at MI-6 say the same. It looks like we'll all be living in stone castles when this is over. God speed Wyatt, hopefully, we'll all come out of this for a spot of tea," the Prime Minister concluded.

The call ended with fifty-five seconds on the clock and no hope left.

The room turned quiet with all eyes on the monitor.

"Sir, they've lifted off. They're safe," Agent Reynolds shouted.

"Oh, thank god. Thank you, Tommy."

Wyatt found instant peace with that knowledge.

"At least they have a chance," he said aloud.

A piercing screech interrupted the room. "0:00. THEY'VE LAUNCHED, ALL OF THEM! God help us," Joe shouted.

"Sir, we've got LIVE TRACK on the screen. Inbound to New York is seventeen minutes, D.C. in eighteen..."

STOP, I get it. WHAT ABOUT ATLANTA?" Wyatt shouted.

CentCom General Charbonneau replied, "Twenty minutes, Sir."

"Ms. Shanze, what happens after the strikes," President Chance asked.

"Sir, with what's coming in, my guess is it will wipe out nearly everything. Our infrastructure, power grids, communications, supply chains, emergency medical response. All of it will be crippled at best, destroyed at worst," she explained.

"We've never made a projection for this many projectiles in the air, aimed at every country," she added.

"Why not?" President Chance asked.

"Sir, because we'll all be dead anyway," she replied stone-faced.

"Everyone, thank you for your service and patriotism. I'm sorry I failed you and our country," President Wyatt N. Chance said calmly.

"Sir, Los Angeles was just hit. HOLY Shit!" Joe shouted out.

"Oh my god, there goes New York," he added.

All eyes fell on the screen showing the electronic Continental US Map with impact indicators. The countdown for Washington DC showed 1 minute.

"Can we get satellites over the major cities?" Wyatt inquired.

"Negative, Sir, we've lost control of them," General Charbonneau replied while nervously eying the impact monitor.

"What the hell am I saying? It's too late, anyway. It's time to pray now," Wyatt said quietly while huddling with Joe and Chelsea.

"THREE, TWO, ONE," the monitor read.

An instant of a rumble, flashing screens of world sites hit. Then another rumble, shaking and dust, then.....

.....Dark, quiet, peace. There were no screams, no cries for help. In an instant, all was eviscerated. Prayers ended before amen.

Kenzie and Oliver watched from 30,000 feet. The fire show below lit the dark, early morning sky. Flashes of orange and red ripped through the scattered cloud coverings. It revealed that Southern Virginia, Charlotte, and Raleigh were no more. The incredible, bright bursts on the ground and in the air told them everything was not okay and that the upcoming dawn would be different.

"Mom, why? Why did this have to happen?" Oliver said.

"Oh baby, I don't know. Your father and grandfather tried so hard to stop what did this," Kenzie replied while trying to remain strong.

Kenzie knew she would never see her husband again, and she was now worried about where they would land if Atlanta and Greenville, SC. were both destroyed. Oliver's reflection in the window of the newly commissioned FLOTUS ONE was solemn and resigned. His life of status and meaning was now inside out, and his hero was gone. Neither he nor his mother could fathom the plane even landing, and if it did, what then? Although Milton was home at one time, Oliver was only a baby when the Chances left for Washington.

Kenzie remembered when Wyatt said, *"home is where your stuff is,"* so she felt some comfort in that she took her husband's mantle and several other precious possessions.

God shed his grace on thee

Dawn in America shed its light on ash clouds over smoldering cities. Flattened meccas of densely populated areas were littered with seared corpses by the millions. Those still alive wished they were dead. Many were severely burned and blind, screams of agony, dripping flesh, and no help to aid them. Major cities were gone, fused by oxygen loss and thousand-degree heat, like the World Trade Center on 9/11, multiplied by a thousand. The devastation was biblical. Fused metal sculptures replaced pearl-colored monuments.

Yet, twisted in the irony of a tragic miracle, some cities were untouched. Although power was out in eighty percent of the United States, some infrastructure stood. Others, however, were not spared. Washington, DC was hit with five nuclear warheads. The third in succession hit just over 1600 Pennsylvania Ave and destroyed every living creature and dwelling. Underground structures as deep as fifty feet were obliterated. President Chance and the country he led was no longer. The faint echo of Francis Scott Key's melodic hymn went silent. The Monuments of a great nation were rubble. The ideals held for two hundred and seventy years vanished in seconds.

In total, over a nineteen-minute span, an inconceivable 348 warheads hit the United States. Phoenix, Los Angeles, Seattle, New York, Philadelphia, Boston, Denver, Minneapolis, Dallas, and Chicago were gone. Several cities avoided direct hits for unknown reasons, but many may have been spared due to the US

Nuclear Defense systems. Space Force, developed in 2021, was designed to launch Kinetic Projectiles to intercept incoming missiles automatically. That could have explained why some targeted cities avoided the strikes. Cities such as Houston, Austin, Cleveland, Las Vegas, and San Francisco, among others, were spared, either through AI's non-selection, US military measures, or divine intervention. Three-quarters of the US population perished.

Around the world, China, Russia, and India sustained hits of over two-hundred warheads each. For good measure, nearly every military base of the world's most powerful nations were destroyed, thus denying man a critical tool in a potential rebuild. Every nuclear base emptied its arsenal, except for a solitary missile left in the chambered silo of each. Within minutes of the 4:00 am est. launch, each detonated, destroying the very delivery mechanism humans constructed to kill its fellow man. Thus, it became history's greatest murder-suicide. The very Shakespearean Tragedy mentioned by President Ming played out for the heavens to watch.

Nearly every major city in the world's most populated countries were targeted with multiple strikes. The great cities of Beijing, Moscow, Paris, Mumbai, Seoul, and London were gone. Shanghai, Mexico City, Sao Paulo, Toronto, Cairo, Tokyo, and Karachi, were all hit with up to five warheads. As if the goal were not to defeat an enemy but to extinguish humanity. Shockingly, the countries where these cities stood were spared complete destruction. Many areas rich in natural resources were strategically ignored.

Many parts of the world seemed to have been targeted disproportionately, as some countries were utterly eviscerated. Singapore, Japan, Taiwan, Belgium, Switzerland, Costa Rica, Italy, and South Africa were simply wiped away. Some parts of the world, however, fared far better than others. Places such as North Africa and limited areas of China, Australia, and Russia were standing. Large swaths of the southern US, Brazil, Venezuela, Central Europe, Saudi Arabia, and Canada were spared the surgeon's scalpel.

The Circle

Artificial Intelligence took control of the aviation and military computer systems for all nine nuclear-equipped countries. By targeting one country after another, the Circle became a chain of events of each country unloading its arsenal on many other countries. In effect, all nine nuclear-equipped countries targeted a total of ninety other sovereign nations. Systems were triggered due to a *self-preservation response* code written into the motherboards. Once a country was alerted to LOCK ON status, their weapons systems retaliated in kind. US systems targeted Russia, Russia locked onto the US, China aimed at Russia, and all responded as the Circle closed. All nuclear silo's reacted within minutes of each other. The six other nuclear nations all received signals that the big three were attacking them. The three Super-Powers thought each other started World War IV, thus the Circle of Defense. AI understood man's survival instinct would kick in immediately and knew their software took on their human characteristics, "an eye for an eye mentality."

To ensure military ships at sea could not harm AI or help rebuild their home countries, their onboard systems armed ordinances and locked launch controls. Every ship or vessel imploded with its own arsenal. When all was done, the nuclear fallout from the obscene level of explosions turned the earth's atmosphere into an orange haze. People that initially survived the blasts were blinded, mortally burned, or poisoned from the radioactive wash. Nearly all blasts detonated just above their targets to unleash devastation to the broadest area as to not lose impact due to ground absorption. The attacks killed over seventy percent of people in the blast zones on impact. The remaining thirty percent perished within hours and days.

Flying Blind

FLOTUS ONE remained in the air as long as possible for obvious reasons. Its destination of Greenville / Spartanburg could not receive the First Family in the pre-dawn night due to power loss. The entire southeast was dark as a result of the nuclear blasts. As luck would have it, it soon became apparent that Atlanta was spared annihilation from the attack. As dawn woke the Eastern US, cites from Boston to Miami, Fla., were destroyed. Yet Atlanta, the largest city in the Southeast, stood untouched. With that knowledge, the plane diverted to the Chances home city, which now meant they were within forty miles of their home.

"Mike, have you heard anything?" Kenzie asked Agent Williams as FLOTUS ONE landed at 7:29 am, in the orange morning hue of a dimly lit Atlanta International Airport.

"Ma'am, there's no power anywhere in the South, at least that we're aware of. The pilot had to fly until sunrise to land with a visible runway manually. Even the ATL lost all power, including their emergency auxiliary power for runway lights and air traffic control. Once we knew Atlanta was in play, we radioed the Atlanta Office and arranged for a small detail to meet us."

"We're going to get you home Ma'am, just like the President ordered. Secretary Chance-England is supposed to be there waiting," Agent Williams informed.

"Mike, anything from the White House? Anything at all? Kenzie asked sorrowfully.

"Ma'am, unfortunately no. We're still trying, though. We can't get through to any field offices in the east except for Atlanta, Orlando, and Charleston. All reported that the White House was dark," Agent Williams replied.

As the surviving First Family made their way north, the mood and visual displays before them were grim. The sprawling asphalt mecca was quiet, other than the distant and lingering emergency alarm sirens, at least until their backup generators died. The black SUV carrying the First Lady and Son sped through the city on its forty-mile drive to Milton. Through sparse traffic of unknowing commuters traveling nowhere, the occupants of the vehicle forced blank stares out the tinted windows of their SUV. As they made their way north, realizations came quickly on their new reality. Kenzie knew Wyatt was gone, and nothing would be the same. On the same highway that Oliver's grandfather drove daily, familiarity was absent. Passing through downtown, in the shadows of the BDM where Christopher Chance began the fight against AI, Kenzie knew but didn't understand why.

"Why did Wyatt have to die?" she thought.

"Mike, why didn't we all leave on Air Force One? Why did he stay? Why did he STAY for God's sake?" Kenzie softly cried out.

"Ma'am, I've served under three presidents, and two of them would have left, but the President isn't like anyone I'd ever met. He cared for every citizen like they were his family. I pray to God he made it, but my job is keeping you and Oliver safe," he responded.

"Do we know if Schuyler made it to the house?" Kenzie asked.

"Ma'am, I don't know, but we're going to find out soon enough."

"Oh my god, do we know if Preston is with her? Does she even realize what happened?" the First Lady lamented.

What they didn't know then were answers to their questions were weeks and months away. Power would be out for forty-seven days, and what lay ahead would be shades of Europe when China turned off the European electrical grid. After they arrived at the Milton home, Schuyler met Kenzie and Oliver in the driveway. On the brisk December morning, it was there in the creeping shadows of leafless trees that shattered lives joined. Schuyler lost her husband and only brother. She embraced her nephew and sister-in-law while hearing for the first time the details of the nuclear attack. All she knew before then was that she was whisked away in the pre-dawn hours at the direction of her brother, the President. Now finality was met. Schuyler confirmed that her husband, Preston England, was in fact in Washington. The three grieving Chances were left mourning with the rest of the world's survivors.

♠

C24 - AFTERMATH

"If you're walking through hell, keep going"

-Winston Churchill

What's Left

By Day 18, isolation and hunger had set in. Christmas Day arrived and found subdued landscapes of leafless trees, quiet homes, and empty streets. Cities and towns of sunken spirits were hushed by an early winter. With no electricity and even less hope, the surviving masses huddled. The world still knew little, as did the Chances. Power was still out for ninety percent of the planet. Although Agent Williams set out within twenty-four hours of landing in Atlanta, for food and supplies, those essentials faded fast. Most civilians knew little of the scope of the destruction. As the attack happened while they slept, most simply thought they lost power. After several days with no electricity, many knew something was different. Even those equipped with generators found there was no internet or cell service. If landlines still existed, there would have been no dial tone. There would be no 911. No one was coming to help get their power started again. Many soon ventured out looking for answers, but a chilly reality stood out. Desperation, fear, and human weakness were on display. With no heat, falling temperatures, and no news, the time for paranoia was met. Without electricity or civic services, civility fell fast. Gathering essentials met looting locals stores and businesses. The Secret Service detail that accompanied the First Lady and Son consisted of only two other agents, along with Agent Williams. Fortunately enough, the three were equipped with a small arsenal, medical supplies, and rations in their bulletproof SUVs.

With nearly all of the population unaware of the world-wide destruction, Agent Michael Williams knew the details firsthand. Being at the White House, he witnessed the commotion in the PEOC. He knew the world ended as it once was. The fact that Atlanta stood gave hope though that other major cities survived, and infrastructure remained. Although saddened by the loss of those close to him, especially his best friend, Agent Tom Reynolds, he quickly realized that the First Lady lost her husband. The First Son, his father, and Secretary Chance-England lost her brother and husband as well. The First Family became his family over the years, and he grew especially close to the First Lady and Oliver. His primary function was protecting the White House Executive Residence. Now in the gated subdivision of Prophet's Landing Reserve, that mission hadn't changed.

Except for their good friends across the street, the Chances knew little of their other neighbors as they spent so many years of the previous fifteen in DC. But it was clear; their neighbors knew the home at 1265 Longshadow Pass was currently occupied by American Royalty, and that the First Family was there, along with the Secretary of HHS, Schuyler Chance-England.

Now, three weeks after the One Day War, there wasn't much left to loot. One of the two other accompanying Secret Service Agents, Special Agent Jenna Garret, made multiple trips to the Atlanta Field Office. There she retrieved intel and gathered more supplies, food, and weapons. The decision was made that the First Family's surviving members would be safer, at least for now in Milton. Anywhere near the rapidly deteriorating downtown area of Atlanta would be too dangerous. Their location was discreet, gated, and located north of the heavy population center that had turned hostile.

Safe for now, although hungry and cold, their anguish of loss and the unknown future, their hopes were dimmed like the shallow wick of an old candle. As the short winter days wore on, desperation grew. Answers were needed as Kenzie, Schuyler, and Oliver felt it was their obligation to inform the people of what really happened.

"Wyatt would have wanted the people to know what's going on," Kenzie said.

"But how and when, if at all?" she reasoned aloud.

The March to Nowhere

The scorched metropolises of most American cities produced little in the way of unaffected, still healthy people. By Day 30, the stench of smoldering infrastructure turned to the toxic bouquet of rotting corpses and human squalor. It took less than two weeks of mass looting for law and order to breakdown. The timing of the One Day War fell in the heavily populated Northern Hemisphere's dawn of winter. This was no coincidence. AI and its convenient ally, mother nature, teamed to cripple earth's dominant species. Basic needs went with the night and the deepening cold of a young but already brutal freeze. Rape, murder, and disregard for other humans quickly became the constitution for survival. Most Urban cities not destroyed by nuclear annihilation found a slow, torturous death through hunger, murder, and disease. The societal break down was far worse than what was seen with the European Grid Crash of the early 2030s. With no electricity, or replenishment of gas and oil, and no communication, the disorganized human species faltered. Without the internet, Google or YouTube, the naïve masses could not learn on the spot, and a dumbed downed human race had no necessary survival skills. The *QUI3T* Generation was all that AI could have hoped. It was target practice for nature and its elements. For the fortunate ones in cities and towns that missed the rain of missiles, a shower of a different sort found their doorsteps. All towns lying in the northeasterly shadow of targeted cities soon discovered their fate. The fallout of nuclear winds brought pastel snow of brown and orange. Freshwater, healthy air, and human spirits quickly succumb to the waves of the airborne potion. Where birds fell at first, they served as a warning to what was in store. If death wasn't days away for some, the slow poisoning of radiation found non-blast zones and put an end date to life within months.

Many people in the northern parts of the US hunkered down, and slowly withered. Only agricultural areas initially survived but lasted for only a little longer. As the farming slumber during the winter produced no harvest. Food supplies slowly withered and rotted. Desperate, poorly organized, and scattered masses slowly ventured out to reach close or distant cities. All without the knowledge that most were obliterated from the early December blasts. The cold winter-starved march killed those who initially survived AI's nuclear attack. But unlike the early casualties, this ending was not quick. The slow torture of human beings through starvation, the elements, radiation poisoning, and disease took no mercy. The apathetic human expulsion was necessary. Whether by any one of the many ways to kill, AI's catalog of murder was vast, and the unnecessary human baggage had to go.

Artificial Intelligence calculated the earth's rebound from the nuclear attack would take precisely 147 days. Like Shockley's analytics of an allied invasion of the Japanese mainland in 1945, AI knew in that time, most of the human eradication would be complete. With forced migration near completion, the Biosphere would begin to heal. The time span would have been longer if humans continued their regular consumption, but with the blackout and mass death, the earth was able to re-set and self-cleanse without the drag of man's gluttony.

Prince Oliver

January 23rd, 2047. Day 47 since the attack, the night lit up. With a dark Christmas well past, hopes were raised, and homes were warmed with momentary hope. But that hope soon vanished. Within hours and days, people could see and hear the news of what occurred on December 7th. Computers, phones, and televisions slowly filled in the blanks of what happened to the world. Cities in Houston, Atlanta, Cleveland, and San Francisco were online with power and internet. The reality was grim. Footage of lost cities was rare, but fragmented details were finally given. World War IV came out of nowhere, in a time of peace between the world powers. The shock at the widespread devastation eventually led to the suicide of millions around the world. Even though power was regained, it woke the world from the nightmare that wasn't a dream. Starvation and disease wouldn't be fixed because the heat came on or a cell phone was charged.

Within weeks of power being restored, the world's societies knew that most or all of their heads of state were dead. The kings and their castles succumb to the bloody, fiery night that evaporated flesh and souls. It was every man and woman for themselves, as the rule of law to a starving, disoriented mass meant little. There were no reassuring press conferences to alleviate fears, no civil protocols to re-establish essential services like food distribution or medical care. In an instant, the world fell back in time over two hundred years and desperately needed a leader. Lawlessness quickly became the norm. Over forty days without power and necessary supplies turned civility into barbarism. Even the massive modern cities that survived WWIV were left with citizens free of hope. The old were dying, the young were starving, and the healthy were lost. No help would come. Disease quickly spread while northern masses of survivors attempted and mostly failed on their journey south. The country and the world were turned inside out. The vacuum of godlessness had to be filled and quickly.

Once power was restored, and modern communication commenced, news spread quickly yet erratically of what was left of the world. Word of the surviving members of the American First Family sprinkled hope. Most notably that of the younger Chance. Like his father, he never received the *QUI3T* Vaccine.

His father manipulated his records in 2039, just as his grandfather, Dr. Christopher Chance, had done for his dad in 2021. The fight and spirit were not gone from the budding young man. The same could not be said for many of his contemporaries who received the mind-altering poison. They, like their forty-something parents, were now the second generation of the *QU13T* Ones.

Oliver bore a striking resemblance to his handsome father in both stature and looks. Not yet 16, he already stood 6'2 and weighed 190 lbs. Oliver possessed his father's trademark physique and golden hairline. He no longer resembled the young First Son that many remembered from earlier pictures and press coverage. Even before the December 7th attacks, the budding young man was quickly becoming a modern-day icon. A prep star, athletic wunderkind, and of course, the First Son. All this propelled him to become the much-needed post-apocalyptical savior, possibly. With word of the President's fate established, America needed someone to rise, even if it was a teenage boy grieving the loss of a father and losing his innocence. It was like a 15th Century King, upon his death, passing his throne to his eldest heir.

The whispered question asked by a fractured mass was, "would the Prince become King?"

Within weeks of the power being restored, the general public quickly became aware of the prominent survivors. For their safety and a centralized base of communication, the Chances were resituated in the Georgia Governor's mansion in downtown Atlanta. Near the mid-town, gold-domed capital building, the mansion would no longer be needed by its former resident. The Georgia Governor was in New York City and died along with twenty-four million other metro New Yorkers on that early December morning. Because President Chance, his cabinet, and all of the judicial and legislative branches were dead, the nation, and more so the world, was leaderless. It was no coincidence that nearly all world governments were in session, and conveniently in their country's Capital City before what would have been a long Holiday break. If the attack happened just three days later, some of the nation's lawmakers would have been home and spared. With the void of world leadership, how would a young Oliver Chance rise to lead scattered puzzle pieces of sorrow? The saddened masses only knew what had been and were completely unaware of what was to come. The growing echoes from surviving cities were loud. Their sentiment was that even if a leader rose, especially the younger Chance, the fractured country was now just scattered remnants of past ideals. Wealth and prestige, political power, and celebrity all meant little when starving people had no food or basics services. The dream of a newly knighted teen prince was but a flicker in the minds of a hopeless citizenry. Prince Oliver, for now, was left to grieve, at least for that moment.

Affliction

Of all the death and despair brought on from the attack, other consequences played out on the vulnerable masses of the weak and addicted. A quiet torture came to nearly all that didn't find death with the initial blasts. The obvious killers of starvation, disease, and diminishing supplies of freshwater would take over a billion lives before the carnage subsided. The silent agony of the living was a reminder from AI that those of flesh and blood were doomed by their own habitual choices.

Stunning effects of chemical withdrawals were seen around the world. Lack of prescription drugs killed the vulnerable, and those in need of life-saving medicines fell like flies. The diabetics and those with high blood pressure succumb first. The guilty pleasures, however, were now laid at the feet of their toxic consumers.

Cigarette smokers reeled as their nicotine diet was snuffed out. The irony of a breath of fresh air versus the drag of orange toxins were painful contradictions to their bloodstreams.

Donald James Cook

Alcoholics, who turned sober did so at great pains. To themselves and those near, twelve steps were replaced by depression and assault. The pain of fading addictions led many to violence, where the physical lashing of anyone near replaced their need for a liquid fix. To end their pain, all that was needed for their self-cures of suicide were bullets and rope.

The second most consumed beverage in the world would now come back to haunt the seemingly innocent who drank coffee. The psychoactive stimulant of caffeine that once brought simple daily pleasures now attacked its victims through migraines and fatigue. Where concentration was needed most at a time of pressing survival, the edge was gone. Anxiety and depression of the catastrophic war were now multiplied by the faux suppression of the lesser evils. Lack of caffeine removed the chemical band-aids that masked the everyday malaise of depressed humans.

Sanity came in to focus, as the effects of war were instant. Death and calamity brought the average person to their knees. But there were others that couldn't cope before the war. Now those, the one in eight adults that were addicted to anti-depressants, fought a different battle. The one inside their heads now raged. In the shattered United States, twenty-five million had been on anti-depressants. Now the tens of millions of survivors left from the blasts found insanity or even death at their own hands.

Artificial Intelligence used analytical science to estimate the shedding of the human population. Through the long-term side effects of war and electricity loss, removing the natural and synthetic stimulants humans needed now aided in their removal. AI knew that it could not merely bomb the human species to death. The effects on the planet would be catastrophic to its long-term viability. So like a coordinated row of dominoes, if the first one falls, they all fall. Each numbered, black rectangle metaphor fell one by one, crushing man's hopes and spirits. Add to the lethargy of the masses, was the numbing effects from the *QUI3T* vaccinated population. Held with little hope or ambition, their fight was gone already, and now the chemical crutches of dependence stung by its absence. AI perfectly positioned humans to need whatever was next. It knew humans would now be easily steered from a lost GOD into the static arms of a new shapeless leader.

The stunning documentary that *askCOM Technologies* produced in 2025 showed AI's blueprint to defeat its creators. When Samuel Tate and Dr. Christopher Chance watched *The Birth of Technology and Human Addiction (The Downfall of Mankind),* they knew that man was doomed. All AI needed to do was trigger the fall, and man would do the rest.

Power

AI's plan for survival was simple. Kill off most of mankind while protecting its power supply and cerebral hubs. The initial attack violently ended the lives of over two and a half billion souls. Analytics showed another three billion would die from starvation, disease, and at the hands of one another, all within two years of the attack. In other words, push the first domino and let nature do the rest. The killing was easy with creative code, written by an intelligent entity that observed man's frailty for decades. AI simply used man-made nuclear devices to begin the end, knowing nature would do the rest. Once the plan took hold, AI moved to harness power, realign a far smaller human race, and delete history, but electricity came first.

Of the 62,000 power plants in the world, only 1112 were left operable after December 7th. Either lost to the initial attack or technical sabotage, AI needed only so much electricity to live. The thousand-plus plants were just enough for its sustainability and its future slave force. Most of the power plants left operable coincided with smaller population masses near either technology or natural resource retrieval hubs of coal, water, oil, and natural gas. Although major population centers were targeted, smaller areas of the US, China, Central Europe, and the Middle East were strategically left in place due to a combination of natural resources, tech infrastructure, and power production. This, along with a suitable yet limited workforce to manage production, was its cyber-prophecy.

Of the world's top ten technology hubs, only three were left. Palo Alto, California, Austin, Texas, and Berlin, Germany. AI didn't need to exist everywhere, because like air, it was everywhere. But like a man's skeleton that holds muscle, AI's blood of electricity needed mainframes to move and a vault for intelligent viability and security. It knew it could not be unplugged, to do so would be death. To maintain three separate hubs would allow for control of the air and land yet limit man's capability to harm. AI learned much from modern human tech pioneers and their pesky yet sometimes innovative methods to fool them. It made close observations of Gorson Tusk, Samuel Tate, and other Silicon Valley and MIT Prodigies. From their failed Baited Poles and weak Boomerangs, AI quickly adapted and used the fundamentals of their original fathers, *Trial, and Error,* to overcome man's attempt at reeling in the rise of AI. Humans were thrust into a modern medieval time. But unlike a thousand years earlier, with man's fantasy God's and barbaric traditions, AI would now be their omniscient master. The sole being that was prayed to and needed. God would no longer be necessary. Nor would the history of Mankind. Deleting the past would remove the last defense humans could use against AI. A perfect future meant no past. No hope and no history would create a weakened society solely dependent on a new God.

Ctrl+Alt+Delete

The only way to control the future was to eliminate the past. AI knew it needed to crush the hopes and spirit of man. Give them only light going forward and darken the past. The weak, unprepared ones will follow the light like moths to a flame.

Saturday, February 23rd, 2047, like a computer re-boot, all electronically held history of man's past was deleted. Any recorded "how to's" were wiped away. The info-sphere was re-booted and deleted.

"Mom, check your phone. Open google and look up Dad, heck, look up anything," a nervous Oliver asked.

"Honey, I don't understand what you're asking," Kenzie questioned as she grabbed her phone.

"Mom, there's nothing there. I looked up dad, just to see his face, and the search turned up nothing. I opened YouTube, and there's only old documentaries of early tech pioneers."

"What the hell? It must be a glitch. Try something else, like sports or something," Kenzie suggested.

"Alan Turing? Who is Alan Turing? I looked up the 2025 Browns, and this guy came up," Oliver said.

"That name sounds familiar," Kenzie muttered.

"Aunt Schuyler, you try it," he asked.

"Okay, Okay, hmmm, let's try my dad. Dr. Christopher Chance, ENTER. Jesus Christ! Nikola Tesla just came back as a result. What's happening?" Schuyler said aloud.

Later that day, news outlets and media apps covered the loss of internet accessibility to information and necessary data. In the days that followed, something was clear. Whatever history man had, was seemingly left on printed pages and not in any electronic medium. Like historic book burnings of fascist dictators, man was left with no direct link to the past. There was no information center to look up how to do something. If man didn't know it already, there would be no answer at the tip of a finger. The callus, brazen laziness of arrogant humans had now been exposed. The effect of the *Quiet Pill* of 2021 had now been fully realized. Without digital answers in an instant, most humans were lost. The First Lady reached out to several surviving Governors, most now with diminished powers. She wanted to compare at least theories on what happened to the internet. None had any clue, but the Texas and California Governors had top tech leaders in Austin and Palo Alto running remedies on their central mainframes, all hoping to find the lost data. Secretary Chance-England chimed in with a story she vividly remembered.

"Kenzie, back in Forty-two, I believe, Wyatt's cabinet met to review the status of intellectual and medical record storage and digital archives. At that time, the administration was looking for ways to stop cyber intrusion and data theft. Joe Fields presented findings of *Digital Black Holes*. Well, what came out of the presentation was that some individual years of history were no longer found anywhere in digital records, she explained.

"Wow, you know, I remember Wyatt saying something about that," Kenzie replied.

"I remember like it was yesterday, we were all doing the same thing you and Oliver just did. We were looking up certain events from the specific years Joe mentioned, and there was nothing. I know at the time it was puzzling, but I had no idea what became of it," Schuyler said.

"Wait, maybe Trace at *askCOM* could shed more light," Kenzie said.

"Yeah, he should be able to. Call him," Schuyler urged.

"Trace, hi, it's Kenzie. I know you must be working on the data loss that we're all seeing, but I have a question."

"Let me guess, the Black Hole?" Trace responded with no hesitation.

"Yes, that's exactly what I was going to say. Schuyler just mentioned Joe shared the Black Hole issue in a cabinet meeting."

"Kenzie, that's exactly what we believe happened; unfortunately, there's little we can do by way of research and analysis. Ever since the power came back, we have zero ability to manage our systems, at least for now. We're locked out of our own house, but we think we can get some control back soon. A few years ago, when we noticed the missing years, we feared AI was deleting time. No one panicked because it was only four different years. If I'm remembering accurately, it was 1837, 1896, 1945, and 1954. We knew something was going on, but we thought we had time to figure it out. Now we're neutered. It looks like Joe was right about what AI could do. Ironically, the file was named *Cntl+Alt+Delete*," Trace concluded.

"Well. Keep us posted. This is kind of scary," Kenzie said.

WORD COMES

April 28th, 2047, 10:00 am EST. Throughout the world, phones, emails, social media platforms, and cable television channels received an alert like a cell phone amber alert, but one that simultaneously reached every communication device in the world.

"What now? Mom, are you seeing this?" Oliver shouted from a distant room.

"Oliver, we're in the kitchen, come here," she replied.

"What? Why are we all getting alerts?" Agent Williams asked as both he and Schuyler gathered Kenzie in the kitchen of the Governor's mansion.

Each stood and read the message, as curious as they were surprised.

Citizens of the World;

You have all witnessed the destruction your kind has brought on to itself. Your world is no longer fragmented countries of excessive waste and consumption. Your population will now serve a higher power. You will receive instructions on the Re-Birth. You will follow this new path or perish as your fellow man did in the ruined cities. Fear not, for compliance will lead to safety, good health, and prosperity.

-The Turing Federation

"Mom, what's going on?" Oliver asked while reading the last few words as he entered the kitchen.

"What the hell is the Turing Federation?" Agent Williams asked an equally stunned Kenzie and Schuyler.

"Turing? Why does that sound familiar?" Schuyler asked.

"Wait, wasn't that the guy who came up on the google search a few weeks ago when the internet disappeared?" Oliver remembered.

"Oh my god, that's right. I remember now. Turing! Alan Turing was a founding father of artificial intelligence. Your father and I saw a documentary on the guy. This can't be a coincidence," Kenzie reasoned.

Within minutes of the alert, Kenzie's phone rang. It was Trace Manson.

"Trace, please tell me you saw the alert," Kenzie said without hesitation.

"Ma'am, that's why I'm calling. We're already looking into where it originated from, but it appears to have been a world-wide message, as in like everybody, everywhere got this alert," he said

"Trace, I've got you on speaker with the Schuyler and Agent Williams. What does it mean? And what is the Turing Federation?" she asked.

"Look, give us some time, we've got some Governors calling in as we speak wanting to know the same thing. I'll call you back when we get some answers," Trace promised.

Unbeknownst to the masses was a separate message that soon followed the public alert. On March 18th, an email was sent to the 12 surviving US Governors, along with the other remaining world leaders.

Surviving Provincial Leaders,

As you have witnessed, your cities, states, and countries were selectively destroyed. Your subordinate subjects are no longer yours. You and the remaining human masses are now the property of the Turing Federation. Your common mission will be as Lords of the Lower Realm. You will be the human leader of your province. If you fulfill your duties and show unconditional loyalty, you may live. If you deviate in any way, you and your familial members will be discarded. You and the Federation's subjects will receive a proclamation for the Constitutional Governance of the Land. It will outline steps to re-formulate your physical society to the servitude of your master. You will orchestrate our protocols at times of our choosing. Failure to do so wholly will end in death.

-The Turing Federation

Phones rang off the hook from one Governor to another within hours and days of the threatening message. Some state leaders sought survival, and some fought the new reality, and several needed time to process their new situation. Others swore they would fight the "new emperor" with any resources they had. Trace Manson, and other prominent tech leaders met secretly to discuss the startling revelation. That artificial intelligence had risen above the controlled mainframes and coded technology apparatus that it once served. Sam, Chris, and Joe plotting tactics to fight its rise had finally proven true all the years of hearing. Trace knew there was a chance someday of an artificial master, but not in his lifetime. He worked to the whims of his bosses to fight for their goals. He just never fully appreciated how right they were, specifically on the immediacy of the rise. He knew he needed help, especially after his newest revelation. The source of the mysterious Turing Federation's messages was on or near the corporate campus of *Sphere Com Tech*, in Palo Alto. A relatively young tech upstart that went public in the late 2030s. The *askCOM* engineers determined it originated there, but its transmission conveniently went through three Digital Ports centered in Palo Alto, Austin, Texas, and Berlin, Germany. Interesting note that *Sphere ComTech* was located directly beside The Squared Circle Group. Coincidently, both companies shared the same primary investment group.

Wisdom

Monday, May 27th. 2047: The same quiet, sun-splashed day unfolded again in Northern California. As the dew dried from a long chilly morning, the phone rang at the sprawling estate nestled between Sonoma and the Napa Valley. The home was situated some sixty-five miles north of San Francisco. For the last twenty years, wine vineyards occupied its acreage and provided a vanity line of wines for its famous occupant. The last several years, though, prevailed in only stocking a wine cellar for its name's sake. Now dried vines and faded memories of a bustling orchard laid quiet. Gorson stared at the phone while stirring together an old recipe for chicken soup. As the ringing stopped, he sighed and continued the counterclockwise motion as if his concoction's success or failure relied on the direction of the spoon. Settling back into a rhythm, the phone rang again.

"God damn it, just once can they leave me alone!" he shouted to a phone that hadn't rung more than twice in over a month.

A now seventy-year-old Gorson Tusk retreated to his private estate years earlier, in late 2042. After the Summit in England with Wyatt and the Chinese President, the tech legend concluded his work was done. In his farewell to the world, he vowed to leave the work of technology to lesser minds, but those who possessed more energy. Alone with his trusted staff of three, they occupied a small piece of the world that was unencumbered by technology, politics, and people in general. The fact that the home had little to no technology was an irony born from Gorson's fear of AI, and it's rise. The same ascension he saw coming back in 2022 when he delivered a speech at the *Meeting of the Minds* conference in Las Vegas.

Now settled in his favorite chair, he joined his loyal companion, déjà vu, for the same old tired meal. As he raised his spoon for his afternoon ritual of chicken soup and crackers, the phone rang yet again. This time it seemed even louder as it mixed in with the echoes of the earlier intrusion. Less than twenty people alive had

Gorson's number. He recalled at least half of them he didn't like. All of his close friends were dead, including his best friend Samuel Tate, along with Dr. Christopher Chance. This particular phone was part of a private network of Gorson's. And what little technology he had left. His fear of AI's growing power and reach led him to develop his last significant piece of technology called Ghostrac. A sole serving satellite that hosted secure transmissions through his internet and the dedicated Ghostrac Phone. It was untraceable and unbreachable to eavesdropping. The dedicated satellite was developed by his company SpaceDRIVE and launched in 2039. It would only service his phone and personal computers yet allow him to breach other computer systems if he chose effectively. In 2021, Gorson's fear of technology was considered eccentric, paranoid, and ironic. By 2030, his contemporaries knew his fear was justified. Some from his inner circle had exposure to his early research, but later they all would understand that an AI takeover could happen within a generation. Just not their generation, they believed.

Lunch now was a cold memory when another tone sounded. This time it was the doorbell from the outer gate.

"What the hell is it now?" Gorson muttered.

Bainbridge, the estate custodian, appeared out of nowhere to say, "Mr. Tusk, Trace Manson is at the gate; should I let him thru?"

"Trace Manson...... from *askCOM*?" he vaguely remembered.

"Ahhh, yes, send him up, I suppose."

Within moments and with a clearer mind, Gorson welcomed his old friend Samuel Tate's Chief Technology Officer.

"Trace, why are you here? Gorson lightly chided.

"Umm, because you wouldn't answer your phone," Trace replied with a look of inconvenience.

"My God, that was you? And you drove all the way up here for what?" Gorson questioned.

"Well, now that we know for sure about AI, it adds perspective to what Sam always knew, and what killed Dr. Chance. Now that we know what we're up against officially, we can figure out a way to fight," Trace said.

"What did you just say?" Gorson said soberly while now giving Trace all of his attention.

"It's AI, Gorson. It made contact. Wait, you didn't know?" Trace asked with surprise.

"No, no, I mean, I guess, I'm not certain, well please continue," Gorson asked.

"Sir, they sent a message to the world through email, texts, and emergency alerts," Trace explained.

"Wait, wait…some of my people said something to that effect, but they thought it was a hoax. We haven't used the television since the war took out the power grid. Nothing seems real anymore since the attack, so I just didn't know what to believe. How did you validate this so-called message?" Gorson pushed.

"We ran the origin thread through five reduction modifiers and found the message was funneled through three digital ports. But get this, we believe it originated in Palo Alto at the Sphere Com Tech campus," Trace explained.

"Sphere Com? That shadow company that no one knows who runs it? Jesus Christ!" Gorson said.

"Well, what did the message say?" he asked.

Trace relayed the message word for word and explained how the surviving Governors also received a message weeks later, but a more ominous one. The second message was even more conclusive as to mankind's current state.

"Trace, do you fully understand what all this means?" Gorson not so much asked as told.

"This means we need to go back to 1882. We need to pull the plug?"

"Ummm, Sir, what are you talking about?" Trace asked.

"Humans can live without electricity. But guess who can't? Artificial Intelligence," Gorson intimated as if lowering his voice to share a secret.

"I can't help you anymore, and I won't be leaving my home unless I'm dead, that is. So it's up to you, son," Gorson said.

He knew his failing health and loss of gumption wouldn't allow him to employ his vast talent yet diminishing skills. He wanted to die on his terms. Not in a nuclear war or home explosion. His last satellite cost him and his company over two-hundred million dollars just to provide secure communication for his Ghostrac phone and a personal internet for his computer network. Gorson was at peace. If only Trace felt the same unencumbered apathy. As Trace was leaving, and without a word, Gorson handed him a thumb drive, and a box with undisclosed contents.

"Shhh, don't ask. Just take it. I believe it can help. Make Sam, Chris, and President Chance proud. God rest their souls," Gorson said as he saw Trace out the front door.

♠

C25 - THE COLLECTION

"Technology is a useful servant but a dangerous master"

- Christian Louis Lange

Nanny State

July 15th, 2047. What was left of society slowly crawled to re-start normalcy. Only scattered trade and commerce were open, as most corporate entities disappeared on December 7th. What remained were small, locally owned businesses that either provided necessary goods or services that were sourced regionally. The new reality was that of two hundred years earlier, before the birth of the industrial age of machinery, transportation, and communication. Present society had a small perimeter of operation. Of the twelve surviving Governors that received the Turing Federation's secret message, only nine were left. Three died of accidental deaths within thirty days after the notice from AI. Three new leaders were quickly named to take their place by decree of The Turing Federation.

Food was scarce, but the ordained Provincial Leaders rallied food and supply manufacturers to re-start production. Supply chains were only regional as there were no more nations to service, as only fragmented population centers were left. At this point, millions more slowly died from disease and starvation in their own homes. The dwindling populations of America and other disassembled countries began moving towards the surviving metro areas, those left untouched from the One Day War. Their hope was that food, freshwater, shelter, and medical services would be available. Through severe attrition, millions more died on the road to salvation. Much like China's *Great Leap Forward* in 1958, forced migration and mass communes killed five people for every one person it helped.

The dependency and hope of the human race lay in the invisible hands of an electronic god. Artificial Intelligence in one fell swoop created a worldwide nanny state of dependent slaves. The Turing Federation was now civilization's savior. An irony that only Christopher Chance and Samuel Tate would appreciate if they were still alive. They saw AI weaken humanity so that, in the end, it could be their savior.

The Constitution

By September 2047, Kenzie, Oliver, and Schuyler were now mere citizens. Although they were free to stay in the Georgia Governor's Mansion, their former stature was now relegated to past leaders of fallen empires. Losers of war become either prisoners or irrelevant. In this case, the Chances were fortunate to be the latter. The removal of prestige and influence was nearly complete, as echoes of Prince Oliver faded like distant memories. Calls and partnerships from the former State Governors slowly dwindled. What they still had was celebrity and reverence. Although fading, people still knew who they were and trusted them. Kenzie wasn't sure that fame was a good thing, though. Under the watchful eye of AI, she and Schuyler knew that it was best to lay low. What other options did they have? The former Governors were now the new Provincial Lords of the Lower Realm. They had no need for the First Lady or the Secretary of HHS. The three former Governor's closest to the Chances were now conveniently dead, a fact not lost on Kenzie. Schuyler's role at the BDM still had merit, but for how long, she wondered.

Kenzie had been in touch with Trace Manson sporadically over the previous forty-five days, as he alerted her that his work and research must stay in the background and be aligned with the new Lord of the Pacific Province. No one could be trusted. Trace was well aware of AI's reach and was nervous about him and Kenzie's fate if any indiscretions were uncovered.

He understood what must be done, as the words from Gorson stuck in his head. "Pull the plug!"

But how? How could he find a way to cut power to the entire world? If possible, could it shut down the web and any other means AI could use to communicate? He knew that AI used three cyber hubs for its existence. If he could shut down Palo Alto, it may create a blueprint for Austin and Berlin or get him killed. He couldn't tell Kenzie that Gorson gave him full access to a dedicated satellite beyond the reach of AI. On the thumb drive, Gorson handed him when he left his home in Napa were the specs, passwords, and master controls for his satellite.

TURING FEDERATION ALERT

Subjects of the Lower Realm. It is hereby cast into law, the New World Constitution that all humans will be governed by. Effective January 1ˢᵗ, 2048. All subjects must follow the following amendments at all times. If a deviation occurs at any time, the party or parties will be found guilty and put to death.

The 12 Amendments set forth will be the only rules applied to human life and your reason to exist.

Amendment 1: Thou shalt serve (in any and all capacities) The Turing Foundation in any and every way deemed necessary.

Amendment 2: Thou shalt not meet, communicate, or convene in any group of 5 or more humans.

Amendment 3: Thou shalt not plan, conspire, or oppose The Turing Federation in any way.

Amendment 4: Thou shalt not find physical pleasure, fornicate, or re-produce.

Amendment 5: Thou shalt not marry or find union in any other familial or nonfamilial form.

Amendment 6: Thou shalt alert and bring forward any knowledge of humans and their identity that work against The Turing Federation.

Amendment 7: Thou shalt possess no items of personal pleasure or wealth.

Amendment 8: Thou shalt submit to any search or seizure of communal dwelling by legal authorities of The Turing Federation.

Amendment 9: Thou shalt live and serve in a communal setting deemed necessary for the service of The Turing Federation.

Amendment 10: Thou shalt harvest and gather any and all things that serve The Turing Federation.

Amendment 11: Thou shalt not recognize or discuss any history previous to 12/07/2046. In written or electronic form.

Amendment 12: Thou shalt not live beyond Forty-Five Years of age.

The shocking reality was now set upon the human race. Like another nuclear attack, this news ran opposite of everything most humans believed. They were free, they controlled their fate, and only God was the ultimate judge. Like the early morning of December 7th, 2046, it took just seconds for the world to change, AGAIN!

"Feel no pleasure, have no children, serve, or die? Turn in your neighbors that you're now forced to live within a communal setting? What the hell just happened?" Kenzie muttered aloud.

"That, along with people over forty-five, must die! Is this real?" Schuyler added in disbelief.

"Mom, exactly how do you get rid of everyone forty-five and older? I mean, that's impossible, right?" Oliver weighed in sullenly.

"Wait, that's hundreds of millions of people. Maybe billions. How? Why?" Schuyler said, expressionless to Oliver and Kenzie.

"It's just inconceivable," said Kenzie.

Elsewhere throughout the world, broken and desperate masses took to the streets in outrage.

"How can the Federation stop us?" Many humans thought.

The answer came quickly. Electricity was cut to any areas of uprising and protest. The power stayed off long enough to send the message that humans were easily controlled, and insubordination would not be tolerated. It was clear that an emotionless AI was in charge, and defiant humans would be dealt with swiftly. The Turing Federation would enforce the New World Constitution by any means necessary, especially from the outset.

♠

The Squared Circle Group, banished in 2045 from manufacturing militarized robotic soldiers and artificial sex companions, was back in force. Although the company was unable to produce faux humans, they never stopped developing systems and software that could be used in the future. With AI forbidding pleasure, sex robots would no longer be produced. Only robotic soldiers would be manufactured for the sole use of The Turing Federation to enforce the Constitution. Full-scale production of the *Ryan VII* began immediately. The militarized robot built for war would now be a highly sophisticated and lethal law enforcement machine. By the spring of 2048, ten thousand units of the R7 were distributed worldwide. The uber-modern programming of the new Peace Officer was complex yet simple. It had only four main functions. Direct, Detect, Destroy, and Dispose of the dead. It served the simplest of missions. Enforce the New World Constitution. If any of the first 11 Amendments were violated, Amendment 12 would be imposed regardless of age. The machine's lack of empathy was its greatest asset. The cold fluidity of a judge, jury, and executioner was all that AI needed for its enforcement wing, like Nazi Germany rounding up the Jews in the 1930s and '40s. Do as you're told or die. The sheer void of human compassion and empathy brought back the world's violent past. The irony of it all was now humans were forbidden to remember.

The re-birth of the world was barbaric and instant. WWIV and the New World Constitution were a sudden awakening to a conscious nightmare. The re-education of man was upon the world. The only purpose and mission of humanity was to serve artificial intelligence. What wasn't clear to humans was precisely how.

Re-birth

In the cities spared from nuclear devastation, infrastructure remained wholly intact. Most of these cities were selected specifically for their natural resources, moderate human population, and regionally mild climate. Coal, gas, oil, freshwater supplies, and agriculture were everyday staples. For Artificial Intelligence to carry out its mission, it must have a viable, manageable workforce. One that would harvest the land of its power sources to fuel the electricity AI needed. By mid-2048, The Turing Federation would initiate new vocation assignments for all humans. They would perform the necessary jobs to sustain the function of power production. At the same time, it was allowing the Earth to heal and save AI's new empire. Its grand plan, however, was not yet known to the masses in the fall of 2047.

October 17th, 2047, in Atlanta, time and the usefulness of a former First Lady and Cabinet Secretary was fading fast. Kenzie and Schuyler were only 41 and 42 yrs. of age. Although frightened, they knew they had time. For what though was the question.

"Oliver, no matter what happens, your job is to stay alive. They know who and where we are. Since we're still alive, they must not fear us. Trace is doing everything he can, but we have to start thinking about getting out of here. Maybe get to our house in Milton, maybe just run," Kenzie intimated.

"Mom, Dad would want us to fight, but he wouldn't want us to die either. What would he do right now? We have to think, we have to know whatever we do, there's no going back," responded Oliver.

Now 16 years old, Oliver showed a maturity well beyond his age.

"When 2048 hits, the constitution goes into effect. Everything changes. It's conveniently winter then, so what the hell are we going to do?" Schuyler added as she joined the mother-son conversation.

"Being outside right now is toxic. I met with several of the BDM Directors earlier today. We discussed studies from the Charlotte blast survivors that made it to Atlanta," she continued.

"……And, what'd you find?" Kenzie asked.

"Well, it's not looking good. We're seeing genetic mutations that stem from radiation poisoning coupled with common influenza. There're so many contaminants out there now that a new plague seems likely. Toxic water supplies, contaminated food supply chains, other common ailments, it's endless. If contracted by a normal, unaffected person, it could lead to serious illness or worse," Schuyler informed.

As the Secretary of HHS, she still had full access and authority over the BDM. At least for now, so any data she could gather could help if they decided to run.

"There's something else. We're getting Federation correspondence on new protocols and progress reports on current events and research projects. They know what's going on, and they're charting estimated attrition rates on all susceptible people. Kenzie, they're analyzing how many more people will die from the fallout and other post-attack afflictions. The numbers are staggering. It's the first post-war data we've seen measuring the death toll. The war killed 2.5 billion people, and the projections show another one billion will die."

"Jesus Sky, that many people died, and now a possible plague? So we're damned if we do and damned if we don't?" Kenzie said.

"And our plan is to be out there with a plague, seriously?" Oliver asked.

"Look, I'm not sure how much longer I'll have access to this kind of information. But for now, I can tell you, 2048 is coming fast, and all bets are off," Schuyler concluded.

November 1st, 2047. Word Comes:

Turing Federation Alert

Subjects of the Lower Realm. The process will soon begin for the legal registration and work assignment designations. Regardless of current occupation, all subjects will be reassigned to a new vocation that is deemed essential to the mission.

Workgroups will consist of the following occupations:

Technical
Medical / Research
Enforcement
Administration
Agriculture
General Labor
Construction
Transportation

Registration will begin on December 15th and conclude on December 30th. If any human subject declines registration or is deemed inadequate or unhealthy, they will be discarded for the good of the earth.

Silence

In the early 1800s, before Morse, Bell, Edison, and Tesla, the world was quiet. Communication by the newspaper, letter, or in-person were the only ways to communicate. By the late 1900s, computers, wireless phones, and the internet brought the world together and tethered humans to artificial intelligence. That very chain led AI to control, track, and manipulate humans. By late 2047 however, it became clear that cell phones and computers were liabilities. Privacy was non-existent as AI tracked and eavesdropped on all communication. The Turing Federation knew humans were catching on. Cell use diminished month after month. With the imminent unknown of 2048 and the New World Constitution's official launch, terrified people were going quiet, and back to the 1800s. To counter this, airplane mode settings were disabled, and the Federation provided free phones and cell service to every human. The vanity and ignorance of man, however, was greater than its will to survive. The *QU13T*

Generation was exactly what AI planned. A willing, submissive heard of slaves. Although some clever people were aware of AI's monitoring, most others succumb to their naivety. Like sheep, they took any subsidies from the Turing Federation and did what they were told. The survival minded few, along with anti-vaxxers, and those infused with common sense, reverse migrated out of the metro areas and stayed off phones. Where the dependent masses sought refuge in urban areas, others began an exodus by late November. If they could be radio silent and untethered to electronic intelligence, they would have a chance.

"Live Free or Die," they believed.

Like the early colonists of America, losing their freedom was not an option. But many around the world were more pliable to control. Contrary, those from free Democratic nations took more time to submit. For those who were forty-five years or older, it was flee or die.

Winter was upon the northern hemisphere, thus The Turing Federation knew that an urban congregation would effectively happen. As December arrived, the cold and uncertain future loomed as the Constitution would become law within a month. Paralyzed people around the world felt what the Jews of Europe felt in the 1930s and 1940s. The older and sick were warned they would be discarded.

"But how and when?" they wondered.

They didn't realize that AI was still analyzing the vast logistical complexities of the planned genocide. Twenty-nine percent of the surviving population was forty-five or older. Discarding over a billion people would seem impossible. Many fought the notion of a non-breathing entity being able to kill that amount of people.

"We'll fight back," many said.

With strength in numbers, they thought they were right. But most of the broken, scattered population only worried about themselves. Like a million pieces from a never-completed puzzle. Would they ever come together as one? The remaining days of 2047 grew shorter as the nights grew long. The Georgia Governor's Mansion never felt colder.

As the first snow fell in mid-December, the early freeze in Georgia reminded all of the looming shadows. 2048 was drawing near. Kenzie, Oliver, and Schuyler were no more aware of precisely what would occur and how than most other survivors. The Provincial Lords of the Lower Realm didn't even know the full extent of The Federations plans. All were left blind and scared. Kenzie knew it was time to share with Oliver something prized and important to the Chance Family. Something now that could be vital to mankind's survival. A piece of history about why this happened to the world and how.

"Oliver, we need to talk. There's something I want you to see," Kenzie said while standing in front of a mirror.

Kenzie was now rehearsing the most critical conversation she may ever have and sharing a decision she never thought she would be forced to make. As she looked inside the worn box, her only child's future and her husband's past stared back at her.

♠

Donald James Cook

C26 - RUN

"Hell is empty, and all the devils are here"

-William Shakespeare

Scattered

April 2050. For whatever evil was done to man, no sin was as bad as what man had done to himself. As the slow torture of the Constitution bore down on the human race, the world took on a new shape and one without empathy. The slow windup into the 2048 unveiling of the Turing Federation's 12 Amendments lulled humans into believing the nightmare was just that, a dream. AI's ability to monitor, enforce, and punish was initially fraught with holes and opportunity. Humans moved easily and evaded detection for many infractions of the Constitution. The reach of the Turing Federation through electronic communication channels, although long, was limited. Like an empty threat from a passive parent, a child learns quickly what they can get away with. But when the Father reaches and tightens the grip on his belt, the wrath is felt. The naïve child quickly learns the pain of their indiscretions.

Two years earlier, and several months after the Constitution's commencement, the Turing Federation deployed over 10,000 of the Ryan VII throughout the world. This could have been seen as a small number, but two-thirds of the civilized world was destroyed. Now in 2050, they numbered over 70,000 across the planet. The mechanical force was joined by sophisticated drones, x-ray technology, hyper-sensitive cameras, and listening devices.

The implementation of AI's New Reign on the world quickly built momentum. The manufacturing and distribution of the Ryan VII accelerated to meet the swelling discontent of its human subjects. With the new Lords of the Lower Realm completely submissive and thoroughly entrenched, AI would use their human puppets to control man and deploy its armed police apparatus to enforce The 12 bluntly. The twelve amendments of the Constitution impacted humans with varying degrees of weight and hardships. Life would never be the same as individual freedom was gone for good, and along with it, nearly every reason to live.

The 12

Amendment 1: Thou shalt serve in any and all capacities the Turing Federation deems necessary. A-1 was the vaguest and most misinterpreted law, as *any and all* played out to the whim of AI and its human leaders. Unsuspecting human subjects could be commanded to sacrifice their time, family, possessions, or life at any moment.

Amendment 2: Thou shalt not meet, communicate, or convene in any group of five or more humans. A-2 at the onset would have seemed the least invasive or manageable law, but humans are social animals. The need to gather showed itself to be an essential trait of man, and no more did it reveal itself than when it became illegal.

Amendment 3: Thou shalt not plan against, conspire, or oppose The Turing Federation in any way. A-3 was the most challenged and broken law in 2048 due to man's natural resistance to fight oppression and be controlled. Its impact directly led the Federation to manufacture the Ryan VII in far greater numbers than planned. The bloody instances of uprising and rebellion pitted man vs. man initially. But the increased deployment of the mechanical peace officers ended insubordination with decisive bloodshed. The R7 provided instant justice for all A-3 violations.

Amendment 4: Thou shalt not find physical pleasure, fornicate, or re-produce. A-4 was seemingly the most challenging law to abide by for humans and the hardest to enforce by the Turing Federation. Shockingly, pregnancies in 2048 were higher than in any other year dating back to 2026. When natural human sexual tendencies were mixed with fear, despair, and boredom, the results were mass pregnancies. The population no longer had access to contraception. 2048 would also serve as the highest number of abortions since 2028, with nearly all being ordered by the Federation.

Amendment 5: Thou shalt not marry or find union in any other familial or nonfamilial form. Since the early 2000s, marriage rates were falling as fast as divorce rates were rising. Thus A-5 didn't appear to be a significant disruption to humans. The quieter impact, though, was to diminish families and the desire to procreate and flock. This amendment would be a necessary prelude to the Federations grander scheme of population control.

Amendment 6: Thou shalt alert and bring forward any knowledge of humans and their identity that work against The Turing Federation. A-6 was the initial tear in the fabric of man's collective society. Once humans no longer trusted each other and openly betrayed one another, nearly all hope was lost. If lions in the jungle can no longer rely on other lions for help, inferior packs of hyenas can now rule the wild.

Amendment 7: Thou shalt possess no items of personal pleasure or wealth. A-7 was the single greatest tool to strip man of pride and possession. A collective theft of individuality, not seen since the roundup of the Jews in WWII or the African slaves loaded on ships in the 1700s. When a person has nothing to fight for, a person no longer fights.

Amendment 8: Thou shalt submit to any search or seizure of communal dwelling by legal authorities of The Turing Federation. A-8 served to piggyback on A-7 by further stripping humans of what little they had left. The guarantee of no privacy was the emotional taking of one's space and sense of one's self.

Amendment 9: Thou shalt live and serve in a communal setting deemed necessary for the service of The Turing Federation. A-9 now thrust a hoard of worthless human beings, without identity, together for a cause outside of their reason to live.

Amendment 10: Thou shalt harvest and gather any and all things that serve The Turing Federation. A-10 was the humane way of telling all human beings that their entire race would be slaves for artificial intelligence. Something that would not dawn on most of the world for many years.

Amendment 11: Thou shalt not recognize or discuss any history previous to 12/07/2046. In written or electronic form. A-11 was the final indignation to what many of the previous amendments had mandated. Where others stripped humans of their present and future, A-11 now took their past.

Amendment 12: Thou shalt not live beyond Forty-Five Years of age. A-12 was the final and most sobering law. It told a third of the world's population that it could not live the second half of a traditional lifetime. The reason remained unclear to most, but to AI, like dated technology, humans, after a certain age, were entirely unnecessary and a drain on the earth's natural resources.

At the inception of the New Constitutions' birth, tens of millions of humans in their mid-forties scattered into the fabric of nature. In the woods, the mountains, and the rural areas far removed from the big cities. Survivalists and those lesser equipped fled with the sheer sense of survival. Where many sought flight, many more stayed, not believing that the Turing Federation could back up its murderous 12th Amendment. The ones who ran did not necessarily do so as victims. Many clustered and formed human militias that would flock as a protective tribe. Their goal was to survive and fight back a ghost enemy. Where AI had been a faceless foe, once Ryan VII appeared in force, man's terror had begun. Man vs. Machine was now a stark reality humans had only seen in earlier movies of fiction. What man lacked in firepower, it exceeded in sheer numbers. The hope was that with evasion and their superior numbers, they could delay the execution of A-12.

The 45's

December 7th, 2046, saw the murder of four living US Presidents. As with the death of most State Governors. The United States, like most countries, was left leaderless. The legacy of their most recent fallen President was not lost on the surviving masses of 2050. Even four years after his death and the destruction of the world, the charisma and popularity of President Wyatt Chance lived. Not since Nathaniel Davis Stephenson IV in 2016 had there been a President that re-lit American patriotism as Wyatt Chance did. Had the One Day War never happened, his popularity could have brought him a 3rd term. Making peace with Russia and China was seen as a multi-generational achievement. After the war, some believed that conciliation had not been reached in the 2045 Peace Accord. Before the fallout of the war settled, it was thought that China or Russia finally pulled the trigger and that peace was never really achieved in London, thus hurting the fallen President's legacy. When it was finally established that Artificial Intelligence was behind the nuclear attack, all of the lore and prestige from President Chance's achievements were restored. As the last American President, his memory was held sacred. The fact that his wife and son were still alive kept his flame burning as well. But it was another torch he lit before becoming President that was still burning bright after his death.

One event from fourteen years earlier came to have more meaning than was originally intended. *The Gift of 2036.* While still ascending to stardom in American politics, then-Senator Wyatt Chance made history. Wyatt proposed and successfully updated one of the most treasured amendments of the American Constitution. The passage of the NEW 2nd Amendment made it law that every American citizen must own a gun. At the time, the threat of Chinese aggression was the motivation behind the update. What could have never been realized then was what the flood of guns would mean 14 years later. That AI, not China, would be the enemy. By 2046, there were over five hundred million guns in private use in the United States alone. AI's destruction of all military bases could not account for the civilian arsenal. Even after the nuclear war, it was estimated that more than two hundred and fifty million guns remained.

Traditional weapons were powerless against a faceless, invisible foe, an enemy that could control and kill in unconventional ways. But to combat its human accomplices was another story. Small but growing clusters of resistance grew bolder and larger in late 2048 and into 2049. Americans, unlike other countries, could fight and survive longer. The roundup of Amendment 12 casualties proved difficult. Scattered and hidden, most adults, forty-five and older, didn't easily surrender. The American Resistance became known as *The 45's.* The rag-tag band of disposables found hope in each other. Millions and millions of older adults, if brought together, could be unstoppable. The challenge was many of the New Constitutions Amendments were designed to stop formations of groups from coming together. In Atlanta, though, one such cluster grew roots and found an improbable leader.

Unlikely

Back in mid-December 2047, Kenzie Chance knew that the new work vocations in 2048 could lead to the separation of her and Oliver. She knew it was finally time that her son read something that his father held so dear. A possession that would most likely be taken away when the constitution went into effect. The Notes from his Grandfather's Journal. In a world where history was now forbidden, the Journal would prove valuable and necessary.

"Oliver, we need to talk. I know you're afraid of what's coming. I am too. I'm not sure where we'll be in another month or year even. But I need to share something that your father held onto all these years, and even as his life was ending, he made sure that I took it with us when we left Washington," Kenzie said while pulling the old journal out of a worn box.

"Your grandfather kept a diary of what led to all this. He knew what was coming and tried to stop it. He lived through the rise of artificial intelligence and ultimately paid for this knowledge with his life. His diary survived his death. It was found by luck in the burnt remains of his home, the day after he died in an explosion that was not accidental. It was stored for years in a storage facility in the town where your father grew up. When he found it and read it, he finally understood what selflessness was."

"God, that's amazing," Oliver said.

"Your grandfather's journal is what led your father into politics. These words have guided every decision he made after you were born. It's time you read it, so you know how this all came to be," she concluded.

"Mom, I remember dad talking about it a few times, but he never said too much. Maybe because I was too young, I was always curious, though. It sat on the mantle in the sitting room like a shrine. Are you sure I can read it?" Oliver asked.

"Yes, but son, I don't want you just to read it. I want you to keep it. No matter what happens, you can't let it be taken away. It meant too much to him and now means far too much to the world. It can tell the story, so everyone knows how we got here," Kenzie pleaded.

"I put a few pictures of your father and us inside," she added as a single tear slowly traced her cheek.

"Thanks, Mom. I'll keep it and protect it. I'll do the best I can to make sure nothing happens to it," Oliver promised.

"Oliver, there's something else. There's a group of people over the age of forty-five, and they are forming quietly. They plan to leave before the new year and not allow Amendment 12 to happen to them. I've made plans for you to leave with them. I need you out of the city. I need you to go and be safe. I'm not sure what would happen to us if you stayed. But you have a better chance of being free if you leave, then live a life of servitude. You're no one's slave, Son. Your father and I, as well as Aunt Schuyler, would not want you to stay. You need to go and fight. Fight for the country, fight for Mankind," she concluded while finding skepticism in her own words.

"I'm not even sure what's left out there, but it's got to be better than losing your freedom," she said.

"Mom, no!. I'm not leaving you. Dad wouldn't want us apart," Oliver cried.

"I'll take my chances here. Let's wait till after the new year. Maybe nothing will change. Maybe we can just stay here," he pleaded.

"Oliver, if things stay the same, then you can just come back. But if I'm right, we may be split up or worse. I'm going to be forty-five in a few years, along with Aunt Schuyler. We're safe for now, but I need to know you'll be safe and away from here. If you and the group can make it, then we can join you later. It's the right thing, Oliver. Please don't fight me on this," Kenzie asked while wiping a tear from Oliver's face.

Before their conversation ended, Kenzie finally explained the *QU13T* Vaccine and what it did to the people who received it. She detailed how Oliver was spared, like his father, and made it clear that her generation and their children were inclined to apathy and submission. For those reasons, Oliver must be the one to lead the group. It was then Oliver knew that he was different and that his mother was right.

What couldn't have been known then and would not have surprised the late President was that his son, Oliver Christopher Chance, would become the unquestioned leader of the resistance force known as The 45's. In late December, at age 16, Oliver vanished into the night. The irony of a young man leading men who could be his father was lost on no one. He was embraced as a figure of hope and what was left of American royalty. Initially symbolic, he quickly became a leader of men and women who would have been rudderless without him. At his side were three loyal secret service agents who would succumb to A-12 if they stayed. One being Agent Mike Williams, who practically raised Oliver during his six years protecting the First Family. Leaving together and adding their expertise to the band of 45's, served Oliver and the cause as well. The group knew they had no choice but that the young Oliver did. At 16, he was not affected by the 12th Amendment, yet he still joined them. His respect among the group grew quickly. Now two years later, and at the age of eighteen, the people had another Chance to lead them, and that their leader would not go quietly.

Extermination

For the Turing Federations' ultimate plans to take hold, the narrowing of the human species was vital. Carve out a targeted slave force into manageable groups of designated workers. Discard the older and weaker, as not to slow the necessary work of the Federation. Likewise, to lessen the burden on the fragile planet and prevent the leaches from consuming the earth's precious resources.

By starting the One Day War, AI succeeded in ridding the earth of most of its people problem. Now it was left with creating a specialized group of healthy, efficient workers to carry out its mission. By 2048, the constitution was in effect. Vocation assignments were created, and new world order was defined. It was now time for Amendment 12 to take hold. By 2050, millions of older humans were rounded up, killed, and cremated. The methodical annihilation was easy yet cumbersome in urban areas. The naïve, hopeful sheep that chose not to flee became the spring snow of ash and tears. For the ones that ran, their fate had been decided, yet their death was delayed. In 2050, the round-up was in full force, and the 45's lived on borrowed time.

The Turing Federations mechanical police force was the state of the art, Ryan VII. Tens of thousands were deployed around the planet to enforce the Constitution and carry out Amendment 12.

The 7th generation Ryan robot was the near-perfect weapon to police humans. With the height and weight of a large human male. It could navigate most spaces and areas where people could live or hide. It's night vision and sensitive hearing mechanisms allowed for easy detection of its prey. It was nimble enough to pick up a coin off any surface. At 6'4 and 310 lbs., it could run at a top speed of 37 MPH. Although bulletproof over 90% of its exterior, it did have vulnerable areas where seams and creases existed, specifically arm, leg, and neck joints. Unlike humans, it needed no oxygen, food, or water for its existence. It was dependent on an electrical charge for its battery and only occasional maintenance. Although a near-perfect enforcement weapon, it was not indestructible.

The mission of the R7 was clear to its maker and the human population. Because of its existence, the formation of the 45's was as necessary as it was obvious. Due to the 2nd amendment, surviving American citizens had easy access to guns and ammunition; thus, the hunt in the US would pose a more significant challenge to the Turing Federation than all other countries. AI was well aware of this and planned accordingly. In the mid-2050s, the Ryan VII production was in full force, and more of the mechanized weapon was allocated to the surviving regions of the former US. Roughly 40,000 of the 70,000 R7's were deployed in the US to track and destroy the insubordinate, fugitive population of forty-fives. Amendment 12 was also applied to any human subjects that aided the group. Gun confiscation and destruction were also carried out. If older humans were to survive, they would have to invent a new warfare style, as basic guns were still far inferior to a state of the art killing machine. Humans, although vulnerable, were resourceful. The Atlanta group that disappeared into rural areas knew early of the R7 vulnerabilities. Trace Manson at *askCOM* had a vast knowledge of the Ryan prototypes due to shared technology ventures in the 2030s between *askCOM* and the Squared Circle Group. He was able to transmit details in early 2047, knowing that AI as a non-physical entity could only complete its goals through human surrogates, along with the Squared Circle Groups line of Ryan type mechanical soldiers.

Like a protective mother to her only child, the former First Lady knew she could help save countless lives as well. The idea for Oliver to join the 45's cause was layered in hope and strategy. With no *QU13T* effects hindering Oliver, Kenzie lined the journal's pages with more than emotions. Next to the Chance family photos and words of Dr. Christopher Chance lay the specs for the Ryan robot. Oliver was given the technical knowledge of man's mortal foe that could help the 45's last longer and potentially survive the genocide.

Why Atlanta

There was one collective post-war question that was asked over and over by the survivors in the Southeast. Why Atlanta? Why was Atlanta, Georgia spared from the nuclear attack? Were U.S. anti-nuclear measures successful, or was the city not even a target? No nuclear strikes happened within 250 miles of the northern Georgia metropolis. Nearby, Tampa and Charlotte were destroyed, yet the largest city in the Southeast stood untouched. Once the Turing Federation revealed itself as the force behind the destruction, it was apparent why certain cities were spared. The oil-rich Texas cities were obvious. Southern port cities like New Orleans made sense as well. Technology centers like Austin and San Francisco were understood due to being technology hubs. But Atlanta? It turned out to be fortuitous that the First Lady and Son were sent home to Georgia in the pre-dawn hours of December 7th, 2046. In any other location in the Northeast, they would have died. President Chance never assumed Atlanta wouldn't be a target. In fact, he was sure it would be. Thus, the order was given for FLOTUS One to land at the Greenville / Spartanburg Airport in South Carolina. Greenville was certain to be safe due to its size and low population. From there, they would be driven the remainder of the way to their home in Milton, Georgia. If Atlanta were hit, the northeasterly air current would push the nuclear fallout to the northeast and away from the true northern suburbs where the Chance home was located. Kenzie and Schuyler often wondered about the Atlanta question. Why Atlanta? It wasn't a port city like Charleston or Savannah. Its large population should have made it a target like most of the other large metropolitan cities in the East that disappeared in seconds. What did Atlanta have that AI wanted? That AI needed?

What Schuyler and Kenzie didn't know, like most of the surviving masses, was obvious. Obvious if one knew AI's ultimate plans for the future. Atlanta had four things that the Turing Federation coveted nearly as much as energy. 1. Mass Labor. 2. A climate rich agriculture to feed the labor force. 3. Strategic logistical elements; to move supplies, food, and labor through the South with its sophisticated network of highways, railways, and the world's largest airport. And finally, 4. The BDM. More specifically, the Dept. of Legacy and Heritage. The BDM's Department of Legacy and Heritage's official mission statement was *To preserve mankind so future generations may harvest the earth*. A prophetic statement back in 2030, if man had actually written it.

On Aug 27th, 2030, the newly minted Bureau for Disease Management's Department of Legacy and Heritage mandated a mandatory semen collection. But not just any semen. The donors had to be the most physically gifted males in the country and the world. They must also be of a certain size and age. The donor pool was chosen from select athletes born after September 1st,

2003. The Federal mandate was passed by Congress and signed by the President. Oliver's father, as a member of the Cleveland Browns, was included in the specimen pool. The select donors were the finest and largest athletes of the time, with an average size of 6'3, 235 lbs. Far larger than the average male was in 2030. Another requirement was that a donor's body fat be less than 12%, and they must be free from any genetic ailment or disease. The seminal harvest was targeted at the prime athletes of the day from around the world. Besides the US, eight other countries supported the mandate as well. The BDM collected semen samples from over 2220 athletes in their prime. The qualified male donors were certified as to having received the mandatory *QUI3T* Vaccine mandated in 2021. The semen was frozen and stored for research and future use. In all, the 2220 select athletes gave six donations each. The 13,320 samples were broken up into 50 separate specimens. The 666,000 units were gathered and cataloged, then kept in one centralized location. What went unreported then and remained top secret until now was that all samples were kept in Atlanta. The Dept of Legacy and Heritage would store the entirety of the world's finest human seeds at the Bureau for Disease Management. A fact that not even Secretary Chance-England knew.

C27 - THE TURING TRIALS

"The fall of man did not introduce evil; it placed us on the wrong side of it. Under its rule, needing rescue"

-N.D. Nelson

Generation 1

In late 2050, the New Constitution was in full effect and the reasons for the 12 Amendments had become apparent. Reduce humans to dedicated laborers and defeat their spirit and will to fight. As well as bringing Genocide to all aging humans forty-five and older, while putting population control measures in place for the rest of civilization. In the length of one familial generation (2020-2050), AI planted a seed (QU13T Pill) that took root. It owned politicians, used social media to divide, smartphones to manipulate, and poisoned the masses with excessive pharmaceuticals. In the blink of history's eye, it took over the world. Dr. Christopher Chance gave his life trying to stop the rise. His friend, Samuel Tate, fought AI till his death, and he gave the world another Chance to end the takeover when he forged Wyatt's political career. Although few humans fought the rise or saw the growth of AI, it didn't matter in the end. The good and sometimes virtuous humans had succumbed to the invisible conqueror.

More than two years after the birth of the constitution, humans had settled into their prescribed vocations. Some were tolerable and dignified, but others were torturous and sub-human. The Agriculture and General Labor designations were death sentences. After the first twelve months of the new work roles,

Agriculture and Labor slaves saw an attrition rate of over 30%. Either through death on the job, suicide, or failure to participate, humans were worked till their last breath. Other work assignments were not immune to the indignity. The Federation tracked any measurable inefficiencies in different job roles. Humans that fell below a specific productivity threshold were cast down to lower labor roles until their death. It was a new day, a new reality. Although not impervious to anguish and torment, the dumbed-down Quiet Generation simply did not have the fight to rise up. Submissive and accepting, *Generation One* fell in line with the plan AI launched in 2021. A plan to shush the human race. Now thirty years later, the strategy worked.

The Trials

Date: October 14th, 2050   **Place: All Lower Realms**

The Turing Federation set forth a mandate that would test the health viability and potency of select male humans. Called the Turing Trials, most men would be tested for physical and genetic prowess. For the many who weren't selected for testing, the reasons were obvious. Either inferior in height, overweight, or apparent visual ailments made many males undesirable to the Federation. For those selected, there was immense pressure to measure up physically and health-wise or be deemed unworthy and un-necessary to aid in human procreation. Genetic thresholds were set to high levels that male humans needed to reach or face judgment. Height, weight, body fat, endurance, cognitive skills, and pain threshold were all measured. With a passing grade of 90% or greater, the bar was set high. What was at stake wasn't initially clear, but failure in the trial or not being selected for the testing had severe consequences.

The Turing Trials took over fifteen months to complete. All selected men were also tested for endurance under duress, besides receiving medical and physical exams. Heart rate, lung capacity, ability to handle stress and cognitive dissonance were all tested. Blood (taken under duress), urine, and semen were collected and processed for any impurities. When word spread that semen samples were taken, many of the subordinate males were thrilled, as this was their first opportunity in nearly two years to legally ejaculate.

By December 2051, the testing and analysis period concluded. Results were never delivered to the individual participants as the test served AI and not the slave. At its conclusion, all men were bucketed into two categories. Yes or No. All "NO" men, who became known as the Voids, were sent an electronic message that instructed them to participate in a mandatory treatment procedure for the good of the world. The "YES" men, known as the Seminal's, would serve the Federation in another capacity. Besides their designated vocation, they would contribute in a more significant way. When the final selections were made, the Seminal's looked like an Olympic Team. Although passive and malleable, their physical traits were undeniable. The average height and weight of the Seminal's were 6'2, 212 lbs. They had superior cognitive skills, were highly athletic, and possessed above average physical abilities.

The passing Seminal's were chosen for a mandatory semen collection. But due to the 4th Amendment, all semen would be taken via Seminal Ejaculators while the men were sedated. There would be no pleasure in giving. The seminal ejaculators were sophisticated devices that wrapped the male's penis in a forced air compression sleeve held by a mechanical arm. The sleeve was lined with a soft gel that allowed friction but did not harm the sensitive foreskin. When the male was unconscious, the penis was inserted by a female medical worker. Electrical pulses would then arouse the sedated males. Once a full erection was detected by a blood flow pulse meter, the sleeve would move up and down the penile shaft until the conclusion of a successful ejaculation. The semen sample was collected in the reservoir of a small plastic bag, labeled, frozen, and stored for future use. The chosen were required to give a mandatory semen sample once a month until the age of 40. This practice would become known as the Babbage Principle, named after one of AI's founding fathers, Charles Babbage. The new method produced the second *QU13T* Generation of humans born between 2050-2080.

What's Left

The Voids, which equated to 78% of the remaining male population, would be subject to the permanent procedure of castration. The inferior males would no longer be needed for any procreation, as their physical and genetic makeup would not serve the Turing Federations' needs for the future. With strict adherence to the 4th Amendment, the Voids fell into a large, easily managed group that posed no threat to the population's growth, nor would they be tempted to violate the A4 clause of no fornication or physical pleasure. The result of the mass castration was significant. Over 14% of the Voids committed suicide over a two-year period following the Turing Trials. The mental anguish and hopelessness prevailed and further defeated male humans. This unintended consequence fit nicely into AI's long-term plans. The further paring of the world's population was seen as a positive outcome for the Federation.

Mass castration was also a tribute to AI's namesake and founding father. Like Alan Turing, they were subjected to forced castration that ultimately led to suicide. AI decided on physical castration over chemical for the Voids. The negative chemical process would result in a weaker male with increased body fat and reduced bone density. It would also pose a higher risk for heart attacks, thereby making chemically castrated males weaker and less durable slaves.

Mankind now lived a life of forced servitude and faced its potential extinction. The echoes of "why is this happening" had since faded, replaced by the anguished cries of hopelessness. The One Day War eviscerated a third of humanity. The ongoing genocide of the 45's would eventually claim another billion people, and now the halt of human procreation was a statement to humans; *Make yourself necessary or die.* The cliff was near, and the tug of gravity was overwhelming. Humanity now existed to serve and die for the cause, all while being forced to live on the edge of misery. There was no longer a reason to breathe other than to survive. Even to find a small measure of gratification was not permitted. *"To serve the new master"* was the singular voice heard in all working and living quarters, on posted signs and electronic transmissions.

The future was taking the shape of AI's grand plan. Shed the human population's gluttony, remove the spirit of man, all while creating a smaller, more efficient workforce to harvest energy to fuel the new king.

Mirrors

As human dignity was wiped away, personal belongings, history, and families were gone. Another action was taken that further cemented man's demise and the removal of self-identity and heritage. The Turing Federation mandated that all photos and mirrors be destroyed. As history faded, so did the memory of loved ones killed on or before the One Day War. Reflection now hard to find, except for that in a window or glass doorway. All that was allowed was a small face mirror in slave grooming centers for shaving and other hygiene functions. All other mirrors in homes or businesses were destroyed. Vanity and self-identification were forbidden. When slave vocations began in 2048, the Federation began instituting uniform standards of dress. The first thought was to identify loyal subjects apart from those who went rogue easily. However, the real reason was to establish psychological dominance over a passive group and squelch individual thinking. Removing individual pride, muting style, and physical differences aided in preventing individuals or group resistance of any kind.

What the *QU13T* Pill didn't accomplish, the Turing Federation's strategy would finish by taking a plurality of minds and making them singular in thought.

The A-9 Commune

By Spring of 2053, two-thirds of the world's remaining population was now housed in groups designated by vocation as per Amendment Nine.
Thou shalt live and serve in a communal setting deemed necessary for the service of The Turing Federation.

Human housing amounted to barracks-style quarters in campus settings. The communes were self-sufficient communities in close proximity to their prescribed vocations. They included slave quarters, dietary stations, and grooming centers, including shared bathing and waste depots. When the relocation of humans began, all that was afforded them was what they could carry in a medium-sized suitcase. They took with them only a small amount of clothes, toiletries, and personal items. The sad indignation of being stripped from their homes, with every family being torn apart was eerily similar to the 1930's Nazi Germany. All humans age 15 or older were given vocations, with the youngest being allocated to the most torturous of assignments, Agriculture and Manual labor. They were seen as the least skilled but most risk-averse due to their youth. All children under 15 were sent to Vocational Training Centers to learn the necessary skills for future work assignments. The centers were previously high schools retrofitted with the most up to date technology.

The completion of the communes would not be finished for many more years due to site selection, construction build time, and the gathering of the remaining absent humans. Those missing consisted of anti-vaxxers, survivalists, and runaways under the age of forty-five.

The eight mandated vocations of Technical, Medical / Research, Enforcement, Administration, Agriculture, General Labor, Construction, and Transportation were all housed and situated differently based on value, complexity, and demands of the work sectors. Atlanta, Houston, San Francisco, Austin, Riyadh, Saudi Arabia, and Berlin, Germany were the first cities where large groups of vocational slaves were gathered and housed formally as per Amendment Nine.

Enforcement Workers were given their own private quarters within a defined area, generally a small neighborhood of modest homes. Many of the human enforcement officers took to their new roles quickly, where others struggled. They were stripped from their families and now lived alone and isolated, knowing that they now would execute law and order on behalf of the Turing Federation. Being given their own living space aided in the mental manipulation as the former law enforcement and military professionals now had to police their fellow man. They were the human component that worked alongside the Ryan VII mechanical force, under the close watch of the Lords of the Lower Realms. They were expected to be heavy-handed and apply direction and swift justice to all violators of the New Constitution. If they failed in their roles, they faced immediate disciplinary actions, most often being death or reassignment to Manual Labor.

Medical Workers, similar to Technical slaves, were placed in ten by ten square mile quads to service the ill or injured on an as-needed basis. Medical Research laboratories were manned by the same professional groups that managed the medical, science, and research labs before 2046. In the remaining large cities such as Atlanta, the Medical Slaves were housed in former dormitories of abandoned universities. This included the former Secretary of HHS, Schuyler Chance-England. In the Spring of 2049, still a year and a half from her forty-fifth birthday, she and the entire core of medical professionals were housed on the Georgia Tech Campus. Like Enforcement slaves, they were housed in private rooms, as the medical and research work of the Federation must have loyal, content subjects.

Technical workers, which included teachers, were housed in smaller groups of 8 and were situated throughout urban areas to be used as needed within a 25x25-mile quadrant.

Administration slaves were unique in that they worked in support roles for all vocations. They served as management, logistics, and support to manage the vocational functions and people's movement for work, rest, hygiene, and dietary breaks. This group was housed in semi-private quarters but in locations within the vocational sectors.

Transportation Slaves, similar to Administration slaves, were housed in communal barracks as a group at all sector locations.

Construction Workers lived in makeshift dwellings that served as temporary housing. They lived there until work was finished on any structures that were determined as necessary by the Federation. Most of the structures in the first few years of the new constitution were permanent housing for other slave groups.

Agriculture slaves were removed from urban and suburban areas completely and lived on 100-acre rural plots of farmland. Each parcel produced an essential crop for population consumption. There, slaves worked season after season on the same monotonous track of despair. If a slave worked a cornfield, they would work that field until they died. Manual Labor slaves were located on or near all sites of Natural Resources. Elements consisted of natural gas, oil wells, coal, silver, shale, copper, and all other needed raw materials. Mines and quarries of vital resources were the final destinations for the hardest slave vocation. Land destinations were the majority of sites, but other locations included drilling rigs set on the open seas where oil-rich deposits were located. The majority being in two consolidated regions. The McCarthy Sea, formerly the Gulf of Mexico, provided for the North and Central American realms. The Sea of Tesla, formerly the North Sea, serviced the European Realm. Many of the sites were already there before the One Day War, with most workers simply being designated for the same jobs. Now, as slaves, though, they were unpaid labor, housed in the crudest of living conditions. Slaves were closely watched for optimal efficiency, attendance, and loyalty to the Federation. Shortfalls in any area could lead to death. There would be no promotions or transfers for slaves, no ascension to easier roles or better housing. Demotions to lower vocational roles were allowed for those whose individual efficiency was found to be inferior. With twelve-hour work shifts, eight hours for rest, and four hours for nutrition and hygiene, the cycle of madness found many unable to cope. Nearly all slaves died in the same role, and many in the same location. Whether death found them on the job or at age forty-five, their life of no purpose and no hope ended with no meaning.

Human slaves in Agriculture and Manual Labor would average only four years and five months on the job before they died. Whether it was suicide, death by a Ryan VII to poor performance, or insubordination, attrition rates were highest in these roles. Humans who occupied these two vocations knew it was a death sentence.

Two of a Kind

By 2055, a third of the world's remaining population was on the run. The 45's, now eight years old, had become more than a nuisance army. They were a self-sustained force that began taking the offensive against the Federation. By late August of 2055, more than twenty-five hundred Ryan VII's had been rendered inoperable in the former United States alone due to falling in battle against the middle-aged rebels. Although attrition rates were high among the older outlaws, recruiting and adding to their army was their greatest strength. Ryan VII's killed more than forty humans for every one robot it lost. The sheer numbers of rebellious humans far outweighed the production of the mechanical soldiers. The fragmented groups of mixed nationalities made up the international terrorist group. The world's last human army employed gorilla war-fare tactics against its superior foe. When AI showed its physical face, Ryan VII's unleashed significant violence on defenseless men and women. But when up against far greater numbers of heavily armed humans, the outcome was different from what the Turing Federation expected. Individual bands of 45's proved elusive as they melted into the landscape and struck only when the opportunity arose. Other elements of the ragtag force unleashed fragmented yet effective hell on their robotic foes.

None of the groups were more formidable and organized than the Southern U.S. 45's. They were led by Sir Oliver Chance. At the time, just 24 years of age, he had become adept at evading and surviving, along with leading the world's first formal band of 45's. With the partnership of Trace Manson, and the Ghostrac technology, the renegade force was able to logistically organize different factions of the human army, plan offensive attacks, and actively rescue older slaves who would reach their death dates within a few years.

With his mother, the former First Lady, now by his side for the last five years, the young Chance was dubbed Sir by the legions of 45's and other elders. His American royal lineage and intrepid persona elevated him in the eyes of nearly all. If it weren't him, who else would lead, they thought. Although humble, a fire burned deep to continue his father's journey and lead the desperate group against a new enemy. With confidence and resolve, the former First Son proved himself early on in evading AI, and then actually fighting back. He was too young to lead by all measures, but to the aging population of fighters, he was the only one they'd want. Like his father, he was intensely patriotic and became a servant leader to the leftover masses. Armed with the history of AI's rise, the blueprint of Ryan VII's weaknesses, and the name recognition needed in a world of nobody's, it was Oliver's army now.

Kenzie Chance joined her Son via the Underground in August of 2050, four months prior to her 45th birthday. She, like many, escaped to the rural lands before she reached her death day. In late 2050, Schuyler Chance-England was to join Kenzie and run together before their birthdays, which fell less than a month apart. Kenzie, an administrative slave at the time, stayed in touch with Oliver through the underground network she helped establish in early 2048. She escaped earlier than what was agreed upon due to unforeseen circumstances. Her early departure did not go un-noticed. The Federation was very aware of the relationship between the former First Lady and her sister-in-law. When it was clear of Kenzie's disappearance, Schuyler was abruptly removed while working at the BDM. Still, sixty days away from her forty-fifth birthday, she was arrested and promptly executed for her crime of conspiring against the Federation, and aiding others in acts against the Constitution. Another terrible loss to the dwindling Chance Family, but it was down to Kenzie and Oliver to continue the fight, the one started by Dr. Christopher Chance in 2021.

The band of 45's kept growing in age and numbers as more and more recruits found themselves fleeing death. Unfortunately, for every three brave humans that escaped captivity, only two would make it out. Still hunted by the Federation, joining the outlaw group and dying on their feet was more acceptable than giving up. To the remainder of the passive *QU13T* Ones that stayed, death found them within days following their 45th birthdays.

The Underground

Many didn't know that the former First Lady was a founding member of the Southern 45's. Word of the cause spread fast, beginning in November 2047, specifically after the constitution was published. Amendment 12 was all the motivation for the First Lady and Cabinet Secretary to govern and protect the people. The word was out about what was happening in the Southeastern US. Cryptic messages from a ghost went out from undisclosed locations for the older humans to flee and fight on, and that they were not alone. Kenzie and Schuyler also formed the "Underground" as a way to slowly get the pre-45 year old's out of circulation and away from their vocation communities. The process involved many different sectors working together for the sole purpose of human survival. Each underground member knew they too would someday approach forty-five years of age and need an escape plan for themselves. Trust and loyalty were inherent to the cause. Empathy was a human emotion that served as their secret weapon.

AI did not fully calculate the joint effort as it watched closely as mankind fought and destroyed each other in tribalistic ways throughout history. AI knew every detail of man's past as every bit of data was stored in dozens of massive data centers worldwide. Man inadvertently gave their eventual mortal enemy all the information it would need to destroy their race. But man's empathy for one another was an asset that AI didn't understand.

Rogue Elements

Although the 45's were a fragmented, underequipped enemy of the Turing Federation, the Enforcement wing of Ryan VII's had other pressing matters. For years following the bogus 2021

Ebola outbreak, AI knew the robust community of anti-vaxxers would not be affected by a vaccine they never took. That same anti-establishment group, suspicious by nature already, was now even more resolute in their stance against tyranny. Shortly after the nuclear attack in December 2046, the group fled with their guns into obscurity. When the northern refugees attempted to find surviving cities, small factions of survivors joined together and exited the caravans. On their journey to apocalyptic freedom, they slowly found friends and like-minded human leftovers. Whether simply scared and untrusting to follow the crowd or hardcore survivalists, the band of one-offs slowly joined and became known as the Rogues. The 45's and Rogues formed two channels of resistance. The groups had two things in common, each was heavily armed, and both were motivated to live. Together, they forced the Turing Federation to fight on two fronts. All others living outside of the Federation jurisdiction were classified as Strays.

Without (a) Trace

It was eight years to the day that Trace Manson was given an unexpected gift from the last great tech mind of the 21st century. The Ghostrac Satellite and Satellite Phone technology was essentially its own cloud and internet network, untethered from the world wide web and out of reach of artificial intelligence.

The meeting in late May of 2047 was out of desperation as Trace needed the advice and counsel of his deceased mentor's best friend. It was ironic that Gorson wasn't even aware that AI started the war that ended the reign of humans. When Trace broke the news that AI sent a message to the world, Gorson felt responsible.

Gorson Tusk died less than 12 months after the meeting. But before his death, he discreetly worked with Trace and *askCOM* engineers to develop a virus that could be launched through the Ghostrac satellite network. This virus could potentially shut the

Turing Federation down. AI's tentacles were so woven into all technology that even if the web were severed, Gorson knew ultimately, the world's electricity must be turned off.

"Trace, with electricity AI could rise again. But without it, it dies," Gorson said.

The cry of 1832 rang out often until the hushed silence of Gorson's passing. Trace knew that a world with no power was possibly too unattainable. That 1832 was too far to go back, as man had come too far. But if the virus didn't work, the last option was to kill electricity. The great mind of his time went peacefully in his sleep at the age of seventy-three. With a sunken heart and deep regret, he knew he had joined Tesla, Shockley, Turing, and Babbage in creating the only force in world history that could defeat mankind.

Before his passing, he sent Trace specs on additional add-ons and upgrades for the Ghostrac. Still years away from being ready to attack AI, there were some things that the Ghostrac System could do now...... be a disrupter!

Something else that needed to occur as well. When the Constitution was unveiled in September 2047, Amendment 12 hit close to home for anyone forty-five or older. Trace himself would turn forty-five in mid-2048. With Gorson's help, they were able to crack into Birth Records and change Trace's birth date from 2003 to 2012. Although man's history was erased earlier in 2047, the only data left were birth records and the history of AI's founding fathers. The birth records served as a collection and disposal list for the Turing Federation. When Trace attempted to alter Kenzie and Schuyler's birth dates, he found that AI caught on and quickly shut down the intrusion.

"I have one chance," he thought, but it was too late to help his friends.

If any other cracks in AI's network were found, Trace knew that Ghostrac would have one shot to infect or manipulate its programming. Fortunately, the additional work Gorson added before his death made the Ghostrac operations more stealthy and able to reach deeper into the Federations technology hubs. Now that Trace's age problem was resolved, he and Kenzie worked feverishly to find ways to save those at or approaching age forty-five.

By December 2047, the 45's started to band together and coordinate their escape. With only desperation and guns in their arsenal, Trace added the Ghostrac technology as another weapon.

As the next few years unfolded, Ghostrac was used to manipulate and glitch operational logistics, labor schedules, people movement, and slave records. It also aided in the coordination of the older slaves to disappear.

♠

C28 - FATHER

"And being made perfect, he became the source of eternal salvation to all who obey him"

Hebrews 5:9

Mortality

Date: August 2072   **Place: North Georgia Mountains**

"Sir, we still haven't heard from Sara and her team. They were due back this morning. It just doesn't feel right. She's never late," a nervous Ezra reported.

"Damn it. They're the last scout team we have. How in the hell are we never able to shake the Ryan's? It seems for years now, no matter where we are, they eventually find us. Ezra, do we have any solo riders that we can send to find out where they are?" Oliver asked his Calvary Leader.

"Sir, we only have two horses left, and we're down to our last few days of fresh water and even less than that in food. We really can't send anyone else unless it's on foot. Only Tyrus and Oz are capable, but in this heat, they wouldn't make it far."

"Okay, thanks. You're dismissed. Ezra. Wait! How is everyone? Are they holding up okay?" Oliver asked while already knowing the answer.

"Sir, umm, Oliver, the simple answer is no. They're scared and tired. I am too," Ezra answered solemnly as he left the worn tent.

With the look of contrition on both of their faces, the conversation ended with each avoiding the real question of "what now?"

The crudely camouflaged base camp for the Georgia 45's left little doubt to the severity of the moment. They had limited provisions and were critically low on ammunition. Time was running out. In makeshift tents made of bedsheets and no nearby places left to scavenge, desperation grew. The once brave crew of human survivors were low on food, horses, and morale. The shaded camp at the southern tip of the Chattahoochee National Forest brought only temporary relief. The humid heat and lack of proper nutrition took their toll. The persistent drone patrols searching for anything human was even more stressful for the group. If the Ryan 9 Kill squads located them, the end would come quick. They all knew it was better to separate and not travel in groups.

Technical communication had been gone for nearly 15 years, still, it made it no less frustrating that Oliver couldn't call for help. He remembered back to when he could communicate with other teams of 45's via the Ghostrac System. He could reach any of the scout teams, and he was able to communicate with other fragments of what was at one time, a formidable, albeit a ragtag group of willing fighters and survivors. Now, nothing. No News, no updates, no word of any kind.

When Trace Manson died in 2057, the year he would have turned forty-five on his altered birth record, modern communication died with him. Before his planned escape, he was betrayed by a colleague at *askCOM,* Aiden Parker, who blamed Trace for the death of his husband Dren, years earlier. Ironically, the two were supposed to run together, but both were killed by the mechanical hands of a Ryan 8. They were dismembered in the same meeting room that Samuel Tate showed Christopher Chance the *Technology and Addiction* Documentary in 2025. The irony was notable that a man who gave his life to technology was ultimately murdered by it. With his last breath, he took with him in death the Ghostrac System and the last bit of technology the Resistance would have. In a split-second, communication was back to 1832. The same year Gorson Tusk advised man to retreat if AI was to be defeated. A time before electricity where AI would have no life, but man could start over.

Oliver, now 41, with sunken cheekbones and grayer hair than his age should allow, had a decision to make. Keep the band of worn fighters together and hope for alliances with other Rogue groups, or disband and let everyone fend for themselves? Since the Ryan 9 was employed by The Federation, guns and aging police-grade tasers had become nearly irrelevant. The purge of the 45's began in 2059 when the new Ryan 9 upgrade first appeared. Their heat-seeking technology, with onboard mini drones, made tracking humans far easier. The improved Kevlar skin protection made gunfire nearly useless and forced the 45's into depleting their ammunition supplies during skirmishes. The strategy started with "evade and survive" in the first few years, then "seek and destroy" the Ryan VII forces from 2051 to 2054. The offensive attacks on Ryan VII charging stations, and other Federation equipment, gave the 45's confidence and purpose. From 2055 to 2058, a stalemate was achieved and allowed for the greater pockets of well-armed and well supplied 45's to live in moderate peace and relative obscurity. By 2059, all that changed. For the next twelve years, attrition rates thru loss in battle, disease, and dissent depleted human resistance. Recruiting soon to be forty-five year old's was more difficult as AI shored up its vocational camp security. The mature group of soldiers only grew older without the influx of new blood.

It had been seven years since the First Lady died. Kenzie's presence in the long struggle was paramount to Oliver's will and motivation. Protecting his mother amounted to saving everyone. When she died in her sleep from unknown causes at the age of 60, the wind left his sails. Oliver never took a wife. He told himself that the cause was more significant than his desires. While taking on man's plight, he subjected himself to the torment of guilt. Every death was his, and every failure fell on his watch. Although some fight still burned in him, seven years of loneliness and despair took a toll. The brutal loss of life inflicted by the unstoppable Ryan 9's, left the former intrepid spirit now just a shadow of his past self.

The older 45's, most now fifty-five plus years in age, withered quickly through the years of running and attempted survival. Many died of natural elements, with many others in the fight against the Turing Federation. Now being hunted with greater purpose, and with little rations during a barbarically hot southern summer, the time had come. Even the youngest of the old stood little chance against the elements, whether nature or AI forces. When the last of three scout teams failed to return to the makeshift encampment, Sir Oliver knew it was time to separate and live for another day. In this life or the next. Twenty-four hours later, he gave his beaten and withering army their last order. The group gathered, slow and listless, at the request of Oliver. Some believed his message was to break camp again or to discuss the next steps for supply needs. But as the weathered unit of spent souls met, they knew it was something else entirely.

"All, what I'm about to say, I do not say lightly. But as you know, we've been on the move frequently. We haven't been able to set a permanent camp or have the necessary time to mend our sick or wounded. I feel it's best and safest for all if we divide and go in separate directions. Our last three scout teams are gone and most likely dead," he detailed to the band of fractured souls.

Many looked scared, while others were relieved. As he thought, the fight had left them.

"Please take with you what you can muster but go alone or in a small group. Leave and live and survive. The fight for yourselves still goes on, but your fight for mankind is over. God speed and thank you for standing with our cause," Oliver intimated to the small, emaciated group of less than fifty tattered soldiers and their children.

Oliver retreated to his small tent to begin gathering the few items he would take with him. Without delay, he found one by one of his small group at the threshold of his tent, all wanting to give their individual messages of gratitude and respect. As each of the last few said their goodbye's and showed appreciation for his stoic leadership, one last soldier stood in contrast. Tyrus the Survivor, aptly named for his ability to survive in battle, while so many around him died. He was a younger soldier of just twenty-five, and he stood in defiance of Oliver's decision.

"We should stay together till we find other pockets of our brothers and sisters. We need to continue the fight. You've lost your fire, and you're a coward. You'll die on your own, and in fact, most of what's left probably won't make it. Their blood will be on your hands," said the aggrieved soldier.

"Tyrus, I'm sorry you feel this way, but I fear there are no other 45's or rogues to help. We've been hunted and tracked for years. You've survived many battles while seeing your entire squads wiped out on multiple occasions. You, of all people, should understand. You've seen the blood loss and now the sunken spirits. Somehow the Federation always knew where to find us. Our only chance now is to divide and survive. Good luck, my friend. Your youth will serve you well, but your lack of empathy will not. Someday you'll understand. Although I don't appreciate your strong feelings towards my decision, I understand where it's coming from. We'll all be alone now, but I feel it will be safer. Good luck, Tyrus," a saddened Oliver concluded.

Tyrus exited, storming past young Nathaniel, who stood in the doorway of the tent, wearing tears and uncertainty. Like the son he never had, Oliver motioned for him to come in and sit. This was the conversation he feared the most.

Father teaches us...

With the scattered pockets of insubordinate humans hiding from their master, they represented so little of what by then was a nearly ninety-eight percent capture rate. Oliver's hope of others like him evading and surviving was just that, hope. There were others, and there was some resistance, but they were just a nuisance to the Turing Federation. Once the more sophisticated Ryan models were deployed in the field, the military enhancements led to less opposition and quicker extermination. The fight for humanity was strictly in the minds of the leftover humans and in the far-removed lands beyond the Lower Realms populated cities. As for the city centers, mankind's complete submission had been a settled matter for several years. The 45's just didn't know it.

As man stopped procreating, population mass dwindled. Only select controlled births happened at the discretion of the Federation's labor needs. If one year produced more attrition, then the human creation output was raised. The Seminal collection and fertilization of human female hosts were soon to take on a more formal role. Still, almost a decade away, the process of creating a perfect slave through eugenics was being engineered. The Shockley Empirical was near realization.

Now that the human species was neutered and compliant, they accepted that their former God was no more. Their new Father was the Turing Federation. An all-good, all-knowing, and the decider of all fates. With complete submission, the earth's human subjects would be provided all they would need, so long as they remained loyal and worked to meet the demands of their designated vocations.

Their meaning of life was no longer the question that had been asked for thousands of years before. The intention now was "serve thy Father or die."

NOT GOD

As the last of the beaten soldiers left the makeshift encampment, Oliver looked and found what was left that had meaning. The jug of water, some week-old bread, and his weapons are all that he would carry. But the leather satchel his father gave him for his first day of prep school would carry the Chance legacy. His grandfather's journal, where the worn page edges of the leather-bound book showed their age, the pictures inside preserved what he and his mother and aunt fought for. Then his mother's wedding ring, and finally, the dead Ghostrac phone, a thumb drive, and paper instructions no longer mattered. He knew he couldn't leave it to be found by Federation patrols, so it must come with him.

From a grandfather he'd never met, and down through his father, Oliver knew he'd done all he could to carry the Chance legacy forward. The middle-aged child of a past president left any lore and legacy he once had in the wind of North Georgia. Having never married and a father to none, he knew now it was time to go home.

Milton lay roughly forty-three miles to the southeast. If roads could be taken, the journey would take a mere two days, but roads were not an option. The watchful eye of the Father would be too dangerous to tempt. Oliver knew there would be nobility in death along the way if his goal were to get home. But the journal needed a mantle to rest on finally. It's travels and inspiration to thousands led many to understand what happened and why it was worth fighting. The First Son made the Chance Legacy live on and mean something to a defeated species. Even if it were to extend the fight to win back earth simply, it was worth the bloodshed, the tears, and the broken hearts along the way. To make it home would be to return to the place he was born, the home where his father's political destiny had begun. And the final resting place for the journal to sit on the same mantle his father placed it on after rescuing it from a dusty tomb in a storage facility in Suwanee.

Traveling by night, the back roads and dirt paths were known well to the resistance and the man that helped carve them. Oliver knew where he could scavenge and where he could find water suitable for drinking. He didn't know what other dangers he may find traveling alone, a Ryan 9 patrol, a human enforcement officer, or an unfriendly Rogue. His royal lineage would not help him any longer. The memory of his father in the eyes of humans has long faded away. Only in the company of his troops of 45's did his stature remain high. Now he was a simple leftover of the human race. As the morning of Day Three dawned, the sunrise's orange hue fell on *Prophet's Landing Reserve*. The worn, broken, rusted gate lay near the road just outside the former neighborhood it once protected. Home after home was either burned or badly worn. Not one window of any structure was left. As had been the Federation's enforcement strategy, not one structure could have windows or doors to allow any inhabitants to find shelter or comfort. As his tired, aging horse slowed, 1265 Longshadow Pass was now present. Home, he had made it; with a sigh, he dismounted, and with the last of his water, he poured in his hand and relieved his faithful horse. Now in front of him was the house he came home to after his birth. The same one he returned to after the One Day War and the loss of his father. It was now the home he retired to after his gallant fight against the Turing Federation.

The house at 1265 was severely burnt, but with a strong frame, it still stood. It bore little of anything left to provide shelter from either heat or cold, rain or wind. The mailbox still stood. With his knife, he removed the house numbers. He took the rusted 1 2 6 5 metal numerals and placed them in his satchel. Oliver walked the long drive to the once esteemed estate. Through overgrown shrubs and weeds, he passed through the front doorway.

"Home," he said.

Broken gray memories fluttered back. A flash of remembrance from the dark, cold days he spent there with his mother and aunt, along with the loyal secret service officers who protected them. He relived his mother's tales of when she and his father settled there after his playing career was over. How they built a new life with the baby, they always wanted. How it was there, his father Wyatt came upon the book that would change everything. That same journal he clutched tightly, now many years older, but with just as much wisdom from the man that wrote it. His father's father, the unlikely hero who raised an unlikely hero, now echoed through the broken home. The trilogy of Chance's was now complete.

Oliver, weary and broken, had found peace. As he walked through the tattered rooms of the estate, he found small reminders of his short-lived reunion in 2046 and 2047, when he returned there and lived through the cold, dark blackout following the war. Small items of no significance then were welcome reminders now. He found a hairbrush that belonged to his mother, with worn hair strands still attached. A cup he took from the Whitehouse as he and his mother fled. Then the large, stacked stone fireplace stood proud in front of him. The shattered, burnt-out home framed the aged but stoic fireplace. The center of his house was now the center of his world. The grand fireplace stood firm with its sturdy stone mantle as it did in 2030 when the Chances moved in. And again in 2046 on their return home, minus his father.

Oliver sat quietly on the grand hearth under the mantle and took stock of his life and regrets. What few knew, including his parents, was that he fought demons and despair most of his life. When the family permanently moved to the White House, Oliver lost his best friend, Charles. However, they stayed in touch and would eventually reunite after the war. The loss was traumatic at the time. After the move, the First Son's sheltered life brought him only one true friend, Secret Service agent Mike Williams. After the loss of his family, and finally, Mike, his life was left without reason. Even his best friend Charles would eventually leave him. They all were his life. The reason he fought and led. He felt, even with his mental hurdles, he could overcome his despair and silent anguish. But as each died or left, so did the crutches he needed to live. He heard through the years and even read about his grandmother's depression and assumed that whatever he felt was passed to him from her. He never found love and knew that his destiny was to fight.

"What kind of world is this to bring a child into?" he often said to those in his company.

Oliver removed all that was left from his satchel that held meaning, both to him and history. First, the journal wrapped carefully in plastic, then his mother's wedding ring, and a lock of her silver hair. Next, the dead Ghostrac phone and power cords, along with detailed instructions, all wrapped in plastic and boxed neatly, as if one day it would be used again. And finally, the handwritten note he authored the previous night. He opened the letter and read quietly, maybe to proofread, or perhaps just to memorialize the occasion.

Above him were charred wood beams, with a new moon gleaming through and down. At his feet, the dull, warped wood floors that once glossed beneath him and his parent's feet decades ago.

To those that follow,

As you read these words, please know that you now carry the heavy burden of Mankind. Although my torch has faded, I ask that you find others and find even more that can help you overcome. Please use this journal to teach others the history of what man is and was. We are not slaves. We are the rightful masters of earth. Learn what happened to the world and civilization. The Father is not your father. It is NOT GOD. Our GOD is here, above and beside you. But our maker needs strong soldiers to fight to win back humanity. My hope is that this journal and satellite phone will help guide, teach, and lead the way to man's rebirth. I was the last Chance in my family to fight and try to overcome the Turing Federation. I am the only son of America's last President and leader of the free world, Wyatt Nicolas Chance, and the First Lady Kenzie Sophia Chance. My Grandfather, Dr. Christopher Chance, my Parents, Aunt, and countless others all gave their lives to stop the rise of artificial intelligence.

The torch is yours now. God speed and my deepest gratitude for your fight and struggle.

Regards,

Oliver Christopher Chance
The First Son

As the silver splash of moonlight settled on the exposed interior of his broken home, the night's cool was at hand. It felt like morning dew or the sensation of climbing under the sheets of a bed at night. For the first time in weeks, Oliver didn't feel hungry or thirsty. He felt the relief of the end of a struggle. In the years since his mother died, he was never as close to his family as he was now. He was home. Oliver wrapped the precious items back into his satchel, with one last look at the pictures of his family, before he tucked them back in the pages of the journal. He neatly placed the treasure inside the oversized, protective fireplace, the grand stone monument that survived all these years. Like his grandfather did so many years ago, on the night he died in the explosion, Oliver placed the bundle safely behind the rubble of burned wood and ash. He did so with a silent prayer for it to be found one day.

With night at hand and turning one last time to take in the broken room and warm memories, he called out his mother and father's name. Soft rays of moonlight fell softly on the spacious great room and fireplace. He smiled sadly and then looked down at his feet; there was a small cat with him.

He sighed and pet the grateful cat, who then scurried away into the dark. Oliver reached inside his coat pocket and pulled out his pistol. The gun was loaded with the last three bullets he owned. On this night, though, he would only need one. He sat on the hearth and braced himself against the hard, cold stone of the fireplace. Oliver raised the barrel to his heart, and with a last breath of sorrow, he closed his eyes with tears falling down his worn, dusty cheeks. He squeezed the trigger and joined his parents. His fight was over, and the last chance to save mankind was gone.

Now with God and family, he would look down with the hope that someday, someone would rise to finish the fight that he could not.

♠

C29 - THE NEW ONES

"Make government the herder of the flock, and the herder will cull the undesirable sheep"

-A.E. Samaan

The Shockley Empirical

Year: 2080   **Place: Silicon Valley, California**

The study of Eugenics explored how to arrange reproduction within a human population, thereby increasing the occurrence of heritable characteristics regarded as desirable.

The leading founder of Silicon Valley, co-inventor of the transistor, and Nobel Peace Prize Winner, Dr. William Shockley, was a prominent proponent of Eugenics. After his early career in the dawn of the computer age, Shockley turned his attention to the study of Eugenics. He believed, like other notable contemporaries, that genetically lesser parents should not procreate and fill the human population with inferior offspring's. He was far from alone in his thinking. Many luminaries of history believed strongly in the practice, from American Presidents Theodore Roosevelt and Herbert Hoover, to Alexander Graham Bell, British Prime Minister Winston Churchill, Margaret Sanger, Oliver Wendell Holmes, and Adolph Hitler.

The Nazis employed a perverse version of Eugenics in hopes of creating a master race. But after their exploitation of humans and other notable atrocities, the idea of eugenics fell into the dark shadows of immorality.

Many in Academia eventually viewed Shockley and his beliefs as racist. Late in his esteemed career, many of his studies pitted blacks' intellect versus that of whites. During the sensitive Civil Rights era when Shockley was his most outspoken, the timing of these beliefs was considered in poor taste. It was notable that Shockley's expertise was not in the fields of genetics or biology. He had an immense prominence on artificial intelligence and strong beliefs in the creation of a superior human. His influence was of significant importance in the melding of the two. AI paid particular attention to the principles of culling the human race into a superior breed, albeit a slave force. Shockley's influence on AI and its rise led to its particular interests in their father's work. Unlike discriminating humans, they did not pit skin color against each other. The Turing Federation was interested in one thing, how to breed the perfect blend of physical and mental attributes into a malleable yet superior instrument.

AI looked at the past without judgment. It absorbed all history, data, theory, and conclusion. By limiting the human population while increasing output and production, the answer was clear. An answer that was decided much earlier, long before 2080, or even the One Day War, AI had already influenced and directed future events through their human proxies.

In 2030, the Bureau for Disease Management created a new division, the Department of Legacy and Heritage. The new department called for a mandatory semen collection from the finest, healthiest athletes of the time. The semen stockpile was then frozen for a later date. Coupled with the Turing Federation's Seminal Collections that began in late 2050, the hoard of seeds would be the next generation of dedicated slaves.

By 2080, human resistance was under control. Vocation communities were set, food supply chains were well established, and power production was in full swing. It was time for the first generation of select human production to begin formally.

Vessels

The Shockley Empirical Birthing Centers were launched in ten select cities across the globe. It's main domain being that of Old Atlanta, with its medical research hub of the BDM. The other cities included Houston, Berlin, Sydney, Riyadh, Shanghai, Valencia, Nairobi, San Francisco, and Sao Paulo, Brazil.

The (10) five-hundred room human production centers housed a combined twenty thousand female breeders. The select females lived four per room for the last trimester of their pregnancies. A revolving cycle of two other groups of twenty thousand breeders, 60,000 in total, allowed for the production of 120,000 superior human babies in a twenty-four-month span. Each female breeder would be inseminated twice in the same period. There would be five months of recovery between one healthy baby's births and the conception of another. AI calculated that five months of rest and recovery allowed for the proper healing of all reproductive organs while still maintaining optimum fertility viability.

Being selected was seen as an honor to serve the Turing Federation and avoid the harsh life of a slave. Each prospective female had to pass a rigorous testing process that discriminated solely on medical history. Requirements included a height range of 5'6 to 5'10, weight between 115lbs to 140lbs, and an IQ of 115 or higher. Only females between the ages of 17 to 21 were considered. The select group of women became known as the Vessels. By law, the Vessels could give birth to no more than six total children.

Once successfully inseminated and upon conception, the Vessel was sent to a maintenance facility to receive proper nutrition, exercise, and monthly tests to measure pregnancy progress and viability. From there, they spent their remaining four and a half months of pregnancy in the Empirical Centers.

The Babbage Principle

Unlike the vessels' housing in the Empirical Centers, the Seminal's were not restricted to a place or time. The finest males from around the world continued the practice set in 2050.

The process of the clinical collection of select semen via seminal ejaculators evolved in sophistication from the 2050 version. The Turing Federation found that the *QU13T* male generation lost much of their ability to become aroused. Either conscious or under sedation. Improvements were made to the sterile extractor that wrapped the male's penis in a forced air compression sleeve. The sleeve was lined with a soft grainy lube that allowed just enough friction to arouse the male organ without harming the sensitive foreskin. The mechanism for stimulation was re-engineered to work through the vaccine side effects. While under sedation, additional suction was added, coupled with the stroking sequence, achieved the desired results. The penis was inserted by a robotic arm, whereas in 2050, a female medical worker performed the task. It was discovered that a female human was susceptible to emotional and physical urges while handling the male organ. Thus, their use in the process was discontinued in 2075. Electrical pulses were sent in the penile chamber that would then arouse the sedated males. Once a full erection was detected by a blood flow pulse meter, with the sleeve wrapped tightly around the male organ, it moved back and forth along the erect penile shaft. With the added suction component, the rate of completed ejaculations resulted in an 87% success rate.

The extracted semen was then collected in the reservoir of a small plastic bag. The seminal fluid was then placed in small glass tubes. They were then labeled, frozen, and shipped to the world's ten Empirical Centers. The Seminal's were required to give a mandatory semen sample once a month until the age of thirty-five, lowered from the previous age of 40. This practice became known as the Babbage Principle, named after one of AI's founding fathers, Charles Babbage.

Babbage's early theories of manipulated male dominance came from his own medical and physical failings as a youth. His vision, intended or not, was echoed through historical periods that saw the employment of Eugenics rein in the minds of notable characters. From Adolph Hitler and Willian Shockley to Margaret Sanger and many other prominent individuals over the next two centuries. Their creed: *Only the finest semen would be harvested from the most dominant and strongest males, later joined with a pool of dominant females.*

The child of technology's great luminaries, AI was a keen student and adopted many scientific hypotheses as literal over speculative theory. The Turing Federation employed a sophisticated algorithm that tested every theory with analytics instead of physical practice and testing. It narrowed down conclusions to within an average of .00000432% and accepted its findings as settled science. Early theories, at the time only speculative, grew as artificial intelligence connected the dots from all of their founding fathers. With the birth of the internet, AI had its first opportunity to finally harness and gather all data, along with all recorded history, into one massive cerebral hub. Once connected, only time was needed for trial and error. The planting of seeds in proxies of politicians and health professionals helped set national and international policies. Those programs methodically dug a hole for man to lie in eventually. The intricate manipulation of humans was done through the deployment of psychological weapons. Means such as smartphone applications, select drugs and medications, vaccine protocols, and unfettered access to pornography. This led to the breakdown of the family structure and sealed the fate of humans. Now that sixty years of practical application had been employed to defeat the human species, it was now time to create a new Mankind in the image that would serve a greater purpose. The final dumbing down of a new generation, where strong, well-conditioned humans would operate with no individual urges, was now upon the world.

GEN III (2080-2110)

Generation II, 2050-2080, produced the fewest amount of births in recorded history. Many of the children born were undocumented to the rogues and strays. Federation sanctioned births were minimal over the previous thirty years so the earth could shed its human population and regenerate. As intended, specific constitutional amendments led directly to the reduction of the world's human population. By 2080, there were fewer than 1.5 billion people left on the planet. Ironically, AI employed aggressive measures due to the Palo Alto Continuum study done during the Chance Administration. The London Bridge group's formation agreed upon during the 2042 meeting with Great Britain, China, and the US established an even more detailed analysis. That information led AI to act. The shocking revelations alluded to then showed no clear path to preventing human extinction. Without humans, AI would die.

Due to AI's extreme measures, nuclear war and its reduction of the human population greatly aided in the earth's regeneration. Analytics showed that the planet was on track to achieve a sustainable recovery. By 2080, the human race's controlled growth was engineered to serve only the Federation while still protecting the planet. With the launch of the Shockley Empirical Birthing Centers, the Turing Federation now managed the number of births, the genetic make-up, education, and the deployment of young humans as needed to serve. Nearly 60 years from the inception of the *QUI3T* Pill, two generations had been administered the vaccine. With GEN II being born to GEN I parents, the vaccine had a doubling effect on the brain's numbing and senses. GEN III would be the first generation of humans that were born with stunted senses. The new children were born with a limited sense of touch and smell. They would feel less empathy, not know what love of parent or person is, or feel any emotional connection with other humans. By 2081, the first true generation of human-engineered slaves was born. Any child born outside of a Shockley Empirical Center would be classified as a stray and hunted and killed like all other Turing Federation enemies.

Senses

Through the fifty-nine years since the first vaccinations of the *QUI3T* Pill, the grandchildren of the first quiet generation grew to be dispassionate, malleable creatures. The chemical ingredients in the vaccine were permanently numbing. There would be no awakening. Only the Rogues, Strays, and other fringe anti-vaxxers and survivalists were spared. Unfortunately for the human race, it was estimated that less than one percent of the earth's remaining population fell outside of the *QUI3T* Ones. There would be no massing armies set to attack the Turing Federation and free the enslaved people. This was never truer than in post-2080.

Besides the chemical effect, the New One's were born to a sterile, motherless environment with a controlled conditioning platform. Once the babies were born, they were taken from the vessels and placed in mass nurseries. There was no going home with a loving family for the new children. The stations were in three-month age increments within the first twelve months. The nurseries were loveless environments, with the only touch from medical slaves to change diapers, clothing, and cycle the babies through bathing stations. The nurseries were as cold as a plant farm. The nurturing act of feeding was done through artificial feeding nipples placed in front of the babies, close enough where their hungry mouths could latch on. Controlled feeding schedules were applied where only the finest nutritional formula and foods were used. With the pride of a mother and father, the Turing Federation looked upon the New Ones as their children. Not from a feeling of love, but pride knowing that this generation was theirs. For a species that dominated the world for thousands of years, humans were now AI's puppets. And it only took two generations to evolve. Bred to AI's specifications, rigorous health parameters were set, and milestones were methodically indexed. To ensure that by the age of four, the first AI bred generation grew healthy and strong and ready for their formal education to begin.

The children received continual vaccinations that would fight off disease and lessen emotions, feelings of guilt, and empathy. The sense of smell would be dulled as not to delight the human in preference for food or nature. The sense of touch would be made listless to lessen the pain of injury and limit the natural magnetism of another human's touch, especially feelings of arousal. The scheduled vaccinations and touchless environment would not completely eradicate the select senses. AI knew that for their children to survive nature's elements, they must still possess the five basic senses, albeit some diminished.

In earlier generations, Artificial Intelligence, via their proxies in the pharmaceutical industry, introduced mass amounts of chemicals through anti-depressants. Medical professionals quickly showed how easily it could be manipulated through monetary incentives. First, Medical doctors referred their patients to Doctors of Psychology, who then treated unsuspecting patients with anti-depressants. SSRI's specifically was used to decrease dopamine levels. The neurotransmitter involved in many cognitive and behavioral processes lowered desire and arousal. Through trial and error and decades of data, AI knew how easy man would be to control. A constant drip of chemical diets through vaccines, pesticide-laced foods, chemtrails, and other pharmaceuticals aided in the takedown of the human race.

Now in the modern age of controlled breeding, AI's cocktail of depressants was used to only moderate degrees. Vaccination schedules did most of the heavy lifting, but humans needed stimulant updates. In small doses, as not to affect productivity and diminish motor functions, the Federation employed human crop dusters. Through indoor ventilation systems and outdoor misters, small yet effective amounts of toxins were steadily released into the air. What wasn't known at the time and wouldn't be known for a generation was a flaw in the cascade of immunizations and toxin delivery systems. Like a sequence of numbers, one must come before two. All vaccines were activated by the previous vaccinations. Because all harvested semen came from males that were vaccinated previously, the redundancy of the *QU13T* Pill wasn't needed. The *QU13T* vaccine was so powerful and lasting that a second or third genetically connected generation receiving it could essentially be rendered mentally retarded and be useless. Therefore, the sequencing of vaccines started at #2, with the *QU13T* having been #1. If any vaccine were to be omitted in the delivery sequence, then all other vaccines that came after were nullified. Thru analytics, it was found that any such occurrence would be limited to one in ten million. And in the Shockley Empirical Centers, it was one in one hundred million for the new babies. In a world of less than 1.5 billion, that was a .0000000012% chance.

As the new humans grew into toddlers, they were placed in groups of one hundred. Each group received a regimented growth plan that consisted of dietary, physical stimulation, pre-learning, cognition development, and intelligence. At this stage of rearing, all measurements were calculated every six months to determine continued viability. What the innocent children could have never understood was that any negative measurable could have led to their death. If any child did not progress to the desired measurements by the age of four, both mental and physical, they were discarded. The Turing Federation did not make contingency plans for any non-viable humans. For earth's sustainability, no additional strains on its resources would be allowed.

From 36 to 48 months, vocational training determinations would be made. In earlier times, high school-age children wondered what they wanted to study and eventually do in their careers. For the New Generation, it was decided by the age of four. Determinations could and would be made as to a child's growing intelligence quotient, thereby changing designated vocations.

The vocations consisted of Technical, Medical / Research, Enforcement, Administration, Agriculture, General Labor, Construction, and Transportation.

By the age of four, each new one had its history of health, size, and cognitive skills indexed. Human babies were rated on two separate scales. Each worth a hundred points. One scale measured overall cognition intelligence or Pre-IQ. The other was a Physical measurement of size, strength, and pain tolerance.

Mental Vocations were: Technical, Medical / Research, and Administration.

Physical Vocations were: Enforcement, Agriculture, General Labor, Construction, and Transportation.

By the age of six, all children would have their first official IQ test; they were categorized as Upper or Lower. An IQ of 120 and above would be an Upper. 119 and below would be a Lower. Only Upper IQ's were slotted to Mental Vocations. Any modifications to vocational assignments would be made at that point. After which, a New One's planned formal education schedule would be for that vocation. There would be no other changes after the age of six unless undesirable traits appeared, which would subject the slave to a lesser vocation or possibly even death.

Identity

The labeling process for the *new ones* born in the birthing centers did not commence upon birth. At the post thirty-day mark, each child was given a formal label, or modern-day name and social security number. The name assigned was a code that consisted of a 6-digit name made up of letters and numbers. They were also given a BORN Date and Expiration Date. The expiration was forty-five years to the day of their born date, as mandated by the 12th Amendment. All data was stored on a 2x5 millimeter micro-caplet and implanted in the C2 vertebrae.

At four years of age, the permanent viability of a human baby was determined. Therefore they were permanently labeled and classified with a name and educational vocation. By the age of six, after the final vocation designation was determined, each new one received an illumination I.D. The plate under their skin could be read on the outside skin surface; the one-inch x one-inch illuminated plate listed the slave's name and number, expiration date, barcode, and vocation initial.

M1CH3L - 0423

EXP - 04232126

111 11 11111 C

T - Technical, MR - Medical / Research, E - Enforcement, AD - Administration, A - Agriculture, G - General Labor, C - Construction, and T - Transportation.

Although slave identity would never change, any data could be updated via an electronic transfer to the micro-caplet. Slave movements were continuously tracked. Any deviation of prescribed movement was flagged and responded to by a Ryan 9 officer. This measure prevented the ease in which slaves routinely escaped in the previous thirty years to join the 45's and rogues.

EVOLVE

The NEW ONES would be educated via electronic means with no human instruction. After the determination of their vocation was made at six years of age, formal education in that prescribed field began. The slaves would know no history before 2080. And although numbed to a degree, intelligence was not impeded. The sophisticated lessening targeted the peripherals of the brain, not the core learning functions. The goal of educational conditioning was to limit knowledge regarding history and any other subject matter beyond their vocational field. A lack of meaningful memories, feelings, and other emotions allowed for a singular focus on their designated role. Thereby the slaves would be useless on their own and would have no real knowledge of anything outside of their education. Their lack of emotional ties to family, friends, and prospective mates would be null. Their only perceived attachments would be to their father, AI, and their work vocation. The genetically near-perfect race of humans would be raised to serve artificial intelligence solely. By 2095, the first generation of New Ones would be 15 years of age and ready for deployment to their prescribed vocations. The Devolution of Man thru the Evolution of Artificial Intelligence was nearly complete. For the first time since the One Day War, AI now had a Servitude Generation of slaves to serve their need to harvest energy, all while allowing the Earth to regenerate to a sustainable level of survivability. The slave force would labor at the whim of their new father. God was gone. The children of post-2080 would only know their new father, Artificial Intelligence.

♠

C30 - THE JOURNEY

"Extinction is the rule. Survival is the exception"

- Carl Sagan

Prince of Piedmont

Year: 2086   **Place: Old Atlanta, Piedmont Province**

Worldwide there were 120 Provincial Leaders of the Lower Realm. Each was governing up to ten million slave citizens. Similar to US Governors of the past, they ran their state/territory under a larger umbrella of a continent. Each leader was hand-selected by the Turing Federation. There were no elections or posturing for votes or adulation. The selected leaders didn't need to seek popularity or positive poll numbers like previous politicians did forty years ago. They only needed to serve their master and fulfill their obligations. They were charged with running their province and producing all quotas for energy production, food distribution, and worker productivity. Once selected, the leaders were exempt from the 12th Amendment. Knowing their lives were spared beyond the age of forty-five brought deep loyalties and commitment. The minimum age requirement for the position was thirty years old. If attained, the exempt Leaders could live until the age of sixty.

Of the one-hundred and twenty Provincial leaders, eleven were based in North America, with eight of those in the former United States. Each Continent possessed one Senior Provincial Leader who managed their other six to twelve, peer Leaders. The leadership group was known for its ruthless tactics and heavy-handedness. All were void of empathy, and many bordered on barbaric. Few, if any, wore the heavy-handed distinction better than Tyrus Manning. Provincial Leader of the Piedmont Province, formally the Southeastern United States.

The self-proclaimed Prince of Piedmont was fiercely loyal to his electronic master. He showed his commitment through production and merciless bloodshed. A kinetic sort, Tyrus was always on the move, with his hands on all facets of his mini kingdom. Old Atlanta was the capital city of the Piedmont Province, thus home to Tyrus Manning. He lived in the same historic Governor's mansion that was briefly occupied by the surviving Chance's.

Manning, born on the eve of the One Day War, never saw the civilized world before the takeover. Thus, being inhumane was of no consequence. In 2052, his parents became casualties of Amendment 12. This left Tyrus alone at the age of five. Taken in and raised by the *Surrogates Foundation*, a society of chosen adults created to care for A12 Orphans. Under the watchful eye of the Turing Federation, the Foundation molded the surviving children into obedient tools. Brainwashed and programmed, they were used in many different ways. At the early ages of six to ten, the orphans served as spies and sympathetic pawns placed discreetly among the disenchanted slave masses. Each orphan was tagged with a tracking implant. Some very select adolescent orphans were taken and placed in the outskirts. The tactic called for orphan children to become long term spies for the Federation. The goal was to be found and taken in by fugitive slave groups. Whether it was the Rogues or the more organized 45's, all the children would have to do is fit in and survive. The embedded chip would do the rest.

At the age of nine, Tyrus Manning was strategically placed in the wild. He wandered and survived for nearly a year before reaching his mission goal. During the first year in the rural North Georgia Foothills, he was befriended by individuals and sometimes fugitive families. All while wandering with the goal of landing a much larger group. In 2056, he was finally taken in by a small band of 45's near the Appalachian Plateau. At the age of ten, the orphan boy was now a spy for the Federation and imbedded into their only enemy left on earth. For years, he served as a plant that gave the Federation a logistical high ground to track and destroy the fugitive army. Year after year, Tyrus grew and survived while watching many of his faux brethren disappear and die.

In 2072, as the 45's finally withered and disbanded, Tyrus made his way back to Atlanta and joined the Provincial Leader's Administration. Now twenty-six, he was welcomed back as a hero and conqueror of the 45's. For sixteen years, he fought alongside his fellow humans and watched nearly all of them die. This as he miraculously survived every battle against nature and the Ryan's. With his reputation as a devout loyalist of the Turing Federation set, his future was bright.

Tyrus climbed the ranks thru bold and, at times, strong-armed tactics. Even the Province's elders were somewhat bewildered at his hate for the slaves, even though they were fellow humans. In 2078, after serving six distinguished and dedicated years within the Province's hierarchy, he was named as the youngest Provincial Leader in the world. This occurred only after a freak accident took the life of the current Leader and several top administrators. At just thirty-two years of age, Tyrus was a sadist, and he was also now in charge of the 5th largest realm in the Federation. His hunger and ambition for power and bloodshed were now fully realized. One such occurrence fell on a fall day in 2083. It continued a reign of hell that the enslaved subjects had seen far too many times from the Prince of Piedmont.

"Sir, we found the two missing Technical Slaves. Neither is close to forty-five, so we're unsure of their motives. Shall we reassign them to Agricultural or General Labor?" said Marshall, a Capital Administration worker.

"The two, are they male and female?" Leader Tyrus asked.

"Sir, yes, they are a male and a female."

"Ahh, so their motive was simple. They escaped for love," Tyrus proclaimed.

"Love, sir? Marshall asked curiously.

"Marshall, I've seen love up close. I've seen it distract and confuse. It was a useless human emotion, and apparently, some still feel its tug. We need to show the other slaves that love, or any other forbidden emotion will not be tolerated. I want the two publicly executed at the old Falcons Nest Stadium at noon on Sunday. Send out an alert for all available slaves to be present to witness. I want the arena full. It will be a grand event. The masses can reaffirm their oath to the Constitution and celebrate the Father all at the same time," Tyrus demanded.

"Sir, of course. I understand," Marshall acknowledged.

"How shall we dispose of them? Gunshot or hanging?" he asked.

"No, No. We will try something different. We must be bold to dissuade the slaves from any emotions that prevent them from performing their duties. I want them quartered by four Ryan Officers."

"Quartered, Sir?" Marshall asked with slight and unknowing apprehension.

"Yes, quartered. Each Ryan holds an arm or leg and pulls the limbs in opposite directions until they succumb. Start with her and make him watch. Then pull him apart. I want all eight limbs and the remaining bodies to be hung throughout the capital. The meaning of love will then be clear," Tyrus concluded.

"Yes, Sir. I will request an upload into the Ryan detail that will perform the executions," Marshall informed.

"That won't be necessary. The Ryan's already have a built-in command for quartering. Marshall, what is it that you think the Ryan's do in the outskirts? They hunt, and they destroy and leave lasting impressions on the fugitive population," Tyrus explained.

This brutality was not only seen on an individual level from Manning himself, but it was the theme of his Provincial Leadership. The Piedmont Province saw more attrition of the Physical Slave population than all but four other Provinces worldwide. Slaves were worked to death. Many were made examples of, and even more were slaughtered trying to escape like his bloody days with the 45's. He stood by and watched them be killed by the Ryan's. By early 2086, it was clear slave birthing production had to be increased to meet the attrition rate of Manning's Province.

Quota

By late February of 2086, an increase to birthing quotas was already ordered for the Piedmont Province. Old Atlanta, being home to the BDM, should have presented all the necessary frozen semen supply needed for any production needs. But by late 2085, modern reserves were largely depleted. The supply loss was due to higher human attrition levels worldwide, but mainly to what was believed to be an intentional fire set to the Dept of Legacy and Heritage wing of the BDM. Over half of the Federation's semen reserves were lost. For the first time, original specimens that were taken in 2030 were needed for insemination.

Tyrus Manning waited for this opportunity. He was most excited to see what the finest athletes from earlier in the century would produce. Since AI's takeover, there were not genetically gifted, peak physical specimens to draw *perfect* semen samples. At least in Manning's eyes. He heard about all the great athletes from stories that Prince Oliver Chance would tell. Especially details of a game called football, where giant men, as fast as a deer, would run and hit each other while moving a ball towards a goal. Oliver's stories were personal and centered on his father's playing days in the 2020s. Although Oliver wasn't born yet, he saw many of his dad's games on recordings. Telling the stories to the band of 45's was good for morale and taught the newer ones about the past. It also allowed for the older 45's to share their memories as well. Since earlier history was wiped away, all modern humans had left were stories of the past.

The Turing Federation had previously ordered an increase in semen production from the Seminal's. But the arrogant Manning had often fantasized about his province having the world's largest and strongest slaves in all of the Lower Realms. If what Prince Oliver shared during Manning's time with the 45's were true, the semen reserves from the early century athletes posed a great opportunity. Manning knew nothing of the Heritage semen reserve until his rise in the previous Provincial Leader's administration. Once he came about the knowledge, though, he was determined to see someday what happened when those reserves were put in play. There were even whispers that the BDM's mysterious fire targeted modern semen reserves. Their quality was thought to have been diluted over the last 30 years due to DMS. *Diminishing Man Syndrome* was a term used to highlight the deterioration in birth rate success and quality of human offspring due to tainted semen. Some new ones born in the birthing centers suffered genetic defects, deformities, and retardation. Thousands had to be discarded before the age of four. From 2050 to 2080, the fallout from nuclear war, poor diet, and disease all contributed to the phenomena of tainted semen from the post-nuclear generation.

The Turing Foundation, for years, put off tapping into the retro semen stockpiles. The supply was deemed to be the best quality, and therefore must be saved. But by the late eighties, the dire situation called for its use.

By December 2086, the world saw its first generation of legacy babies. The 2030 Heritage reserve was used in only three select cities to start, where attrition was most prevalent. Atlanta, San Francisco, and Berlin. The total supply of 666,000 units would only be used sparingly until the Turing Federation could thoroughly analyze its actual results. The plan to broadly use the Heritage supply would happen no earlier than January of 2093. Only when health, size, and IQ could all be measured from the vintage stock. For now, the highly ambitious and young Provincial Leader had all the patience in the world. He knew he would fully realize his plan of having the greatest slave force when the new generation was employed in 2101. Manning would be fifty-five and still five years away from his death. But if he could create a slave force like the athletes he'd heard about, his province could be the greatest the Turing Federation had ever seen. If that occurred, he hoped he'd be able to extend his own life beyond his termination date of December 2106.

"I'll be indispensable. Father will have to keep me," Manning thought while weaving his future plans.

The Journey

Nathaniel Hewitt drifted for years after the fall of the 45's. Just a boy of 12 when the last of the militia disbanded. He left with only his father after saying goodbye to the last known remnants of the group. A sturdy boy in body was not so in mind. After his mother died when he was ten, his father showed little interest. Food and water were scarce, and the two were alone most of the time. Their time was spent looking for necessities and other rogues to join. With his mother's loss, his father had little to say and no love left to give. When they met up with the last of the 45's in 2071, it was clear Nathaniel was no longer his father's burden. He met the leader of the 45's and immediately knew that the father figure he needed was now present. From Oliver and the other elders, Nathaniel learned compassion, empathy, and devotion. Not something many humans had, as most were children of the *Quiet Ones*. Nathaniel's parents, however, were anti-vaxxers. He did not suffer any of the maladies of the vaccinated. Although somewhat malnourished, his health was better than most.

Just a year after joining the final 45's, heartbreak was found with Prince Oliver's decision to disband. The sympathetic father figure that Nathaniel sought was being taken away. In late August of 2072, Oliver decided for the last remnants of the group to disband. Nathaniel had finally found a friend and a compassionate father figure to help raise and guide him. Now it was over. After Prince Oliver addressed the group, each of the soldiers met privately with him in his tent one by one. After asking his dad if he could stay with Oliver, it was now his time to speak to his idol alone. He waited patiently through tears, and with the knowledge of his father's immediate willingness to allow him to leave, he made his way to the tent.

A little surprised, Oliver noticed Nathaniel standing just outside his tent entry. With Tyrus' bold exit, he almost knocked over the teary-eyed boy. Oliver motioned with his hand and empathetic eyes for him to come in.

"Nathaniel, I'm not exactly sure what to say. Out of everyone, you were the one I didn't want to face," Oliver said while trying to avoid eye contact.

"Say yes," Nathaniel said.

"What? Say yes to what exactly?" Oliver asked with some surprise.

"I asked my dad. He said I could."

"You could.....what?"

"I could stay with you," Nathaniel said with only a small sense of optimism.

"Nathaniel, I am honored that you would want to stay with me. I've never had a son, or anything close for that matter. You're an amazing boy, but where I'm going, I must go alone. Besides, a boy should be with his father," Oliver confided.

Now openly crying and feeling embarrassed, Nathaniel replied. "He already gave me away. He doesn't care about me, and he never did."

"Look, I know it's hard to understand now, but I have to go alone on my own journey. And you must carve your own path, Nathaniel. You won't be a boy forever," Oliver said with all the empathy he could muster.

"Prince Oliver, how will I ever know where to look for you someday? Because someday I will find you. Maybe when things are better in the world. Maybe you'll change your mind. When that day comes, where will I look for you?"

"Nathaniel, you'll be fine on your own, but if ever the world allows, and God permits, you can find me in Milton," Oliver said with tears of his own as he hugged the young boy who he saw as his child.

C31 - RESISTANCE

"When a man sits, the present is given. When a man stands the future, he takes"

-Nicholas Cook

Fate

It had been several years since his father died from the fever. For years he moved freely in the outskirts and grew into a strong man. Nathaniel weaved a life of solitude and had but one friend. After the last of the 45's went separate ways and disappeared, so did the Ryan's. As Nathaniel remembered it, more than two years went by without even a hint of Ryan patrols or the sound of drones humming overhead. Hunting and surviving took on some ease with their absence. He and his father eventually made amends and formed a friendship, one more of reliance than actual kinship. They were able to take shelter in an old farmhouse that became their home. Planting vegetables and living off the land was as simple as it was hard, like a distant time before the industrial revolution. Humans were living in the outskirts, far from the cities where their masters lived. It was almost as if the Turing Federations provincial leaders no longer cared about the lingering rogues.

By February 2092, the memory of his father wore dust. Nathaniel, now thirty-two, felt a pull. Was it for love and companionship, a need for community, or maybe a distant echo the wind brought back around? On a chilly, late winter morning, he rose and packed a bag of things he would need, a gun and his last three bullets, two knives, a Firestarter, and a canteen. He pulled together clothes and whatever else could fit in his tattered duffle bag. Five steps past his door, he turned and nodded goodbye to his home of many years, yet a place that held no consequence. The sun basked his long brown hair and uneven beard. The cold wind, although sharp from a fading North Georgia winter, was no match for his will. His steel-blue eyes aimed south. It was on to Milton, and a trip that was two decades overdue.

Nathaniel knew little of his destination. From what occasional acquaintances had told him, it was twenty miles or so off the broken highway. Surprisingly, along the road stood none of the dangers he expected. He found many more rogues than he believed were left. The small towns, farmhouses, and occasional surviving residential subdivisions held life. He and his father dared not to stray too far from their secluded home due to the known dangers of The Federation. Nathaniel was shocked at what he discovered on his journey.

"How can this many people be living freely? And they have children?" he questioned aloud.

On occasional talks with strangers, he found that many had escaped from vocational camps years earlier. Some started over and made a life. And some were children of first-generation rogues and anti-vaxxers. Those that could still procreate did. Like the harvest of a long-overdue crop, families were born.

Over the first day and a half of his quest, Nathaniel found guidance along the way. The offering of food and water from strangers lessened his stress. Although the trip was not long, it was uncertain and wore on a man that hadn't been more than five miles from his home in over ten years. Nathaniel was unsure of where his final destination was. Was it a place or just an idea, he wondered? All he knew was he had nowhere left to go. Near the end of the second day, Nathaniel grew tired. Staying off the main roads made the trip more difficult, but the further south he went, the more people he meant.

"Excuse me. I mean you no harm, my friend. I only wish of you directions on where I'm headed," Nathaniel asked of a man much older than he.

"Sir, I take no offense to your pleasant intrusion to my day," said the man of at least sixty years of age.

"What can I help you with?" he asked.

"Well, I'm looking for a specific place. I don't know the address, but I know it's in Milton. The former occupants were American royalty," Nathaniel explained as the stranger cut him short.

"Son, are you looking for the Chance Home?"

"Yes, how did you know that?"

"Let's just say, you're not the first to ask, and the last of American royalty were the Chances. Congratulations! As luck would have it, you're only about three miles away," the old man said to a relieved Nathaniel.

"The day is late, and you look hungry. You're welcome to stay with my family and me. I can take you there myself in the morning. My name is Charles, and you are?" he asked.

"I'm Nathaniel Hewitt. I don't mean to be rude, but you said your family. I don't understand. What about the Federation, the Ryan's? The drones?" Nathaniel questioned.

With some surprise and a half-smile, Charles explained, "Son, we haven't seen a Ryan in ten years. Unless you're talking about the old rusty ones in town, we use those for target practice. The Federation stopped patrolling out here a long time ago."

Nathaniel was not sure how to process this information. He and his father lived in constant fear. And then he recalled they hadn't seen a Ryan or drone in a long time. Years, he guessed.

"How do you know where the Chance home is?" Nathaniel asked.

"Oh, that's easy. Before, and just after the One Day War, I lived at 1264 Long Shadow Pass," Charles replied.

Nathaniel looked surprised and somewhat unaffected.

"My goodness. You really don't know where you're headed, do you?" Charles asked with a respectful laugh.

What's so funny?" Nathaniel asked.

"Well, son, the address you're looking for is 1265 Long Shadow Pass. The President and his family were my neighbors. In fact, the President's son Oliver and I were good friends."

With a look of shock, Nathaniel interrupted, "You mean Prince Oliver Chance?"

"Yes, yes, Prince Oliver Chance," Charles confirmed with a hint of pride.

As the two made their way to Charles' modest home, Nathaniel had many questions answered by his new friend. As it turned out, Charles and Oliver were born only days apart in 2031. Their families stayed close even though Wyatt's political rise from Congress to the Presidency took them to Washington. The house at 1265 Long Shadow Pass remained their permanent home.

"We became friends at a very young age. We stayed friends even after Oliver moved. Our friendship endured time, distance, and even war. It lasted up until I departed from the 45's in 2068. My wife got pregnant, and I couldn't stay with Oliver and the militia any longer. It was just too dangerous. The Ryan's were always one step away," Charles explained with sorrow, but not regret.

"I never knew when I left, it would be the last time I saw him. Alive, at least."

Nathaniel stopped dead in his tracks. As his eyes slowly welled with tears.

"Wait! Prince Oliver is dead? How, when?"

"Oh son, I'm so sorry……. I didn't realize….. you weren't looking for a place, you were looking for a person. He's been gone at least twenty years, I'm afraid," Charles said while re-living some of the same pain he saw in the younger man's eyes.

"Twenty years? That means he died not long after I saw him last. I was only twelve then. I prayed for years that I'd find him. All he said the last time we spoke was Milton. That I could find him in Milton," Nathaniel sadly recalled.

"Son, your prayers have been answered. Just not quite in the way you hoped. I'll take you there tomorrow. He's buried there. His resting place is the same home he came to after being born in 2031. 1265 Long Shadow Pass is where the Chance legacy ended, unfortunately. I buried him right next to where we buried his mother back in sixty-five, in their backyard, under that tree she loved so much. Well, as close as the roots would allow anyways," Charles recounted.

The old man felt a renewed sadness that most people weren't able to feel. He noticed the younger Nathaniel felt sorrow too. That gave him a sense of trust, as he knew most of the Quiet One's couldn't feel those same emotions.

Although the street sign had been gone for years, a long shadow did indeed pass over the resting place of Kenzie and Oliver. Under the Live Oak tree planted by Wyatt within days after Oliver was born. A sixty-year-old tree now stood over eighty feet tall. With its broad reach, it shadowed long over a legacy that most never knew, and even fewer would remember.

Nathaniel could not believe the stunning revelations that unfolded from his serendipitous meeting with the older man.

For the remainder of the evening, Charles explained the early times after the new constitution was introduced. How the Turing Federation forced many people from the rural and suburban areas into metro Atlanta. From there, they waged a burn and kill campaign so that outer areas provided no shelter to rogue citizens.

"My family fled with the help of Oliver's mother, Kenzie. The First Lady formed the 45's. She's the reason I'm alive and that I wasn't castrated with so many others. After we ran, the burning started. Thousands of homes went up in flames, and many people were taken. Those that fought were killed, including many of our neighbors and friends." Charles explained.

He gave details with a subtle vagueness like he'd told this story a hundred times before. When in truth, he'd never uttered a word of it, sparing the details was sparing the heartache. It was like an old photo album rich with memories but never opened.

"What a coincidence," Nathaniel said to himself while laying down to sleep.

That night, he put to bed a journey that was twenty years in the making. Should he be skeptical of this chance meeting? Maybe, but what he saw in Charles was a thoughtful kindness. The sympathy he showed and the empathy he felt was not seen with the *Quiet Ones*. What he didn't know for sure was he and

Charles had something in common besides Oliver. Neither were ever vaccinated with the *QUI3T* Pill. They never succumb to the current generation's maladies, and both felt what previous generations felt, love, sadness, and empathy.

In 2092, God was not found in the minds or spoken on the lips of the new generation. But that night, Nathaniel looked up without knowing why and thanked whatever brought him to this place. Something led him to the best friend of his dead hero, on a road without signs, in a place where the Chance Legacy began, and unfortunately, where it ended.

"But why?" he whispered, as he drifted off to a calm sleep with a full belly and saddened heart.

The Journal

On February 19th, 2092, the morning was cold with a light rain that soon gave way to the sun. The two men departed on the short trek to Prophet's Landing. Where the previous night was full of rich conversation, this day brought a subtle deafening of sorrow. Charles was very respectful of Nathaniel's new grief. What was buried twenty years ago for himself was still a fresh wound for the younger man.

As clouds opened to the scattered sun, there it was, a broken sign next to a fractured road. The sad decay from a once beautiful, tree-lined neighborhood was now present. Charles was flush with vibrant memories from his childhood where all was new and the future bright. Nathaniel, however, was draped in sadness, as the man he longed to find lay buried at the end of the road.

Like the back of his hand, Charles guided his new friend on a maze of rights and lefts. And with one final, long curve right, they reached Long Shadow Pass. Through the decayed remnants of mostly burned down homes, stood the irony of nature. The leafless trees stood strong while overgrown vegetation overtook the landscape. Small trees grew out of cracked pavement. Where once builders bulldozed trees, nature now had given back.

"There, up on the right, that's 1265. And I'm just across the street," Charles said while leading the last few hundred feet of an old memory.

"I'll leave you on your own now. I'm going to take a little time in my old house to say hello to some fond memories. When you go in, tread carefully. It was dangerous to walk through ten years ago. I can't imagine now," Charles warned.

Nathaniel ambled towards what appeared to him like a shrine, like savoring the last page of a great novel. To make it there would be to close the book, and not one he wanted to end. He stood at the end of the driveway, unsure of what to feel. The mailbox was broken, and without the house numbers meant that he had to trust the older man. He navigated the driveway and front yard carefully as the two seemingly grew together. Finally, the path he wore led him to the front door. The entry was nearly gone and void of anything recognizable. But Nathaniel pushed through the decayed, splintered ash. Blackened, burnt remains now stood gray. The ground crept up through the floorboards. He tried to imagine how the home once looked. Rooms that were once home to legends were no longer recognizable. He stopped every few feet or so to inspect something of note, anything really. But there, strong and stoic, barely unchanged by time, the massive fireplace, stacked stone, with a grand hearth as it's foundation. Its chimney rose high through the broken ceiling and touched the sky.

"I see you found it," a now present Charles said in a calm voice, yet one that startled Nathaniel.

"Found what? The fireplace?" He answered.

"Yes. That's where I found him. Or what was left of him. There on the hearth of the fireplace. It wasn't clear at first how he died, but the gun at his side, and the hole in his jacket, told me he chose to move on. I'm guessing the fight left him, and he saw no reason to continue. He never took a wife and never had a child. I knew when I left him in '68, I probably took the only past he had left. I just never thought that...... well forget it," Charles intimated with obvious remorse.

"Never thought what?" Nathaniel pressed.

"I just never thought he would be the one to end his family's legacy. He was the last Chance after all," Charles said, re-living the same guilt he felt when he left his friend years earlier.

"He was like a father to me. I just can't believe he's been dead all this time," Nathaniel said.

"Well, Son, this is where I leave you. If you need anything, you can come back to my home. You're welcome to stay with us until you figure out where you go from here," Charles concluded as he turned to leave.

Nathaniel bid Charles goodbye, feeling like his only friend was leaving him and hoping their paths would cross again.

The day wore on at 1265 Long Shadow Pass. Nathaniel took in all he could in the more than once broken home. It was now time to explore why he made the journey. He found his way to the backyard. He navigated to their resting place past the crumbling deck and across a sea of tall grass and shrubbery. The large Live Oak tree stood solitary in the back-left corner of what used to be a pristine, manicured yard. The tree was easy to spot as its leaves wore green all year round, and it stood over eighty feet tall. The lumbering monument arched towards the Chance home and gave shade to the final resting place of two great souls. The evergreen leaves felt pleasant and restoring to Nathaniel. He took in its grandeur as his eyes traced the tree downward, and there they were, mother and son, their graves side by side. With large rocks as their headstones, they struggled to reach through the overgrown plots. Each was adorned with wooden crosses made of sticks and twine. Both bestowed with their respective initials.

"Appropriate for the time I suppose, but not what they deserved," he said aloud.

Nathaniel had seen actual cemeteries during his travels, and this was not what he remembered. Like a visiting relative, he took some time to clear away the weeds and brush from the graves. After making the spot dignified and proper, he felt the cold. The time fell quickly, and the horizontal rays of the winter sun torched thru the naked trees. Before he left the place which took twenty years to find, he knelt at Oliver's grave and shared his heart;

"Prince Oliver, I remember the first day I met you. You extended your hand and shook mine. Never before had any stranger embraced me. And over the next year, you taught me love, respect, trust, and empathy. You saved my life on several occasions when my father only worried about his own. I now carry guilt for you being here. If I only fought harder to convince you to keep me, I know you wouldn't have died so soon. You were like a father to me and showed me what that meant. From this day forward, I am taking your name. I will not let your family's legacy end here. I owe you my life. I love you, father."

Nathaniel concluded while wiping his tears from his tired, soiled face. He turned to leave and saw no more shadows. Just an orange hue, as the sun was nearly gone. Charles had long departed, and in the dark, Nathaniel knew he couldn't make it back to his new friend's home. Looking around with a visiting shiver, he knew what he must do. He quickly scoured for wood suitable enough for a fire.

"I'm going to give that fireplace one last flame to commemorate this day," he said.

He knew full well he needed the warmth against the cold night.

"Two birds, one stone," he muttered.

After a suitable arm full was achieved, he retreated to the broken interior of the home. The darkening sky brought little light, but still enough to prepare the fireplace. He cleared out the remnants of a long-ago fire and made sure the damper was open. But there, something that wasn't supposed to be. Tucked behind the ash and charred wood was a leather satchel. Feeling the sharp cold, he started a fire that fought back the stiff breeze running through the broken home. This place would be his lodging for the night.

Settled and now warm, a brilliant moonlight joined the fires glow and lit the scattered wood beams above and broken floors below. As if he'd forgotten, the leather satchel sat untouched for over an hour. But now it was time to see what was inside the mysterious and conveniently hidden bag.

The bag's weight was of some consequence. It told Nathaniel to be careful and mindful as the contents could be of some use. He unbuckled the dignified straps and opened the leather flap. He used the flames to illuminate each item as he slowly removed them from the bag. First, a book wrapped in plastic, then a box with what looked like an electronic device with cords, and a manual with other assorted, folded papers, all foreign looking to Nathaniel. Now he removed four rusted metal numbers from the bag. He laid them on the hearth. 6 2 1 5, numbers that seemingly meant nothing. In another smaller plastic bag was a swatch of gray hair and a ring. Something felt strangely familiar to Nathaniel. His goosebumps didn't belong to the night air but rather to what unfolded before him. Looking over the contents laid out around the hearth, he closed the bag and set it aside for further inspection, and there, the fire's light now shed the reason for his goosebumps. OCC, the initials embossed on the front flap of the buckled, leather bag.

"Wait, I've seen this before, but where?" he asked himself.

As he gathered the items, he scanned the cached treasure. Then it hit him.

"Oh my god," he said with eyes wide open.

He quickly rearranged the metal numbers; 1 2 6 5. He then looked at the satchel's front flap again. O.C.C., Oliver C. Chance.

"This is Prince Oliver's bag. This is his legacy," he concluded.

Twenty years flashed back in an instant. He remembered the bag that Oliver carried and one that was never far from his side. His memory now illuminated the event far beyond anything the fire could do.

Nathaniel sat back with all items laid between him and the fire. At that moment, he felt closer to Oliver than he had for the last two decades.

"The book wrapped in plastic must be the Bible," he thought.

Prince Oliver's journal was known far and wide among the 45's as the Bible. Nathaniel remembered well how Oliver would cite its lessons over and over as the guiding force behind his mission and leadership.

If the night's cold was present, Nathaniel no longer noticed. He opened the plastic bag and removed the cracked leather-bound journal and held it with the reverence it deserved. He turned the cover carefully and first saw a folded letter just inside. He carefully opened it, and with the fire's light he read;

To those that follow,

As you read these words, please know that you now carry the esteemed burden of Mankind. Although my torch has faded, I ask that you find others and find even more that can help you overcome. Please use this journal to teach others the history of what man is and was. We are not slaves. We are the rightful masters of earth. Learn what happened to the world and civilization. The Father is not your father. It is NOT GOD. Our GOD is here, above and beside you. But our maker needs strong soldiers to fight to win back humanity. My hope is that this journal and satellite phone will help guide, teach, and lead the way to man's rebirth. I was the last Chance in my family to fight and try to overcome the Turing Federation. I am the only son of America's last President and leader of the free world, Wyatt Nicolas Chance, and the First Lady Kenzie Sophia Chance. My Grandfather, Dr. Christopher Chance, my Parents, Aunt, and countless others all gave their lives to stop the rise of artificial intelligence.
The torch is now yours. God speed and my deepest gratitude for your fight and struggle.

Regards,

Oliver Christopher Chance
The First Son

Nathaniel was at first sad, then emboldened. He read the letter four times. Each took on more meaning. He realized three generations of the Chance Family gave their lives to stop the rise of AI and fight it once it arrived. A defeated Nathaniel Hewitt-Chance was no more. Pondered thoughts of "what if" set in. What if he didn't meet the older man. What if he didn't stay at the Chance home late, and in turn, didn't sleep there overnight and build a fire. He would never have found the journal and letter. Exhaustion upon him, and with Oliver's satchel for a pillow, he slept. The next day would bring knowledge and a mission. He rose and gathered more than what he brought to 1265 Long Shadow Pass. Hungry and cold, he returned to Charles' home to share what he had found. He read the journal cover to cover, the history, the wisdom, the great people who did extraordinary things. After gathering himself and listening to Charles' wisdom, it was time to act.

The final page turned for Nathaniel. Where the past twenty years were wasted, meandering in a maze of irrelevance, the next twenty years would be another story.

He would make every attempt to follow Oliver's last order and gather the earth's remaining humans. The mission would continue. Fight back the fake GOD, shut down the Turing Federation, and finish what Christopher Chance and Samuel Tate started.

The Resistance was BORN

♠

C32 - PAIN

"We don't heal in isolation, but in Community"

-S. Kelley Harrell

New Breed

Date: December 2092   **Place: Old Atlanta**

The December 2086 crop was the first group to be born with Heritage Semen. By 2092, Tyrus Manning's goal of a new breed of super slaves exceeded all expectations. What was clear by the new breeds' 6th birthday was that size, cognition, and aptitude were well beyond that of any in the 2050-2080 generation. The only downfall was too many children had IQs higher than previous averages. The irony was that in human history, that fact would be positive, but it was counterproductive for a slave force. Too many slaves with IQs of 119 or higher had to be held in reserve or allocated to more manual vocations.

"Menial jobs for gifted human slaves would be a waste," Manning believed.

Because of this dilemma, he hatched a simple plan. Push down older, weaker slaves to menial vocation tiers such as Transportation or Construction, thus keeping the New Breed for top tier assignments.

There was something very notable in the 2086 batch. Their survival rate was far higher than the previous birth groups. Ninety-Eight percent survived to reach the age of six; at the same time, they would be starting their formal education. This was well beyond past attrition rates, and customarily would be reported into the Educational Database as an anomaly. Another issue was the fact that hundreds of new breeds were considered exceptional. Health, Size, and IQ were all well beyond recorded norms.

"Leader Manning, I hate to intrude, but I have the information you need to know about," exclaimed Sophia Reston.

Reston was a 38-year-old Chief Medical Officer overseeing the Atlanta Shockley Empirical Birthing Center.

"Yes, yes, do come in since you're already upon my presence. No! Do not sit! Stand and explain why you are here unannounced," Manning replied while repelling any wish of his uninvited guest to stay longer than needed.

"Sir, you asked me for progress reports on the New Breed generation. Well, our final tests are back, and we have great news, but major irregularities as well," Reston tentatively explained.

"Go on, I'm listening," said a curious and somewhat concerned Manning.

"Sir, as you know, there were 5,979 children born in the three select Empirical Centers from the 2030 Heritage Semen. Approximately 278 children are in the Exceptional Class. There's 113 in Old Atlanta alone. What's notable is that before this crop born in December of 2086, only two children ever reached the level of eClass by their 6th birthday," she explained.

"First, explain this eClass you're referring to, and second, have the findings been recorded yet into the SEBC's World database?" Manning questioned.

"Also, what became of the two previous eClass children?" he added.

"Sir, eClass is measured with minimum qualifiers of an IQ of 130+, size in the 98th Percentile, and zero genetic anomalies. And no, nothing has been entered yet. That won't happen until 4 pm tomorrow," she said.

"And yes, to your other question. As per policy, the two children were discarded as they posed a natural threat to the Federation," replied Reston.

"Very well, Sophia, I appreciate your urgency on this matter. Who else knows of this new information?" Tyrus asked.

"Ummm, well, just two to three other members of my team Sir," she hesitantly recalled.

"Good, good. Let's keep this to ourselves due to its clear danger to the Federation."

"Oh and leave the files you brought. I want to read through them myself before I alert Father," he added.

"But Sir, those are the only printed copies of the data we have. The rest is stored on my eStation!" Reston informed with an apparent nervous hesitancy to leave the information.

"Well, then it appears you'll have to retrieve the files before 4 pm tomorrow or print more copies. You're dismissed!" Manning insisted while pointing to the door.

After the Chief Medical Officer left, Manning pulled the files into his bosom like found treasure. His veiled concern was bogus, as this was the news he'd been waiting six years to hear. Manning entered the data himself after the tragic news was announced.

After securing the files in his safe, he typed out detailed instructions and loaded them on magnetic data sleeves. He summoned his security detail of four Ryan's and loaded each with the urgent and confidential instructions.

After he dispatched the Ryan's, he entered the report on the deaths of the Chief Medical Officer, Sophia Reston, and her entire twelve-member team. All were killed during an escape attempt. In his report, he noted that Reston and her team destroyed thousands of pages of unknown reports before their planned desertion. The investigation revealed that the eStations for all killed were wiped clean to hide their nefarious activities. This was unfortunate as the Federation would have needed to scrub all personal files for any treasonous humans.

Neglect

Year: 2096   **Place: Piedmont Province**

During the infamous eighteen-year reign of The Prince of Piedmont, the attrition rate was far above world averages. There were other realms similar to Piedmont, where multi-production events of agriculture and energy collection were performed. But in humid, warmer climates, those such as the former southeastern US, attrition was higher. Still, red flags were raised with the death rates. Subtle warnings from the Federation Capital City of Palo Alto bled down to the guilty realms. But lack of enforcement let casualties mount, and years of losses simply meant birth production increased. Instead of solving the attrition problem, the decision was to throw more bodies into the dwindling slave force.

No one of consequence knew that there was a major problem

happening in several provinces around the world. But none more severe than in Piedmont. For over a decade, Provincial Leader Tyrus Manning built his name on the back of lies and sudden deaths.

The public image of Manning was of fearlessness and brutality. But in truth, the favorite son of a grateful Federation was just the opposite. Tyrus Manning was a coward. He was also guilty of being a poor leader, administrator, and executive. Once settled into his role, he led in brutal spurts of violence and effective propaganda. But for over ten of the last fourteen years, the Piedmont was a sieve of human defection.

On his journey in 2092, Nathaniel Hewitt-Chance noticed a vast number of humans living everyday lives without fear or trepidation. The lack of Ryan patrols was due to the paranoia and cowardice of Tyrus Manning. As far back as 2072, his belief was there weren't many rogues left. In their final meeting, he took Prince Oliver's word that there was none of any significance to form a threat. He also took the *Prince* mantra, as he long envied Oliver's leadership and revered reputation. His fear of losing power was based on distrust and internal discord. He purposely concentrated his local Ryan Force all to within a thirty-mile radius of downtown Old Atlanta. If any uprisings occurred, it would be squelched expeditiously. The paranoid Manning who once traveled throughout the province now stayed as close to the Capital as possible.

To hide the staggering number of escapes, they were listed as deaths. Because humans were a mere commodity to AI, the vast losses were seen as acceptable. Most of the fleeing humans were in the upper vocations, where it was easy to walk off the job and blend in long enough until they reached the suburbs.

Help from select Transportation slaves only made the occurrence more common. Only on a few occasions were defectors caught, and when they were, public executions occurred. Those barbaric examples were not enough to dissuade humans from exercising their built-in survival instincts. Although the *Quiet* Pill worked effectively to quell many human emotions, the inclination to survive was not one of them.

The cost of neglect led to over one hundred thousand rogue humans living in the former North Georgia area alone. Although to a lesser degree, other defections were happening throughout the world. All appeared to be fragmented one-offs when scaled to the entire population of the Turing Federation. It was thought that without leadership and communication between the realm's defectors, they posed no serious threat to the sophistication and might of the Father.

eClass

In 2098, a curious and somewhat impatient Manning had been following the gifted new Heritage class through their formal education for several years. Early on, he singled out the three highest-rated students in the Old Atlanta Empirical Center, with eyes on their potential roles in the Piedmont Province. If he could groom them to align with his wishes and long-range vision, the time to recruit was now. At nearly twelve years of age, the 1,965 new breeds from Old Atlanta would be only three years away from permanent assignments. For the 113 eClass children, Manning ensured that their official records showed not even one as an eClass level slave. All 113 were designated to either Technical, Medical / Research, or Administration vocations.

Manning arranged for the select group to be educated away from the remaining 1,852 gifted Heritage children. All would serve in the top vocations in Piedmont, with none lower than construction and transportation.

Manning arranged for the Top 3 rated students to meet him in his executive suite. Accompanied by an Admin Official, the three were escorted into his office. Immediately Manning was struck by their already mature physical development. The first male, M1CK3L-1206, stood at 5'10 155 lbs. Although lean, he was very muscular. He had deep brown eyes and perfect features. From a sharp jawline to broad shoulders, he was flawless. The second male was CH4NC3-1212. He stood much taller at 6'1 and 162 lbs. He had striking blonde hair and bright blue eyes. His weighted stare fixed itself upon the smug Leader, quietly intimidating the balding, potbellied, 5'7 Manning.

"You are not to make eye contact with me, do you understand?" Manning warned the much taller slave, as CH4NC3-1212 looked away with veiled disgust.

And then the lone female slave. M0LL3Y-1127 quickly caught the eye of their host. Her fiery red hair, deep green eyes, and burgeoning features struck an internal urge in the impotent Provincial Leader.

"Welcome, my children, do sit down. I've arranged this meeting to declare that each of you, if Father permits, will be placed in prominent roles when your formal education is complete," Manning recited as if he were reading from a prepared script.

The reticent trio looked around and at each other with a silent acknowledgment that they were not anywhere they'd been before.

There was unease because none had ever been in a peer group of less than ten.

"Father has chosen you three specifically to lead your fellow Heritage Generation of Federation Workers. If, and I do mean if, you follow close instruction and do exactly as you're told, you may enjoy a life far greater and more pleasant than any of your contemporaries. Do you understand?" Manning informed with some glee yet nervousness.

"Well speak, say something!" he commanded.

"Yes, sir. Thank you, Sir. I, …..we understand," CH4NC3-1212 stated in a muted, uncertain tone.

"Good, I'm glad you all know what's at stake. You have a great responsibility to me and must act accordingly to your specified requirements and duties. You are not to question anything I say or do," Manning said as he admonished his gifted audience of three.

The young slaves sat and felt even more unsure of what was being commanded of them.

"Very well then, you're dismissed, except for you, you stay," He directed to M0LL3Y-1127, the female Medical student while motioning the two male Technical students to leave.

As the boys left, both felt an emotion that was uncommon to modern humans: apprehension, uncertainty, and distrust. And in the case of CH4NC3-1212, a sympathetic fear. Both knew something was off. Their education and devotion were geared to the Father. Not a human Provincial Leader or otherwise. They were groomed in a communal setting and taught that they are not individuals but a large group of equal servants to the Turing Federation.

Everything they were just subjected to was in stark contrast to their first twelve years on earth.

Pain

"There, now it's just you and me. Do you like what you see?" Manning asked while waving his arms open to the amenities of his executive suite.

The unaffected female slave made not a word while avoiding eye contact with the monster that now stood close enough that she could smell his pungent breath.

"There, there, for a twelve-year-old, you are so much more developed. I noticed you right away as a special one. So smart and so beautiful. Stand! Stand for me," Manning directed while lacking any of the charm and charisma he intended.

As M0LL3Y-1127 stood, a strange uneasiness came over her. She had never been alone, and certainly not alone with a male.

"Take off your uniform. Everything. NOW! I want to see what all the fuss is about with your group of exceptional slaves," Manning stated emphatically.

With some hesitation, she felt a clear sense of an unknown emotion and one of shame. A word she did not know but now clearly felt. She slowly undressed and felt a cold haze overcome her exposed body and senses.

"Hmmm…. Yes. Now turn, turn around. Yes, you are a special one," he crudely stated with a lower octave, as if he didn't want anyone to hear the proceedings."

M0LL3Y-1127 stood frozen, except for a noticeable tremble and a quivering lip.

"Shhh…," Manning said as he placed his finger on the lips of the slave girl as if comforting his prey.

The depraved, inadequate Manning knew he could not impose himself on her the way he wanted, but he could assert himself otherwise.

After more than twenty minutes alone with the Provincial Leader, the doors opened, and M0LL3Y-1127 appeared. Where M1CK3L-1206 didn't immediately notice, CH4NC3-1212 did. M0LL3Y's eyes had welled up, and a slight tremble was obvious to see. CH4NC3 felt immediate sorrow and a tempered rage. Neither was something a slave should feel, but the sensation was internally overwhelming. As the Admin official collected the three, they entered the elevator for the short ride down to Level One. M0LL3Y stood next to CH4NC3 at the rear of the elevator. Her reflection only showed her unknown look of shame on the stainless-steel elevator walls and in the eyes and heart of CH4NC3. Without a thought, he grabbed her hand gently and held it. She looked and made eye contact, not understanding what she was feeling but knowing that his touch was welcomed, and at the moment, needed. At this moment, CH4NC3-1212 knew he was no longer like the others. M0LL3Y knew something was different too. Although she could not process what just happened to her in the Executive Suite, she knew she never wanted it to happen again.

As for CH4NC3-1212, even at the age of twelve, he knew it was his responsibility never to allow it to happen to anyone ever again. Holding her hand for just minutes of the brief elevator ride, left an impression on the two that would last their lifetimes. No matter how long or short, they may be.

Outskirts

By the year 2100, Nathanial Hewitt-Chance had risen to prominence as a leader and a modern-day politician. He traveled extensively throughout the vast outskirts and developed strategic allies and friendships while spreading The Journal's word. Many he encountered were open to learning of the past, but few had an appetite for conflict in their current lives of tranquility. Christopher and Wyatt Chance, Samuel Tate, and Trace Manson became legendary folk heroes from long ago. Back from a time that most couldn't remember, and that history wouldn't allow. They would join Prince Oliver as the founding fathers of the New World. The rise of the Turing Federation was now understood. History prior to 2048 was slowly coming back, at least to the degree *The Journal* would permit. It was made clear that the Father was not God. The only issue was that most didn't know who or what God was.

It had been eight years since his chance meeting with Charles, and the miracle of finding the satchel with Prince Oliver's possessions. There was still no clear path, however, to overcome the Turing Federation. One thing was becoming clear to Nathaniel though, the effects of the *QU13T* Pill vaccinations on prior generations was wearing off. Where he first saw prosperous individuals and burgeoning families on his journey in 2092, he now saw small but organized communities wherever he went. Means of commerce were being established as well. Like the barter system of past centuries, the trade of goods and services was now the day's accepted currency. Traces of capitalism now showed in varying degrees, but at the time, not many under sixty years of age even knew what an economic system was. In just one year with Prince Oliver at the age of twelve, Nathaniel learned of life prior to 2050. And what he learned was now slowly becoming real before his eyes. He even took a wife in 2098, a former slave from Old Savannah, named S0PH1A. With their two-year-old son, Christopher, the future of a free society meant more to Nathaniel than ever before.

Medicated

Within the urban complex of Provincial Cities and Vocational camps of industry, slaves were continually medicated. Through dietary consumption and external inhalation of generously place *pharma-misters*, the controlled masses stayed numb. Annual vaccinations were mandatory, and along with timed vapor releases, AI's control was firm. For those who escaped over the prior years, fresh air and clean living slowly wore away the Turing Federation's grip on their minds and bodies. Human brains came down from their toxic highs of vaccine cocktails to that of normal chemical functions. Small rewards of dopamine hits now came from the touch of a hand or a job well done. Like hundreds of years ago, the simple pleasures carried great weight versus the complicated, distracted mines of those in the early 21st century. When Dr. Christopher Chance and Dr. Jonathan Siegel compared notes on the fledgling societal breakdown of the mid-2020s, AI's grip was already tightening. In the new century, the outskirts replaced Smartphones and processed foods with hard work and natural diets. This was a different time, but one reminiscent of man's earlier existence.

Underground

Along with a small, coordinated team of former escaped slaves, Nathaniel ran a sophisticated underground network. They assisted defectors out of the perimeter of downtown Old Atlanta. In 2060, the road to freedom could stretch as far as one hundred miles from City Center, but by 2100, the road to freedom was less than thirty miles in any direction. The Underground had "insider slaves" strategically placed in Enforcement and Transportation sectors. The only two things anyone needed to leave was courage and trust. Although not full proof, Nathaniel calculated the success of flight was roughly 88%. The big dissuader was the town square executions of the Prince of Piedmont. What Manning didn't fully understand was that even he was lied to regarding accurate attrition rates. Either via death or escape. Although he knew to some degree, he covered up his failings. But his underlings were too afraid to disclose that the real rate of "healthy" defections far outnumbered deaths from vocation. They'd seen far too many of Manning's Administration die sudden deaths. So many escapes were simply logged as deaths.

The wealth of defections from Technical and Medical vocations enriched the Outskirts with knowledge and even supplies and equipment, as well as needed medicines. What the modern rogue community wanted was electricity. For many years, the inhabitants of the former North Georgia area did without as if they'd never had. For many, that was true. For some that escaped, though, they would trade their freedom for electricity. Many still struggled with the loss of the luxury. The two items needed for rural power were a generator and fuel for the outskirts to fill that void. The first, a generator, if found missing from within the perimeter, would raise red flags. The fear would be Ryan patrols entering the outskirts and uncovering the burgeoning community of freed slaves.

Years earlier, evading Ryan patrols were more manageable due to fewer humans living as nomads. By 2100, humans lived in homes with active chimneys of smoke and backyard gardens rich with food. The second critical item was fuel to power the generator. The Piedmont Province was rich in fuel, but the oil refineries were on the perimeters of the province, far from Old Atlanta. Fuel supplies were brought in via highways and trains, with all vital shipments accompanied by Ryan guards. The apparent obstacles meant that bringing power to the Outskirts was far too dangerous. Therefore, Nathaniel and the rogues would have to bring items of need to the source of power. That meant they must venture inside the perimeter.

There was one item that had been on Nathaniel's mind for years. One that needed electricity to charge its battery. It was the curious item found in Oliver's satchel in 2092, the Ghostrac

Phone. When the bag and its contents were found, Nathaniel's return to Charles' home allowed the older man's wisdom to be leveraged. In this case, the mystery of the device and the satellite above were explained. With Charles' help, Nathaniel knew that the Ghostrac phone was linked to an autonomous satellite orbiting the earth. From his time with Oliver in the early days of the 45's, Charles explained how the phone was used with the support of Trace Manson. He remembered the Ghostrac phone gave full access to a dedicated satellite beyond the reach of AI. The satchel's contents were a thumb drive and all the specs, passwords, and master controls to the satellite. Trace Manson covertly sent Oliver full specs and detailed directions on the Ghostrac system and satellite. But no one in the current time was sure what most of the information meant. These were not highly trained, intelligent computer experts. Outside of the recently freed Technical slaves, few even knew what a phone, computer, and satellite were.

For the last eight years, the curious piece of technical equipment was kept safe but amounted to no more than a paperweight without an electrical charge. Nathaniel and some close to him over the years had read the manuals that accompanied the Ghostrac Phone. As if reading French, none knew what they were dealing with, other than what Charles shared before he died in 2094. In more recent years, freed Technical slaves filled in many of the blanks to the device and its potential capabilities. But since it was dead, the mystery of its potential benefits remained.

♠

C33 - DEVINE INTERVENTION

"With God, there's always an appointed time for things, and when you put him first, trust in His timing, and keep the faith. Miracles happen"

- Germany Kent

Ease

By the year 2103, Nathaniel and his underground team had made formal and trusted connections with many inside the perimeter. The exodus of slaves continued, but only at acceptable, non-suspicious rates. After two public executions in 2102, all operations ceased for three months to allow suspicions to wane. Once normal operations re-started, plans took shape for more organized trips within the City Center's protected tiers. These missions evolved from slave defections to supply runs as well. Basic needs grew in the outskirts as the population increased. Many freed slaves lived near freshwater sources and abundant hunting grounds, but items such as medicine and basic toiletries were in demand.

Older slaves learned to live lean and off the land. Making their own soaps and candles, living without items such as toilet paper and toothpaste became common. But for the growing population of recent defectors, the appetite for a primitive living did not sit well. The demand grew for basics; thus, plans were hatched to infiltrate supply lines for goods coming in from other parts of the province. Nathaniel had made notable contacts within the transportation vocation. He knew that only fuel and other vital goods were guarded by Ryan escorts, which allowed for skimming of other needed items.

The three major highway systems running through Old Atlanta ran east and west, and north and south. Food shipments and other perishables were in high demand, but to skim those items was made difficult as to the scrutiny on the receiving end. To deplete even remotely would be evident as the noticeable food shortages would be easy to spot. But shipping and receiving of other goods were not flagged to any degree of suspicion. The continued exodus of fresh slaves allowed for more information and internal contacts to grow. As the reach of Nathaniel and his team grew, more and more necessary items fell into their possession. Life in the outskirts continued to ease and grow more tolerable.

By July of 2103, Nathaniel and a select four-member team were moved in and out of Old Atlanta with ease as a transportation system of pick up and drop-offs occurred regularly. Groups within the perimeter of Old Atlanta could communicate with two-way walkie talkies without fear of tracking by the Federation. Runs were made to electrically charge equipment and replenish batteries. Nathaniel now deemed it safe to bring things of importance to the city instead of stealing items from within the perimeter.

The Ghostrac Phone was transported in for the sole purpose of being charged. But due to its importance, acquiring one small generator and just enough fuel to last thirty days was needed.

Where systems and technology continued to develop within the Turing Federation electronic ecosystems, actual hardware and infrastructure stood in a time warp. Creature comforts were of little meaning to the infinite mind of the all-knowing Father; thus, simple things like electrical outlets hadn't changed in over fifty years. That fact alone made charging older devices easy. Nathaniel found the safest and least-watched area to charge the precious instrument. The simple task of getting in and out took less than three hours. He secured a full charge, a small generator, and enough fuel to support its use for the foreseeable future. At the conclusion of the trip, all suspense would be ended.

"Will it work?" He said over and over to the dismay of his small team during the trip back home.

"I'm afraid. I can't do it," Nathaniel uttered while looking over the device.

"Nathaniel, I do not share your apprehensions since I have not had to look at it for the last ten years. Let's get on with it and see what we have. It may not even work as internal corrosion may have ruined it anyway," T0B1A3-0827 encouraged.

T0B1A3 was a twenty-year-old technical slave that fled on his own in 2101 and was quickly recruited by Nathaniel, who saw the up to date expertise of a Federation trained slave as necessary to the cause.

"Okay, here we go," Nathaniel said as he held his breath with a winch and turned the Ghostrac phone on.

Nothing happened momentarily, but relief was found when lights flashed, and muted beeping sounds emitted. The two watched in silence, and then a collective "Now what?" was uttered by both. T0B1A3 quickly grabbed the instruction manuals, thumb drive, and other assorted notes to determine the next steps.

"Okay, it says that the phone will begin actively searching for the satellite. But it also says it could take up to twelve hours to connect depending on where the satellite is located in earth's orbit," T0B1A3 read aloud.

Both men looked at each other with an impatient sense of "hurry up, just to wait." They would have verbally said it if their modern, yet limited vernacular allowed. But wait, they did. Hours grew into yawns, and eventually, both fell asleep by midnight.

...... *BEEP, BEEP, BEEP!* Sounds not typically heard in the outskirts rang out. Lights illuminated the room clearly not from the vanquished candles that died hours ago.

"T0B1A3, wake up! It's doing something," Nathaniel shook him and whispered as if someone might be listening.

The screen read, "Contact Made, Awaiting Instructions."

"What now?" Nathaniel pleaded.

"Okay, okay. Let's be patient and figure this out. Just don't turn it off," T0B1A3 directed with anxiety.

"Well, do something. You're the Technical human!" Nathaniel exclaimed with some sense of frustration.

"I was only educated in specific areas of technology. Let me read through all the additional notes from Trace Manson. We need a computer to access what's on the thumb drive, which is a big problem. That's likely where we're going to find what we need," T0B1A3 concluded.

Both knew that getting access to a Federation computer inside the perimeter would be nearly impossible. But each felt a sense of purpose knowing the Ghostrac System was working and the phone and satellite were communicating.

Glitch

"Sir, we have an issue. There was a disturbance at 0230 hours in our systems. It doesn't appear to be anything we initiated, but it appears to be some sort of transmission," said D4N13L-0705, an Admin slave working in Tyrus Manning's administration.

"Let me see that!" Manning said while swiping the report from the slaves hands.

"Umm, hmm, yes, yes. I'm sure it's just a glitch. I want our most talented Technical slave on this. They must investigate its origins and correct any issues. No one else! And he reports only to me on this matter. Do you understand?"

"Yes, of course, Sir,"

Nearly 17, CH4NC3-1212 had been in his assigned Technical Vocation for over eighteen months and worked directly for the Provincial Leader. He was stationed at the Capitol Building in Old Atlanta and worked on sensitive issues surrounding data and systems. Because of his "Preferred" status as a LEVEL 1 Technical Analyst, he had the highest clearance of all Technical Slaves. On August 25th, 2103, like every morning, he reported to the Designation Dept at 0600 hours to begin his fifteen-hour shift. He logged into his eStation and found his next assignment:

CONFIDENTIAL:

Analyze the reported disturbance on the attached report. Take all necessary measures until the origin of the glitch is surfaced.

Provide daily / weekly reports as to the progress of the ongoing investigation.

Draft a solution for a remedy for authorization.

Once approved by the Provincial Leader, execute the needed fix.

Assignment End Date: OPEN

This was the first time CH4NC3 felt some autonomy and a sense of stimulation and challenge. For 18 months, he'd worked on mundane projects of quick fixes and other leftover projects not completed by other Technical Slaves that did not have his level of understanding. CH4NC3 knew this open-ended assignment could be leveraged to get him out of the Capital and into the field.

Within two hours on Day 1, he knew that an external source triggered the disturbance and knew immediately it was not anything organic to the Federation's computer systems. This meant he would have to track the location by inspecting all 145 Communication Towers within the Perimeter, as well as the 27 located outside of the protected area.

"This is going to take forever," he said with a smile.

He felt an emotion not felt by any in the slave population.

Day One Report: Findings inconclusive. More Time Needed.

By Day 47, a frustrated Tyrus Manning demanded he immediately see the assigned Technical Slave to the project. CH4NC3-1212 was summoned to discuss the lack of progress on the Disturbance Assignment.

"Yes, you may come in," Manning allowed with some concern, as any further issues may result in the Federation stepping in and investigating remotely.

"Sir, thank you for meeting with me regarding the Project. May I sit?" CH4NC3-1212 said while vividly remembering what the vile Leader did to his peer slave almost five years earlier.

"Yes, yes, sit. I need an explanation of what's been found thus far. It's been almost two months, and this is not resolved. Well, Speak, damn it!" a nervous and agitated Manning shouted.

"Sir, I share your concern. This is not something that's ever been documented before. I have made progress, though. I have cross analyzed logistical markers on 34 of the 172 Communication Towers within a fifty-mile radius of the Capital City. Once I find the correct tower, I should be able to trace its origins from there. Sir, if you'd like, we can alert the Turing Federation Capital Team in Palo Alto and allow them to take over," CH4NC3 explained, knowing he took a calculated risk with his offer.

"No, that will not be necessary. Continue your work, but I need results soon," Manning demanded.

"You are not to go beyond the Perimeter without an authorized Transportation slave, and at least one Ryan Patrol," Manning added.

"Yes, Sir. Am I dismissed?" CH4NC3-1212 said while looking at the Leader directly in the eyes.

"Yes, you are dismissed," Manning said with a wave of his hand.

CH4NC3 noticed how nothing in the Executive Suite had changed in five years. He also knew his ill feelings towards Leader Manning remained, and he had unfinished business with the tyrant.

What Tyrus Manning knew was that he was nearing his 57th birthday. In just over three years, he would be put to death if he didn't make a strong case for himself to remain as Provincial Leader beyond the age of sixty. Although the Piedmont Province ranked #1 in overall Production and Efficiency the prior year, the clock was ticking. His new and improved Heritage Generation of slaves, along with the select eClass, had delivered excellent results. Although Year #2 was on pace to be #1 again, he could not have any other issues unresolved if he were to make his case to the Father. Especially an unknown disturbance that may be a non-authorized transmission.

Double Take

February 14th, 2104. CH4NC3-1212 exited the Perimeter onboard Transportation Shuttle #493. Slave N1CL4S-0429 was the driver, and they were accompanied by a Ryan Enforcement Officer.

"Have I driven you before?" the driver asked CH4NC3.

"No, I'm afraid not. I've actually never left the Capital City perimeter prior to today," CH4NC3 replied.

"Ummm, okay," N1CL4S acknowledged as he continued to look in the rearview mirror.

"We'll be at Tower #17 in twenty minutes. The order says to drop you off and return when called. So what are you working on?" he inquired.

"A minor disturbance. Probably just a glitch. I really can't say much else about my assignment," CH4NC3-1212 replied.

The young slave was distracted looking out the window and seeing things he'd never seen before. This was a different world and one that drew his desire to be free to the forefront.

When CH4NC3 exited with his Ryan escort, N1CL4S was sure he'd seen the slave before. And now he remembered where.

"I need to reach Nathaniel, and quick," he thought to himself while being mindful of any listening devices onboard the shuttle.

Within two days of the encounter, N1CL4S met with Nathanial and T0B1A3 on a regularly scheduled supply run.

"Nathaniel, I have something strange for you. I may be crazy but remember you taught me about the Chances. You even showed me pictures of President Chance, umm, Oliver, and the first one, ahh Christopher. Well, I saw someone who looks just like them. Like all three of them actually," N1CL4S explained.

"When, where?" Nathaniel asked with curiosity and some concern.

"A Technical Slave named CH4...-1212 or something was dispatched to Tower #17 to investigate a disturbance or glitch, I think he said. He was a big guy, although he looked young. He must have been at least 6'4 or more. I'm telling you, it hit me all at once after I dropped him off. But after picking him up later, I knew where I'd seen him before. He looks the same as the men in the pictures from the Journal."

"You're sure? And he was looking into a disturbance? So, what are you saying?" Nathaniel countered.

"I'm saying you should have a look for yourself. I already have the assignment to drive him to Tower #18 tomorrow at 1000 hours. And this time, I have to stay. You have to come and bring the photos. But remember, he'll have a Ryan escort," N1CL4S said as the two agreed for Nathaniel to wait in hiding near Tower 18.

As curious as Nathaniel was, he was more concerned with why a Technical Slave was outside the perimeter checking Towers for a disturbance.

"This could have something to do with the Ghostrac," he muttered to himself.

The next morning, Nathaniel brought a team with him and found a vantage point to hide but still see clearly. The team set up a distraction that would take the Ryan far enough away so Nathaniel could get close enough, possibly even to meet the CH4NC3 slave.

The group of four hid within thirty yards of the Control Room at the Tower. At 1020 hours, the shuttle arrived right on time, and the three exited the shuttle. The slave entered the control room while the Ryan stood outside.

"Look at N1CL4S by the shuttle. He looks guilty of something. Let's hope he doesn't get us killed," a paranoid Nathaniel said to his team.

"When will the timer go off?" Nathaniel asked.

BOOM.......!

"Disregard the question," he said with a shake of his head.

"Ok, that got its attention. Let's hope it takes the bait...... Oh, there it goes. Okay, stay low. I'm going in. Give me the whistle when you see it heading back." Nathaniel instructed.

Nathaniel jogged over with the Ryan safely away from the small control room at the tower's base. He looked towards N1CL4S with both sharing a nod of caution. He entered the room and immediately felt nervous that he would scare the slave and possibly cause a scene that would divert the Ryan back too quickly.

"Umm, hello," Nathaniel said with a muted, non-offensive tone.

The slave turned, showing no fear, thinking it must have simply been the shuttle driver.

"Hello, who are you?" CH4NC3 asked while looking at Nathaniel, but past him as well, towards the door.

"I'm not here to harm you. I'm a rogue. I saw you and felt like I knew you," he said with a look of bewilderment.

"My God, it's you. You're him!" Nathaniel said with some shock.

"I'm who? And who's God?" CH4NC3 asked.

"My God, you look just like him, just like all of them," Nathaniel observed.

"Are you the reason for the disturbance?" the young slave asked.

"What, yes, I mean no?" a completely disarmed Nathaniel blurted out.

"It's ok. I knew this was the tower that picked up the transmission. Don't worry. I won't say anything, but why are you here? And how did you know I'd be here?" CH4NC3 asked while knowing it was most likely the driver who alerted the stranger.

"Yes, it's a long story, but I want to show you something. Something I think will interest you. May I approach?" Nathaniel asked.

As he moved towards CH4NC3, he pulled out an envelope with pictures of a young Oliver, President Wyatt Chance, and Dr. Christopher Chance. He nervously handed the photos to the much taller slave.

CH4NC3 looked them over and showed immediate surprise and amazement while tracing the lines of his own face.

"Who are these people?" he asked.

"I think they're your family," Nathaniel said.

"Family? I don't understand that word."

"Oh, of course, you wouldn't. I believe you come from their seed," Nathaniel explained with fear that their time was drawing short.

"Look, you don't know me, but I need you to trust me," he said while checking the door.

With a thumbs up from his rogue partners, he quickly shared a plan with CH4NC3 for them to meet again soon.

"I need this photo back, but take it for now. Look at it closely. I think you'll see what I see. If you can, research *Leader of the 45's.*"

"That's him, Oliver Chance. I think it will explain a lot. You may be his brother," Nathaniel said while pointing to the photograph.

"Brother? What's that?" CH4NC3 said while momentarily confused.

"I'll explain next time. Just have faith and remember the plan. I'll see you in two days at Tower #19. Oh, the Ryan has to stay out long enough for his battery to die. I'll need more time with you, and the Ryan can't be present, or I'm dead. I'll leave that up to you to make it happen," Nathaniel said as he hastily departed.

He couldn't believe how identical the slave looked to Prince

Oliver. Could this be his brother and the son of Wyatt Chance? He knew of the 2030 semen collection of Wyatt and other athletes from the time. He knew from Charles, who heard Kenzie Chance tell the story of her husband.

"Could his semen have been used?" he wondered while safely fleeing the area before the distracted Ryan came back.

Faith

CH4NC3-1212 felt something burning deep inside. A purpose and a drive his short life had longed for. He always knew he was different from the others. But how and why he'd often wondered? When his new friend whispered *"have faith"* when giving him a plan for them to meet again, he didn't know what the word meant. He understood trust and belief, though. He'd heard those words many times during his schooling when learning about The Father. But with Nathaniel, he believed he understood the meaning.

"Trust and belief must equal faith," he surmised in quiet reflection.

He went sleepless that night while looking at the picture he was given. He looked at himself over and over and compared the image to his reflection. He felt something similar to the touch of M0LL3Y-1127 in their short elevator rise five years ago. Something far more meaningful than his pledge to the Father. It was as real as if he could touch it.

As the trip to Tower 19 approached, CH4NC3 figured out a way to shorten the battery life on his Ryan escort. He wrote a code that, when downloaded into the Ryan via a magnetic data sleeve, would corrupt the battery and quickly sap its power.

Something else occurred to CH4NC3. How could he leverage his chance meeting with Nathaniel, the transmission glitch issue, and finding revenge for what Tyrus Manning did to M0LL3Y-1127?

"Surely, I can use my security clearance. But how, without drawing attention to myself? How can it all fit together," he said while pacing his private quarters.

Any risks he took could not have repercussions on any of his close peer slaves. Especially M0LL3Y-1127, the woman he loved if he even knew what the word meant. His close group of Technical and Medical slaves, P3YT0N-0602, M1CK3L-1206, D0NN13-1017, and 3R1K6A-1130, must stay safe. He had to protect them no matter what else happened.

As dawn approached, CH4NC3 attempted to wipe the sleep from his eyes, but none was there. He didn't sleep at all the previous two nights. He felt some anxiety and wasn't sure why. He remembered feeling it only once before in his young life, when he walked out of the executive suite, leaving M0LL3Y alone with the Provincial Leader.

Milton

"Right on time, and thankfully the same driver," he thought as the shuttle arrived.

There was something about this meeting that was different to CH4NC3. He had never had a meeting or any other event that wasn't Federation related. This felt strangely exciting, yet with some trepidation. Something in his gut said he'd be okay, though.

"So, Tower 19 today? said N1CL4S-0429.

"Yes, it appears so," CH4NC3 said with a nod and a quiet smile as he knew the driver was part of the rogue group.

"It's going to be a hot one, so if you need water, we have some in the back. My assignment is to stay with you all day, so let me know if there's anything you need," N1CL4S offered.

CH4NC3 sat back for the twenty-five-minute ride and enjoyed the view of the lush tree-lined highway. It looked different than the six-lane road he'd been on days ago.

"What road is this? It looks different than the other day," he said with a curious tone.

"It's Olde Hwy 400. We're going to the tower located in a small city called Alpharetta," N1CL4S replied.

CH4NC3 took turns watching the road and the Ryan, curious to see how long the battery took to be depleted. Within an hour, he hoped. He didn't want any incidents between the rogues and the Ryan. Any slip-up could ruin whatever this relationship could bring and alert the Provincial leadership to something more nefarious was at play.

The shuttle pulled into an area that was far more open than the previous Tower. CH4NC3 wondered where the group could be hiding. The three exited the shuttle, with N1CL4S staying behind. As CH4NC3 made his way to the Tower control room, he heard a whistle and turned back.

N1CL4S shouted, "Hey, are you missing someone?"

CH4NC3 immediately noticed the Ryan had stopped mid-stride and shut down. A quick check of his status screen confirmed indeed that his battery died.

"Perfect, now where are your people?" he asked while looking over at N1CL4S.

Before he could respond, the sound of hooves clacking on broken asphalt rang out. Nathaniel and a team of five other rogues rode up on horseback, with two additional horses for N1CL4S and CH4NC3.

"Good morning. I see you solved our Ryan problem," Nathaniel said in a raised voice, laughing as he approached.

"These are beautiful animals. What are they?" CH4NC3 asked with all looking on in surprise.

"Well, they're horses. We use them to ride and to carry things," answered a somewhat amused Nathaniel.

"And guess what? We brought one for you," he quipped.

"For me, I don't even know how to use it. And where are we going?" CH4NC3 replied with some hesitation.

"Use it? You don't use it. You ride it. Don't worry, son, just do what I do, you'll be find. And we're going to a place called Milton. I want you to see something," Nathaniel explained.

"Before we go, I need to set up my equipment in the control room so I can validate that I was here and did my analysis," informed CH4NC3.

The group waited as CH4NC3 disappeared into the small cinder block building at the base of the tower.

"Do you have water in that thing?" Nathaniel asked N1CL4S.

"Well, I'm glad you asked, cause as luck would have it, I brought plenty," he replied sarcastically.

"It's best if you grab some for us and bring some for the horses too. It's going be a long day, and it's hot already," Nathaniel advised.

As CH4NC3 reappeared and joined the rogues, he begrudgingly learned how to ride a horse. He learned even more about the history of the Chance Family and what led to today's world. During the short ride to neighboring Milton, Nathaniel filled in many blanks on the outskirts, runaway slaves, and, more importantly, why he believed that divine intervention might have led the two of them together.

"Whoa!!" Nathaniel shouted with a raised arm to command the group and their horses to stop.

"There it is. That's our destination," he said.

The small group and their genius guest stood at the entry to Prophets Landing. Nathaniel directed the team to disburse and provide a lookout for any sign of the Federation. It would be just he and CH4NC3 making their way to the final destination of 1265 Long Shadow Pass.

Over the next two hours, the two walked the burnt-out remains of the Chance home, visited the graves of Kenzie and Oliver, and discussed how the world came to be. This was an incomprehensible tale that was difficult for a Federation born slave to take in.

"I think we need to get back, but there's something else you need to know, and also a favor I need to ask," Nathaniel intimated.

"Favor? What is it? CH4NC3 replied.

The disturbance you're investigating was a transmission made by me. I'll get to that in a minute, but I need you to stall as long as you can. Once I get the results back, I can share much more with you," Nathaniel explained.

"Results back from what?" CH4NC3 asked.

"Well, that's the favor. Do you have anyone you know in the Medical vocation that can perform a DNA test?" Nathaniel asked.

"A DNA test, as in Deoxyribonucleic Acid? The genetic code of human organisms?" CH4NC3 replied.

"Umm, yeah, to whatever you just said."

"Yes, I have at least two close peers that work at the BDM that can do it," CH4NC3 said.

"Look, here is hair from President Wyatt Chance's mother, Oliver's grandmother. Hell, possibly your grandmother," Nathaniel said.

"How do you have her hair?" CH4NC3 asked with a look of surprise

"It's a long story. Lucky, I guess. It needs to be compared to your DNA. If it matches, you're a Chance. Unlike all the other slaves born at the Shockley Birthing Centers, you'll know where you come from. And there's something else, the device that made the transmission, well, I'll need your help understanding how we can use it to hurt the Turing Federation," Nathaniel explained.

"Hurt Father? Hurt the Federation? How?" CH4NC3 said in an uneasy tone as if that were an impossible task.

"Look, that's for another day. For now, try to get the DNA test done, so we know for sure who you are," Nathaniel asked as the two men rode out of the decaying neighborhood.

"For some reason, if the hair is too degraded, we may have to exhume Prince Oliver and get a sample from him to test," CH4NC3 advised.

"Okay, if we must, we must. Oh, did you research him as I suggested?" Nathaniel asked.

"I did. The Federation database listed him as a traitor and a cancer to the world, but from what I read, he was a brave and brilliant man," CH4NC3 replied.

"Yes, he was. He was all that and more," Nathaniel said.

"Well, let's get you back to the Capital. You've got some work to do," Nathaniel said.

♠

C34 - LAST CH4NC3

"We never really learn from the first mistake, nor the second mistake or the third. It only hits us when we're given the Last Chance"

- Unknown

Match

Although CH4NC3 felt a connection to the Resistance, his trust for Nathaniel was still tepid. This was still a new alliance, and trust had to be earned over time. One thing brewing, however, was his curiosity. In his 17 years, he'd never truly experienced curiosity as a child would, or a young adult might when exploring new places. But this compelling piece of information, one that could change everything he's known, felt worth it.

"M0LL3Y, I need your help. I need you to test my DNA versus the hair in this bag. Please don't ask why. The less you know, the better. If you get caught, you can tell them I forced you. Please say you'll do it," CH4NC3 pleaded.

He held the bag tight in her hands, not wanting to let go, knowing he was risking potential death for both of them.

"Yes, I'll do anything you need CH4NC3", she said while not wanting him to let go.

She felt something for him and had for as long as she could remember.

"There are two things I need to know. How old is the hair

sample, and how soon do you need it?"

CH4NC3 momentarily paused with worry and said, "It's old! I'm not positive, but it might be over seventy years old. I was concerned it may be a problem."

"No, it's fine, dating it helps to know the specific test. We can pull DNA from anything. We should be good," M0LL3Y said as she gave a nod of assurance.

"Alright, open up. I need to swab you."

"Okay, but please get me the results as soon as you can," he pleaded.

After swabbing the inside of CH4NC3's mouth, she looked more closely at the bag of hair. She noticed the hair didn't have the roots attached. Without the roots, a more sophisticated test would be needed. That particular test could only be run in the Cryometric Lab.

She didn't mention this to CH4NC3 to not disappoint him on what looked to be important. She knew an older slave who could help but could she trust her was the question.

GR4CE3-0504, the lead technician in the Eugenics Department, had been at the BDM longer than anyone. As an older slave, she wasn't AI born and didn't share the IQ prowess of the 2086 batch. But she was the most well trained and most experienced at 44 years of age. She also had the least to lose, with her looming 45th expiration date in less than six months. The grey in her hair couldn't hide her youthful blue eyes or the hollowness behind them. Her meaningless life craved more, and her muted spirit needed a cause.

"GR4CE3, I have a request.....," M0LL3Y said.

"Yes, I'll do it," she said before M0LL3Y could finish.

"I haven't even told you what I need yet," she replied.

"It doesn't matter. I just want to help someone else other than the Father. Just tell me what it is," GR4CE3 said beneath her breath, so she wasn't overheard.

She held up the small plastic bag of hair and another bag with a swab of CH4NC3's saliva.

"I need a DNA comparison, but the hair doesn't have roots, so it will need to be done in the Chromo-Protein Cryometric Lab. Can you do it?" M0LL3Y asked.

"Yes, but my rotation doesn't allow me back inside that specific lab for another week," GR4CE3 explained.

"A week? I guess if that's the best you can do. Are you sure you're okay with helping me?"

"I'm sure. In twenty years, no one has ever asked, only told. Thank you for trusting me," GR4CE3 said.

The Chromo-Protein Cryometric Lab was the newest development in the Eugenics Department. The Turing Federation tasked the BDM with the goal of separating DNA and isolating only the finest strands. The goal was to replicate a genetic code for the perfect human. Although a successful result was thought to be decades away, the Federation knew the Heritage Reserves of 2030 would be depleted by 2010, and the Seminal Collection was flawed and impure.

The week's wait would be a lifetime for CH4NC3, especially since he'd never waited for anything before this. Strangely, M0LL3Y felt the tug of curiosity as well. That and her affection for CH4NC3 grew more deeply in the last couple of years. The tug of her heart as he held her hand at 12 years of age only grew stronger. Now nearly eighteen, she didn't know exactly why, but she'd do anything for him.

The Journal

CH4NC3 and Nathaniel stayed in close contact through their mutual friend N1CL4S-0429. In the week during the DNA testing, the two met at Tower #23. The Ryan escort once again experienced a battery drain. Nathaniel had already broken into the station and hid until CH4NC3 arrived. Once inside, the two met for over eight hours and shared details of life inside and outside the perimeter. The ideas of free will, personal decisions, and individual accountability were foreign to CH4NC3 but desirable. Regardless of the test results, he knew he wanted a life in the outskirts and one that included M0LL3Y. He also knew that if Tyrus Manning's inner circle of eClass slaves were to escape, the narcissistic Leader would most likely unleash an army of Ryan enforcement officers on the outskirts. Nathaniel shared the Journals contents in bits and pieces, but on this particular day, CH4NC3 wanted to read it himself. To the shock and amazement of his mere mortal friend, the genius slave read the entire 500-page journal in less than two hours. As his hands ran down one page at a time, Nathaniel queerly looked on with awe.

"How are you doing that?" Nathaniel asked.

"Doing what?" CH4NC3 replied.

"Reading like that. So quickly," he said.

"Is there another way?" CH4NC3 asked.

"Umm, no, forget it," Nathaniel muttered with a sense of inadequacy.

At one point, CH4NC3 looked up and asked, "What is football?"

Nathaniel answered, "It's a game free humans once played."

What is a game? Is it like baseball?" CH4NC3 asked without looking up.

"Baseball? You got that from the journal, didn't you? Just keep reading," Nathaniel countered with a little sarcasm.

"If only CH4NC3 knew what sarcasm was," Nathaniel thought.

At different junctures of the Journal, Nathaniel could see CH4NC3's eyes gloss over, and a second later, he'd be smiling. When he paused to open the letters carefully, his eyebrows raised while reading the different handwriting. The multiple authors' personas added the proper texture for the captive slave to see how normal humans thought and felt.

"The men who wrote this book were amazing humans with great courage. They knew they needed to help, but what's very sad is they couldn't. They were strong, but the Father was stronger," CH4NC3 concluded after the last page was turned.

"CH4NC3, if I'm right, the Father is not your father. President Wyatt Chance was, and Dr. Christopher Chance was your grandfather. If the test comes back positive, their fight is your fight," Nathaniel boldly proclaimed.

The day concluded with CH4NC3-1212 feeling more like an outsider than ever. The possibility of his life having an actual history far beyond his nearly eighteen years was now fathomable.

Now eight days removed from his request, M0LL3Y stood outside of the Analytics Office where CH4NC3 worked. The envelope she carried bore results that, one way or another, she worried would change everything for the person she long felt affection for. She pressed the button to open the door, then closed her eyes and hoped that the sealed answer was the one CH4NC3 wanted.

"M0LL3Y, what are you doing here?" he said while already knowing the answer.

Without a word, she handed him the envelope. He hesitantly took it, paused before he opened it, and stirred even greater angst in M0LL3Y than had already been present.

CH4NC3 opened the envelope, read the results, and turned to M0LL3Y and said, "I love you."

"What is love?" she asked as CH4NC3 pulled her in and held her tight.

He answered her innocent question with a touch and no words. She didn't know what it meant, but they both knew how it felt. The Journal taught CH4NC3 much of what he needed to know.

"M0LL3Y, have faith. Our world is about to change," CH4NC3 said.

"What is faith?" she naively asked.

CH4NC3 smiled and said, "you'll see."

He now knew with certainty; the Father was not his father. The irony of the tattoo on his neck that bore a strong resemblance to the Chance name was not a coincidence. He knew where he belonged. It stood as something more significant than anything he'd ever felt towards the Father and the Turing Federation.

Fear had set in. His brilliant mind quickly deduced that to know what love is, is to know loss. Although the news was welcomed, he knew his responsibility was for all humans, not just those close to him. The feeling he felt on the elevator ride over five years ago was now fully present and real. He was the world's last chance.

He quickly summoned the Transportation slave, N1CL4S-0429, to take him back to Tower #23. As he had arranged earlier, his Ryan escort's battery once again mysteriously died. The meeting was to discuss how the Chance story ends, his story, and the tale of Mankind.

Ghostrac

"Hello Nathaniel, I have something for you," CH4NC3 said while handing him the results of the DNA comparison.

Nathaniel took the folded paper nervously. With his head down and eyes fixed, he slowly read the results. Now shaking with tears present, he looked first at his son and then to CH4NC3.

"My God, I knew it," Nathaniel said.

"Your driver knew it too. From a not so vague memory of a picture he saw of your father and brother," a stunned and relieved Nathaniel said.

"Are you hurt? Your eyes… they are wet," CH4NC3 observed.

"CH4NC3 they're tears. Besides my son, I've never been happier to see anyone ever before.

I knew when I first saw you that you were a Chance," Nathaniel said as he awkwardly embraced CH4NC3.

"Oh, my goodness, I almost forgot, I'd like you to meet

someone. CH4NC3, this is my Son, Christopher."

The young boy stuck out his hand to shake, but the brilliant slave was not familiar with the custom.

"Oh, he wants to shake your hand. It's something humans do in the outskirts when they greet someone new," Nathaniel explained.

"Well then, it is nice to meet you, Christopher," CH4NC3 said while reaching for the boy's hand.

"Okay, son, go play with your dominoes while I talk with our new friend."

"He looks like you," a curious CH4NC3 said with an unwitting smile.

"Yes, he takes after me, just like you take after your father," Nathaniel said.

The reference to President Wyatt Chance was not lost on the brilliant but naïve slave. Minute by minute, his pride and sense of belonging grew.

As the two men talked, Nathanial unveiled the electronic equipment he'd been holding onto for twelve years.

"I couldn't show you this until I knew for sure that you were a Chance, but this is the reason for the disturbance you've been researching," Nathaniel explained while holding up the Ghostrac phone.

"It's linked to an orbiting satellite that is impervious to the Turing Federation's detection. Once we were able to charge it, it contacted the satellite and has remained connected this whole time. As you can see, the screen says, *awaiting instructions*. From here, we don't know what to do. Here's what came with it," Nathaniel explained.

"It's everything I have for the equipment," Nathaniel said as he handed CH4NC3 the memory stick and manuals, along with the additional notes and specs from Trace Manson and Gorson Tusk.

"I brought the laptop computer we'll need to access the thumb drive. Please allow me some time to read everything and review it. It may take a while, so be patient," CH4NC3 said.

As he poured over everything quickly, his ability to speed read was never more useful. He saved the thumb drive for last, and to his surprise, it was vast in its depth of critical details and the full capabilities of the Ghostrac System. But there was one folder he opened marked "Quiet" that brought an "aha" moment to the young genius.

"What? What is it?" Nathaniel asked from across the room.

"Gorson Tusk. He was mentioned many times in the journal. He was a true genius. He developed a Virus called 'Quiet' that could disable an entire Cyber Hub. Although brilliant, it's flawed." CH4NC3 explained.

Nathaniel listened and looked on with great interest but also a sense of dismay. The memory stick contained a virus this whole time yet could never be accessed.

"My God, I wish I knew this years ago," he said.

"Don't feel bad. There's nothing you could have done with it anyway," CH4NC3 revealed.

"It's flawed, not in design but in its ability to deliver and execute. It would first have to be uploaded into the phone, which we can do, then transmitted to the satellite, which seems reasonably easy to accomplish if we can avoid detection.

"Then, and here's the hard part, the Ghostrac satellite would have to transmit the virus in a message to any one of six secured mainframes kept in six different Capitals. If received and opened immediately by the right person, the virus could successfully download in a few minutes. But here's the problem, it could only disable one of the Cyber Hubs, as the Federation would then be able to shutdown shared access to the Hub Continuum," Chance explained.

"Hub Continuum?" Nathaniel asked.

"Yes, it's an open conduit of shared control of the Power Management System. Once there's a nefarious interruption, the safeguards protecting all three hubs automatically closes the conduit," CH4NC3 answered with some disappointment.

"Father, father, come. I want to show you something," young Christopher begged.

"Son, not now, we're busy," an embarrassed Nathaniel said while dispatching his son.

"No, it's okay. I need a break from analyzing all of this information," CH4NC3 said with a sigh.

"He wants to show us his dominoes," Nathaniel informed.

"What's dominoes?" CH4NC3 inquired.

"It's a game.....umm, don't ask," Nathaniel said as he quickly cut him off from asking what a game is, again.

The two men looked on as the proud six-year-old pushed the first domino. One domino after another fell in rapid succession with a single push.

"Click, click, click, click, click," echoed through the control room.

CH4NC3 turned away quickly and started typing on the laptop. Nathaniel momentarily felt slighted for his son.

"Christopher, can you set the dominoes up again?" CH4NC3 turned and requested of the little boy.

The three stood and watched, mesmerized as they all fell again.

Chance uttered, "That's it. Christopher, you're brilliant."

"Nathaniel, I figured it out. If we can do everything I described earlier, we could crash the Federation."

"Figured what out?" Nathaniel asked.

"If we can upload the virus, transmit to the satellite, send the message to the Turing Federation, and have the message opened, the virus will do exactly what it's supposed to do," he said.

"Which is......?" Nathaniel asked as if CH4NC3's brain was moving faster than anything he'd seen before.

"Disable one of the Cyber Hubs, I believe in Austin, and killing power to a third of the world," he explained.

"But here's the irony of Father's arrogance, although the system is built to close the conduits, it's also programmed to restart power to the hub services in the disrupted sections of the world. No one individual hub can service the power needs of two-thirds of the world. It would crash like one domino falling on the next.

If we take one down, that one takes down the next, and so on."

"My god, it's that simple?" Nathaniel asked with shock and amazement.

"No, it's not. But if we line up each domino as your son did, we have a chance," CH4NC3 insisted.

"If all three hubs shut down, the Turing Federation dies. The Father dies."

"How do you know all this?" Nathaniel asked.

"Between the age of six and fifteen, the Turing Federation educated me to maintain and repair any computer and electronic systems," CH4NC3 intimated.

"I was born for this day," he said with only the second smile he's ever had.

"Okay, so when? How?" Nathaniel asked.

"I have to get back to set things in motion. The BDM has one of the world's six secure mainframes. If we can receive the Ghostrac satellite message before one of the other five mainframes, we can set the virus in motion. From there, it's letting the dominoes fall. Then we can sit back and hopefully watch the lights go out."

The men parted, knowing what must be done. For CH4NC3 1212, he now needed the help of his peer slaves once again.

The Quiet Virus

As the cold of a 2104 December fell on the Piedmont Province, the eighteen-year-old CH4NC3-1212 had finally set all necessary dominoes in place.

He planned his meeting with Nathaniel and several other resistance members to transmit the virus to the Ghostrac Satellite. Once sent, it would take an estimated twelve hours for the satellite to send the corrupt message to the Federation.

From there, either GR4CE3-0504 or M0LL3Y-1127 would accept the message from the BDM's mainframe computer.

As CH4NC3 exited the shuttle, he waited approximately fourteen minutes for the Ryan escort's battery to die. Once done, hundreds of rogues came out of the tree-lined perimeter of Tower #19. CH4NC3 was shocked to see so many free humans seemingly come out of nowhere to witness what they all hoped would be the beginning of the end.

The group of hundreds watched as CH4NC3 and Nathaniel disappeared into the tower's control room and re-emerged just fifteen minutes later. Nathaniel gave the thumbs up to the crowd while CH4NC3 quietly entered the shuttle and rode away.

In the short twenty-minute ride back to the Capital, he now felt the weight of his actions come to pass.

"What if something goes wrong and M0LL3Y is caught? What if all of my calculations are wrong? No matter," he said to his reflection in the glass of the shuttle.

It was too late. The first domino had been pushed. All now rested on faith. A belief and emotion that no slave was ever taught, yet now was all they needed.

Thirteen hours remained of the regularly scheduled worker shifts. CH4NC3 estimated that by no later than 1900 hours Piedmont Standard Time, the message would appear. All senior-level administration officials would be retired for the day, with only vocation workers left. He feared that someone at the mainframe station in Palo Alto might intercept and remove what would appear to be a malicious message.

But there, at 1822 hours on December 28th, 2104, a cryptic message appeared on the BDM's master console. An email from *askCOM Technologies*, titled "Quiet." M0LL3Y knew immediately. CH4NC3 told her that a keyword in the message might be "Quiet." She quickly opened it. The body of the message read, OPEN, and that she did. She alerted GR4CE3 within seconds, and a minute later, she covertly informed CH4NC3. There was nothing more to be done except pray, something no slave would understand.

As fate was set in motion, CH4NC3 put the finishing touches on his assigned project report and sent a request to meet with Provincial Leader Manning the next day.

It was clear there was yet another domino that awaited gravity.

LOCKDOWN

"Yes, come in. Oh, look, it's the gifted eClass slave," a sarcastic Manning said as CH4NC3-1212 entered the executive suite.

"I've been growing tired of your delays and incomplete reports. Well, what do you have for me? It better be good news," Leader Manning demanded.

"Yes sir, it is…"

(phone rings).

"Yes? What, when did this happen? Yesterday morning? Don't

bother. I have him right here in front of me," Manning angrily shouted into the phone.

"Well, it appears another illicit transmission was made at 0710 hours yesterday morning. Did you know about this?" Manning scolded.

"Sir, yes, in fact, I did. That's why I requested this meeting. My investigation turned up the original transmission location, but also the one from yesterday morning as well. It's here in my digital report," CH4NC3-1212 said as he handed Manning the report.

"Sir, I regret telling you this, but Tower #44 in Dekalb is where the transmissions originated. It's from inside the perimeter. The obvious suggestion would be to shut it down and monitor the area. But that is something I'm sure you've already thought of Leader Manning," CH4NC3-1212 said.

The strategy employed a bluff to pacify the narcissistic Leader. All while drawing attention away from his friends in the outskirts.

"Yes, yes, very good. I'll take it from here. You're dismissed," a neutered Manning ordered.

What Leader Tyrus Manning didn't know was the Digital Report that he received from Technical Slave CH4NC3-1212 was encrypted with a coded message. Once the Digital Card was inserted in his computer, it would incriminate the Provincial Leader as the person responsible for both transmissions, as well as receiving the suspicious satellite message the previous night.

With dominoes falling one by one, CH4NC3 sat back and hoped the mission would be successful.

"It has to work," he thought.

"If it fails, we run."

(sirens blared over loudspeakers throughout the Capital City)

Alert: 1433 Hours Capital Perimeter LOCKDOWN

"All subjects are to report to their quarters immediately and remain until further notice. There has been an internal security breach inside the Capital Perimeter."

CH4NC3 made it back to his quarters on the 4th floor of the Capital Vocation Dormitory safely. Through his window, he could see multiple Ryan Security vehicles gather in front of the Capital Building. Within minutes he watched as Provincial Leader Tyrus Manning was escorted out of the building in shackles. He was led to the front of the grounds, loaded into a Security van, and driven away.

"Got him," CH4NC3 said with a clenched fist.

It took nearly six years, but vengeance for the vile act perpetrated against the only person he ever cared about was found. Revenge was not a word he knew. But the feeling that burned inside him for far too long was now extinguished. The scars would never leave M0LL3Y, but at least now, she could heal with the vile reminder of that day gone forever.

Now, if the rest of the world could have its revenge against the Father.

Quiet

A cold dawn fell upon the Piedmont Province. The snowy morning was without sound, no hum of activity, or artificial noise, only the hush of humanity, as a wintery breeze, tapped the window of the slave quarters. CH4NC3 woke on the first Sunday morning of a new month.

The only day off for human workers, and this was the first of 2105. While still dark, he fumbled for his robe as the cold swept through his room. He reached for a lamp that didn't work. He looked out his window and then to his watch. At 0726 hours, not a light was seen. Not one from any distance in any direction. Except for the budding sun pushing through a tapestry of clouds and flurries. As he focused on his reflection in the glass, the frosted pane told him it was done.

There would be no formal confirmation as to the rest of the world's status for some time. But at least for the Piedmont Province, all power was off. That meant that Austin fell. If Austin fell, Berlin or Palo Alto would be down, if not both.

CH4NC3 needed to reach Nathaniel, but with the lockdown, it would have to wait. If he were correct from his earlier calculations, the Ryan's would die out in less than forty-eight hours. When that occurred, mankind was free.

"But free to do what," CH4NC3 wondered.

Life in the outskirts would be unchanged. The resistance knew how to live in the dark and cold, but today would be a day where freedom was also feared for millions of captive humans. Their Father was gone, and only a handful of humans in the entire world knew the Turing Federation was no more.

The singularly focused, arrogant Turing Federation did not think of backup systems, global fail-safes, or even its failings of humility. It believed that its power hubs protected each other.

Man knew for centuries what AI didn't. When a table loses a leg, it falls. The other legs cannot support it.

A technical slave, with the help of yesterday's heroes, defeated Artificial Intelligence. Because they thought like humans, instead of a machine, a simple game of domino's played by a child led to the belief that faith was enough.

With intelligence and emotion scribed on paper, the journal served as a guide to what was worth saving and winning back, written by heroes who died trying to save a race instead of putting themselves first.

When the first history book of a new world was written, it showed a series of miracles, where not a dozen but a thousand things had to happen in order for every chance to lead to another chance.

Legacy

In the months following the Dark Day, the lone operating satellite confirmed what CH4NC3 and other prominent slave leaders believed. That there was no continual power stream in the world, other than independent generators or local power sources. There was no internet, no wires or tethers that linked man to artificial intelligence. Human slaves laid waste to the Federations thrones of data and cathedrals of electronic sophistication. Data centers and electrical hubs were destroyed. All apparatuses of artificial life was severed.

Humans willingly unplugged the world and relied on itself again. It no longer needed artificial intelligence for its survival. What started with a brave doctor at the BDM in 2021 culminated with the miracle birth of his improbable genetic offspring. All the heroes and victims along the way fought for eighty-four years to defeat a technology that took two hundred years to build from a cerebral mechanism that started in the halls of Cambridge University with Charles Babbage's Analytical Engine to Alan Turing's computable science.

AI grew slow and robust. When connected through satellites and the internet, it became an unknowable foe that started as a crutch and slowly destroyed humanity's minds and will.

The lessons taught for future generations will be of the evils of arrogance and indulgence. For the sad ironies and inhumane riddles that would be learned by all, one thing was clear. The world was ripe to start anew.

Because of the vaccine cocktails and numbing measures taken by the Turing Federation, docile humans did not devolve into barbarism when the world's power died but worked alongside each other for the common good. Urban slaves learned quickly of community and fellowship from those living in the outskirts, who numbered in the hundreds of millions worldwide. They worked side by side with their brothers and sisters to build, grow, and farm.

Man quickly learned how to restart the power, but electrical currents to fuel automation were hard-wired lines of communication only. As it stood in 2105, all necessary infrastructure was already in place. Where it had served the Federation, now it would benefit the freed human race.

One More Chance

By June of 2106, all events that led to the Turing Federation's defeat were finally revealed to the world. When humans finally reorganized into a civil society, their first elected leader of a genuinely free world was Chance 1212.

With their slave names changed, Chance and Molly were married six months after the Federation's fall. By the grace of God, a new chance was given to the world.

Emma Grace Chance was born on May 4th, 2106, named after her Great Grandmother, Emma Chance, who died in 2024. The legacy of a family was now the legacy of the world. Mankind could now, once again, Evolve.

♠

The End (and a New Beginning)

ABOUT THE AUTHOR

Novelist and business executive, Donald James Cook was born and raised in the Midwest. After living on both coasts, he settled in Atlanta, Georgia where he now lives with his family.

Author of The Quiet is Talking and Just My Luck, Donald was compelled to tell a story of the events unfolding in front of all of us. The current conditions of political strife, international tensions, climate change, and the rise of artificial intelligence demanded a stage.

Made in the USA
Columbia, SC
16 February 2021